THE PRODIGAL SON

SARA CATE

For you.
You know who you are.

If you or anyone you know are ever feeling
hopeless, please reach out for help.
You are not alone.
U.S. Suicide Prevention Hotline
1 800 273 8255
There are further resources included in the
back of this book.

DEAR READER

I'm going to be straightforward with this content warning. There are some very heavy themes and potentially triggering content in this book. Please read this list before embarking on this story.

In Isaac and Jensen's story, you will encounter: homophobia, parental abuse (physical and emotional), sexual assault of a minor (off the page), conversion therapy, violence, attempted suicide (on page), alcohol abuse, religious trauma, and death of a parent.

As always with any Sara Cate book, a happy ending is promised. But the journey there is fraught with struggle, fight, resistance, and perseverance.

It shouldn't have to be this way.

It feels this story is more important now than ever. I hope when you read it, you see the joy and love within these pages and remember that it's worth fighting for.

For ourselves and for each other.

Love always,
Sara

PROLOGUE

Isaac
Nine years old

"Go ahead, Isaac," my mom calls from the couch. "Your audience is ready."

I'm hopping up and down nervously on my feet as my brothers, Luke and Caleb, mumble back and forth on the other side of the curtain. There's a guitar in my hands, and I practice putting my fingers on the right strings to make sure I'm ready before walking through.

When a few more seconds go by, my brothers start cheering for me to encourage me, but it only makes me more nervous.

I feel stupid. What if they laugh? What if my dad hates it?

"Hey, buddy, what's up?" I turn to find Adam kneeling down behind the makeshift stage—which is just my mom's old curtains we draped over a string we tied from one banister to the other.

"I'm nervous," I whisper.

He smiles, ruffling my hair. "Don't be nervous. You're a natural. I've heard you practicing in your room."

"You won't laugh at me?"

His face contorts as he looks at me with confusion. "I would never laugh at you."

My biggest brother is a grown-up now. I miss when he lived here because out of everyone in the family, he's always the nicest to me.

"They will," I mumble. I can still hear Luke and Caleb bickering. I'm sure my mom is still waiting patiently and my dad is probably reading something on his computer or some papers from work. He's always working.

I don't know if they can hear Adam and me talking, but for some reason, I feel the urge to cry. Then Adam puts his hands on my shoulders and turns me toward him.

"Isaac, listen to me. We're your family. Even if we do laugh sometimes, we're not laughing at *you*. The good thing about family is that we always take care of each other—no matter what. Okay?"

I take a deep breath. Sometimes, when I get nervous or scared, I just think about how confident and sure of everything Adam is. He's never scared.

"Okay," I reply, nodding my head.

"Everything all right back there?" my mother drawls sweetly.

Adam taps the front of my cowboy hat and winks at me before he crawls out from behind the curtain. Addressing my family seated in the living room, he says, "Trust me. It will be worth the wait."

Instantly, my other brothers hush and the room goes quiet.

"Ladies and gentlemen," Adam announces. "For your listening pleasure, we have a real treat for you tonight. For a completely sold-out show, he's here straight out of Austin, Texas, the best country singer this side of the Mississippi, our very own... Isaac Goode!"

My family starts to cheer. Luke and Caleb holler and woot as my mom whistles. Then, as soon as Adam draws the curtain open, my father bellows proudly, "That's my boy!"

There are a few lights we borrowed from the church stationed around the living room, and they're so bright they make me squint. As my family cheers, I smile so widely that I have to cover my face in embarrassment.

Caleb mimics the sound of a crowded stadium as Luke mouths, *You got this.*

Another deep breath.

Looking down at my guitar, I place my fingers on the right strings and start to strum. The first chord is off, and it sounds terrible.

"Wait, sorry," I mumble uncomfortably.

"It's okay," my mom whispers.

Another deep breath.

I fix my fingers and close my eyes. Then, I strum again.

This time, it's perfect.

The music plays as I imagine the chords on the paper playing in my mind.

C chord.

D chord.

My mother starts to clap along, and I open my eyes to see my dad smiling.

"I love this song," he says, and my brothers quickly hush him. "It's Hank Williams," he adds, ignoring them. Caleb throws something at him, and everybody laughs. Even Dad.

I just keep playing.

"Heeeeey good lookin'

Whaaaaatcha got cooking?

How's about cookin' something up with me?"

My mom sways from side to side as she mouths the words along with me. Adam takes a seat on the recliner and rests his elbows on his knees as I play.

Soon, everyone is clapping along, and I even start to dance a little like Hank does in the videos.

The switch from the G7 chord back to the C is tough but as I get in the groove of playing, it happens easily.

"I got a hot rod Ford and a two-dollar bill,

And I know a spot right over the hill."

Mom's smile grows brighter as I continue to put on a show. And no one laughs.

In fact, their encouragement only makes me more comfortable. So I put a little more into the performance, a little more twang in my voice, a little more bounce in my dance, strum a little harder, and even throw in a little yodel.

When the song comes to an end, I sing the loudest and strum one last time before holding my hands in the air.

My family is on their feet in a second. They're all cheering and clapping.

"Bravo, bravo!" Luke shouts.

"Hot damn, boy!" my dad bellows. "He's got some talent!" He nudges my mom with his elbow.

"That was so good, baby!" she calls as she crosses toward me, swallowing me up in a hug. I have to reach up to hold my cowboy hat in place as she kisses my cheeks. "You're amazing, Isaac."

"Encore, encore, encore," my brothers all chant in unison.

"I know one more," I say. Which is a lie. I know a lot more than one.

Quickly, they take their seats, and I put my fingers back on the guitar.

As I play them another Hank Williams and then a George Jones and even a Marty Robbins song, they keep clapping and dancing and cheering me on. It's the most fun I've ever had.

And not once do any of them laugh.

✝

After I'm done performing, my brothers and I are in the kitchen around the large island. Luke pops some popcorn and Caleb cracks open a Coke. The four of us laugh and poke fun at each other as brothers do.

When I hear my parents' voices from the living room, I hop down from the stool and walk out toward where I hear the fireplace crackle.

"He's such a sweet boy," my mother says.

"He sure is," my dad replies.

"Where did he get such talent? Certainly not from my side," she jokes.

I stop in the hallway and listen when I realize they're talking about me. It's quiet before he adds, "I think he gets it from me."

My mother giggles softly. "Since when do you play the guitar?"

"I played when I was his age," he says.

"You did?"

"I was damn good too. Probably could have been a star."

A smile stretches across my cheeks as I lean against the wall.

"Oh, Truett." My mom giggles.

My dad gets mad a lot, sometimes at me and sometimes at my brothers. So when he's in a good mood, the house feels nice. Everyone's happy. I wish it was like this all the time.

Tonight, he seems like he's in a good mood, and I don't want to miss it. Taking a step forward, I enter the living room to find my parents sitting next to each other on the couch. My mom is cuddled up under Dad's arm. She has a glass of wine in her hand and he has something stronger-smelling in a short glass.

"There's the star now," she says softly as I enter the room.

"Get on over here, Hank Williams."

With a bashful smile, I cross the room and climb onto the couch between them. My mom strokes my hair and kisses the side of my head.

"You sure did good tonight," my dad says, patting my leg. "Where'd you learn to play that guitar so well?"

I shrug. Truth be told, the music director at Dad's church taught me the basics when he passed down his old guitar to me, but the rest I learned on my own. But I want to be humble for my dad.

"I'm so proud of you," my mom whispers.

"Here, boy. You earned this." My dad passes me his short glass, and I scowl at it as the acidic stench reaches my nose.

"Truett!" my mom hisses. "He's nine!"

"So? I was younger than him the first time I had my first taste of whiskey. Besides, he proved himself tonight, didn't he?"

She huffs and looks away.

"Just a sip," my dad says, holding it in front of my face.

It smells terrible, like fire and cinnamon. I don't want it.

But he looks so proud. So I take it.

Just a sip.

"There you go," he says as he watches me tip it back. There's a large ice cube in the middle of the glass and it clinks loudly as it rolls around. When I inhale through my nose, it burns, so I try not to breathe as I wait for the liquid to touch my lips.

When it does, I sip a tiny bit of the alcohol into my mouth.

It's worse than fire. Worse than acid, cinnamon and smoke all rolled into one. It doesn't just burn; it screams its way down my throat, but I'm not sure it makes it all the way because suddenly I'm coughing like the devil. I end up spitting saliva and whiskey all over my lap.

My dad laughs loudly as he pounds his palm against my back, but it doesn't help. The fire won't go away. I want to throw up, but since my dad is laughing, I smile up at him.

"It's good," I say, but my voice won't come out, so it's just a strangled, raspy sound, which only makes my dad laugh more.

"That's enough," my mom scolds. "Isaac, go into the kitchen and drink some water."

"Yes, ma'am," I reply as I climb off the couch. As I walk to the kitchen, my head feels light and fuzzy, and I blink a lot as I reach the room where my brothers are still cracking up and teasing each other.

"The hell happened to you?" Caleb asks.

My eyes are still watering as I shove my shoulders back proudly. "Just sharing some whiskey with Dad."

"Whiskey?" Luke snaps. He looks angry, which makes me feel bad. Luke hates everything Dad does. But he doesn't understand.

I can still make Dad proud. It's too late for him. They fight too much, and Luke says stuff just to make Dad mad.

But I saw the way Dad smiled at me tonight. I saw how proud he was. I can still be a good son, like Adam.

I glance up at him to gauge his reaction. As Adam fills a glass of water, I catch a glimpse of concern on his face.

When he hands it to me, he bends over so his face is level with mine. Then he places a hand on my shoulder and stares into my eyes.

"You don't have to do that to make Dad proud, you know?"

"I know," I say with a shrug. Taking a sip, I try to act nonchalant, like the whiskey didn't burn and my brother should have nothing to worry about.

Adam chuckles and ruffles my hair. "You're a good kid, Isaac. Stay that way."

My head still feels heavy as I give my brother a smirk.

"We won't always be around to take care of you." I glance over at where Luke is resting his elbows on the kitchen island. He picks up a piece of popcorn and tosses it at me. With a laugh, I pick it up and toss it back at him. My laugh turns into a giggle and suddenly, I can't seem to stop. Maybe it was that nasty drink Dad gave me, or maybe it's just because I have all my brothers together. Or maybe because acting like a real country star tonight made me feel so good.

"Sure you will," I reply, looking up at each of them. "We'll always be together."

"Of course, buddy," Adam says as he shakes my shoulder. It doesn't sound true and it makes my laughter stop.

"You'll always have my back. You said." I don't like the sound of my voice. It shakes a little like I'm about to cry.

"How much of that whiskey did he drink?" Caleb asks with humor on his face.

Luke looks guilty, and Adam is trying to smile, but it's a lie.

"Drink this," Adam says flatly as he forces me to take the glass of water and tip it back.

The good feeling starts to fade, and it makes me sad. The lights of the kitchen are bright, and I focus on the black-and-white towel hanging from the handle of the oven. It has a cow on it because Mom loves cows.

As I stare at it, trying to shrink away from my brothers' attention, I'm relieved when they eventually go back to talking to each other and not to me. Sipping my water, I realize for the first time that my brothers lie, especially to me.

Soon Luke and Caleb will be done with school and move away. Adam won't come around as much. It'll be like I don't have brothers anymore.

And if I don't have my brothers...then I have to be tough and take care of myself.

PART ONE
THE STAR

ONE

ISAAC

"What's *his* name?" Lola asks as soon as I open the door of her car. I slide into the passenger seat, sweating inside this dark-black hoodie that's about two sizes too big.

As I clip my seat belt in place, I make a contemplative expression. "Brady...no, Brody?"

She makes a laughing sound as she pulls out of the apartment complex's parking lot. "You better be careful, Theo."

It should probably feel stranger to be referred to as Theo by my closest friends, but I've had this stage name for so long that it's honestly what I prefer to be called. I'm not Isaac anymore. It's just easier to be Theo Virgil. Theo Virgil is the life of the party. Theo Virgil has a song on the Billboard Top Ten and a sold-out tour. Theo Virgil doesn't have any skeletons in his closet.

"I'm always careful," I reply haughtily as I kick my cowboy boots up on the dash.

Lola smacks my leg. "I just had it detailed, you prick."

Laughing, I take my feet down and blow her a kiss. "Sorry, Mommy. Don't be mad at me."

She rolls her eyes but can't fight her smile. "Did you check his phone?"

"Yep. He didn't take a single picture of us, and he doesn't even listen to country music."

"You got lucky," she mumbles.

"Damn right I did," I say with a wicked smile and a wink, but she doesn't laugh. Tilting her head in my direction, she levels me with a sober expression.

"I'm serious, Isaac."

My smile fades as I turn my gaze forward, my insides souring from her use of my real name. Lola has known me long enough to know my history. My real name. How I ran away at seventeen. How I don't really keep in touch with my family anymore.

Except for Lucas. And that one night I shared a couple of beers with Caleb.

And a few cryptic letters back and forth with Adam.

I call my mother from time to time, too. I'm not a monster.

But that's it. I haven't been in the same room with all of them at once in eleven years, and I don't really plan to anytime soon. It would feel too weird. I don't mind being called Isaac every once in a while by those who know me best, but I don't want to *be* Isaac.

I built all this on my own. I created Theo to get away from that life.

"I'm just looking out for you," Lola adds with concern in her voice. "You should be able to come out on your own time, not when some asshole in a bar leaks a few photos or, God forbid, videos."

"I know. You're right, but I'm careful, though. I promise."

"You better be," she replies sternly. "You're a big deal now, dude. People are going to start recognizing you, whether they listen to you or not."

I love Lola. She's a badass with a real soft side, and she's been my bassist since I moved to Nashville, like, six years ago. But I have to admit, it irks me when she tries to mother me.

It's not her fault. I'm a fucking mess, and most people either jump onto the hot mess express alongside me or do their best to try and fix the course I'm on.

Lola tends to fall into the latter, but she does it out of love.

"Besides, the tour schedule is tight. You can't be doing these little one-night stands while we're on the road," she says as she turns down the road that leads to my apartment in the city.

"Why do you think I'm getting it out of my system now?" I ask, trying to remain calm whenever she brings up the tour.

I can tell she's doing the same.

"According to the tour manager, we'll be taking off hours after each show and sleeping on the bus between stops," she says with a hint of excitement in her voice.

"On that big fat sleeper bus with my name on the side," I add.

"On a sold-out national tour."

"No big deal," I reply with a shrug, keeping my cool.

"Yeah, it's nothing."

As she pulls up to my house, we make eye contact momentarily before completely losing our shit. Lola and I scream in unison as we dance around in our confined spaces.

We've done this no less than a hundred times over the past couple of months. And who could blame us? Our last tour nearly wiped us out financially, and that was after skipping hotels to sleep in a tiny, pre-owned camper van packed to the brim with our instruments and gear while the rest of the band followed behind us in Rio's old VW hatchback.

Now, we're traveling like real stars. Like we've made it. Surely, every country star has these little freak-out moments before their first major tour.

"Aaaaah," Lola cheers excitedly. "You fucking did it, Isaac. This is really happening."

"We fucking did it," I correct her.

"Sure, but you just wrote the songs, built your following, and performed in front of them every night."

"Stop, stop, stop..." I say as I playfully shove her shoulder. "Okay, keep going."

We laugh together for a while before I reach over the console and place a kiss on her cheek.

"Thanks again for picking me up. You are my savior, my queen, my goddess, and I love you."

"Love you, too," she replies as I open the door to climb out. Before I shut the door, she calls out, "Get some rest, Theo! We have a big day tomorrow!"

"Aaaahhh," I say quietly with a big grin on my face.

With that, I shut the door and walk up to my apartment. After I signed with the Austin-based label, they offered to put me up in my own place. They want me to be able to focus on songwriting, but really, I know it's just one more way they can own me, which is fine. They can own me if they keep paying me.

In the shower, I stand under the hot stream of water for long enough to make my skin wrinkle and turn red. Sometimes it feels like the shower is the only place I can focus and think clearly.

I relive moments from last night at the bar and with the handsome stranger. I conjure up feelings and turn them into words. Those words turn into lyric pieces I may never use, cataloged in my mind where I know they're safe.

Blue jeans wrapped around my waist
That tequila trance on the dance floor
A one-night understanding

Shutting the water off, I grab a towel from the hook by the shower and wrap it around my waist before stepping out onto the mat. A man with dark hair and dark circles under his eyes stares back in the bathroom mirror.

Sometimes, I find myself wishing those lyrics could mean something more. More than drunk nights and meaningless hookups. More than moments, more like forevers. Real feelings.

Am I even capable of that?

Why does it feel like all I'm meant for is hookups? Every time a guy tries to get close, I push him away or sabotage the relationship. The moment anyone tries baring their soul to me, I immediately stop taking him seriously. I crack jokes. I find a flaw, and I fixate on it.

I have erected some chastity belt around my own fucking heart, and most days, I don't care. I like it this way. I joke that I'll be a slut until the day I die, but then I have sobering moments like this when I look in the mirror and hear the man staring back say, "You'll be alone forever."

I talk a big game, but even I don't want that.

After getting dressed in a pair of joggers and a Nirvana T-shirt, I head down to the spare bedroom turned gym on the main floor. It was their not-so-subtle way of telling me to build some muscle. No one likes a scrawny country star.

But I have the attention span of a squirrel, so I scroll social media while doing leg extensions on the big machine with pulleys and weights.

My workouts are never more than half-assed.

While setting down the weights to do some shoulder presses, I get a text from Luke. It's a picture of his eleven-month-old baby, Henry. He's sleeping in his arms with his chubby fist perched under his chin, but one tiny finger is sticking out, so it looks like he's flipping me off.

I laugh as I type out my response:

> Your baby has an attitude problem.

Staring at the photo for a minute, I put off my shoulder workout. Henry has a tuft of copper hair on his head and the cutest damn nose.

Luke's reply comes in.

> This is his way of saying good luck on your tour.

I chuckle to myself.

> That's sweet of him. Tell him I said

Putting my phone on the bench, I do a few lazy sets, pulling the wide bar down without really counting. When I'm tired, I stop and pick up my phone again.

No messages. Just a couple thousand tags on social media that I can't check anymore. It's nice, but I miss being a real person on Instagram instead of a celebrity.

Not that long ago, I could respond to fans and message people. Now, all I'm allowed to do is post stuff to my stories to appear "relatable," and even that has some very strict guidelines from my publicist.

All in all, it's fucking lonely.

But how the fuck can I be lonely? I've got two point nine million followers. I have a loyal band who are my best friends. And Luke is always just a phone call away.

It would just be nice to have someone around—always around. To share meals with and come home to and bitch about nonsense. Not a phone call away. Not a stranger in a club or on the internet. More than a friend. Like a long-term fuck buddy.

I'm pretty sure that's a boyfriend, idiot.

Eventually, I give up on my lazy workout when I hear my stomach rumbling. After ditching the gym equipment, I order some Thai food from my phone and lounge on the couch until it arrives about thirty minutes later.

The girl who delivers it does a double take when I answer the door. She stares at me dumbfounded while I'm reaching my hand out for the bag of food.

"Uh...here you go," she stammers before passing it over.

"Thanks," I laugh.

As soon as she smiles back, she curls a strand of hair behind her ear. "I know who you are," she stammers sweetly. "I'm a huge fan."

I start to close the door but stop to soak in some of her adoration. I mean...who doesn't love attention?

"Thanks," I reply, showing off the signature Theo Virgil dimples. She giggles again.

"Would it be rude to ask for a selfie?" she asks.

"Of course not." Laughing, I set down my food and step outside as she pulls her phone from her pocket.

"Oh my god, I'm shaking," she says. "This is crazy."

When she eventually gets her phone up, selfie camera on us, I lean in next to her and throw up a cheesy backward peace sign as I grin brightly.

She snaps no less than a dozen pics before pulling away. When our eyes meet again, her gaze lingers, and I realize she's working up the nerve to ask for something else. Maybe my number. Maybe a conversation. Maybe more.

She's thinking right now that she has a chance. But she doesn't. Not on God's green earth or any other planet, for that matter. I have about as much interest in getting in bed with her as I do with a cactus, which is to say, *none*. No offense to her, of course. Just not my type.

Still, I'm thinking that I should flirt with her for no other reason than to keep up the whole straight-guy charade. But I'm too fucking hungry, so I back away as she works herself up to say something more. I slowly close the door, politely saying, "Have a good one."

Taking my lunch to the kitchen, I dig in and scroll through videos on my phone. They're all pointless, mindless entertainment. And for a while, it works to distract me from the loneliness.

It's fine. Everything's fine. I'm at the top of my game. Living on top of the world. I'm going on a fucking tour—a real one.

It doesn't matter that I'm hiding this super intimate part of myself from the world. It doesn't matter that all of my fans think I'm straight. Or that I haven't seen my entire family together in eleven years.

Like I said, it's fine.

The loneliness, the shame, the fear. All of that shit is Isaac's problem, not Theo's. Because things will probably never be as good as they are right now.

So who the fuck am I to complain?

Two

"Brothers and sisters, let us remember that God's love is steadfast and his grace is sufficient for all our needs. No matter the trials we face, His word is a lamp to our feet and a light to our path."

Heads nod in the congregation. Thousands of eyes point in my direction as I speak, but my attention catches on the few who momentarily glance down, distracted by something on their phones or carrying on a small conversation with their neighbors.

When I raise my voice, just a hair for dramatic effect, they all turn back to me. It lights a fire in my veins. My heart thrums harder.

"Let us walk boldly in faith, trusting in his sacrifice and sharing his love with the world around us."

More heads nod.

Preaching is a performance. One I've prided myself on getting pretty good at over the years. It's an art form, really, turning Bible scriptures into narratives, compelling and relatable.

"Have we not our own sins by which the good Lord has sacrificed himself for?" I ask softly as I rest a hand on the pulpit. As I stare out into the audience, I try to bare a piece of my soul to each of them. Like casting a line and hoping to catch a bite. Except it's not fish I'm after, but kinship.

There's a buzz under my skin as my eyes connect with a woman near the middle. She's clinging to every word, hope and desperation in her eyes. She's not here because she's been ingrained with a responsibility to worship. She's here because she needs this.

We all need this.

This hope. This faith. This harmony.

To stave off the loneliness, or the shame, or the fear, or all of the above.

"Let me ask you, my friends, what are you doing with your life to honor Christ's sacrifice? How are you spending your time before your final judgment day? Are you wasting it on hatred and judgment of your brothers and sisters? Or are you using the blessing of time you've been given to look after one another? Love each other as Jesus loves you."

The woman in the middle grows misty-eyed and I give her a soft smile and a simple nod.

After concluding my second sermon today with a prayer, I breathe a sigh of relief at the pulpit. I make my way down to the floor to mingle with the congregation, and before long, a crowd forms, waiting to shake my hand or share their kind words.

After they've all cleared out, I make my way through the back halls of the church toward my office. The team has everything else under control, and I have a meeting to get to that I don't intend to miss. It took me months to set it up.

As I reach the office, I quickly change out of my formal shirt and into something more casual. My phone chimes with a text message and I quickly pick it up to check while standing in my black slacks in my private office.

> Dad: Beautiful sermon this morning, son. I'm so proud of you.

Smiling down at the screen, I type out a quick response.

> Glad you liked it. Thank you.

Before I can put it away, I notice an incoming email and a sense of guilt gnaws at my stomach.

From: Eternal Harmony
To: Jensen Miles
Subject: Invitation to the Annual Conference, Harmony for All

---

I don't open the email. I just stare at it in my inbox and mentally berate myself for not being more enthusiastic about responding.

Deep down, I don't want to attend or contribute to the organization, and I haven't for years. But there's a deep gnawing guilt for putting off their requests. I'll deal with it later. It's a heavy topic to tackle in a rush.

After getting dressed, I throw my phone in my pocket and check my watch. Twelve fifteen. I'm going to be late if I don't hurry.

Rushing out of my office, I wave at everyone who congratulates me on a job well done this morning as I pass by them on my way out to the parking lot. I thank them all and burst out into the sunlight behind the church where my Lexus is parked in the first spot.

Zipping out of the lot, I make my way to the location on my car's nav system. It's in an older part of town, and there's not a spot to park in at first, so I circle the block a couple of times until I find something.

It's a couple minutes past ten thirty when I pull open the door to Sal's Diner. The bell above me chimes as I enter, drawing the attention of the people lingering around, waiting for a table to open up.

I see a hand waving from a small booth near the window, so I squeeze through the crowd and make my way over.

Adam Goode stands up to shake my hand as I approach him.

"Thanks for meeting me," I say as I take a seat across from him.

"Of course. I watched your sermon this morning. It was good."

I smirk as a waitress comes over and fills up his coffee cup. When I turn mine over, she fills it as well.

"I'll give you two a couple minutes to look at the menu," she says before walking away with the coffeepot.

"Thanks," I mumble to her as I stir cream and sugar into my mug.

Adam doesn't say a word at first, and judging by the tepid, unwelcoming expression on his face, he's skeptical of me and probably doesn't want to be here. I don't blame him.

To him, I'm on the enemy's side. I'm filling the shoes he probably once thought he'd fill himself. The Goode family drama has been the talk of the town for nearly two years now, and Adam wanted it that way. He made a spectacle of himself the year his father was arrested.

I decide to start with small talk in hopes that I can get him to relax and trust me. I want him to see that I'm a nice guy and nothing like his father.

"Interesting location for a meeting. Do you come here often?" I ask.

"I used to write my sermons here," he replies as he glances out the window. "Met my wife here."

He doesn't look like the same man I knew when he was in the spotlight. He looks more comfortable, laid-back. Softer around the face with a bushier beard and crow's-feet blossoming around his eyes. All the signs of a comfortable, happy man.

"You don't preach in your church on Sundays?" I ask as I lift my coffee to my lips.

"No," he replies, sitting back. "I'll never preach again. And it's not my church. We use it to feed the homeless and offer support to the community."

"Noble," I reply with sincerity. "So, no congregation."

"We have a congregation," he replies smartly, and I worry that he's taking my tone as sarcasm. "It's just a lot smaller than yours."

"Equally virtuous."

"Don't patronize me, Mr. Miles."

I put up my hands in surrender. "I promise you, I'm not."

"Then what can I help you with?"

He wants to get straight to business, which means my attempt at small talk has failed. That's fine. I can still make my case.

"I used to preach at a much smaller church in Georgetown when I had the opportunity to preach at Redemption Point. When I arrived, the congregation was weak, jilted, wary. But a lot of them stayed because that church was their home."

"You've built it up nicely, I see," he replies flatly. "So, what do you need from me?"

"I'd like to invite you to join us."

His eyes narrow at me from across the table. "Join you where?"

"To our service at Redemption Point. Join me at the pulpit. I'd like to really show the people our solidarity."

"Mr. Miles, we do not have solidarity. I won't step foot in that church again. Do you even realize what you're asking of us? My father built that church. The man who has tormented our family. Nearly killed my wife and kidnapped my niece. He broke my mother's heart and..."

He cuts himself off, grinding his molars as he glances away from me and around the diner.

"I expected this reaction from you," I say softly. "And it's warranted. Trust me, I know."

"Then why would you ask?"

"Because your father is gone. He's behind bars and that church might have been his creation, but the people are just as hurt as you are. They want to know you haven't abandoned them."

"Most of those people you speak of rallied around my father after his conviction. They supported him even after finding out what he did."

"Who are we to judge?" I ask calmly.

He huffs with a shake of his head. "You have a lot of nerve, Jensen."

The corner of my mouth twitches. "So I've been told. And I don't often take no for an answer."

"I'm telling you no," Adam says bluntly, this time staring into my eyes.

I lean back and let out a sigh. I'm not giving up. I just need to find another angle.

The waitress comes back and takes our order. I keep it simple with just an order of bacon, eggs, and toast. Adam gets the biscuits and gravy.

"What about your brothers?" I ask casually, taking another sip of coffee.

"What about them?"

"You have three, right?"

Adam tenses and glances up at me skeptically. "How much do you know about my brothers?"

"Not much," I reply casually. "There were some photos left over at the church. I did some light research. Saw you had twin brothers, Caleb and Luke. And one younger, but I couldn't find much on him."

He nods before crossing his arms over his chest. "Do you always stalk the personal details of everyone you have breakfast with?"

I laugh, although he remains stoic. "It's hardly stalking, Mr. Goode. Your family has been local celebrities since that church opened. More so in the past two years. You made sure of that."

His eyes narrow again. "Well, if your research was any good, then you'd know that I am the only Goode son who had any chance of following in his father's footsteps. Luke and Caleb don't give a shit about the church and never did."

"And your youngest brother? What happened to him?" I ask.

"He's gone," Adam responds coldly as he takes a drink and avoids my gaze. "Ran away a long time ago, so leave him out of it."

My blood runs a little cooler with the severity of his tone. "It's not my intention to pry. I assumed he was no longer in the picture. I couldn't find anything on him except for a photo of a little boy your father kept on his desk. I figured it was him."

"I don't want to talk about him anymore, if you don't mind."

"Of course."

What the hell happened to his brother? I get a nagging suspicion that there's something darker and more serious there than I realize.

We sit in silence for a few moments as I weigh my options. Our food arrives and I spend the time boasting about the church and all we've accomplished since I've taken over. I'm still trying to win him over. I could press him some more to attend for the people's sake, but it's obvious he feels as betrayed by them as they do by him.

And I'm not trying to manipulate Adam into something he doesn't want, but the truth is...Redemption Point will never be as good as it once was until we've made it clear that Truett Goode's scandal is behind us. We have to make peace as a community.

"You know..." I say carefully once our breakfast is mostly eaten.

Adam glances up at me skeptically.

"RP can offer resources for your cause. I'm sure what you have going on at your church is wonderful, but we could give you more. You've seen what we have at our disposal. You could feed more mouths, reach more people, offer more—"

He holds up a hand to stop me. "Are you bribing me?"

I watch his features and remember that Adam Goode is not a

virtuous man anymore. He's not as pious or as obedient as he once let the world believe.

I've seen the videos.

"Maybe," I reply with a shrug as I meet his gaze.

"You've got some fucking balls, Jensen."

I smirk at him as I set down my fork. "Yes, I thought we've established that."

He watches me as if he's just now noticing something about me. Then, suddenly, his expression changes. It hardens. Placing his fork down, he pushes his plate away. Then he reaches into his back pocket and pulls out his wallet. I watch with confusion as he slips a twenty-dollar bill from the fold and drops it on the table.

"What are you doing?" I ask.

"It was nice meeting you, Mr. Miles. I wish you all the best with Redemption Point. I'm sure it's in good hands."

As he stands up, I reach out a hand and place it on his arm to stop him. "I don't understand. What did I say?"

He lets out a sigh with hooded lids, a look of disappointment on his face. "It's not what you said," he murmurs. "It's who you reminded me of when you said it."

With that, he pulls his arm away and walks out of the diner. I'm left alone and reeling.

If he's implying what I think he's implying, it's a cold punch to the gut I wasn't expecting.

He thinks I'm like his father—like Truett Goode. It's a sobering realization. One I wish I could argue. I might have the same job and even the same demeanor, but if only Adam Goode knew the truth, he'd know. I am *nothing* like that man.

THREE

The lights are blinding as I clutch the guitar pick between my fingers and sing into the mic. Beyond the brightness, I don't see individual people but a tidal wave of bodies and voices. Arms reaching overhead, phone flashlights gleaming, my own lyrics being echoed back to me as I reach the bridge.

To my right, Lola smiles so brightly I can see it in my periphery. And behind me the band plays, and it's all I hear in my earpiece.

Being on tour is like nothing else I could have imagined. After my music really took off online, I knew the fan base had grown. Now, being here in a stadium where fans fill literally every seat, and they sing every word of my music, is incredible.

A fucking dream come true.

On the bridge, I let go of my guitar and swing it behind me so I can hug the stand and sing directly into the mic. I manage to make eye contact with some screaming fans in the audience as I bare my soul through the song.

Some lyrics I wrote when I was drunk or feeling emotional or pissed at my dad. It's a song about being on my own, about saying goodbye, about finding myself. Most people assume it's a breakup song, and I guess, for all intents and purposes, it is.

They just don't realize it's Theo Virgil breaking up with Isaac Goode.

I open my eyes and stare into the eyes of a young woman in the pit as she screams my own words back to me, and there's a connection so visceral between us that she starts crying immediately.

Damn, girl, who hurt you?

On the last chorus, I pull the guitar back to my front and play even louder, giving a little jump as I strum. Lights flash, and my name in bright bulbs behind me pulse as the song ends and the crowd goes wild.

"Thank you, Los Angeles!" I say, breathless, as I hold up a hand. I toss the pick into the crowd and the people scurry for it desperately.

Sweat drips down my brow and my muscles ache, but I wouldn't trade this for anything. As the band and I bow, I'm already excited just thinking about doing it all over again two nights from now in Portland.

The four of us make our way offstage and meet in the back for a postshow celebration. Lola and I hug each other as the other guys share some high fives and cheers. Every show feels like a celebration.

Granted, we've only been on tour for a week now and this is only the fourth show, but I don't know if I'll ever get sick of it. The energy is amazing.

The *only* downside, and I'm going to chalk this up to beginner's stress, is that I haven't written a word all week. In fact, since that day in the bathroom, when I stared into the mirror and wondered if I'd be a slutty loner for the rest of my life, the words just stopped coming.

No music. No lyrics. No feelings whatsoever.

Someone passes me a water bottle and I quickly chug it down, dousing the last third over my head. Lola and I make our way to the tour bus out back while the rest of the guys hang back. The tour bus is big enough for all of us, but they like to stick around and make sure their instruments get packed up correctly.

All I have to do is pass my guitar to the nearest roadie. As he takes it from my hand, he looks into my eyes and smiles. "Got it, boss," he says with a wink, and I hesitate.

He has dark-brown hair that curls from the front to the back, cropped shorter on the sides in what I like to call a country mullet. He has nice eyes too, something I've noticed nearly every night of this tour.

"Thanks," I stammer after clearing my throat.

Lola would have my head if I tried hooking up with one of our roadies. As he walks off with my guitar, my eyes follow him, and Lola notices.

"Don't even think about it," she barks, grabbing the back of my arm and hauling me toward the backstage door.

"What?" I ask, feigning innocence. "I was making sure he had my guitar."

"Right," she replies, unconvinced.

"Then let's go out. I need to get laid, Lo. It's been a week!" I complain as we reach the door. The moment the security guard opens it, I hear the fans screaming. The short distance from the door to the bus, I turn and wave to them as they snap photos of me and beg me for an autograph.

Lola passes me my cowboy hat, and I slip it on quickly before jogging over to the crowd of mostly ladies to sign what they have. I sign pictures, hats, shirts, and one pair of breasts. I wink at the girl as I hand her back her black marker.

"I'm never showering again," she says with a sigh.

Gross.

"Hope you enjoyed the show," I reply with a laugh.

After the tits, I move down the line to a younger woman who is staring at me with wide, tear-brimmed eyes. I smile at her and she starts to cry. Just when I expect her to ask me to sign something of hers, she reaches out her hands and clutches onto mine.

"Your lyrics saved my life," she says with a sob.

I freeze, staring at her as emotion burrows itself in the back of my throat.

"You have no idea how powerful your music is," she continues. "I ran away from home because of your songs and they've gotten me through the dark times. You're amazing."

A tear slips down her cheek and I scan her features, trying to discern how old she is. Does she know that I ran away too, or is it a coincidence? Does she have any support, or is she sleeping on the streets?

My heart swells as I stare at the young woman. I don't know what the fuck to say. I've had interactions like this before on my indie tour, but never this intense. My music reaches further now. More ears. More fans. More exposure.

"Thank you," I stutter. "Take care of yourself. I'm proud of you for putting yourself first," I say, and she cries more. Then she puts out her arms, and I let her wrap them around me, engulfing me in a hug as my security guards in their yellow shirts approach.

"That's enough," one of them says, but I let the girl embrace me a few moments longer.

Finally, when she pulls away, she whispers, "Thank you, Theo."

"Uh...you're welcome," I say as I let the guard pull me away and guide me to the bus. The girl's voice echoes in my ears.

Thank you, Theo.

I want to tell her that Theo didn't do shit. He didn't run away or write those words. He might have performed them, but it was Isaac who shed the blood, sweat, and tears in those songs.

"Everything all right?" Lola asks as I climb aboard the bus. She's already pulling out her clothes for a shower. I always let her go first.

"Yeah," I reply, shaking off the interaction.

"The driver said we're not leaving until five," she adds as she rummages through her stuff.

My head picks up, my interest piqued.

"In the morning?" I ask.

"No, next Tuesday," she replies with sarcasm. "Yes, in the morning."

I glance down at my phone. It's only eleven thirty, and we don't have a show tomorrow.

"Does that mean we can go out?" I ask with excitement.

She turns around and gives me a stern expression. "Yes, but just a few beers and *no* hooking up."

I huff in frustration. "What? You think I can't make it back in time?"

"If anyone can go out, find someone to fool around with, and make it back in five hours or less, it's you," she says coolly.

"Aww...you're just saying that." I smile brightly.

"I'm serious, Isaac. Just a few beers."

"Yes, Mommy."

She takes a quick shower and I'm right behind her. The tour manager isn't going to just let us leave on our own, so we have to have a driver take us with security nearby. But at this point, I don't give a shit. It's been nothing but work for a week straight, and tonight, I'm ready to have some fun.

Lola and I are the only two going out. The rest of the band, Hugh, Rio, and Waylon, rarely party with us, anyway. Hugh is married and travels with his wife, Rio is like sixty, and Waylon prefers to stay in and unwind alone.

Lola picks a local bar that seems low-key enough, and we climb into the back of a black SUV together with two security guys dressed a little more discreetly than before. It's not a gay bar, much to my disappointment. But I get it. It would blow my cover, big time.

I never set out to spend my career in the closet. This isn't how I wanted it to be, but my image grew too fast before I had a chance to say something.

Not to mention, the country music fan base isn't exactly the same crowd who cheer on the pop stars who come out. I don't know how they'd react, and I'm terrified to find out.

And then, of course, there's the issue of my label not knowing I'm gay. They asked me to sign on the dotted line and I never thought to stop them and say, "Hey, by the way, you should know, I enjoy sucking dick. Will that be a problem?"

So, yeah. The likelihood of getting that tonight is very slim to none, but I'll happily settle for getting drunk at a bar on a rowdy Saturday night.

I slip out of the SUV with a pair of shades on, and Lola looks back and laughs at me.

"What?" I ask. "I want to be incognito."

She loops her arm through mine as we make our way inside. It's a loud, busy bar with a dance floor to the right and a long bar that is brimming with people. Feeling instantly exposed and uncomfortable, I'm in desperate need of a drink.

Just when I think this is a stupid idea, the security guard ushers us to a set of stairs on the right.

"Where are we going?" I ask.

"Someone called ahead and reserved you a VIP table up here," he says.

Lola and I make eye contact, sharing an expression of surprise. We're not really VIP people. We're more dive bar, hole-in-the-wall-type people, but this I could get used to. Especially when they show us to a large area with a private bar, servers, and large tables occupied by others.

"Welcome," a cute server says as we sit down at the table. "What can I get you guys to drink?" she asks.

Before long there is an entire bottle of Tito's on the table between us because neither of us felt right ordering beer in a place like this.

"Holy shit, isn't he an actor?" Lola asks as she nods her head to the table next to us.

I turn around to see some fancy action star behind me with a throng of women around him.

"Oh fuck, yeah, it is. He's even hotter in person," I whisper back to her.

It feels strange to be at the table alone with Lola, and I wonder if this was a mistake, but before long, others start to approach and see our empty seats and spare alcohol as an invitation.

The vodka goes down easy and the party blurs nicely around us. Some people recognize me, but it's not like being surrounded by fans. Most of them are other celebrities or friends of celebrities.

As the night goes on, I let loose. I get flirty. Typical Theo behavior. I'm touching people and making inappropriate jokes, and I lose track of Lola because she caught the eye of some hot young actor.

A very good-looking guy ends up sitting next to me and telling me all about his Instagram page devoted to fitness, which I can't be less fucking interested in. But I'm drunk, so I fake it and focus on how nicely muscled his thighs are and how good he smells and how nice his lips would look around my cock.

But I never make a move. I just listen to him go on and on about his career, his *message* and his values, and I never once nudge him to go to the bathroom with me to fool around.

Why? Because he knows I'm Theo Virgil, and it's not worth the risk.

One pic of me hurrying off with a guy would ruin everything and at the beginning of my big tour.

Even when he places a hand on my thigh, I manage to talk him off, and I've never done that before. It all just feels so fucking unfair. Lola is in the corner of the bar making out with some dude she just met and I'm denying myself this fitness god because I'm afraid the world won't like it.

When Lola and I finally stumble our way back to the SUV, I'm in a bad mood. I should be proud of myself for making the smart choice, but I'm not. I'm just pissed and still a little horny.

Deep down, it suddenly feels like I'm living in Truett Goode's house again. Like the whole fucking world is Truett Goode's house, and I'll never be able to escape.

FOUR

JENSEN

When I walk through the automatic doors of the bowling alley, the crashing sound of the pins greets me as I notice my parents in the center lane. My mom throws her hands up and cheers as all ten of the pins crash in a strike.

My dad gives her a high five as I approach them. As soon as they see me coming, they greet me with big smiles and warm hugs.

"You made it," my mother says excitedly as she wraps her arms around me.

"Of course," I reply, slinging an arm over her shoulders.

My parents are in a Monday night bowling league and I try to join them as often as I can. My dad is in his late seventies, happy in his retirement, standing just a few inches shorter than me, with light-gray hair and a cropped beard.

"How's work been, son?" he asks as he runs a towel over the blue marble ball in his hands.

"It's been good," I say with a nod. "Had nearly twelve hundred at our last service."

"That's wonderful, baby," my mom says, hugging her arms around my waist.

"Yeah. We can seat up to two thousand, so we're getting there. I'm proud of how far we've come."

My dad takes his turn to bowl, and I pour myself a drink from their pitcher of soda. My parents are hardworking people. My mom was a high school English teacher for nearly forty years, and my dad is a retired cop. We really are the quintessential American family.

They had me in their thirties after years of trying to conceive, making me an only child, but I have no complaints about my upbringing. They are the best people I know, and they did everything they could to give me a good life.

The door to the alley opens and I turn to see my parents' longtime best friends, the Kozacks, walk in.

"Well, look what the cat dragged in," Mr. Kozack says, clapping a hand on my shoulder. He's a burly man with a large belly and a receding hairline.

He and his wife greet my mom with hugs and handshakes. Then I watch their daughter walk in behind them.

Gabrielle Kozack is younger than me by twelve years, meaning she was just a child when our parents became friends. We've barely gotten to know each other, although it's been over a decade. She is only twenty-eight and recently out of a long relationship.

It's not at all her fault why her presence makes me instantly uncomfortable.

"Jensen, you remember Gabby, right?" my mother asks sweetly.

"Of course." I reach out a hand to shake hers, but she goes in for a hug first. It's awkward, but I try to play it off, feeling my mother's lingering gaze on us as we embrace.

"Good to see you again," she says while curling some hair behind her ear and avoiding my gaze.

Gabby is a beautiful woman, but she's also very shy and a little awkward. I never know what to say to her when we're alone.

Which doesn't make things better when our parents strike up

a conversation with each other, leaving me and Gabby to fend for ourselves.

"You still working at the library?" I ask, taking a sip of my soda.

She nods. "Just a library tech for now. But I'm thinking about going back to school to get my master's in library science."

"That's great," I say, nodding and not knowing what else to say. Normally, I'm great at small talk. But every time I speak with her, or any woman for that matter, I feel so lost. I wish I could understand the disconnect.

"And you're still preaching, right?" She picks at a hole in her jeans as she lets her gaze rake over my body.

"Yeah. Over at Redemption Point. You should come sometime."

Please let's talk about the church. I could do that for hours.

Her head tilts back and forth with little interest. "Maybe someday," she says, which means never. "That's so cool, though," she adds. "I bet they love you there."

For the first time tonight, her eyes meet mine, and I think there might be a spark of something. Hoping it's a real connection, I hold her eye contact for longer than usual.

"I hope so," I reply slowly, in a deeper timbre.

She definitely notices and licks her lips. I let my eyes scan her features, gauging my attraction with each pass.

Soft lips. Cute nose. Light-blue eyes. Bombshell-blonde hair.

I could see the attraction here. I could imagine myself kissing her lips if I tried hard enough. I imagine what it would feel like to hold her body against mine. To roll on top of her and settle between her thighs.

I could do that easily.

Gabby and I make small talk for a while. Then we make our way to the bar, leaving our parents behind. She orders a spicy margarita, and I get a pint of Guinness. We share some nachos and talk about work, life and dating.

She teases me for my age and I tease her for hers, and before long, it feels more natural than it's ever felt before.

I can do this.

Then, a song comes on the radio, playing through the speakers of the bowling alley. I mouth the words and tap my hand on the bar.

"I love this song."

"Oh my gosh, me too!" she says, grabbing my arm. "I am obsessed with Theo Virgil!"

"His new album is incredible," I reply, which is true. I am a big fan of Theo's LPs, but this new one, *Unholy Ghost*, is his best work yet.

"His lyrics are so good," she says, still holding my arm. "He just has a way of speaking to my soul."

"Same," I reply, but when I catch my reactions growing too enthusiastic or excited, I bite my tongue and school myself to keep it under control.

"I have tickets for his show in Phoenix."

My eyes dart to her face and I freeze. I've been wanting to see Theo for so long, but I seem to miss all his shows.

"I'm very jealous," I reply. I love that we have even more to talk about now. If she's truly a big Theo fan, this could give us even more to bond over.

Then her eyes meet mine, and they widen. "Well, I was going to sell them. My friend had to cancel because of her anniversary, and I don't want to go alone."

Is she inviting me to go to Phoenix with her?

When I don't respond, she continues. "You should go with me!"

"To Phoenix?"

"Yes! Flights are cheap there, and it would be such a blast."

Instantly, I start thinking about plane rides and hotel rooms, and anxiety builds inside me.

But for Theo Virgil tickets...

"Oh, and did I mention they include backstage passes?" She gives a coy smile as she brings the straw of her drink to her lips.

My jaw drops. "You're joking with me."

She shakes her head slowly.

"Yes, let's do it," I say without hesitation. "When is it?"

"Next Tuesday night. But we could do one night in Phoenix and fly back Wednesday."

"I'll buy the tickets now," I say, picking up my phone. Gabby starts to giggle excitedly, and it's a sweet sound. Bubbly and warm.

She really could be perfect for me. I just have to get over my hang-ups.

Again, for backstage Theo Virgil tickets, I'd do just about anything.

I book the plane tickets quickly on my phone and she works on getting us a hotel room, picking a nice one near the venue. We settle on a single room with two queen beds and agree that for just one night, we can share.

I don't miss the excited energy written all over her face as she books it. Judging by the way she leans in, touches my arm, and smiles flirtatiously at me, it's clear that Gabby is interested in more.

So am I.

So am I, so am I, so am I.

If I say it enough in my head, it will make it true, right?

Our parents head over shortly after their game, and I notice my mom's eager expression as she takes in just how well Gabby and I are getting along. She's been hounding me to find a nice girl and settle down for a while anyway, so I know that's what she's wishing for now.

And if I did it with her best friend's daughter, she'd be on cloud nine.

"Jensen is going to go with me to Phoenix next week for the Theo Virgil concert!" she says excitedly to her parents.

My mom's eyes light up. She's watching me with an enthusiastic smirk, excitedly wringing her hands.

"That's wonderful!" Gabby's mom says. "You two will have a great time."

As the six of us leave the bowling alley together, I sense my mother hovering behind Gabby and me, but when I move to say goodbye to her, she gives us space.

"I'll see you next week, then," Gabby says while staring up into my eyes.

"I can't wait."

Gabby moves in for a hug, and I start to panic, afraid she's coming in for a kiss. To my relief, she's not and we just share a quick, platonic embrace.

Leaving her at her car, I walk over to my own, where my mother is waiting.

"Well, that sounds like fun for you two," she says with mischief in her eyes.

"Yeah," I stammer.

"Gabby is such a nice girl. I think she's perfect for you, Jens."

I clear my throat. We're getting dangerously close to uncomfortable topics of conversation. I don't want to upset her. All I want is to make my parents proud, so I put on a brave face and remember to breathe.

This is how it's meant to be. It's not too late to change.

Old mantras come back, echoing through my mind like habits.

Growth is possible. God makes everything possible.

"She is a nice girl," I say with false confidence.

"I'd love to see you two together," she murmurs innocently. "A mother could dream."

"She's a lot younger than me. That doesn't bother you?"

"Why would it bother me? Gabby is in need of guidance. She needs someone to take care of her, and you could do that. You two would make a lovely couple."

"Enough, Mom," I say with humor in my tone.

"I know, I know. I won't meddle."

When she touches my arm, the love in her words and her

touch is apparent. How could I suspect my mother of anything less?

"I just want you to be happy. Is that too much to ask?"

I pull her into a hug and kiss the side of her head. "Not at all, Mom. But you don't have to worry. I am happy. I promise."

"Good, baby."

As she pulls away, she pats my arm and stares into my eyes. I catch something in her expression that sours the warmth in my stomach. It's like she's acknowledging the elephant in the room with her eyes. The thing we don't acknowledge anymore.

She stares a moment too long. A little too serious. A little too concerned.

But instead of talking about it or giving this awkward thing room to breathe and grow, we shove it in a drawer and slam it shut. We don't need to look at it, or remember it, or think about it.

Why would we when we can just move on and pretend it doesn't exist?

With that, I say goodbye to my mother, opening her door so she can climb into the passenger seat. My dad waves to me before I slam her door shut and send them off.

When they're gone, I take a deep breath. And when I'm alone, I don't open the drawer. I don't take out that nagging truth or memories from the past. I don't revisit any of that. I just keep it out of sight and get into my car.

Next week, I'll go on that trip with Gabby. Maybe we'll have a few drinks at the concert and end up making out before the end of the show. Maybe we'll catch a cab back to the hotel together and end up having wild, uninhibited sex in one of those queen beds. Maybe we'll cuddle and talk about our future and make plans to see each other again.

Maybe it will all end up okay. Maybe, maybe, maybe.

The more I play out the scenario in my head, the more it feels like someone else's life.

Because it certainly doesn't feel like mine.

FIVE

ISAAC

The crowd chants the words of the song back to me, and the echo of voices is incredible. Tonight's show is in an amphitheater, and I think I love this even more than stadiums. The dark night sky covered in stars makes for an amazing backdrop that even the bright lights over the stage can't dull.

It's enough to distract me from the fact that I still haven't written a word in almost two weeks. The muse will come back. It has to.

We always start off the show with a loud banger to get the crowd excited. It's not my most recently popular song, but it's familiar enough that major fans know the words and sing along.

As it comes to an end, my band and I play the strongest and loudest, laying hard on the guitars and drums. The crowd cheers for a while before I take to the microphone and address them.

"Hey there, Phoenix. How y'all doin' tonight?"

They scream in response. As the lights overhead scan out to the crowd and off me, I gaze out into the throng of people, finding eyes in the masses to connect with.

Tonight, my gaze connects with a tall, handsome man near the front. He's standing in the pit with a short blonde woman at his side.

I smile at him a moment before tearing my eyes away. "What a beautiful night to be together," I say. "Y'all have no idea how grateful I am to be on this tour and get to spend my nights with lovely people like you and this amazing band of mine."

The crowd cheers, and I find the man in the front of the crowd again.

Damn, he sure is cute. Tall and handsome and rich-looking.

Jesus, Isaac. Focus.

"Now, if you don't mind," I say, pulling my guitar to the front slowly. "I'd like to slow things down for a moment and play you a song that is very near to my heart. It's something I wrote a long time ago when I was feeling down..."

I strum a few chords on the guitar, and some of the audience picks up on it immediately, clapping with excitement.

"This song is about being really fucking lonely. You know that feeling when you just get in your car and you just start driving, not knowing where you're going?"

"I love you!" someone shouts from deep within the amphitheater.

"I love you too," I mumble into the mic, making people laugh.

Then, for some fucking reason, I find that man again.

"This song is called 'Lonely Pilgrimage.'"

Mr. Tall and Handsome cheers and claps, and we actually stare at each other as he mouths my song back to me. *He knows my songs.* He's not just here because of his girlfriend, like I assume a lot of guys are. My demographic is about sixty-forty, women to men.

But this guy...he's smiling and cheering and seemingly a real fan. Well, fuck if that doesn't go straight to my dick.

As I play the song, it starts out acoustic. For a while, there's nowhere for my voice to hide as I sing, closing my eyes and hearing only the metronome and guitar track in my ear. This is one of my least favorite songs to play live because, for one, it's incredibly personal.

I wasn't lying to the crowd. I did write it when I was feeling lonely, missing my family. I was in Nashville alone when I got in my car one night and just started driving. I went southwest, not planning to stop until I hit Austin.

About halfway home, it hit me. I was alone. And they weren't.

Obviously, I had Luke if I needed him, but Luke's devotion to me was not the same. He stepped up because I needed him. He stepped up because no one else would.

I missed my *family*. I missed the promise Adam made when I was a kid that they would always have my back.

That night wasn't the first time I felt resentment for my family. It wasn't the first time I wanted to curse at them.

But I was the one who left. I disappeared and I left them no choice. And yet, there I was, mad to be alone.

Digging my own grave is a running theme with me, it seems.

So yeah, the lyrics—*running from you was like running from myself. Running out of breath and running out of steam but not quite where I want to be*—were real.

When I gaze out at the crowd, hearing them sing backup for me, I see the faces of the people who share that pain. I don't know what they went through, but whatever it was, it leaves similar scars, that's for sure.

As the song comes to an end, they lose their minds again. Screaming and cheering on their feet.

I smile out into the lights and the dark sky, and I feel fucking grateful.

✝

After the show, the band and I hang out backstage for a while. The record label has some people we need to meet, so after going to the greenroom for a minute to get cleaned up, we're led to one of the suites that overlooks the stage and the mountains in the distance.

"I need a fucking drink," I grumble under my breath to Lola as we enter the throng of people.

Everyone cheers as they see me come in. Guys in suits with beautiful women with rhinestones on their arms come to shake my hand. I don't catch their names or titles as I search the room for some fucking alcohol.

VPs of something, marketing directors, associates, whatever. I don't fucking care. But I need to keep the record label happy, so I give them all warm smiles and keep them engaged.

Finally, a waiter walks by and asks if I want anything.

"Yes," I say with too much enthusiasm. "Tequila soda with lime. Make it a double."

"Easy," Lola says under her breath.

"Stop mothering me," I whisper back so no one can hear.

The suits are all talking, trying to keep my attention, and when the tequila eventually hits my lips, everything calms inside me. I crack jokes with them and get comfortable for a while.

From what I can tell, these men are all like my father. Conservative, haughty, self-indulgent assholes who only care about themselves and their own pockets.

But more importantly, they're filling mine, so I have to say and do the right things. In the back of my mind is the cruel and nagging reminder that if they knew the truth about me, they might not be so nice.

Then, as I'm taking a drink from my glass, my eyes catch on someone familiar across the room. Mr. Tall and Handsome is here.

Holy shit.

He's standing by the window with the blonde woman, both of them looking nervous as they watch me. Are they just fans who managed to snag some backstage passes?

He's clearly straight, so it's stupid of me to want to talk to him, but I do. I worked hard tonight. I deserve to indulge in a hard drink and a conversation with a hot man.

"Excuse me, gentlemen," I say politely when the conversation dies down. The men carry on talking without me as I make my way over to the other side of the room. There's a buffet that I use as an excuse to head in that direction.

I snack on a few chips before making eye contact with him. Even more handsome up close, I see. Dark hair swept to the side with high cheekbones and a strong jawline. I could cut fucking glass with that bone structure.

"Hey there," I say, picking up a shrimp from around the bowl of ice. "You guys enjoy the show?"

The man clears his throat, and I realize that he looks a little more starstruck than the woman. She's shy, I can tell, but he can't take his eyes off me like I'm over here sparkling.

"Absolutely," he says as he comes closer. "You were incredible out there."

"It was so good," the woman chirps quietly at his side. She tries to cling to his arm, but he pulls it away, reaching for a handshake from me.

"I'm Jensen Miles. It's such a pleasure to meet you, Mr. Virgil."

I nearly choke on the shrimp cocktail as I laugh. "Jesus, please don't call me that. Theo is fine."

There's a twinkle of interest in his eyes as I slide my hand into his. He squeezes my palm so firmly that it sends a jolt of excitement down my spine.

Easy, Isaac.

"I'm Gabrielle," the woman says, and I have to tear myself away from the dark oak-colored eyes of the man to remind myself that she's standing there.

"Lovely to meet you, Gabrielle. Thanks for coming to the show."

"I'm so starstruck," she says with a giggle as she covers her mouth.

"You two from around here?" I ask, wanting to make small talk. I'd rather talk to them and stare at him than go back to the boring suits.

"No, we flew over from Austin for the show."

I wince at the sound of my hometown. I don't openly claim Austin as my home, not as Theo, at least. Theo is from all over. A little Nashville. A little New York.

But the idea that this guy resides somewhere in the vicinity of my family makes me feel suddenly uneasy. Does he know my family? Does he recognize me?

Surely not. I've done enough digging to know that the only photos of me associated with my father or his church are from when I was very young, with lighter locks, no facial hair, and a bit more pudge on my boyish face.

I look almost nothing like Isaac anymore.

"My record label is actually based out of Austin," I say because it's an innocent thing to admit. "I'm there quite often."

I do not miss the way Jensen's eyes widen and sparkle with interest at hearing that.

Because he's interested in my music, of course.

"A friend of mine got these tickets because her dad works for your label, actually," the girl says, beaming brightly. "But she had something come up, so Jensen was nice enough to step in last minute."

"Oh, that's nice," I say as my eyes bounce back and forth between them. Something about the way she said that caught my attention.

I decide to be bold because I'm just straight nosy.

"What a good boyfriend."

Jensen flinches. It's not even subtle. I could have seen it from a mile away.

"Oh, we're not," he stammers, quickly correcting me while the woman looks mildly offended. "We're just friends."

Interesting.

Lola would tell me to walk away. Drop it. Don't risk it.

My subconscious is not as convincing. Because I don't want to drop it. I want to keep pushing and flirting, even knowing that he's probably straight, even if he isn't dating this woman.

Digging my own grave, per usual.

"You guys want a drink?" I ask, looking directly at Jensen while I ask it.

"Sure," he says without tearing his eyes away.

We walk to the bar together, and I notice that he's just a couple of inches taller than me. And I'm six-three. It's rare that I have to look up when talking to a guy.

"Can I get another tequila soda, please?" I order when we reach the bar.

"I'll have the same," Jensen replies.

His friend doesn't order anything. Instead, she chews on her bottom lip nervously.

As he and I make small talk, talking about random shit like Austin and the album, she sort of hangs back without joining in.

Across the room, I can feel Lola watching me skeptically. I can already hear her in my head telling me to be careful, and I know she's right. I should be careful.

But I've never been careful before, and I don't intend to start now.

Six

JENSEN

I can't believe I'm standing at a bar with Theo Virgil. I can't believe he's real and talking to me.

I can't believe he's even cuter in person than he is onstage and in pictures. His smile is adorable, creating little creases in his cheeks when he smiles. His entire face lights up and it's impossible to look away.

No matter how much I train my behavior not to flirt with him, I can't seem to help it. I lean in too much. Stare at his pouty lips too much. Laugh too hard at his jokes.

Gabby is at my side like a harsh reminder that I'm supposed to be here with her. But Theo Virgil takes up the entire room. His mere existence drowns out every voice in here. He is the only person I see.

And the more tequila I drink, the more I let my guard down. Those voices in my head that usually pop up with the mantras I learned decades ago are too quiet tonight.

Change is possible. With God, all things are possible.

It doesn't quite resonate when it feels like God himself is standing right in front of me.

"So, what do you do for a living, Jensen?" he asks with one elbow on the bar.

Instead of his usual worn-out cowboy hat, he has a baseball cap on flipped backward. His dark-brown curls peek out of the back with still-wet tips like he recently got out of the shower.

At his question, I hesitate. I consider telling the truth, but for some reason, I don't want him to know I'm a preacher.

Don't lie to yourself. You know exactly why you don't want him to know.

"I, uh, work for a nonprofit." It's close enough to the truth.

"A benevolent man," he says before his tongue slips out and wets his bottom lip. A spark of arousal travels down my spine, and I reach into my pocket to pinch the flesh of my hip to stop it.

It doesn't work.

He includes Gabby in on the question, and she answers, talking about her work at the library, but I'm not listening. There is too much going on inside me.

"You said you two were just friends. I take it neither of you are married then?" he asks, again just looking at me.

I shake my head with a smirk on my lips. "Nope. Not married."

His gaze breezes down to my lips and back up to my eyes. *Am I imagining things? Did Theo Virgil just check me out?*

Is he...

It doesn't matter.

It doesn't.

By the time we order our third drink, Gabby is growing restless beside me. I'm no fool. I know she had hopes for this trip, and maybe I led her on. Only a few days ago, I was supposed to want that, too. I was supposed to have hope of something happening, too.

As of right now, I can't grasp that hope. It's slipping through my fingers, and I can't remember why I wanted it in the first place.

Theo talks for a while about his tour and traveling with the band and what it meant for him to hit it big, and I soak up every word. I could stand here for years and listen to him talk, and it's not just because he's a celebrity and my favorite singer.

It's just his energy. I'm addicted to it. It seeps into my bloodstream like a drug, and I just want more.

"We should get going," a black-haired woman says as she taps Theo's arm. "The bus takes off in a few hours."

It takes me a moment to recognize her as the bassist in his band.

Theo looks disappointed before giving her an obedient nod. "You're right."

Then he looks at me, and I realize he's about to leave. Instantly, imagining him walking away from me tugs painfully on my heart. I've never felt that way about anyone, but I don't want this night to end.

"Hey, this was fun," he says, looking at me. "Why don't we exchange numbers? You know...to catch up back in Austin."

My heart picks up in my chest. Swap numbers with a man? Alarms are going off in my head, and I know this is not what I should be doing, but he's Theo fucking Virgil. It's not like he's hitting on me. He just wants someone to hang out with.

Beside me, Gabby clears her throat, but I ignore her.

"Definitely," I say, pulling my phone from my back pocket. As I hand it to him, I can practically hear my pulse throbbing. I watch as he pulls open a new text message and types his number out before texting a small message.

"There, I texted myself, so I have yours too."

He hands it back to me, and our fingers brush. A phantom tingle echoes on my skin long after the contact is made.

Then he says his goodbyes to each of us before being dragged out by the bassist. Once Gabby and I are alone, I still feel like I'm reeling. Turning toward her, I notice that she has less excitement on her face. She seems almost annoyed.

"Can you believe that just happened?" I ask as I guide her toward the door.

"He was very nice," she says with less enthusiasm.

"So down-to-earth. That was amazing."

"He really seemed to like you," she says under her breath, but I ignore it. Maybe she's just jealous that Theo preferred to talk to me more.

We catch a taxi in front of the theater and ride to the hotel in silence. I'm still in shock that that happened, replaying everything we said over and over in my head.

It takes me by surprise when Gabby leans on me in the back seat. Her shoulder is pressed to my arm and her knuckles skate delicately over mine. I tense immediately as everything inside me turns to stone.

Now it's time to pay the piper, I guess. I had my fun with Theo, but now I have to put my energy and attention where it belongs. Where it *should* be.

I rub her knuckles back to show that I acknowledge her. She intertwines our fingers and gazes up at me with something warm and excited in her eyes.

Then, the distance between us starts to close, and I brace myself. If I try hard enough, I could enjoy this.

As her lips brush mine, I imagine Theo's pouty lips. I remember the way his tongue darted out to wet them. When I softly run my tongue into her mouth, I picture his.

There's a quiet rumble in my chest as I kiss her deeper. There's even a stirring of heat in my pants. But when I touch her jaw and it's soft skin instead of rough stubble, the heat extinguishes.

I pull away and drop my hand. Her eyes are dilated with arousal as she gazes up at me.

We're about to share a hotel room for the evening, and I hate myself for dreading it. When we reach the hotel, I keep her hand in mine as we make our way up the elevator. The entire time I'm debating on what I'll do.

I could tell Gabby that it's too soon to be intimate. As a pastor, it's wrong of me to be with a woman I'm not married to. I could tell her that I think we should just be friends. I could suck it up and take her to bed anyway.

When I press the key card against the lock, it opens with a beep. Once inside, I still haven't decided on my next move, but Gabby hasn't released my hand yet either.

She tugs gently on it, and I pull her into my arms. "I have a secret," she says.

"What's that?"

"I didn't come here to see Theo Virgil. I came here to spend time with you."

"Oh," I reply in a deep tone. "That's nice."

Damn, I'm so bad at this.

"I wanted to spend time with you too," I say, but even I hear how unconvincing it is.

She giggles before tugging me down toward her. "Just kiss me again, please."

With a deep breath, I do. Her lips are too soft. Her skin is too soft. Her kiss is too soft.

After the kiss ends, she breathes a sigh and relaxes against my chest. "I know you're not the kind of man to take a woman to bed on the first date, but I was thinking we could at least share the bed tonight. We don't have to do anything."

Everything she's saying grates on my nerves. I'm forty fucking years old. I don't need to share a bed with another adult like a teenager. I need another consenting adult to fuck. And I don't like being patronized.

Taking her chin in my hands, I force her gaze up to my face. "I'm not the man you think I am, Gabby."

Her eyes go wide. Then I take her mouth in a punishing kiss, and she lets out a yelp as she clings to my neck to keep from falling over.

I know I'm not supposed to, but I picture Theo anyway. His lips, his mouth, his body. With my hands gliding down her back, I hook a hand under her ass and lift her up so her legs wrap around my waist.

Carrying her to the bed, I toss her on the mattress and rip my shirt over my head. She's smiling as she reaches for me.

"I knew I was wrong about you. I knew *everyone* was wrong about you."

There's a giggle in her tone that makes me pause. Hovering over her, I stare into her eyes.

"How were they wrong?"

Her smile fades as she lifts onto her elbows. "Well, you know…"

Ice shivers its way down my spine. *Fuck.*

The problem is that I do know. Fucking everyone knows—unofficially, of course. It doesn't mean I like to be reminded about it right before I'm about to have sex with a beautiful woman.

When she sees my expression change, I sense her panic. "Shit, I'm sorry. I didn't mean… I thought…"

"It's fine," I say as I climb off her and pace away from the bed.

"I didn't want to push you into doing anything if you didn't want to. But my parents told me about how you were a part of that Harmony-whatever program. I just thought…"

"It's fine, Gabby," I say coldly. "I was only a kid. That was a long time ago," I add with annoyance.

"I shouldn't have brought it up," she replies sadly.

"No, you shouldn't have."

I want to feel bad, but I'm so fucking sick of this. My participation with Eternal Harmony was over fifteen years ago, but it keeps popping back up in my life. When do I get to move on? When do I get to live this life they were so insistent that I live?

I drop onto the other bed and run my hands through my hair. Her eyes still bore into me and I can feel it burning.

By the time she opens her mouth to ask a question, I'm not surprised because I can feel it coming.

"So does that mean you're not…"

"No, I'm not."

"It's okay if you are."

No, it's really not.

"Let's just get to sleep. It's late," I say as I drop back onto the pillow. I'm so tired and ready to put an end to this day. I'll sleep in my clothes if I have to.

"We can still do it if you want," she murmurs sadly, and I close my eyes to keep from wincing.

Maybe I should. If I had any good sense, I would take this beautiful woman to bed and fuck her like any normal straight man would.

But I don't.

Because I'm not.

SEVEN

Climbing on the tour bus, I can't get the sound of Jensen's voice out of my head. Deep, smooth, and sexy.

He was definitely flirting with me. There are times I lie to myself and pretend a straight guy is into me for the fun of it, but by the end of the evening, it was obvious.

Whether he knows it or not. He was flirting with me.

Lola drops onto the couch next to Rio, who is already lounging back with the TV on. He didn't go to the after-party, it seems. Not that I would have noticed. My attention was elsewhere.

Our bus is gigantic. There's a couch and a couple of recliners, a small kitchenette, four bunks for the band, and a room in the back for me. It's almost unbelievable how massive it is.

Instead of hanging with the band in the main area, I move toward my room at the back and close the door behind me. I play it off like I'm just tired, but really, I want to unwind and decompress by myself.

Once alone, I toss my hat on the hook and shuck off my jeans and shirt. Down to my boxer briefs, I crawl into my bed and collapse against the pillows. With my phone in my hand, I scroll mindlessly. And before long, I end up doing exactly what I knew I would.

I pull up his text message. It's the one I sent myself, of course, but I stare at it anyway.

There's no time to hook up with him tonight. The bus is already fired up and ready to go. But if there's any chance I could end up wrapped up in those meaty thighs somewhere in the future, I'd like to make that happen.

Thanks again for coming to the show.

My finger hovers over the send button, but I hesitate. Am I being too desperate? Too clingy? He's going to think I'm a loser if I text him already.

I'll wait until tomorrow. Or what is the rule? Three days?

Instead, I open a private browser on my phone and settle on some tried-and-true visual stimulation. Then I reach into my briefs and wrap a hand around my cock. It relieves the stress in my body after a long night.

It's no six-and-a-half-foot daddy, and it doesn't rev my creative engine, but it still gets the job done.

✝

By the time I wake up, we're in Salt Lake City. Our show isn't until tomorrow, so the crew can get everything set up, which means I have a day off. The moment I wake up, I think about texting Jensen. Did he go back to Austin? Did he sleep with that woman last night? If I had stayed longer, could he and I—

What the fuck has gotten into me?

I stay in bed as long as I can. I figure I need the rest after last night. Around noon, I finally get up. My phone has messages from the tour manager and Rio. Just because there's no show tonight doesn't mean I'm off. I still have to meet with my marketing team and agent about brand endorsements. They want me in an ad for jeans, not my songs, *me*. We're not shooting that until next month, but there's still stuff to be coordinated.

I take a quick shower after getting up. Then I find Lola on the couch outside my room.

"Hey, I texted you. We're all going out for lunch if you want to come," she says casually.

"Fuck yeah, I'm starving."

I pull on my boots and hide my hair under a ball cap as we step off the bus together. A black car waits for us as we climb in. As soon as my ass hits the seat of the SUV, my phone buzzes in my back pocket.

Assuming it's just my agent, I pull it out and swipe it open.

> It was great hanging out with you last night.

My brain takes a moment to catch up with itself. I stare at his message too long before it finally kicks in. Jensen.

Oh shit.

My mouth tugs into a smile as I type out my response.

> Had a blast. I don't think your friend had as much fun, though.

I bite my bottom lip and wonder if I overstepped. I don't know how close they are or if I've offended him by bringing her up.

> She had other plans for the evening, but she's fine.

Other plans? Instantly I wonder if that woman would have rather spent those two hours horizontal with him instead of talking to me. I don't like the visual, so I push it aside.

> You headed home today?

> Yeah. At the airport now.

We just made it to SLC today.

You have another show tonight?

Tomorrow.

Nice. Busy guy.

Very. But it's a good busy.

Yeah. I bet it is.

The show really was amazing. You're a natural.

I promise I'm not just saying that.

"What's got you smiling like that?" Lola asks from the seat beside me.

"Nothing," I mutter as I hide my phone from her.

"Wouldn't happen to be that tall stranger I saw you talking to last night, would it?" She gives me a haughty smirk.

"Maybe," I mumble quietly.

"Please don't tell me you're fucking around with married men."

I let out a gasp as I turn to her with offense. "When have I ever?"

"Never that I know of, but that girl on his arm looked pretty cozy at his side."

"They were just friends," I argue.

"Good," she says. "And you're texting him because…"

"Because he was fun to talk to, *Mom*."

Without responding, she rests her head on my shoulder. "Just be careful. I happen to love you, and I don't want to see you get hurt."

I softly pet her hair and kiss her on the head. "I love you too, but I promise, I'm being careful."

We arrive at a diner, and Lola and I climb out of the SUV. They seat us at a table in the back, and when I pick up the menu to browse, my phone buzzes again.

> God, I was being a neurotic fan, wasn't I?

> Shit, I'm sorry.

> Forget I said anything.

> I'm actually not a fan at all.

I chuckle to myself.

> Thank fuck.

> What a relief.

> I prefer talking to guys who don't actually like me.

My cheeks start to burn when I hit send and realize that the last text was far too revealing. Why did I say that? He's going to freak out. He's going to realize I'm not texting him as a friend. He's going to know everything.

The typing bubbles pop up, and turmoil boils inside me. Biting my lip, I wait for his reply.

> Well, that's too bad. Because I do like you.

My heart hammers wildly in my chest. I feel like a teenager, staring at his message while my insides do somersaults. I just met this guy last night. Why am I acting like such a kid?

Because he's hot. He's so fucking hot.

And we had real chemistry.

"Earth to Theo." I look up from my phone to find Lola staring at me with a look of exasperation. Then I notice the woman standing to my left with an apron on and a notepad in her hand.

"Oh shit, sorry. I'll uh...have a Coke and a cheeseburger, please."

"Everything on it?" the woman asks, sounding annoyed.

"Yes, ma'am."

She scribbles something down and walks away. When I glance at Lola, she looks in shock.

"Wow, you got it bad."

"Okay, but if you saw how cute this last text was, you'd be in a daze too." I bite my lip as I read it again.

She doesn't look as excited. The skepticism in her eyes kinda bums me out.

"You're a celebrity now, Theo. People love you, but you need to be careful."

"I am being careful," I say, trying to brush her off. I'm a little annoyed that she's trying to rain on my parade right now. I found a tall, beautiful man who wants to flirt with me. Let me live.

When I take too long to respond, Jensen texts again.

Too much?

Not at all.

Maybe I'm feeling rebellious, or maybe his last text has me feeling bold. But I type out something a little crazy.

You should come to my show tomorrow.

I continue to chew on my lip as I wait for his response. It's wild that I'm asking a guy I just met yesterday to fly out to Utah to see me after just two days. What am I thinking will happen?

I know what I *want* to happen. Does he?

No matter how many times I tell myself and Lola that I'm being careful, I can see my own behavior plain as day. I'm not being careful at all. In fact, I'm being downright fucking reckless.

Are you serious?

Fuck. I went too far. I made it awkward.

I mean, sure. If you want.

You've probably got work and a life

and you can't just drop everything to come hang out with me again.

I'll be there.

I have to cover my smile with my own hand as Lola scrolls on her phone across the table.

"Don't even try to hide it, lover boy. They can see you grinning from the parking lot."

"He's coming to the show tomorrow," I murmur behind my hand.

"I figured as much," she replies flatly. "Just text Jill and tell her to save you a ticket. He can pick it up at the will call."

"You're not mad at me?" I ask, propping my chin on my hand and gazing at her in the opposite seat.

She drops her phone. "No, but if he outs you or hurts you, I'm going to find him and cut his nuts off and wear them as a necklace." She nods at my phone. "Text him that."

"I will."

Are you sure?

I know it's last minute.

We can hang out again, right?

Yes. Definitely.

I don't think there's going to be any fancy guys in suits this time,

so we can just go do our own thing.

Perfect.

I can cover the flight too.

Don't worry about it. I'll be fine.

Awesome.

Your tickets will be at the will call.

Should I tell them one or two?

My knee is bouncing wildly under the table. If he says two, then I'll know he's just a fan and not interested in me in that way. I can live with that...I guess. Not what I want, but I'll deal with it. Just to get to see him and soak in all of his hotness would be enough for me.

But if he says one, then I'll know he wants to be alone with me.

One.

The single text practically pulses on the screen. I'm never the guy to reconsider moving too fast. If I had my way, I would have dragged his tall ass all the way onto that tour bus last night without a second thought.

So what's with the fucking butterflies? What on earth has gotten into me?

Then I guess that means I'll see you tomorrow.

See you tomorrow.

EIGHT

"**P**lease stow away all tray tables and return your seats to a fully upright position."

I stare out the window of the plane, a nervous energy building inside me as I look out at Salt Lake City below me.

It feels as if someone else is piloting my life entirely. I'm no longer in charge; I'm just coasting down this hill without brakes or a way to stop.

And somewhat shamelessly enjoying every second. Whenever the guilt creeps in, I use the lies in my arsenal as a defense.

We are just friends.

I have no inappropriate intentions.

He's my favorite musician—I'd be an idiot to turn this down.

It's enough to ease my nerves.

As soon as the wheels touch down on the runway, I pull out my phone and text Theo.

> Just landed.

> I'm sure you're busy getting ready, but I'll see you tonight.

> Thanks again for the ticket.

I don't check for a reply until I'm in the taxi on the way to the venue. I really should work on this Sunday's sermon. There are things to do at the church, and I do feel a little guilty that I've put off a lot of that work on my team.

But I've worked so hard over the last year to get the church where it is today. There was quite a hefty mess to clean up after the Goode scandal.

I deserve this break. I deserve to have a little fun and indulge.

A *little*.

By the time I arrive at the stadium, the doors are open, but it's still early, so I kill time by grabbing a bite to eat and a couple of drinks. I'm not a big drinker, but I enjoy taking the edge off when I can. Those three tequila sodas were the most I've had in a long time.

While sitting down at a small table near a food vendor, I take some time to do some people-watching. There's something wildly fascinating about watching strangers in a setting like this. I like to imagine their life stories and their values. What matters most to them? How do they function—with fear or with faith?

This is a country music concert in a very conservative state. Which makes it even stranger that I'm here to see a man I'm fairly certain was flirting with me. A man I'm very attracted to. If any of these people knew that, they'd probably be outraged.

The first time I knew I was different than all my friends was when I was thirteen. Going to the movies with some friends, I found myself lusting after Brendan Fraser in *The Mummy* while they were drooling over the female librarian.

I brushed it off for so long. But it felt like the elephant in the room of my childhood. Like everyone knew before I did. It was the thing no one ever wanted to speak about and it was eating me alive.

When I was fifteen, my mom encouraged me to check out

Eternal Harmony. She called it a *special* youth group. "The most important youth group you'll ever attend," she said.

When I went to the first meeting, my world had changed. I felt like I had finally met people like *me*. The pastor of the group was a guy named Derek. He was in his late twenties and seemed like he had his whole life together. His confidence and charisma drew me in. But more importantly, he was married to a woman. It all seemed so perfect.

He promised us that he was like us. And that if we stayed the course, we would not only save our own lives, but our own souls.

He gave me direction when I felt like I was lost.

At first, my dad seemed worried. He often asked me what Pastor Derek spoke about, but it felt like a secret to me then. Eternal Harmony was *mine*. Something to be proud of. Something that was going to help me.

I was terrified of losing that.

So I told him nothing. Every year in the program, I moved up a level. I became a mentor, then a counselor, then a leader. I made friends and felt like I was truly part of something.

People around town started treating me differently. When I spoke, they listened. Girls began taking an interest in me.

On the outside, I was flourishing, and everything was falling into place.

For a teenager, that was all that mattered.

On the inside, I felt like I was crumbling. Rotting. Dying a slow, agonizing death.

Music starts playing in the distance, distracting me from my thoughts. It's the same opener I saw two nights ago, so I don't rush out to my seat like everyone else.

Instead, I text Theo.

> Good luck tonight.

I'm shocked by how quickly he responds.

Are you here?

Yep.

Come backstage.

I've got an hour before I go on.

Really?

I don't want to bother you.

Not at all.

You know how to find it?

I'll figure it out.

See you soon.

Standing up in a rush, I toss what's left of my food in the trash and walk toward the VIP section. There's a man in black with *security* written across his shirt. I show him my backstage pass and he points to the correct door.

I'm not normally a nervous guy, but right now, the nerves are there. I'm about to see Theo again. And he actually wants to see me. How is this real?

I walk down a long hallway before coming to another security door. I show them my badge and they let me through without question. Suddenly, I'm behind the stage, music blaring from the opening band.

It's a little chaotic, and I feel like a fool asking the nearby person in black where Theo Virgil is. But he hardly gives me a second look before pointing toward a banged-up black door. I press it open hesitantly and find another hallway. This one is quieter.

There are doors on either side, so I stroll down slowly.

Just then, a head pops out of one of the doors. Theo is wearing that adorable, dimpled smile when he sees me. There's no hat on his head, so his dark-brown curls hang over his forehead until he brushes them back.

"You're here," he says excitedly.

Forcing myself to look and feel confident, I stride toward him and hold out a hand. "All thanks to you."

He takes my hand, and the moment our palms touch and our eyes meet, it's like fireworks.

I deserve this, I tell myself. *A little indulgence won't hurt anyone.*

"Come in," he says, tugging me toward the room. I notice the way his gaze dances from my eyes to my lips and down to my throat.

The room is small, like a greenroom with couches and a fridge with drinks. No one else is in here, so as soon as the door closes, we're alone. My skin pricks with nervous energy.

At this point, I'm just terrified of reading the situation wrong. What if I've conjured all of this up, and Theo isn't into me? What if he's straight—or worse? A homophobe who gets the wrong idea about me. What if this ends badly?

I won't make the first move. I'll just follow his lead.

"You want a drink?" he asks, heading straight for the fridge. "We don't have much in here, but we've got beer."

"Beer is perfect," I reply, watching him walk away and letting my eyes trail over his ass in those tight jeans.

After pulling out two longneck bottles, he hands one to me. I flip the top and keep my gaze on him as I take a swig.

"So your work doesn't mind you taking so much time off?" he asks.

As he leans against the counter next to the fridge, I step closer so there is only a couple of feet between us.

"I'm sort of the boss," I reply.

"Oh, nice," he says. Then there's silence between us again.

I can't take my eyes off him. He has such a glow to him, like the sun itself is in the room I'm standing in. And just like the sun, his gravitational pull draws me closer.

But I don't move. I won't risk it. Instead, I stare at his blue eyes, his full lips, and the scruff of hair on his face.

"So...forgive me for asking this," he says, grinning with the bottle near his lips. "But how old are you?"

"Forty," I reply with a wince. I've never looked it up. But I'm willing to bet that Theo is still in his twenties, which means I might be too old for him, as a friend, even.

Instead of grimacing at my answer, he nods. "I'm twenty-eight."

"And you still want to hang out with an old guy like me?"

He rolls his eyes with a smirk. "You are not an old guy."

"I feel like it sometimes."

He takes another drink. "So, no spouse? No kids?"

"Nope. Just never really happened for me. Never found the right person," I reply vaguely. It's true. Although, deep down, I knew I was never getting married. I'd never find the right person.

"And what does the right person look like?" he asks, and my heart starts to hammer wildly in my chest.

"Sorry," he stammers while glancing downward. "That was too personal. I'm not really much into dating either." Then his gaze lifts until we're staring at each other. "It's hard to do for guys like us."

"Like us," I reply, not exactly in the form of a question.

"Yeah, guys who...work too much. You clearly own a nonprofit, and I'm on tour."

Nodding along, I stare into his eyes, noticing the way he dances around the topic we both are so desperate to bring up. He's thinking the same thing I am. We're both afraid of reading the situation wrong and won't make the first move.

"I'm not here to talk about work," I say with a casual smirk on my face.

"Then why are you here?" he murmurs without looking into

my eyes. There's a hint of fear in his voice, and it makes me step a little closer.

For a brief moment, I see Theo Virgil for what he is—a man. A young man with fears and feelings and loneliness like the rest of us.

I'd like to wrap him up in my arms and make all of that go away.

"To see you," I say softly. Maybe too softly. My voice is nothing more than a raspy whisper, and it's definitely not something two friends would say to each other. That much is true.

Theo looks at me with expectation. So, I take another step forward.

"My new friend," I add.

Reaching toward him, I place my beer on the counter behind him, but it brings our bodies closer. So close I can feel his breath on my cheek. So close I can smell his cologne and feel the heat radiating from his body.

Theo isn't the first man I've lusted after and he won't be the first man I've slept with if it gets to that point. I have my secrets and my ways of hooking up and keeping it discreet. I keep my secrets buried so deep no one would ever know the truth. But Theo is the first man I've ever wanted *this* badly.

Our eyes bore into one another's. "Friend," he replies in a daze.

I wait for the moment when our lips will brush, wondering if we're moving too fast. If I kiss him now, will we have sex later? Will that be all? Just a dirty one-night stand, and then he'll move on to the next guy on his tour?

So what if he is? It's not like I could ever be in a committed relationship with a man. Not for a multitude of reasons.

Our lips are nearly touching when someone bangs loudly on the door. Theo and I pull apart quickly. He clears his throat as he answers the knock.

"What?" There's frustration in his voice.

"Fifteen-minute warning," the person calls.

"Shit," he mutters to himself. "That hour went by too fast."

"I should let you get out there," I stammer. "And I'll go to my seat."

He picks up his brown, weathered cowboy hat from the back of a chair. "You could always watch from the wings," he says. "See it from a different point of view."

"Really? I wouldn't be in the way?" I ask.

"Fuck no."

As he heads toward the door, I grab his arm to stop him. As he looks into my eyes, waiting to hear what I have to say, I briefly consider asking him what the hell we're doing.

"Have a good show," I say instead.

He smirks, looking so fucking cute it nearly takes my breath away. "I will."

Then he rushes out the door. I follow behind him as he meets up with his band and crew. Sticking to the wall and out of the way, I watch as he gives them all a pep talk before the show. It's inspiring and I find myself attracted to how talented of a speaker he is.

"I'll tell you guys the same thing I tell you every night. We're here for the music."

They cheer.

"We're here for the fans."

They cheer again.

"And we're here to have a good fucking time!"

His band starts howling and clapping as he builds the energy among them. Finally, he puts his hand in the middle, and they all follow suit.

"I love you guys," he calls before they echo his words back to him. I can't help but grin as I watch. After splitting away from the band, he finds me again, winking across the dark space. Then he takes his place behind the back of the stage, where I know it will eventually split, and he will enter when the music crescendos.

I find a place in the wings where there aren't people moving and working. Crossing my arms over my chest, I watch the band take their places. The crowd starts to cheer at the sight of them. The music blares through the speakers, and I watch in amazement as he eventually enters.

He commands the crowd as he plays his guitar, and the crowd is so loud it's deafening. I can't help but think about the fact that he's obviously hiding this major secret from them. Is it something he's proud of or ashamed of? Will he ever truly come out, or is he content with telling no one about his sexuality? Not that he owes it to anyone.

Does it fucking matter? Anyone could see just how happy he is.

More than once during his show, he takes a peek at me, and our eyes meet.

Suddenly, it's like the ride I've been on this whole time has just picked up speed. I'm still not in the pilot's seat and I have no control. At some point, this thing is going to crash. But until then, I'm going to enjoy the ride.

NINE

Isaac

The show had a different energy tonight. Suddenly, it felt like I wasn't performing for twenty thousand people. I was performing for only one.

And the main event wasn't even the show. It's what could happen after.

I run off the stage with the band after the encore, and Jensen is there waiting. I feel disgusting, covered in sweat, and my fingers ache from playing so hard, but I don't care. When he wraps his arms around me for an enthusiastic hug, I fall right into them. We're both too thrilled and hyped up from the show to care.

When we pull apart, our eyes meet again. It's brief. This isn't the place to be so open with our attraction, and he knows it.

After putting some shit away and making sure my guitar is taken care of, I walk out to the bus with Jensen by my side. The fans are there like always, waiting for me to cross from the building to the tour bus.

As they scream my name, I leave his side for a second and sign a few of their things, more than usual, if I'm honest. The entire time, I feel him watching.

Lola is there to pull me away when I don't give up signing shit.

"I have to get cleaned up. You can wait in the bus and then we can head out to a bar or something after," I say to Jensen once we climb aboard.

He glances skeptically at Lola, who is doing the same back to him. I'm a little afraid of leaving them alone with each other. I hope she doesn't threaten to cut his balls off to his face, but I wouldn't put it past her.

I shower quickly, and by the time I come out, they are enjoying small talk with the rest of the band. Rio has poured some drinks for everyone, and I toss back a shot of tequila in the kitchen to settle my nerves.

Why the fuck am I nervous?

"Ready to go?" I ask Jensen after slipping a baseball hat on my head.

He stands from the recliner. "Ready."

We say goodbye to the band before we leave. "Don't stay out too late," Lola calls like a mother.

There's a black SUV waiting for us, but Jensen and I don't even have a destination in mind. As we climb in, Jensen asks, "When does your bus leave?"

"Four hours," I reply with disappointment. "Where are you staying tonight?"

"I got a hotel downtown. Just a few miles away. I think it has a restaurant and a bar."

A hotel bar. Perfect.

"Sweet. Let's go there."

As the driver takes us to Jensen's hotel, there is a sense of haste between us. For sex, maybe. For that first kiss. For a moment alone with him. It's like a race.

When we get there, we head straight for the rooftop restaurant. I keep my eyes down as we go so no one recognizes me, which honestly isn't often. Without the cowboy hat, I'm just a regular guy. The server puts us in a quiet corner with a palm tree and a large planter to hide us from view.

As soon as we sit down, I look into his eyes.

"Is this okay?" he asks. I'm not sure what he's referring to, but I have a feeling it's the date-like situation we're in. Out on a date in public? No, it's not okay, but not for the reasons he's thinking.

It's not okay because I don't date. The idea of having a meal with a complete stranger to put our compatibility to the test sounds like torture to me, but for some reason, with him, it doesn't sound bad at all.

I'm far more used to hooking up with guys I click with at bars or online, and nine times out of ten, it's a one-time thing. Sometimes, we repeat the hookup so much it starts to feel like a relationship. That hasn't happened in a while, though.

"This is great," I reply, leaning back in my chair and giving him a crooked smirk.

The server comes by and takes our orders. The need for a drink is visceral. I'm desperate for something to settle the unease in my bones.

As she leaves and Jensen and I are alone, the air feels heavy. That almost-kiss we shared in the greenroom is dying for us to acknowledge it.

Jensen has such an air of confidence about him, and I've never been with a guy like that. As he leans back in his chair with one arm slung over the back, my mouth starts to water. I imagine him sitting like that while I unzip his pants. I imagine pleasing him, feeling the weight of his cock on my tongue, and hearing him tell me how much he likes it.

My cock twitches in my pants.

"Do you date a lot?" he asks with interest.

"No," I reply with a shake of my head. "I'm sure you can understand why."

His eyes narrow as he nods slowly. "I do understand." To be fair, I know almost nothing about Jensen so far, but with that look in his eye it gives me the impression that he's harboring secrets.

"What about you?" I ask.

"Same."

The server brings our drinks, and I reach for mine quickly. Jensen watches me with concern as I take a long gulp. I don't know what's gotten into me. I just feel...nervous.

We order some food, and I feel Jensen watching me. He wants to say something. He seems almost...bothered. Is this not what he wanted? The tension in the air feels thick.

My drink goes down fast, and I start to feel at ease.

"What made you want to be a country singer?" he asks.

With a smile, I lean against the table. "I don't know. Ever since I was a kid, I loved performing. I love music. Being able to convey so much with so little. I love writing lyrics in my songs that mean something to me and then mean something to a complete stranger, too. Is that stupid?"

"Not at all," he replies softly. "Your lyrics mean very much to me."

"That's good."

"I can tell you feel very lonely sometimes," he says, and it's like his eyes are boring into me. The weight of those words drags me under. "It's all right," he says, noticing my discomfort. "I feel that too."

"Yeah?" I whisper.

"Why are you so lonely, Theo?"

Something about hearing him call me Theo and not Isaac burns, and I don't like it. But the comfort of his voice is too inviting.

For some reason, I want to bare my soul for this guy, and I barely know him. Glancing down at the table, I pick at the place-mat. "I ran away from home when I was seventeen," I mutter. "And I haven't been back."

"Really?" he asks, leaning in.

"I came out to my dad, and he made me feel like dirt. Like I wasn't worthy of his love. Like I'd never make him proud a day in my life."

"I'm sorry," he mumbles softly.

"God, why am I telling you all of this?" I ask. As I look at him again, I feel something like trust, and it's impossible to explain.

"You're safe with me, Theo."

Suddenly, I'm flooded with a feeling I don't understand. Something incredibly unfamiliar. This feeling of safety.

When our food comes, I order another drink, and we finish our meal with a sense of haste. We continue to make small talk, but I'm so shaken by his offer to keep me safe that I can hardly relax into the conversation.

After we're finished, we battle over who will pay, but I insist and give my credit card to the server first. Then, he gets up from the table and puts a hand on the small of my back.

As we make our way toward the elevator, my heart thrums quickly, and I feel every small movement. I'm a bomb about to explode.

We walk onto the elevator, and I know the moment we're alone, something will happen. I *need* it.

He hits the button for the lobby, and the doors close slowly. The moment they do, he spins toward me. He presses a large hand on my chest and shoves me against the mirrored wall.

There's hesitation on his face as he leans in to kiss me. For just a split second, he stops himself.

Wrapping a hand around his neck, I haul his mouth toward mine. The moment his lips touch mine, the hesitation is gone. Our lips tangle in a needy, passionate kiss.

I nearly melt to the floor when his tongue brushes against mine. The rough texture of his facial hair feels delicious under my fingers as I run them along the side of his face. And when he groans into my mouth, I practically weep. When was the last time I was kissed so well?

The hunger. The sensation. The power. It's all so intoxicating. I want to drown in this kiss. Bury me now because it's enough to kill me.

His teeth nibble on my bottom lip, tugging gently until I whimper. At the sound, he drives his hips against mine, our steely erections rubbing against each other's.

Just before we reach the bottom floor, he pulls away just an inch. With his mouth hovering over mine, he softly whispers, "You scare the fuck out of me, Theo Virgil."

I don't know what that's supposed to mean, but I laugh it off. A moment later, the elevator beeps and the doors open.

We each subtly adjust ourselves in our pants before waltzing out into the lobby of the hotel. I stay back while he checks in for the night and gets his room key. I'm practically bouncing with anticipation.

I watch him from across the lobby, brushing my lips as I think about that kiss, reliving it over and over.

Before I even know what I'm doing, I'm writing lyrics in my head.

Elevator indiscretions
Hard-pressed, soft kiss
A touch worth waiting for

When Jensen gets the key and walks back toward me, there's hunger in his eyes. But I can't help noticing the time. I have to go back to the venue soon. Fuck my life.

"Come on," he says with authority as he guides me back to the elevator. This time, we don't make out during the short trip to his floor.

And when we get out, I can already tell something has changed. Before pressing his key to the door, he turns to face me.

"Listen, Theo—"

"Stop," I say, putting a hand up, wanting to save him from the torture of hard conversations.

"No, let me talk."

"If you don't want to do this, that's fine."

"I want to," he argues. "Trust me, I really, *really* want to."

"Then what's the problem?"

He seems so torn, and it's making me uncomfortable. This is the last thing I want.

"You don't have much time. And I..."

Midsentence, his eyes connect with mine again, and it's like something inside him changes. He dives in for another kiss. It's harsh and warm, and he nibbles hungrily on my mouth.

Fuck.

As our mouths part again, we're both breathless and hard and ravenous. And yet, still both so hesitant.

Inches from his lips, I whisper, "I really like you, Jensen, and I can't believe I'm about to say this."

"Say it," he growls in return.

"I don't think I should come in that room with you."

Who am I? What is happening?

He pulls away to stare into my eyes, and I can't read his features. Jensen is such an enigma to me. There's something beneath the surface that I don't understand. And for once in my life, I want to understand him more than I want to fuck him.

"I think you're right," he says, clearing his throat.

When he takes a step away from me, his absence feels like an ache. Reaching for him, I rest a hand on his side, strumming my fingers along his rib cage.

Reckless, reckless, reckless.

Releasing a heavy breath, he adds, "I don't want to be a tour stop."

I wince as I press my body against his. "I don't want you to be a tour stop, either."

Our words say one thing, but our bodies say something completely different. He presses me against the wall in the hallway, where anyone could walk by at any moment, but I don't care. Right now, there's only his mouth, his hands, his body.

When Jensen kisses me, it feels like he's been starved for so long. It's ravenous. His large hand engulfs my throat as he tips my head back to dive deeper into my mouth. It's so intense that my legs begin to weaken, and I forget how to breathe.

Then his hips grind against mine again, and I feel his rigid length align with my own. We moan in unison.

"I'm starting to rethink this decision," I mumble into his mouth.

"Me too," he pants, grinding again.

I do not want to come in this hallway in the same pants I have to ride home in. I'm thinking about pushing him away, but I don't have the strength. He feels too good.

Thankfully, he's the one to put distance between us again. "Fuck," he mutters as he runs his hands through his hair and paces away from me.

I'm feeling the same. Tense and needy, and I know if I let my body have too much control, I'd say fuck the rules and let him pull me into that hotel room.

And I'll admit, it's cute to see him so flustered. I love the effect I have on him.

"I should probably get going," I say as I step away from the wall.

"When can I see you again?" he asks.

He wants to see me again.

"We'll be in Vegas this weekend," I say with a shrug.

His eyes narrow with a wince. "I have to work this weekend."

"Okay...Denver? Tuesday night."

As he watches my face, I feel so vulnerable. The cryptic expressions are starting to go to my head.

"Talk to me, Jensen. I can't tell if you're deliberating how much you want to see me again or if there's something else worrying you."

Closing the distance, he crowds me again. His tall frame and handsome face fill my vision as he touches my cheek.

"I want to see you again. I was just wondering if I could wait that long."

Why the fuck are my insides being assaulted by butterflies? I think I'm melting, actually fucking melting. I have never swooned so goddamn hard in my life. This guy is going to fuck me up, isn't he? When he says things like that and looks so fucking good, I know I'm in for something.

Please don't hurt me.

"Five days feels like a hundred," I murmur in return.

Leaning in, he kisses me again, but it's softer this time. After a few minutes, he pulls away for the fourth time tonight and looks pained while doing it.

"I'll see you in Denver," he whispers.

As he puts his hand on the hotel door, I take a backward step toward the elevator. At this point, I'm probably late, and Lola will have my head when I get back, but this was worth it. *So* goddamn worth it.

"See you in Denver," I reply as I press the elevator button.

A moment later, it chimes, and the doors open. I leave his sight and step into the elevator, collapsing against the back wall as I let the last three hours wash over me.

Then, just before the doors close, Jensen shoves his hand in to stop them. Bursting into the elevator, he says, "Just one more."

Taking my face in his hands, he kisses me hard again, and I grin like a fool against his mouth.

Oh yeah, I'm fucked.

Part Two

The Preacher

TEN

JENSEN

Standing in the pulpit with the eyes of the congregation on me, I should really not be thinking about how good Theo Virgil's lips felt against mine. But that's exactly what I'm doing.

Through the prayers and the hymns and the blessings, he's in the back of my mind.

Somehow, I pull it together and finish the service. Never mind the fact that I wrote the sermon late last night. This isn't like me. I normally put pride in my work.

But Theo has this hold over me, and I don't want it to stop.

As soon as we reluctantly parted ways Thursday night, I couldn't sleep all night. I kept reliving that kiss. I meant what I said to him—he scares me. How good I feel with him. How much I want him even when he's not around. How much I wanted to drag him into my hotel room and have my way with him.

We've been texting each other ever since. We mostly talk about our lives, childhood stories, likes and dislikes. We send each other selfies and have even video chatted a couple of times when we're not too busy.

"Let us pray," I say as we all bow our heads together. The

moment I close my eyes, that familiar shame creeps in. It's as if the moment I'm alone with God, there is nowhere to hide. No lies to protect me. I have to face my sins.

"We thank you, Lord, for your unending grace and mercy. May we leave this church filled with your peace, carrying your light into the world."

I lead the congregation through the prayer, and when I'm asking for forgiveness for them, I'm really asking it for me.

"Amen," I murmur, my voice echoing from the speakers.

"Amen," they reply in unison.

As they all stand and greet each other, congregating near the doorways and aisles, I stay at the pulpit and stare down at my sermon. My phone is in my pocket, and I've felt Theo text multiple times throughout the service, or at least I assume it's him. These days, it's always him, and I'm not complaining.

He still doesn't know I'm a pastor because I haven't told him. Just one more thing to feel guilty about. But I don't want that part of my life to mingle with this one. I don't want Theo to have to grapple with the conflict that paralyzes me nearly every day when it comes to him and whatever this thing is between us.

For once, I just want to be me, and I want him to be him.

Finally leaving the pulpit, I walk down from the stage toward where the people are mingling. I do exactly what I do every weekend. This is my favorite part, really. Getting to talk to them. Getting to hear how my words—or rather, the word of God— helped them get through a challenging time or the dark internal thoughts that tend to creep in.

A woman I recognize takes my hand with tears in her eyes and tells me how good today's sermon felt, and it means the world to me. That's why I'm here. That's my duty in this life—to bring hope and camaraderie to the people.

My phone buzzes again. It practically stings where it's pressed against my thigh.

I should feel terrible for what I'm doing with Theo. For jeopardizing this position I'm in.

But I'm flawed and imperfect, and I can't help myself as I touch the woman's shoulder. "Please excuse me," I say politely as I take my leave.

Walking away, I pull my phone out of my pocket and check the messages. It's a photo of him in front of the fake Eiffel Tower in Vegas. He has on dark sunglasses and no hat. He's always wearing a hat of some sort and I wish he'd leave it off more often. His hair is beautiful. Dark-brown curls on the top of his head. It highlights his blue eyes and the lighter scruff on his face.

Have a great show tonight!

I text with a smirk. Disappearing down the long hallway, I stare at his photo and my heart starts to pick up pace in my chest.

Closing myself in my office, I lock the door behind me as I take a seat behind the desk.

Thanks. Wish you were here.

Me too.

Two more days.

How long will you have in Denver after the show?

We don't leave until Thursday.

Apparently, I'm scheduled to do some photo shoot there on Wednesday, so I'll have all night after the show.

I shift in my seat at the idea of having all night with him. God, I want it. I want it so fucking bad.

What started as an indulgence has turned into an all-out

addiction. I know it could end badly and likely will. But I'm beyond caring.

I'm no fool, and I'm not a child. The things they tried to drill into my head at Eternal Harmony didn't stick quite as much as they wanted them to. I know there is no way to "pray the gay away." I was "cured" of nothing. In fact, I've had plenty of sex with men since leaving their program.

But it doesn't change the fact that they rewired things inside my brain I can't fix. They buried themselves in my subconscious. Their lies and mantras play on repeat, whether or not I want them to. I can't escape them, and I probably never will.

At this point, my sins are between me and God.

It's about more than sins now at this point. It's about my job, my life, my position in this community. I mean something to people, and I can't lose that. Because if I lose that, then who am I?

As I type and delete and type and delete my next message, it's like I'm being torn apart. There is a rational part of my brain that knows this isn't a good idea. Don't toy with the idea of having sex with Theo Virgil because that is a threat to my entire life. And certainly don't fucking string him along like we have any real future together.

We're both closeted professionals who can't risk their own careers for a love affair.

But then there's the other part of me. The man. The heart and soul and body that craves him so badly I can hardly sleep. I want to pull Theo Virgil into my life where I can protect him. I'd like to plant my feet at his door and be the one who keeps him safe at all costs.

I'll get a hotel close to the venue.

I know the mere mention of a hotel is a point of tension. If I have another hotel room, will he enter it this time? Will he sleep by my side? Will he let me undress him and explore his body the way I so desperately want to?

"With God, change is possible."

"Shut up," I mumble to myself as I drop my phone on the desk and run my fingers through my hair.

I can practically hear Pastor Derek's voice in my head.

"You don't have to live this way, Jensen. This is not what God intended for you, but there is still hope."

I shove the voices down and focus instead on the gorgeous picture of Theo. Suddenly, I find myself closing my eyes again. And then I do what I've done a thousand times already this week.

I pray.

In my mind, I reach for God. I want to feel the comfort only He can give. I want him to tell me I haven't failed him. I need to feel his love.

My phone buzzes again, and I open my eyes to see Theo's response.

I've got some time before the show.

Can we FaceTime?

My blood pressure spikes. Turning behind me, I stare at the large painting of Jesus on the wall. I certainly can't let that be my backdrop if he calls. Turning the chair the opposite way, I show only the white plaster wall of the corner of my office.

Yes.

A moment later, the phone starts ringing. Quickly fixing my hair, I answer it. It takes a moment for Theo's face to appear on the screen. And when it does, my jaw drops and all the blood in my body courses straight for my cock.

Theo is standing in nothing but a white towel wrapped around his waist. He winces when he sees my reaction.

"Too much?" he asks.

"Too much clothing?" I ask with a smirk. "I'd say so, but I happen to think you always have too much on."

He smiles, and it's so fucking cute it has me beaming.

"Wow, we're really going for it today, aren't we?" he asks.

"Well, you're the one who answered in nothing but a towel."

He starts to blush, and I love it. It's true that Theo and I have kept our conversations pretty tame since Thursday. Those kisses and light rutting were about as hot and heavy as we'd been.

But I quite like that we aren't rushing it. We're taking our time with each other. I don't want this fire to burn out.

"I just got out of the shower."

"You look good," I say in a low tone.

"You look good, too," he replies. "Where are you?"

I glance around at the wall behind me. "In my office," I say. "We had...a meeting today."

"Cool," he replies.

Part of me thinks that Theo doesn't pry about my job because he doesn't truly want to know. Either that, or he doesn't care. He's young. Twelve years younger than me. He's less interested in careers and meetings than I am.

I keep telling myself that when we see each other in person, I'll come clean. It's a big deal, and I never felt the desire to tell him before because I didn't see this going as far as it has already.

He leans back on his bed, and I can tell that it's his room on the tour bus. It's not huge, but the bed is at least a queen. It has a dark-brown comforter and white pillows. He reclines and holds the phone up so I can see his face and bare chest.

"You sure you can afford all these flights and hotels? I can help, you know." He says it so innocently, as if he's not bothered by talking about money, and he's not afraid to discuss just how much he has now.

Reassuring him with a warm smile and soft nod, I reply, "Yes, I can handle it. My job pays well."

"Good." He doesn't push the subject and I'm grateful for that.

It's sweet of him to offer and be concerned. Aside from the money, these trips I'm making are easy for me. My team is well delegated, although I'm getting the sense they find my frequent trips odd. As long as the work is getting done and I don't slack on my duties, it's really none of their business.

"I wish I were there with you right now," I say, which feels a little like crossing a line.

Theo's smile turns into desire. "I wish you were too."

"Imagine me lying right next to you. I'd like to hold you to my chest and let you relax there before your show."

"That sounds amazing," he murmurs softly. Then, with a contemplative look, he says, "Can I ask you a question?"

"Of course." I swallow down a sense of unease as I wait for him to ask it. I think in the back of my mind, I know what he's curious about.

"Have you been with a man before?"

My jaw clenches, and I force myself to swallow. Although Theo has spoken about his dating life and coming out to his family, I've skirted over the issue.

"Yes, I have," I reply plainly, and I can tell that he's waiting for more from me.

"Sorry to pry," he says, burying his hands in his hair. "You're just...such a mystery to me."

"I can be an open book if you want. Ask me anything." Reclining back in my chair, I smile at him as I wait.

"Are you gay or bi?"

"Gay," I reply flatly, but keep my voice down in case there's someone on the other side of the office door. "I've been with a couple of women. I just didn't like it very much." I can see his brow furrows delicately.

"Have you been in a serious relationship before?"

My jaw tightens. I told him I would be an open book, and I am, but he can't help that some of these questions are difficult.

"No. I did date a woman for over a year in college, but it was... complicated."

"It sounds complicated."

"I haven't seriously been with a man, if that's what you're wondering."

"Because of your job?" he asks, and I see the youthful innocence on his face. I'd like to kiss him so much right now.

Solemnly, I nod. "Yes."

I watch the way he processes this information and how heavy it weighs on him. Right now, he's realizing that I can never be serious with him.

"Is that what you want, Theo?" I ask. Why do I want him to say yes?

He takes a deep breath and scrubs his hand over his face. "It's never what I wanted before."

"And what about now?" I ask.

He stares into my eyes through the screen as he shrugs. "I don't know."

The corner of my lips tugs upward subtly. Then he continues.

"Obviously, my job won't make that easy, either. I just know that I fucking like you, and not in the same way I've liked anyone before."

This level of honesty and transparency is refreshing. It makes me feel like Theo knows he's safe with me. I want him to always feel safe with me.

"I really fucking like you too."

"Then I say we just take this day by day. See where it takes us."

As he buries a hand behind his head, making his biceps bulge and my mouth water, I smile. "I like that plan."

"So, on Tuesday..."

"On Tuesday, we'll see where it takes us."

Eleven

Isaac

The show in Vegas is rowdier than normal. Which I guess is to be expected in Vegas. Afterward, security has to escort me from the venue to my bus, and they won't let me stop for pictures.

"This is crazy!" Lola says as she runs by my side. As soon as we're alone on the bus, she collapses onto the couch. "You're getting to be a very big deal, Theo Virgil."

"Who knew there were so many fans in Las Vegas?" I ask, pulling a beer from the fridge.

"Theo, these fans are everywhere," she says, unlacing her boots. "Have you even seen how viral your songs are getting online? Or are you too busy flirting with that hottie from Phoenix?"

Grinning around the bottle as I bring it to my lips, I reply, "Obviously, the latter."

"Well, either way, I think you should prepare yourself for how popular you're getting. This is the kind of fame that changes a person's life."

"It's already changed my life," I mumble, leaning against the counter.

"I know, but I'm trying to say...this is the kind of fame that makes it much harder to keep secrets," she adds.

"Maybe I'm tired of keeping secrets," I reply.

When she stands up, she gives me a look of sympathy, and I already know what she's about to say. I just wish it wasn't true.

"Just make sure *you're* the one coming out before someone else does it for you."

"I know, Lo."

She touches my shoulder before walking toward the back of the bus to steal the bathroom first. I know she's right, and I wish I wasn't stuck in this limbo. Afraid to come out but more afraid of being outed. Afraid to be myself but tired of having to keep myself hidden. Wanting to date, but afraid that dating would ruin my career.

✝

When I get out of the shower, there's a new text on my phone, but it's not from Jensen. It's from Luke.

> Hey. We have to talk.

That doesn't sound good. I hope everything is all right with him and Sadie and Henry. Or maybe it's about Mom. Or one of my brothers.

Before I start to panic spiral, I call him. He answers on the first ring.

"Hey," he says into the line.

"Hey," I reply as I run the towel over my head to dry my hair. "What's wrong?"

"Nothing's wrong," he says with concern. "I just want to give you a heads-up about something."

"That doesn't sound good," I reply. Sitting on the couch, I brace myself for bad news.

"Caleb just called me," he says. "Apparently, our dad has won an appeal in court."

"What does that mean?" I ask.

"It means that whatever judge they put on the case has decided to lessen his charge from attempted murder to aggravated assault. They still have to go through sentencing, but there's a chance he could get out early if he wins."

"You're joking," I say as I let this news hit me.

"I wish."

"What did Adam say?" I ask.

Lucas huffs. "He's still too angry to speak to anyone. I'm afraid of what he might do if Truett does get out."

My knee bounces nervously. "Yeah, that would be bad."

"Honestly, Isaac, I'm more worried about you."

"Me?" I ask with surprise. "Why me?"

"Because you're famous now. Once Dad does get out, which I assume he will someday, he can easily find you. He could make some sort of statement about you. He could use your fame to his advantage. You're the key to saving his reputation. And I don't want it to get to that."

Staring at the floor with the phone against my ear, I try to imagine my father doing that to me. Lucas is right that he absolutely could. And maybe he would.

But I remember a very different man than my brothers do. I have this theory that my father feels more shame for me leaving than they think he does. But I don't verbalize any of that.

"We'll cross that bridge when we get there," I say. "For now, I'm not worried. Truett Goode can't hurt me anymore."

Lucas breathes a heavy sigh. "I wish that were true."

For the rest of our call, we make small talk about Sadie and Henry and my tour. I hear the baby crying in the background, and Lucas says he has to go change his diaper, which makes me laugh.

Doctor Lucas Goode changing a diaper will never not be funny to me.

After we hang up, I lie back on my bed and think about my family. I wonder who is taking care of Mom now that Dad is gone and has ruined everything. How is she holding up during all of this? She and I talk from time to time, but always about me and never about her, and definitely not about Dad.

I wonder about Adam and Sage and their baby girl, Faith. I wonder about Caleb, who is now dating my ex, which isn't weird at all.

It's not often I truly think about my family like this. Mostly because it gives me more guilt and discomfort than I'd like. I'm a runner through and through. When things get tough, I get out as fast as I can. Never one to stick around to talk about feelings or, God forbid, feel them.

Suddenly, without reason, I call Jensen. He picks up after three rings. He sounds out of breath.

"Hey. How was the show?" he asks.

"It was good," I reply, sounding despondent.

"What's wrong?" he asks, picking up on it immediately. "Talk to me."

"Can we FaceTime?" I ask.

"Yeah, give me a second. I'm just walking through the door."

"Where were you tonight?" I ask to kill the time.

"Dinner with my parents. I try to go over there at least once a week."

"That's nice of you and actually kind of appropriate for what I want to talk about."

I can hear Jensen rushing. A door in the distance closes, and then, a moment later, he requests to video chat. As soon as I accept it, his picture comes into view.

"Naked again, I see," he says with a low growl in his voice that makes my dick twitch.

"I promise I don't do it on purpose."

"You can call me however you want to," he says. "Now, tell me what's wrong."

Jensen is on his couch, holding his phone and giving me his attention. I chew on my bottom lip as I consider how to say this.

Just say it, Isaac.

"I'm thinking about my family," I say.

"Okay," he replies with concern. "What about them? Did something happen?"

I have not told Jensen about my dad, and I don't plan to. It's embarrassing to have to admit to someone that your dad is a pervert and a hypocrite on top of being a homophobe and bigot. Not to mention, I'll never let Theo and Isaac cross.

"I'm thinking that I might be ready..."

"Ready to go home?" he asks.

"Yeah."

"First of all, do you feel safe doing that?" he asks. I've noticed that Jensen has a very protective side. He's constantly trying to shield me, even when there is no threat.

"Yes," I reply with a nod. "Let's just say...my dad was the problem, and he's no longer in the picture. I'd just be with my mom and brothers."

"And they support you?" he asks.

"Without question."

"Then talk to me. Tell me why you're second-guessing it. What are you afraid of?"

I lie down on my bed and prop the phone up on the pillow next to me. Then I turn toward Jensen as if he's lying on the bed with me.

"It's been so long. What if I feel like an outsider? What if they've all moved on, and it doesn't feel like my home anymore?"

"Then fuck them," he says, which makes me smile. Jensen doesn't often curse, but when he does, it's that much more enjoyable. "Listen, Theo. They are your family. But if they don't have your back and love you unconditionally, then you have every right to distance yourself. You will find people out there who will be there for you without question."

"Why the hell are you so wise?" I ask with a yawn. "I still feel like such a kid sometimes."

"You're not a kid," he says. "And you don't give yourself enough credit. But have you thought that maybe running away at seventeen might have impacted the way you grew up? That might be why you still feel so naive. Because you didn't get a chance to mature."

Jensen lies down on his couch, propping his phone up on his coffee table so it's like we're both lying together.

"That's a really good point," I say.

"If you want, I could go with you," he replies.

Immediately, I tense. I've never taken a boyfriend home, ever. If that's what he is. My boyfriend.

"You don't look too excited about that," he says with a chuckle.

"No, I am," I lie. "I mean...I want to be. That offer is amazing. And I think I'd like that very much..."

"But it's moving too quickly," he says, finishing my sentence. "I understand."

"I've just never brought home a guy before."

"Neither have I."

"Except for a boyfriend I had in high school, I guess," I add, thinking about Dean. "But he started as my best friend, and no one really knew we were messing around."

Jensen growls low in his chest and it causes a flash of heat to gather in my cock.

"I don't like hearing about your past boyfriends," he says with a serious tone.

"I think I like you possessive."

He growls again, and it makes me smirk.

"Well, if it makes you feel any better, that guy is now sort of married to my brother."

Jensen's eyes widen. "What do you mean...sort of married?"

I haven't seen Dean or Caleb's wife, Briar, in over a decade, but I find their story too fascinating not to share.

"Well, my brother is married to a woman. But then...they sort of brought this other guy into their marriage."

"Your ex," Jensen says to clarify.

"Yep."

"Wow... Is that weird for you?" he asks.

I shrug. "I used to worry about Dean. But now, he seems happy. I mean...who am I to judge how people live their lives?"

"None of us should," he replies.

I yawn again.

"Why don't you get some rest? I'll see you in two days."

"Thanks for letting me vent," I reply sleepily.

"Anytime. And there's no rush to make a decision. When you're ready, you'll know."

I nod before rolling over to hit the lamp on the wall next to the bed. But I don't hang up. I don't want to say goodbye.

"I'll stay right here," he whispers when my eyes finally close.

"I can't wait to see you," I reply, half-asleep.

"I can't wait to see you either."

"Jensen," I whisper.

"Yes, Theo?"

"I'm coming into your hotel room this time."

He growls softly into the phone line, and I smile with my eyes still closed. Just before I drift off, I hear him say, "I wouldn't have it any other way."

Twelve

Jensen

The moment my Uber drops me off at the venue, I bolt toward the entrance. There's a massive line to get through security and into the stadium, which is a bit different than last time and it makes me irate. I'm practically bouncing.

I just need to get to him. It's only been five days, but it feels more like five weeks.

You here yet?

Waiting in line at security.

Fuck, I should have given you access to come around the back.

I wish I could come out there.

Don't even think about it. You'll only make things worse.

I'm coming to you.

I don't have a private greenroom this time.

I'll be on the tour bus.

I'll get to you.

I can't wait.

It's unbelievable how close Theo and I have grown in the past week. Everything between us feels so natural. Nothing is ever awkward or uncomfortable. We text each other all throughout the day. We FaceTime as much as we can. He's like a drug I can't get enough of.

When I finally get through security, I bolt toward the VIP section that leads to the backstage area. They are more skeptical this time, and I nearly lose my mind when the security guard almost doesn't let me through, claiming it's only for after the show.

I'm about two seconds away from threatening to get Theo himself on the phone when a supervisor comes over and tells him to let me through.

Next time, Theo definitely needs to get me access to come around the back instead of through the stadium. Which is wild to even think.

Not all that long ago, he was just a favorite singer of mine. Now...he's so much more to me. He's a man I'm growing feelings for. A real person with wounds and scars. After only a week, he has me wishing I could be the guy who makes sure he never gets hurt again.

But I can't. Not really. Not unless I make some very serious changes in my own life.

When I reach the backstage area, I recognize a few faces from the last time.

"I'm here to see Theo," I say to a guard, and he gives me a skeptical look as if I should be detained for even daring to say that sentence out loud.

"He's on the bus," a woman calls. Turning toward the sound of her voice, I recognize the bassist Lola. She waves a hand. "Follow me."

Leaving the security guard behind, I rush after her. But the moment I catch up, I see the hard, skeptical expression on her face and realize she's not going to give me what I want that easily.

Instead, she leads me toward a doorway that's secluded from others. Before pushing it open, she turns to me.

"Theo is my best friend," she says flatly. "And he might seem like he can brush off anything, but he's been hurt before."

"I know, and I don't want to hurt him," I say with severity. "I want to protect him."

"Before you can protect him, you need to know him."

"I'd like to," I plead.

"He doesn't let most people in, you know. So if you get that privilege, I hope you don't abuse it."

"Never." She stares at me for a moment, and I start to grow antsy. "Can I please see him now?"

"Be gentle with him," she says with sorrow in her eyes. "He really likes you."

"Thank you for looking out for him," I reply. "But I promise I like him a lot too, and I don't want to let anyone hurt him."

"Good."

With that, she turns and presses the door open that leads to the back lot. I spot his tour bus behind the other rigs that must have transported their gear and set. After a few feet, Lola stops, letting me finish the walk alone.

I practically sprint. The door to the bus is unlocked as I pull it open and climb the stairs in a rush.

Theo stands from the couch and faces me from the other end. There's a brief moment of hesitation as we each take in the sight of the other. I know deep down that he is as anxious to see me as I am to see him.

"Hey," he mumbles.

"Hey."

Then, we both move at the same time, rushing to close the distance. I grab him by the back of the head first and haul him toward me. His facial hair scratches my lips as I kiss him hungrily, and I savor the burn.

It's only been five days since I kissed him last, but it's as if I've been starving for his touch my entire life. His mouth moves so perfectly with mine; it's like we were made for each other. Our tongues glide as we explore each other's mouths. He clings to my arms, leaning his weight on me as I devour him.

After a moment of kissing, I take a step forward and he lets me press him against the small counter. Without breaking the seal of his mouth, my hands roam down the black fabric of his shirt and over his hips.

Theo's body is slender but muscular. I'm dying to see the definition of each of his abs and that delicious *V* line that leads down below his pants.

"How long do we have?" I hum against his lips.

"An hour, I think," he replies raspily.

I tug up his shirt to get my fingers on his skin, and the moment I trail my touch across his waist, he sucks in a breath through his teeth. My mouth moves to his neck as I kiss and nibble on his sensitive skin. I treasure every little rigid muscle under my fingers as I explore him, but it's not enough.

Meanwhile, he's doing the same to me. He's tugging up on the back of my polo to run his hands along my back.

I can't get close enough to him. That fear I once had of burning out is gone because I don't see a world in which I would tire of kissing Theo. I want more. *Need* more.

Cascading my hands down his ass to the backs of his thighs, I bend my knees enough to get a grasp and hoist Theo up in the air. He clenches his legs around me to hold himself up before I deposit him on the counter. It's much smaller than a real kitchen counter and the upper cabinets get in the way, but at least it lets me feel his legs wrapped around me.

I pull up his shirt again, and this time, I lean down and kiss my way up from his navel to his pecs. He hisses and buries a hand in my hair.

There's a patch of chest hair between his nipples that fades on its way down to his navel. Then there's that delicious trail of hair that disappears under his jeans. I run my fingers through it as I move my mouth to his left nipple. The moment I wrap my lips around the tight bud, he jolts on the counter and drives his hips toward me.

"Fuck, that feels good," he says while I flick it with my tongue and give it a little suck. I move to the other side and do the same there. He's trembling on the counter as I play with his nipples, and it gives me a sense of power that I love.

"Jensen," he cries out. "You're going to make me come in my pants before the show."

"Good," I reply with a smile. "Then you'll have no choice but to think about me the entire time you're up there."

"I'll be thinking about you anyway," he replies, making me stop with his nipples. Standing upright, I kiss him hard on the mouth again.

It's like I'm still on that ride without brakes, but I'm no longer on it alone. We're both speeding toward something we weren't expecting.

As our kiss ends, I reach for Theo's ass and drag him toward me again so I can grind myself against him.

"I won't really make you come in your pants," I murmur as I kiss along his jaw.

"Maybe you can make me come *out* of my pants later," he replies, arching his back for me.

"Oh, definitely. I think we're ready for that."

As much as I'd like to spend our hour preshow kissing and grinding against each other, I'm not just here for that. I want to look into his eyes and speak to him.

Pulling away from the kiss without it getting too heated, I stand a foot away from him with my hands on his legs.

"I'm so glad you're here," he says softly.

"Me too," I reply, running my hands comfortingly up his thighs. "How are you feeling about tonight's show?"

"Good," he replies with a nod. "Are you going to watch again?"

I lean in and kiss him softly. "I wouldn't miss it."

"I kind of like you in the audience," he says with a crooked smile.

"Then I'll be in the audience."

We kiss again, this time softer, as if we're breathing each other in.

"Jensen," he whispers.

"Yeah?"

"You scare the hell out of me."

Hearing him say what I had told him last week hits me with intensity. It means a lot to know that I'm not alone in the shock of this relationship. It's grown faster and more intensely than either of us expected. There is a chemistry and a draw between us that is beyond what either of us has felt before. And it's not just because he's a celebrity or the first man I've been with in a while.

It's because everything about Theo Virgil is compatible with everything about me.

We fit together. And it doesn't make sense.

There's a bang on the door, and I groan into his neck as he answers it.

"I'll be there in a minute!"

We kiss for a while longer before begrudgingly tearing ourselves apart.

Then, I do the same thing I did last time. I watch him give his band a pep talk. I watch him walk out onto the stage, only this time I head out to my seat and enjoy the rest of the concert from there.

It's amazing to see him again from this angle. He gives the crowd exactly what they want. He dances with them, sings with them, and becomes a part of them. He's not up there to be a star.

He's up there to be an artist. He looks out at the crowd as if he's looking out at every single person in the arena individually.

I have a new appreciation for him every time I witness his show. I loved his music before, and now I'm growing a new appreciation for him as a person. I'm still a fan. I still scream the words of his songs and cheer for him after each one. Only now, I do it with the taste of him on my lips.

THIRTEEN

ISAAC

The crowd is massive and so energetic tonight that I never manage to find Jensen among the thousands of faces. But I feel him out there. Having his eyes on me is what gives me the spirit to sing louder, strum harder, jump higher.

It's like he gives me life.

And knowing what's waiting for me after the show *really* gives me life. In fact, it's all I'm living for at the moment.

The crowd is the loudest yet. It's still so fucking surreal. All of these people know my songs. They *like* my music. They are not laughing at me or making me feel inferior.

In some sick and twisted way, I wish my father could see this. I wish I could rub it in his face. *Look at me, Dad. I did all of this without you.*

I don't need you.

When we run offstage before the encore, I rush over to the backstage crew to help me change quickly for the last two songs. The crowd is deafening. It's almost unsettling how loud they are.

I guzzle some water and tear off my shirt as someone helps me into another one. For these last two songs, I like to be more casual.

It's an homage to the old Theo Virgil—the one who started in bars and tiny venues and traveled around in a used van.

It's for the fans who have been with me since the beginning.

After we're all ready, the band and I run back out to the stage, and somehow, the crowd cheers even louder.

"Wow, Denver!" I shout into the mic. "Y'all really showed up tonight."

I stare out through the bright lights and try one last time to find Jensen, but it's futile. It's just a sea of faces blurring together.

"Well, we have a few more songs in us if you could stick around for a bit longer."

They cheer with enthusiasm.

As I strum the guitar, they quiet. Then I lean into the mic. "This is the first song that really took off for me. It changed my life. And it came from the heart. So if you relate to these words, then just know you're relating to me."

After a few more shouts from the crowd, I get started on the song, and it takes me back to the beginning of my career. When I didn't quite know who I wanted to be. I remember feeling like I never fit into any boxes as a musician. I wasn't quite country enough or quite folk enough. I was just me and the music that came from my soul.

Then, out of nowhere, someone got a hold of it, and everyone started to connect with it. Like lightning, it went viral. Overnight, my life changed.

Ironically, it's a song about wanting to fuck someone I'm not supposed to. And most of them have no idea.

Our last song of the encore is a huge hit at the moment, and the crowd really loses it. They sing along as the band and I jam with our instruments. On the final note, we all leap in unison before the lights go out, and we rush offstage.

To my surprise, Jensen is in the wings, waiting for me. I nearly slam right into him and smile brightly, fighting the urge to kiss him.

"You were amazing!" he says with a hand on my shoulder.

"Thank you, but you've seen the show three times now," I reply with a laugh.

"I don't care. It's phenomenal every time."

"Thank you."

His gaze holds mine for a few seconds, and my heart swells in my chest. I'm really losing my fucking grip with this guy.

All I want is to get him to my tour bus, but I'm immediately pulled in different directions. The crew takes my guitar, and Jensen and I lose each other in the chaos backstage after the show. The tour manager and crew want to meet with me for a few minutes to discuss some minor things onstage tonight.

Jensen stays close by, and I keep making eye contact with him, fire burning between us, even when we're apart. He wants exactly what I want. It feels like forever, but the moment no one needs me, we sprint off together.

"Finally," I mutter under my breath. His arm brushes mine, and I notice the itch in my palm with how badly I'd like to hold his hand. Instead, I settle for feeling the breeze off his body as we run toward the back door that leads to the lot.

We don't make it to the door, though. Out of nowhere, his hand wraps around my bicep and tugs me into a dark corner. I gasp as my back hits a black brick wall.

Then his lips are on mine. With shock, I push him away and glance around to be sure we're really alone. When I notice we're hidden behind a mountain of black boxes and a forklift, I smile and haul his mouth back to mine.

Our movements are rushed and rabid, hands roaming and pulling and grabbing. His large hands squeeze my hip and my ass. I explore his chest and shoulder while devouring his kiss.

"Shhh," he whispers against my mouth as his hands fumble for my belt.

My heart is hammering in my chest. Is he really going to touch me here? As much as I want to tell him this is a bad idea, I'm too fucking eager to feel his hands on my cock.

"Jensen," I whisper with my head against the wall as he

quickly undoes my pants and tugs them open. Then he stares into my eyes as he reaches a hand in and wraps it around my length.

I let out a husky gasp, so he slams his other hand over my mouth. "I said to be quiet," he whispers against my cheek with a smirk. Pulling back, he spits into his palm and returns it to my cock to cover it with saliva.

Moving his hand away from my mouth, he kisses the moans from my lips as he starts to roughly stroke my dick to life. It is already half-hard, and he quickly works it to throbbing.

"Fuck," I whisper. There are voices and people shuffling around us, but we are hidden out of sight, at least until someone needs to move these crates and climb into that forklift.

As his hand squeezes my cock, stroking it hard, he kisses his way along my jaw. I'm putty in his hands. I can hardly move.

When his lips reach my ear, he bites the lobe, making me whimper.

"What are you doing to me?" I gasp.

"I'm showing you how good I'm going to take care of you," he replies. "I want you to be *mine*."

On that word, *mine*, he squeezes just under the head of my cock, and my eyes start to roll.

"I want to be yours," I breathe.

"I want to be the one to make you feel good, Theo. I'll be here after every show, and I'll take care of what's mine. I've got you, understand?"

"Yes." My voice cracks as the pleasure builds.

He's stroking me fast, taking me to the brink of pain and pleasure. My body is tight and ready to explode, but there's a sense of panic under the surface, keeping me from finishing.

But then he growls in my ear and says, "Now be a good boy and come for me."

And that's it. I clutch tightly to his body as I'm pummeled by the euphoria. It crashes into me like a storm, causing my muscles to tighten and my body to contort as I ride the wave. There is no keeping in the sounds as I come hard. The sensation spreads through my body like wildfire.

I fist his shirt and bury my face in his neck as it pulses over and over and over again.

"That's it," he whispers in my ear. "Good boy."

I'm panting against his shoulder for a while before he laughs and kisses my head.

"You'll have to let me borrow a shirt for the ride over to the hotel," he adds with humor.

As I pull back, I look down to find his red polo covered in cum stains.

"Oh fuck, I'm sorry," I say.

He kisses my forehead. "Don't be sorry. I'm proud to wear your cum on my shirt."

Goddamn if that doesn't make me hot.

"Now let's get the fuck out of here," he adds as he buttons my pants back up and replaces my belt. I watch him with fascination as he does.

There's a dynamic between us I've never had before, and I'm intrigued by it. He's so dominant and possessive, and I actually like it. I want him to own me, control me, take care of me, brand me.

I want to be his.

I must still be in a daze because he laughs a little as he pushes me out from behind the boxes. I can't help but smile over at him as we reach the door. It's like we have a dirty secret, and he has a very dirty shirt that he's tried to wipe up without much success.

The security guard greets us at the door. "We've been looking for you," he says, and I laugh off the guilt.

"Sorry, we got...uh...caught up with the crew," I stammer. I'm really fucking bad at lying, apparently.

"You ready?" the guard asks. "They're wild tonight."

I'm confused by that statement until we step out of the building and I hear the screams. Jensen crosses his arms over his chest as if that hides anything on his chest, and I laugh to myself when I see it.

Every part of me wants to reach for his hand as we rush out the door. Unlike last time, I want to greet the fans tonight. So I walk over to where they're all corralled and waiting. I imagine they've been standing here for a long time, and they deserve to get at least a signature and a photo out of it.

Jensen stands back with his arms crossed and watches with a pleased expression as I greet as many of the fans as I can.

"You're my favorite singer."

"Your songs saved my life."

"I love you so much, Theo Virgil."

"Will you marry me?"

The cacophony of voices gives me another boost of energy. It's incredible to have so many people who are really here for *me*.

Although, if I'm honest, I'm only really concerned with one of them. And he's watching proudly from behind me.

As soon as I've seen as many fans as I can, I say my goodbyes to them and rush with him toward the bus. When we climb aboard, the rest of the band is there, so there is no privacy to touch each other.

"I should get cleaned up," I say to him as I move toward my room at the back.

"Of course," he replies.

Then I glance down and see the mess again. "Come back here. I'll get you a new shirt."

Rio glances up from his phone as Jensen passes by, watching us skeptically. The only member of my band who really knows the truth is Lola, although I'm sure they have their suspicions. I'm just not as close to them.

When Jensen and I are behind the closed door of my room at the back of the bus, I open up my closet and pull a clean shirt down from the hanger. "Here you go," I say with a smirk.

"Thanks," he replies almost sheepishly.

Then I stand back and watch as he tugs his dirty shirt off and tosses it on the bed. When I get a full view of his chest, my mouth starts to water and I grow more excited, looking forward to the night ahead.

Jensen is beautiful. He's all broad shoulders and bronze skin. With a light patch of chest hair, I stare at his pecs with interest.

"Theo Virgil, are you checking me out?" he whispers quietly.

I step toward him and lay my hand on his chest. "I am." Then I lean in and press my lips to his collarbone.

"You are going to hurry so we can get back to my hotel," he murmurs quietly.

"Yes, sir," I reply before looking into his eyes. His commanding presence catches me off guard, and my blood quickens in my veins when I realize just how much I like saying that to him.

Honestly, who the fuck am I?

FOURTEEN

JENSEN

When I'm with Theo, it's amazing to me how quiet the voices are. I know they'll be waiting for me after this trip. I will pay my penance tomorrow when the guilt and shame built into my psyche come calling, but tonight with Theo will be worth it.

He's sitting beside me, looking as anxious and as tense as I feel. We're not nervous with each other. The only time it's uncomfortable is when we're together and can't touch. Every moment I'm with him without my hands on him is torture.

All I can do is relive the feel of his body against mine. His slender frame and taut muscles. His cock in my hand. The sound of his whimpering orgasm.

I meant every word I said to Theo. I want him to be mine. I want to be the one who takes care of him. Not because he needs it, but because he *craves* it. And I crave it too.

As we reach the hotel, I climb out, but Theo stays back a moment to have a word with the driver. I don't hear exactly what it is, but I definitely pick up the word tomorrow.

He's staying the night.

I am both elated and anxious at the sound of that. It's not that I don't want to fuck Theo's brains out because, *God*, I do. I want everything with him. But I also want to take my time with him. I don't want to waste all this fire in one night.

I want to savor this man.

While Theo talks to the driver, I head into the lobby to check in. The woman behind the counter gets me my key with a flat expression. But as she looks up and sees Theo Virgil walk in the door with a hoodie pulled over his head, she pauses.

Fuck.

He doesn't approach me because that would look too obvious, two men checking into a hotel late at night together.

I clear my throat. The woman behind the desk smiles to herself before getting back to work, typing in my information and getting my room ready.

"Did you see that?" she whispers with a grin. "Theo Virgil just walked past you."

I don't respond. This feeling of protectiveness consumes me as I glare at the woman.

"I'm sure if it was," I mutter, taking my key card from the counter, "your guest's privacy is more important."

Her smile fades as I lift my brows with annoyance. "Good evening," I snap before walking away.

Theo is hiding near the elevators, out of sight of the woman behind the counter.

"What's wrong?" he asks, noticing my foul mood.

At seeing him, I soften and force a smile on my face. "Nothing," I say under my breath.

We enter the elevator together, and I press the floor. I want to slam him against the wall again and kiss him until he can barely breathe, but I'm realizing now just how reckless we were last time. If we're not careful, we'll be caught, and it will be detrimental to both of our careers.

On the ride up, I think about the woman behind the counter.

This constant reminder that Theo is a celebrity pops up around every corner. His shows, backstage, online, in public.

I should be proud that he chooses to be with me, but there's a possessiveness in me that hates that the world seems to think they own a part of him.

But what am I even thinking? Theo and I can't be a true couple. Our relationship will never be genuine. It's cruel and selfish of me to hold so much of his attention and loyalty when I know in my heart that I can't give him anything serious.

This all started as an indulgence, but it definitely doesn't feel that way now.

The elevator doors open, and I place my hand on the small of Theo's back, leading him out to the hallway. We walk in silence to the hotel room. Before I press my key to the lock, I turn to look at him.

"Are we sure about this?" I ask.

"Fuck yes, Jensen," he mutters, leaning into me. "Please open the fucking door."

With a wicked smile, I unlock it and push it open. Taking a step in, I turn back toward Theo and reach out. Clutching the top of his hoodie in my fist, I drag him inside and bring his mouth to mine for a kiss.

He moans against me, and I swallow it down, licking my way into his mouth.

"God, you taste good," I murmur.

He's already fumbling with my shirt—or, technically, his shirt. But I don't want to rush this, so I press my hands down on his.

"Slow down," I whisper.

"I don't want to slow down," he says, biting my bottom lip. We're stumbling into the room, and he's trying to aim us toward the bed.

"Theo," I say with authority.

"What?" he asks without breaking the kiss.

"Get on your knees."

Immediately, he tenses. I'm not normally so controlling with the people I sleep with, but I have such a desire to try it with him. He may not like it, and I can handle it if that's the case.

He glances up into my eyes. Lifting a hand, I slip off his hoodie, letting my command float in the air between us, waiting to be acknowledged.

Then, to my surprise, he lowers to his knees in front of me. The sight is delicious. The feeling, even more so. I don't want to control him for my own enjoyment. I want to do it for his, too.

Theo wants clear expectations. He yearns for trust and connection. And as he gazes up from the floor, his face perfectly positioned in front of my groin, it's written all over his face just how much he likes this.

"Good boy," I whisper as I pet his curls back. His eyes close with a look of pleasure on his face. Leaning forward, he presses his face to the front of my pants, resting it there intimately. I wind his hair through my fingers as I grip him near the scalp.

"You are so fucking beautiful," I whisper, making him hum. When was the last time someone told Theo how wonderful he was? Not Theo, the star. Theo, the man.

"And you want to be good for me, don't you?"

He looks up at me as he nods. "Fuck yes, I do," he replies with a growl in his voice.

"You know you can trust me, right? Theo, you can always trust me."

I notice a wince in his expression, and even when he nods, I don't buy it. He's holding back. I imagine after being betrayed by the people meant to love him most, trust is an issue for him. I want to cure him of that. Nothing matters more to me in this moment than to prove to Theo that I will always be the one to never turn on him, never leave him, never hurt him.

After only a week, I know that in my heart. It rings with truth that defies logic or reason.

Taking his chin in my hand, I tip his face back and force him to look at me. "Say it. Tell me you understand I will never hurt you."

"I...understand," he whispers.

"Good," I reply. "I want to earn your trust, and I will never do to you what they did."

His mouth tics with a hint of a smile. As he rests his cheek against my leg again, I stroke his hair. The feeling in my chest is so intense. How can I be falling for this man so quickly?

Theo's hands creep up and hook onto my belt. His pupils are dilated, and his mouth is parted as he gazes up at me from the floor. "Jensen, please," he whispers. "I need to feel you."

"Then take it out," I reply sternly.

Still stroking his hair, I watch as he unbuckles my belt. Once it's undone, I pull it from the loops and toss it on the floor.

The sight of him unbuttoning my pants is one I'll have etched into my memories forever. He looks exquisite on the floor, and I can hardly wait for the moment he touches me.

"There you go," I murmur with adoration.

Theo yanks open my pants and stares at my cock, pointing upward and straining against my boxer briefs. The tip is poking out of the top, ready for his mouth.

He waits for my instruction. "Go ahead," I mumble. "You want to taste it, don't you? Let me see what that pretty mouth can do."

Licking his lips at that exact moment, he eases down my briefs and leans forward, letting my cock rest on his face. The image is unbelievable. His eyes close as he savors the contact. He darts out his tongue, and the warm, wet sensation hits my skin. As he draws his tongue up the length of it, my head falls back with a moan.

When he reaches the tip, he kisses it with his wet lips, focusing on the underside of the head. My toes curl, and I groan even louder.

"That's it," I growl. "Good boy."

When his lips part, and my cock disappears into his mouth, I nearly lose my mind. The wet heat consumes me, and I feel it everywhere. Covering his teeth with his lips, he moans hungrily as he slides me to the back of his throat, gliding his lips from base to tip.

"Fuck," I mumble, my voice like gravel. "Don't stop. Don't you dare stop that beautiful fucking mouth."

He growls around my cock as he picks up speed. With both of his hands on my hips, he takes me deeper and deeper each time. When he gags, I tear his mouth off with a harsh grip on his hair.

"You're going to make me come already," I bark.

As he smiles up at me with saliva-wet lips, I hold his head in place as I lean down to kiss him. I lick into his mouth and nibble his lips as if I'm trying to eat him and make him mine.

Holding him by the hair and jaw, I force him to look at me. "I am fucking obsessed with you," I growl. "What are you doing to me?"

He smiles wickedly and makes it so clear how he has me under his spell. He is sex and sin incarnate. All of my temptations wrapped up into one. Theo Virgil will be my downfall and my destruction, and right now, I welcome it. Let me burn in the fires of hell forever for that mouth of his. I won't regret a thing.

Bringing his mouth back to my cock, I slide my length down his throat until he gags again. He takes over and sucks with purpose. He wants to please me.

And when the pleasure begins to crescendo, I don't stop it. I let it wash over me.

With a roaring sound, I come, filling his mouth and throat with my seed. He takes it with eagerness, groaning as he continues to suck and swallow, licking his lips when he pops his mouth from the head.

"Fuck." The word comes out like a breath as I collapse onto the bed behind me. My head hits the mattress and I stare up at the ceiling with my cock still hanging out and the aftershock of my orgasm tingling through my body.

A moment later, Theo crawls up and reclines at my side.

Using my arm as a pillow, he cuddles up to me with a proud expression on his face.

"Can you move?" he asks.

"Soon, I will," I reply.

He kisses my jaw and nuzzles my neck.

Opening my eyes, I turn toward him and kiss his mouth. He tastes like a delicious sin.

"You're incredible," I mumble.

His only response is a chuckle as he kisses me again. "Actually, I'm starving."

"Let's order in," I reply, forcing myself to sit up.

He reclines on his back with his hands behind his head. "You really are going to take care of me, aren't you?" he asks.

Leaning over, I press my lips to his forehead before picking up the room service menu. "Always."

FIFTEEN

ISAAC

There is a pizza box on the hotel bed between us as Jensen and I stuff our faces and wash it down with a six-pack of beer.

I'm still reeling from the interaction when we first got into the room. It's become increasingly clear that if Jensen says jump, I say how high. Which would be a red flag if I didn't know deep in my heart that he means it when he says he'll take care of me.

Am I being naive to judge him so quickly? Probably.

But my gut is telling me I'm safe with him.

He smirks at me over the pizza. Lifting the bottle to his lips, his eyes stay glued to mine. I desperately want to stay the night, but I'm not going to just invite myself if he's not ready for that.

And oddly enough, I don't want to stay for sex. In fact, I think I want to wait a while before we take that step. I haven't had this much fun with foreplay since I was a teenager.

The making out. Groping. Yearning. It's all too good to rush it.

"I don't want to be too forward..." he says before taking another pull off the longneck.

"You gave me a hand job backstage surrounded by crew. I think we're past too forward."

He chuckles, and I can't get enough of his smile. It's crooked and warm, lighting up his eyes with delicate wrinkles sprouting at the edges.

I've never really been into older guys before, but Jensen is the exception.

"Well, in that case," he says, looking almost bashful. "I would love it if you spent the night."

I bite my bottom lip to keep from grinning. *What is happening to me?*

"I'd love to," I reply.

"But I'll warn you now," he says, leaning back with a smile. "I'm a cuddler."

"I think I can handle that."

His foot nudges my leg. The energy in the room changes. He takes another drink, finishing his beer but never taking his eyes off me. Then, he sets the bottle on the nightstand, followed by the pizza box.

Then it's just us and a bed.

"Come here," he says in a cool, quiet command. With nothing between us, I crawl toward the head of the bed. When I reach him, I lean forward to press my lips to his. He kisses me tenderly at first and then wraps his hand around my neck to pull me closer.

Before I know it, I'm climbing onto his lap. Straddling his hips, I kiss him without anything but clothes between us. The room is silent except for the sound of our subtle moans and lips smacking.

He moves his hands under my shirt and up my back. His touch feels phenomenal.

As he slides my shirt over my head, his mouth finds my chest. When he pulls my nipple between his teeth, I let out a hissing sound and grind my hips against him.

More, I chant in my mind.

I tug at his shirt as he flicks my right nipple with his tongue. I'm desperate for the feel of his body against mine. He leans forward to allow me room to take his shirt over his head. Then, our chests are pressed together as we kiss again.

My hips grind again and again. With his fingers in my belt loops, he guides my movement, pulling me closer and harder.

Out of nowhere, he flips me onto my back, following behind and settling his body between my legs. From this angle, he grinds me into the mattress, matching up the stiff lengths of our arousal, seeking friction together.

"Pants off," I mumble against his mouth.

As I'm working to undo his pants, he's working on mine. We are frantic and fumbling, desperate to touch each other. I want all of him.

He shimmies my pants down first, taking my underwear with them. I'm naked on the bed in front of him, reaching to remove the rest of his clothes, too. He stands from the bed to remove his pants but is only gone a second.

The moment he's fully naked, he drapes his body back over mine, and the sensation of warm skin on warm skin is incredible. Everything with Jensen feels like I'm experiencing it for the first time. It all feels so different than it does with other people, which frightens me a little. Normally, I'm just looking to get off, but with him, I want to experience it all—because, for the first time, I'm not experiencing it alone. And if that's true, then I might be careening headfirst into a *real* relationship. God, I pray I don't mess it up.

When he kisses me again, our dicks are aligned, and he ruts against me slowly, drawing a desperate moan from my mouth.

"You feel so good," he murmurs.

"Just keep doing that," I reply.

His mouth is fused to mine as he moves, grinding cock against cock. Sweet, delicious friction fills my senses, and I feel myself coursing straight for my climax.

We stop kissing as Jensen lifts onto his hands, meeting my gaze as he continues to move. The combination of his dark-brown eyes and his smooth, hard cock rubbing against mine is enough to send me over the edge.

The sounds I'm making aren't quite moans. They're more like whimpering cries, and judging by the euphoria on his face, he likes it. It feels amazing and I don't want it to stop, but it's not quite enough pressure or friction to make me come. And for once, that's okay. I could stay like this forever. Caught up in a wave of passion with him.

There's nothing outside this door. No fans or careers or families or pressure. It's just us.

Jensen kisses me again, this time trailing his lips down my jaw to my neck, and I cling to him for dear life. I wish I could live here in this moment forever.

At any moment, I expect him to ask to fuck me, and at this point, I would let him. I did want to wait. But I'm so caught up in him that I'll say yes if he asks.

But he doesn't. He seems just as content as me to explore this passion just outside of full-blown sex.

Reaching down, he wraps a hand around us both together and strokes.

"Unh," I groan. "Harder."

Jensen leans back onto his knees and gazes down at my rigid cock. Then he dives down to wrap his mouth around it, taking me by surprise as I let out a needy cry.

"Fuck!"

He moans around my shaft in response, coating it with saliva. He's teasing me on purpose, taking me for a ride without letting it end. I'm tortured by the sensation.

After a few moments, when my dick is good and wet, he kneels again, lining them up and stroking them together.

"Oh God, I'm gonna come," I mumble, throwing my head back. Everything feels so good. The warmth of his hand. The weight of his balls against mine. The pressure from when he squeezes the head on every upstroke.

"You look so fucking hot like this," he says and jacks our dicks together.

"Please make me come," I beg. "I'm ready."

His stroking picks up speed. My legs are writhing with Jensen between them. I'm gripping tight to his other arm, waiting for the climax to pummel into me.

And when it does, I let out a strangled, drawn-out noise as I dig my head into the mattress. He makes a similar sound, and I feel him jolt and shudder against me.

A moment later, warm, wet spurts of cum land on my chest. There's even some near my neck and collarbone.

"Holy shit," he whispers, and I can only imagine it's in appreciation of the mess on my body.

When my orgasm releases me from its grip, I glance down at the mess to see our cum mixed on my skin. There is some pooled in my belly button and mingled in my chest hair. It's a hot fucking sight.

"Don't move," he mumbles as he sits upright. "I need to commit this image to memory forever."

I laugh as my hands fall to the sides. I am wholly spent and sated.

"Go ahead," I say, letting him stare at me, covered in sex.

"I don't think I've ever seen anything hotter in my life."

"That can't be true," I reply.

He drapes his body back over mine, squeezing the mess between us. Then he kisses my lips and looks into my eyes. "Theo, *you* are by far the hottest thing to me, and I think you always will be."

My smile relaxes as I gaze back up at him, overcome by the intensity of his words and his tone. Words like always and forever normally make me panic and bolt, but hearing Jensen say them has me feeling almost...hopeful. It's only been a week, and there's no telling what the future holds for us, but for once, I'm not actually terrified of it.

Which might actually be the scariest thing of all.

†

Jensen opens the door for the large white tile shower for me, and I step in under the hot spray. As he steps in behind me, I sense him watching me with interest.

There's a gravitational pull between us because I'm almost immediately falling into his arms the moment we both meet under the water. Pressing my cheek to his shoulder, I try to breathe and focus for a moment.

It's a while before either of us moves or speaks.

"What are you thinking?" he whispers.

"How crazy this is," I reply without lifting my head.

"What exactly is crazy about it?"

"The fact that I've only known you for a week, but it feels like longer."

"It does," he mumbles against the side of my head.

"Are we moving too fast?" I ask.

He chuckles. "We haven't even had sex yet."

"I don't mean the sex part," I reply. "I mean…"

Pulling away, I only glance into his eyes for a moment before getting self-conscious. Maybe it's just me who feels this way. I don't want to say something stupid. It's embarrassing.

"What is it?" he pushes.

"I just mean that…I don't normally get this close to the guys I'm with. The sex is what normally happens fast, but the relationship…that's what's freaking me out."

"Do you want to slow down?" he asks.

"No."

"Me neither."

"Are you afraid that I'm going to break your heart?" he asks, and I have to let out a heavy breath. Relationship talk is not my favorite. Feelings and fears and all that shit is not for me. It's much easier to find a guy I find hot, have my fun with him, and say goodbye forever. The heart has nothing to do with it.

Staring at the ceiling, I let out a huff of frustration. "Yes, I am."

Jensen wraps an arm around my waist and pulls me toward him. Then, with his fingers on my chin, he forces me to look at him.

"I won't."

"It's okay if you do. It'll give me more songs to write."

He doesn't laugh. "That's not funny."

"I know it's not, but I cover up fear with humor. You should know that about me."

"You cover a lot up with humor," he replies. Then, after a moment, he adds, "But you don't need to hide anything from me."

Suddenly, it hits me that I've been keeping a secret from him this whole time and if we're going to talk about trust and relationships, I should probably come out with this.

"My name's not Theo."

Okay, maybe I should have worked my way into it instead of just blurting it out because he's staring at me as if I've grown a dick on my forehead.

"What?"

"There was never a good time to tell you, so I'm telling you now." I wince as I wait for his reaction. Is this a big deal? Will he storm out in anger?

"So..." he asks.

"So what?"

"What the fuck is your name?"

"Oh," I mutter with a chuckle. "It's...uh, Isaac."

"Isaac."

"Yeah," I reply, hoping he's not about to leave. "Theo is a stage name. I didn't want to use my real one, so it was easier to just make one up, but you know you can still call me Theo if you want—"

"No, I want to call you by your name. I hope you know I'm

not here because you're a star or a celebrity. I don't care about that. I'm here for *you*."

His mouth curves with a crooked smile as he runs a hand down the side of my face. Then he leans in and presses his lips to mine. "Isaac."

Hearing him say it feels like cracking open the last layer of my heart and letting him all the way in. Now, there is nothing between us. No secrets. No boundaries. Jensen has full access to my heart, and I pray he keeps his word and doesn't break it.

Sixteen

Texas in the summer is blistering. The humidity makes everything miserable. But the one thing that Austin has going for it right now is that for the next two weeks, Theo—I mean, Isaac—will only be twenty minutes away.

It's been ten days since I saw him in Denver. He had a photo shoot there the day after our night in the hotel. I flew home while he worked, and we've been texting each other every day since.

They took a couple of days to travel, and then once he got back, his work schedule was crazy, but I can be patient.

I still can't wrap my head around this thing between us. What he said in the shower that night was so true. This relationship is blossoming so fast it's almost terrifying. But at the same time, I've never been happier.

Waking up the next morning in the hotel with him in my arms was divine. Heaven on earth. Ironically, Isaac and I fit so well together. Like he was made to be there. Our dynamic is effortless.

But I can't deny the obvious...that Isaac does not fit well in the life I've built around myself. More than once, I've considered what my life would be like if he did. What if, instead of trying to fit him into my life, I built my whole life around him? How happy would I be?

No more church. My relationship with my parents might be strained. My community. My friends.

But I'd have him.

Hell, it's too soon to start thinking like this already. It's only been a few weeks. He still doesn't even know what I do for a living. Somehow, I've gotten by talking about work without any real specifics. The guilt of that omission is weighing on me.

Especially after he came clean about his real name. I won't pretend that wasn't a big deal for him. He let me into his life. His *real* life.

Now it's my turn.

I have to tell him the truth. We'll get through the rest together.

For the first day in weeks, Isaac is off work. He has a pool at his place, and he invited me over. We're going to do nothing but sit in the sun, cool off in the pool, and be together. It sounds like a dream. Am I putting this day at risk if I tell him the truth? I don't know if that's a risk I want to take.

I should probably be working on my sermon for Sunday, but I can do that later. There are enough drafts on my computer to work with. I'm sure I can pull something together tonight.

If I do spend the night, there's just the small issue of needing to leave early for service. God, I feel like such a monster for keeping this from him. The longer I hold back, the worse it will be when I finally come clean.

I'll know what to do when I see him. My knee bounces on the entire drive over to his place. After ten days apart, the idea of having him all day today is what I'm choosing to focus on.

When I pull up to his place, I send him a quick text so he can open the gate. Immediately, there's a beep, and the gate starts to move. As I creep up the drive, I find him standing at the top in front of his house in a pair of black shorts and a tight-fitting shirt. He looks so good that I'm grinning from ear to ear.

His house doesn't seem too big. It's tall, sleek, and modern, with lots of windows and little natural landscaping. Just the kind of place you'd expect a single musician to live in.

He's beaming as I step out of my car, with dimples piercing his cheeks like parentheses. It would be too dramatic to run to him, although that's exactly what I want to do. So, instead, I walk quickly over to him, and he does the same.

When I get my arms around his slender frame, his lips press eagerly to mine, and I manage to lift him off the ground by a few inches. I can feel his smile against my mouth.

"Oh my god, I missed you," he mumbles.

"I missed you too," I reply, pleased to hear his enthusiasm. I don't want to be alone in my excitement. I like knowing he feels the same passion I do.

Holding his body tightly against mine, my hands roam down his back and over his ass. He groans huskily into our kiss, and it immediately awakens my cock. The front yard is very private so no one can see us, and it feels amazing to be able to be with him in the open like this.

I wish we could always do this.

"Let's go inside," he says, tugging my hand. The modern interior of his house has very few personal items and honestly doesn't strike me as a place Isaac would decorate or prefer. I imagine more color and warmth for him. Soft, personal touches.

"The label technically owns the place," he says as he guides me through.

"Do you like it?" I ask, still holding his hand.

"Not really, but it's a free million-dollar house. How could I complain?"

I pull him toward me, placing my hands on his hips. "And what would you do differently if it was yours? What would your house look like?"

He smirks, looking surprised. "Well..." he starts before looking around. "I want an entire wall of vintage country album covers. And at least one Dolly Parton poster. I'd have a whole room for music and not a studio. Like guitars and a piano and a drum set just to play for fun. And I'd want a big fat cozy chair with books stacked around it."

"You like to read?" I ask, pressing a kiss to his jaw.

"Uhhh...I want to like to read if that makes sense."

I laugh, kissing him again. "Makes perfect sense."

We kiss a bit more, and it isn't long before I'm backing him up to the wall of the kitchen. As my lips trail down his neck, I mumble, "I promise I came here to swim."

"Who cares about swimming?" he murmurs. "That feels so good."

He reaches for my hips and pulls me closer, looking for friction. I'm already hard and aching for him, and as much as I want it, something stops me from taking this any further.

I can't lie to him anymore. The guilt of my omission is starting to pop up in moments between us, and I can't live with that. I promised he could trust me. I promised I wouldn't hurt him, and I'm going to keep that promise.

"Isaac," I whisper, pulling away and putting my forehead against his.

"God, I love hearing you call me that."

"I need to tell you something." My heart starts pounding uncontrollably. What if he kicks me out? What if he's so mad he never wants to see me again?

The thought is too awful to bear.

But I have to, for him.

His eyes grow serious as he stares back at me.

"It's about my job, and after you came clean with your name last time we were together, I realized that I should come clean, too. I don't want to lie to you." My voice sounds tight and uncomfortable.

He pushes me away a few inches to really look at me. There is nowhere for me to hide.

Gazing into his eyes, I decide to just come out with it.

"I said I worked for a nonprofit because I didn't think you'd want to see me again if you knew the truth."

"You're scaring me," he mumbles.

"The nonprofit I work for is...a church."

His brow furrows. "You work for a church?"

"Yes."

The corner of his mouth lifts in a smirk. "That's your big secret?"

I step away and run my fingers through my hair. "Yes, Isaac. Because I don't just work there...I'm a pastor."

His brows lift in surprise. "Holy shit."

I nod. "Yes, holy shit, indeed."

"I didn't know pastors could be..."

"Gay? Well, technically, yes, of course we can. But I'm not out about it. Just like you."

He paces away from me, walking around his kitchen island before coming back to stare at me. "A pastor? Really?"

"I'm sorry for lying and not telling you."

He watches me, his face tense in concentration. He's trying to figure out if he should be mad about this, and honestly, I hope he's at least a little mad. He can't be so forgiving of people when they lie to him or abuse his trust.

But at the same time, I want to earn his trust more than anything.

"A pastor?" he asks, rubbing his jaw. "Really?"

"Really," I reply once again. My shoulders tense as I wait for an outburst.

"You're not like any pastor I've ever met," he says with his eyes narrowed, almost as if he has a bad experience with men of faith and he's trying to reconcile how I can be one of them.

"I'm sure I'm not," I reply calmly.

He contemplates this for a while, staring at me like he's looking for answers. "Okay," he says with finality.

My eyes widen. "Okay?"

"Yeah, Jensen. Okay. I have no reason to judge you for your job or being in the closet. I'm obviously in a similar situation."

Walking toward him, I take his face in my hands. "Do not trust so easily," I say.

"I trust you, Jensen." He's so confident, and something about it breaks my heart.

"Yes, but I've kept this from you for weeks."

"So?" he argues. "I kept my fucking *name* from you. So, we have boundaries. It's not that big of a deal. You can be a pastor, and I can be a country singer, and to the world, we'll just be friends. And everything will be fine."

I let out a huff of frustration. I don't want the world to think we're *friends*. I don't want Isaac to think it's not a big deal.

It irks me to no end that he's so forgiving and accepting of this news. This is why Isaac needs me. Someone has to protect him because his family has fucked him up too much.

"Relax," he says with a smile as he grabs me by the back of the neck. "If it were any other guy who lied to me, I'd tell him to fuck off. But I don't normally let people get this close to me, Jensen. I don't date, and I rarely trust anyone, but I really, *really* like you. And I know you were just as guarded coming into this relationship as I was. Of course, we kept intimate details close to our chests. But it's fine."

I let out a heavy, surrendering breath and relax my shoulders. He leans in and kisses me. The moment his tongue brushes against mine, it silences all the fears and doubts in my mind.

He always has a way of doing that.

"Now, let's fire up the grill, crack open a few drinks, and relax by the pool. Please?" he says with an adorable plea. When I don't immediately relent, he sticks out his lower lip, and it's my undoing.

"Fine," I mumble with a crooked smirk.

It feels like a weight has been lifted, but at the same time... there is still something heavy burdening my soul. Maybe it's the tireless claws of Eternal Harmony buried deep within my psyche.

Maybe it's the fear that either of us could be caught and our liveli-hoods put in jeopardy. Maybe it's the fear that my presence is a threat to Isaac's success.

Or maybe it's the nagging reminder in the back of my mind that Isaac and I have many more hills to climb in our future. And we're a long way off from anything resembling a happily ever after.

Seventeen

ISAAC

Jensen is flipping burgers on the grill in nothing but a pair of tight swim trunks with a cold beer in his hand. And I'm just relaxing in my pool and enjoying the view.

Having him in my house is surreal. This is boyfriend shit. And I don't normally do boyfriend shit, but I'm enjoying this.

He's seemed to relax since the conversation about him being a pastor. If only he knew the reason his being a pastor in Austin is slightly strange for me, the fact that it reminds me of my father. But Jensen is nothing like him. It's like he's rewriting history.

And maybe that's why I like him so much. Because he is righting the wrongs of Truett Goode.

"Let's eat," he calls as he plates our burgers and shuts off the grill.

It's so fucking domestic. Eating together. Spending our Saturday together, talking about the weather, the house, and the food. And you know…I don't fucking hate it.

Jensen Miles looks good in my house.

He looks good in my life.

For a moment, it feels like everything will be okay and we can actually make this work. And if I'm honest, him being a pastor only makes it look more appropriate for a guy like me. Who would possibly suspect us of anything inappropriate?

I'm just a country music star with a good Christian friend.

After we eat, we both get in the water to cool off. He leans against the side of the pool with his arms propped up on the edge behind him. Swimming up to him with a grin on my face, I let the water drip down my shoulders as I slide my hands up his body.

He reaches up and tousles my wet curls, letting one drip over my eye. Then, he smooths them over the top of my head as he leans in to kiss my lips.

Something is different about Jensen today. He seems tense.

"Everything okay?" I ask, wrapping my arms around his neck so our bodies are flush.

"Yeah," he says flatly. "Wish I didn't have to work tomorrow."

"Oh yeah," I say with a smirk. "Kind of a big deal to show up on the only day of the week you do work."

He shakes his head as if he can't believe I'm being so casual about this. "I do work other days, but yes, it is a big deal that I'm there."

"You don't have to spend the night if you don't want to," I say, secretly hoping he does.

His eyes meet mine with sincerity. "No, I do." Then he draws his fingers along my jaw before stealing another kiss.

"Good," I mumble. "I want you to too."

"And what exactly would you like to do?" he whispers with his lips close to my ear.

Heat travels down my spine at his words. "I think you know exactly what I'd like to do."

"I want to hear you say it," he replies with a rasp in his voice, teasing me with his mouth on my ear.

There's a flutter of embarrassment in my gut but also intense arousal at his dominating tone. He has me practically purring with his mouth on my neck.

Then he spins us until my back is against the pool wall. Without moving his mouth, he adds, "I'm waiting."

I'm nearly panting, my heart going a mile a minute when I say, "I want you to fuck me."

Heat cascades down my spine as soon as the words leave my mouth.

He growls against my skin, making my cock ache with need. How does he do this? How does he make me feel like some virginal teenager who blushes at the mention of sex? I've been fucked and asked to be fucked countless times but never like this. Never with such anticipation.

I have never wanted it *this* much.

"God, hearing you say that makes me want to do it right now," he mutters, driving my ass into the wall as he grinds against me.

"I'm ready," I whimper.

He chuckles as he moves his mouth to my collarbone, licking up the droplets of water. "Tonight."

"Fuck me tonight and then give a sermon tomorrow. Sounds perfect," I say with sarcasm.

He tenses, groaning against my skin. "Please don't say it like that."

I can't help but laugh. "There's my dark humor again…"

"I've noticed."

"Just one of my many endearing qualities."

He pulls back and looks into my eyes before brushing another strand of hair from my forehead. Then he kisses it as he mumbles, "Many, many."

We swim for a while longer, mostly lounging in the water and making small talk. The longer we're together, the more Jensen opens up about himself. With everything I learn about him, my heart grows more and more attached.

For the first time in my life, I look at him as someone I might actually want around for the long run. What's really strange is that the more I picture Jensen in my life, the more I see him in the context of my family. He offered to come with me to see them.

Could I really take him up on that?

Half the reason I fear going home is that I know I'd be doing it alone, and I'm not sure I'm ready for that. Sure, I have Lucas and Sadie. And yes, I know my mother and brothers love me unconditionally and would never do anything to hurt me again.

But I'd still be just Isaac, walking in that door alone. Without that sense of comfort and protection I have with Jensen. He makes me feel stronger. Like I'm safe.

Regardless of whether or not he comes with me, there is definitely, without a doubt, a desire on my part to reenter the Goode family fold. I'm tired of missing out on Sunday dinners and birthdays and parties and get-togethers. I'm missing out on my nieces and nephews, and I won't ever get that time back. Caleb's daughter doesn't even know who I am.

So whether or not Jensen comes with me, I'm ready.

But I really hope he does.

†

Jensen and I take turns in the shower after we get out of the pool. I go first and take a little longer to do some extra...prep. While he's in, I relax on my bed, pull out my phone, and check my notifications. There's a message from Luke updating me about our dad's case, but I only skim it with little interest.

> The sentencing has been scheduled for next month. He must be filling someone's pockets because everything is moving much faster than it normally does. Caleb is getting worried, but I don't want to stress you out. It'll be fine.

> Thanks for the update

I reply.

With my knee bouncing, I type out another message.

I'm seeing a new guy.

Oh yeah?

Yeah. I really like him.

In Nashville?

No. In Austin.

Wow.

Is that bad?

I just don't want our family drama infiltrating your career. But as long as you like him and trust him, that's all that matters.

I do. And I was thinking...

I'd like you to meet him.

I'd love to, Isaac. You know that.

How would you feel if I brought him with me next weekend when we were planning dinner?

Of course, that's fine with me.

No matter what, Sadie and I have your back.

I know.

My brother has always been like this. Adam and Caleb were protective too, but Lucas took on the role for multiple reasons.

Obviously because he loves me, but also out of spite for our father. No one hates him more.

Which is why I can't explain to Luke that I am not afraid of Truett. Not in the way he thinks.

Biting my lip, I'm renewed with a sense of excitement at the idea of bringing Jensen around my family. This is the first step. First Lucas. Then the rest of them.

It's surreal to even imagine. Back with my family. Back to being Isaac Goode again. Maybe it's because Truett is finally out of the picture, but suddenly the thing I've been avoiding for over a decade has turned into something I'm anticipating. My family has changed a lot since I left. Adam had a major change of heart and quite a public crisis. Caleb came out as queer and is now in a poly relationship. Even Lucas settled down and has a kid, something I never expected for him.

It seems like the family I was running from at seventeen has been replaced by a family I'm eagerly running to at twenty-eight. After eleven years, I can really come home and share with them everything I've done since I left.

I'm lying on my bed in my underwear when Jensen comes out of the shower. He has a white towel wrapped around his waist and I drop my phone as I stare at him.

Goddamn, is this man really mine?

"How are you feeling?" I ask.

He nods as he walks toward the side of the bed. "I'm with you," he says softly. "I'm feeling great."

"And you still want to do this?"

He growls in response. There's my answer.

Leaning down, he kisses me softly at first, and then it starts to crescendo in passion. I reach for the towel, but he grabs my hand to stop me.

"You'll have to take that off if you want to do it," I say, making him shake his head at my joke.

"I know," he replies, but then he spreads his body on the bed between my legs. Lying on his stomach, he tugs at the waistband of my boxer briefs. "But I just want to play with this a little first."

Blood floods my groin as I recline a little deeper into the pillows behind me. "Well, by all means," I say. "Be my guest."

As he tugs down my underwear, he lets out a hum as if he delights in the sight of my cock and balls. After he has me completely naked, he just lies on the mattress between my legs and kisses his way up my thighs and across each hip bone.

With my head against the headboard, my eyes close. When his mouth reaches my cock, he presses his wet lips to my balls first, kissing and licking each one delicately.

"You're driving me crazy, you know that?" I mutter tightly.

"Just relax and let me take care of you." He gives my cock a lazy stroke and continues to trace the entire area with his mouth, taking his time. Lifting my balls, he licks behind them, and my knees fall open from the bliss.

"Goddamn, Jensen. What are you doing to me?"

"I just told you," he mumbles before licking there again, getting closer to the hole.

What kind of fucking preacher is this guy? If only the people in his congregation knew he spent his Saturday night slathering up a country star's cock, they'd be shocked.

The more he toys with me, the needier I get. He's worshipping my body like he finds it exquisite. Like I'm a work of art. Like he loves every inch.

His tongue laps at the tight ring and I melt into the mattress. Humming with every stroke of his tongue, he seems to delight in my pleasure.

"Please," I beg when his lips kiss wet circles around the base of my length. "I'm ready."

"Ready for what?" he mumbles lazily.

I bark out a laugh. "Fuck you, Jensen. You know exactly what I'm ready for."

"I know, but I want to hear you say it."

"You've been edging me all fucking day."

"Say it, Isaac," he commands.

"Fuck me, please."

"Not yet," he replies mercilessly, and I want to curse at him.

He hums as he brings his lips to the head of my dick and slowly engulfs the hard shaft. I bite my bottom lip to keep from letting out some embarrassing sound. It doesn't work. I still release a slew of garbled noises that resemble words.

Slowly massaging my sack in his hands, he bobs his perfect, sinful mouth up and down on my cock. I'm writhing, my eyes still closed as I grip the pillows on the bed in my tight fists.

Then he presses his finger around my saliva-covered hole, and I stop moving. Knees parted and pulled up, I breathe as he leisurely teases the entrance. Still sucking my cock, he continues to edge me.

"I could worship this cock all night," he says after pulling his mouth away. Those words send a shot of heat down my spine.

"You're torturing me. You know that, right?" I ask, staring down at him, sprawled out on my bed.

"Yes, I do. But I'm enjoying myself," he says before drawing his tongue up the length of my cock again.

I think I'm going to explode or go mad when he finally asks, "Where do you keep the lube?"

"Nightstand drawer," I say with relief.

"And condoms?"

"Yes."

He leaves my cock to reach into the drawer. It gives me a minute to breathe, collapsed on the bed in anticipation. Riffling through the nightstand, he finds the pack of condoms and a bottle of lube, tossing both on the bed before returning to his spot between my legs.

The torture continues as he kisses and licks my balls again. When he reaches for the lube, it's a miracle. He spreads it generously on his fingers before hiking my legs up higher.

Slowly, he works himself in, and it's such a relief I could cry. He strokes with one finger until I'm begging him again.

"More," I groan with my head thrown back.

"Patience, baby."

I don't want to be patient. I want to be fucked.

Finally, Jensen eases in a second finger, working me open to accommodate him. I reach down to stroke my cock as he's prepping me, but he bats my hand away.

"I'll take care of you," he says defensively.

"Really? Because right now, you're killing me."

With a smirk, he kisses my inner thigh. Then, a third finger stretches my hole even more, and I'm finally as ready as I can be.

Jensen moves up to his knees, dropping the towel to reveal his throbbing erection. He gives it a lazy stroke as he reaches for the condoms. I watch as he tears one open and slides the rubber onto his length. Then he takes a moment to slather it with lube and even adds a bit more to my ass.

Climbing over me, he takes my mouth roughly, and I moan against his lips. "I want to be close to you," he says as he rolls me to my side. Then he settles his body behind mine, my back flush with his chest.

With one arm under my head, he grabs his cock with the other and guides the warm, blunt tip to my hole. Sliding his hand up my hip, he grips me tightly as he presses himself inside.

The moment his cock breaches the tight ring of muscle, I let out a husky groan of relief, the burn familiar and delicious. He slides in deep before freezing so we can both savor the feeling as he holds me close, an arm across my chest.

"You feel incredible," he whispers against my ear. "Your ass is so fucking tight. It's like heaven."

"I need it rough," I mutter as I squeeze his hand with mine. "Please fuck me hard."

His mouth traces warm kisses along my neck and ear. Then, his free hand grasps my throat and forces my face toward him. Our tongues tangle as he pulls out to the tip and thrusts back in. He swallows my cries of pleasure.

Picking up speed, he holds me tight in an intimate embrace.

Placing a foot on the bed for leverage, his movements grow harder and faster, and it's like I'm being swept up in a storm with him.

"Harder," I cry.

His hand is still around my throat as he thrusts relentlessly, still going slow to savor the sensation. We are gripping each other so tight I don't know where I end and he begins. Hands, arms, legs, mouths, breaths. We are a mingled, sensual mix of sex, desire and pleasure. He continues his unhurried movement, letting seconds stretch into minutes, and I love every delicate, perfect moment of having him inside me. The sensation is like nothing I've felt before. Gripping the bedsheets, I thrust my ass back toward him, matching the jacking motion of his hips.

My heart swells in my chest for him because this is about so much more than fucking. It's about our souls meeting in this intimate, safe place together.

When he tilts his hips, almost fucking me down into the mattress, his cock hits my prostate, and my cock leaks at the tip.

"Like that. More," I plead, my mind unable to put together more than one or two words at a time. It's all moving a lot faster than I think either of us meant for it to. We're no longer savoring—we're indulging.

"Like that?" he grits through his teeth. "Fuck, baby. I'm not going to last much longer. I wanted to take my time with you, but I can't."

"I need to come, Jensen," I beg. When I reach for myself again, he swats me away.

Then his hand wraps around my length, stroking me in time with his thrusts.

"Yes, God, please," I shout.

"Don't scream for God, Isaac. Scream for me," he mutters in my ear.

"Yes. Jensen, please. Make me come. I'm so close."

His hand picks up speed as his cock continues to peg the spot that makes my eyes flutter. Then I'm swept away with an orgasm so fast I stop breathing. My own cum lands on the mattress and my chest while the pleasure sparks like fire in my bloodstream.

My muscles are still shuddering as Jensen comes. The moaning, groaning sound of his orgasm is so fantastic I could write songs about it. The melodic feel of his cock. The symphonic way he draws a hand up my side and clutches my throat possessively.

Everything about what we just did is like a song—sung in perfect harmony.

EIGHTEEN

After discarding the condom in the garbage, Isaac and I take another quick shower together. Every time he presses his head to my shoulder, I wrap my arms around him and hold him close. He does this a lot. It's almost as if he's starved for affection. When was the last time someone held him and made him feel comforted?

He gives me a spare toothbrush to use, and we both get ready for bed together. When I eventually emerge from the bathroom, he's already under the covers in his bed, and I look at the opposite side where it sits empty as if it's waiting for me.

Isaac grins softly from the pillow, and I crawl in behind him, giving him my arm to lie on. His damp hair keeps falling in his face, so I tenderly brush it back.

"This is nice," he whispers.

I nod with my lips against his head. It is nice. And he seems so at ease, which is what I want.

If only my head could feel that relaxed, but there is some mental block for me that never allows me to fully release the tension in moments like this.

"What are you doing next weekend?" he asks.

"Spending it with you," I reply.

"Good," he replies sleepily. Then, adds, "How would you feel about meeting my brother and his girlfriend? I told them I'd have dinner with them Friday, and I asked if I could bring you."

My body tenses, but I try not to let it show. "As your boyfriend?"

He picks up his head and stares at me with innocence. "They won't tell anyone. They're safe. They obviously know about me."

Immediately, I'm filled with discomfort. Inside, warning signs are going off, and cruel, old mantras fill my mind, but I push them away.

I want to tell Isaac that I can't be anyone's boyfriend, at least not in public. But everything is a contradiction, and I know it. I can't have Isaac, but I want him. I shouldn't think about a future with him, but I do. I'm not supposed to be gay, but I am.

"You don't have to," he says with a sense of worry in his tone. "I can tell you don't want to."

"I do want to," I reply, squeezing his shoulder. "It's just...hard for me."

"I understand. It's hard for me too."

Tell him. Tell him everything. Tell him about Eternal Harmony.

But what good would that do? Make him think I'm broken? Make him pity me or worry that I'll suddenly bolt from his life because of some stupid brainwashing I went through as a kid? That's my trauma, not his.

"Let me think about it, okay?" I say, trying to ease his nerves.

"Okay," he replies.

When he rests his head back on my arm and stares into my eyes, I consider telling him again. He'd be sympathetic. I know he would, but it's all so complicated. Even to me, it's complicated. My feelings for that program, the pastor, and the people in it are still a blur. It's not black and white.

I'm angry and resentful, but there are good memories there too. Enough to make me less angry.

Like I said, complicated.

✝

When I wake up, the windows are still dark, but the bed next to me is empty. I get up and go in search of Isaac.

Padding silently through his house, I follow the sound of a soft melody and find him on the couch, strumming quietly on his guitar.

"What are you doing?" I ask as I run my fingers through his hair. He looks up from the acoustic guitar on his lap to smile sleepily at me.

"Did I wake you? I couldn't sleep and I had a song in my head."

There's a pad of paper on the table in front of him with scribbled notes and lyrics.

"Not at all," I whisper. "Can I hear it?"

Looking almost bashful, he replies, "Sure."

I recline on the couch next to him, my feet touching his thigh and my head on the pillow as he starts to strum.

"It's messy, so don't judge," he says.

"I would never judge you."

In the dark living room, my eyes slowly adjust to the sight of him playing. It's a gentle melody that somehow just sounds like him.

When he starts singing, it's just above a whisper. Delicate lyrics over a sweet melody. And the longer I listen, the more I realize something that takes my breath away...

> *Out of the crowd and into my life*
> *Turning the noise into silence*
> *Elevator indiscretion and late-night calls*
> *Your hard-pressed, soft kiss*
> *My lips were waiting for you all along*

This song is about *us*.

Freezing on the couch, I stare at him as tears begin to brim in my eyes. And just like that, it's the most beautiful song I've ever heard.

You told me this was terrifying
But I was never one for heights
Now, I think I'm fallin'
Fallin' like flyin'
Flyin' home to you

The chorus plays again and I realize in that serene moment that I'm falling in love with him. It's still so early, but I've never felt this way before.

What started as an indulgence turned into an addiction, but now feels like it was love all along. I never intended for it to happen like this, but it has.

And it scares me. It scares me not only for the sake of my own heart but for Isaac's, too.

What if I can't be the man he needs? Coming out was never in the cards for me, and he deserves more than a lover in secret. He deserves vows. He deserves everything.

When the song ends, he waits for my reaction, but I can hardly move. What could I possibly say to properly convey how amazing that was?

"Isaac," I whisper.

He turns his head to face me, so I sit up on the couch to be closer to him.

"It needs work," he mumbles quietly.

"No, it doesn't. It's perfect."

"You think so?" he asks. "To be totally honest with you, I've been struggling with a bit of writer's block lately. I haven't written a single lyric in months until...I met you."

I can't bear another second without his touch, so I grab him by the back of the neck and drag him toward me for a kiss. The guitar falls loudly to the floor as I climb onto his lap. Straddling his hips, I fuse my mouth to his. Our tongues glide against one another's as he groans against my lips.

With my ass in his hands, I grind against him. We are only in our boxer briefs, and I feel him getting hard against me.

Before it can get too heated, I pull away and hold him by the back of the head.

"I wrote that about you," he mumbles, making me smile.

"I love it."

"I want to record it and put it on the EP."

"Isaac," I whisper. The idea that some part of me will be forever ingrained in his music feels too daunting and intense to wrap my head around. What if I fail him? What if I can't be what he wants me to be? I don't want to be some ex-lover hidden within the tracks of his music.

I will never let him down.

That voice suddenly echoes louder than all the rest. Louder than my subconscious, louder than the mantras and the brainwashing. It screams with confidence.

No matter what happens, I will never, ever let him down.

And for now, that's enough. We can face whatever life brings if I can hold true to that. I want him, and I never want him to be hurt, so nothing else matters.

"Thank you," I whisper, pulling back to look into his eyes.

"Thank you," he replies.

"What did I do?"

The corner of his mouth lifts in a smirk. "You were my muse."

Running my fingers through his hair at the nape of his neck, the weight of these emotions hits me like bricks on my chest. I am falling for this man, and I think he is falling for me, and we have the whole world stacked against us.

I want to scream from the rooftops how I feel about him. I want to love him without guilt or shame in my heart. I want to love him out loud.

Instead of speaking promises we can't keep, I lean in and kiss him again. Against his lips, I mumble, "That was the best song I have ever heard."

"I'm glad you like it."

After kissing for a few more minutes, he grabs tightly to my ass and murmurs, "Can we go back to bed and get rid of these boxers?"

With that, I climb off his lap and stand. The moment Isaac is on his feet, I throw him over my shoulder and carry him to the bedroom. He howls with laughter while screaming my name.

I can honestly say I've never been so happy in all my life.

And never filled with so much dread.

Nineteen

Why did no one tell me relationships could be so good? I've been avoiding them my entire life, but I had no idea it would be like this.

Jensen has come over nearly every day this week. We've had more sex than I've ever had in my life. And he makes me so fucking happy. His touch is my addiction.

And if that wasn't good enough, the songs have been pouring out of me. I hear music differently now. Every kiss is a melody. Every orgasm, the lyrics.

I only have five days until I'm back on the road, and as excited as I am to be onstage again, I don't know what I'm going to do without him.

Call me a fool, but I think I'm falling in love with Jensen Miles.

I'm having dinner with my brother tonight, and I'm still waiting to hear back from Jensen on if he'll come or not. Secretly, I'm praying he does. I want to show him off. I'd like my family to see just how good I'm doing, even if it is just Lucas, who has been there for me since I was seventeen. It's a soft launch of our relationship, but I can tell Jensen is nervous about it.

Behind closed doors, he's the world's best boyfriend. Doting, affectionate, possessive. But he's nowhere near ready to be public, which, obviously, neither am I. At this stage of my career, it's not the time to make any major announcements, or I'll risk losing the fan base I'm building.

But Jensen seems even less enthusiastic about being seen together. Even if it's just my family who would never out us or judge us. He clearly struggles with that idea. And I wish I understood why.

I get that he has a reputation in this community. Trust me, no one understands that more than me.

But I'm afraid there's more under the surface I don't know about. Some deeper reasoning as to why Jensen won't ever come out. And if that's the case, and a public relationship is never in the cards for us, then what kind of future do we have?

I know I said we could just be friends who fuck, but every day I sense myself changing. Maybe that's not what I want in the long run. Maybe I do want a committed public relationship.

I'll be patient. I have to be—for him and for me.

Coming down the stairs from my room, I turn the corner and find Jensen leaning against my kitchen counter in nothing but a pair of jeans and a mug in his hand.

Goddamn.

"I could get used to this," I say as I pour myself a cup of coffee. "You in my house looking like that."

He smirks up at me. He hasn't shaved a lot this week, and I like the look of his beard growing in. Stepping up to him, I run my fingers through it.

"This is nice."

"I need to shave," he says, scratching his fingers down the column of his throat.

"No, leave it. It's sexy."

He smiles again before taking a sip. "So, I've decided."

"Decided…"

"I want to go with you tonight."

The calmness in his tone makes me smile. "Really?"

"Yes. As long as you're sure our secret is safe with your brother."

I tilt my head. "It is, I promise."

"And we're just going to his place?"

"Yep," I reply. "Just us."

He sets down his coffee and approaches me, pinning me against the counter. "You're ready for this? To meet family? To be…official."

"Are we…official?" I ask with a crooked smile.

He kisses my lips before leaning back to stare into my eyes. "I hope so."

"So that makes you my boyfriend, and you're okay with that?" I ask.

Taking my chin between his fingers, he holds me in the way I've come to realize is him being serious. He wants me to pay attention and take his words to heart. I love it when he talks to me like this.

"You are mine, and I am yours. We were official the moment I laid eyes on you that night in Phoenix."

I'm doing my best not to grin like a fool, but he says stuff like that, and my restraint goes out the window. It makes my heart beat so hard I nearly pass out. I have no response. I just let him kiss me.

✝

I drive Jensen's car to dinner since I know the way. He sits by my side, looking handsome beyond belief, with his dark waves combed to the side. I have on a casual button-down and a pair of dark jeans.

When we pull up to the house, he picks up the bottle of wine from the back seat and opens the car door. We walk up to the front of the house, and my hands itch to hold his, but Lucas lives in a suburban neighborhood with meddling, nosy people around. It's bad enough being a celebrity. Privacy is almost nonexistent.

"Ready?" he asks with a smirk as I raise my hand to knock on the door.

I glance around to be sure we're hidden from view before I lean in and kiss him on the cheek.

Fuck, I am disgustingly lovesick.

Then, I rap on the door, and only two milliseconds later, it opens. My brother's girlfriend, Sadie, begins shrieking with excitement at the sight of me and nearly bowls me over with a fierce hug. Naturally, I shriek in return, hugging her back and spinning her around like I haven't seen her in twelve years instead of two months.

"Oh my god, I missed you so much," she cries before taking my face in her hands and planting a kiss right on my cheek.

"I missed you too."

At that moment, Sadie notices Jensen standing there. She pulls away from me and grins sweetly up at him. "Hi, I'm Sadie," she says before pulling him in for a hug.

He laughs. "Nice to meet you, Sadie. I'm Jensen."

"Oh my god, you're so handsome," she says, and I nudge her side.

"Sadie."

She blushes with a shrug. Then whispers to me, "Okay, we'll talk later."

I place a hand over my face as she welcomes us into their house. Spotting Henry in his little bouncy plaything, I grin wildly. His hair has grown in so much since I saw him last. He's holding himself upright and jumping on his tiptoes, both things he certainly wasn't doing the last time I saw him.

"Henry!" I say as I rush over to him. He's beaming and giggling, and I can't get over how cute he is.

"Isn't he getting big?" Sadie asks. "He's almost walking."

"Holy shit."

"Yeah, he gets into everything. It's exhausting."

"I bet," I reply.

Jensen is hovering behind me, being more quiet than normal. I nearly forgot how nervous he was for tonight. So I step back to be next to him, hoping my presence offers him some comfort.

He forces a smile, and I start to worry a little. Did I push him into this too fast?

"Where's Luke?" I ask, but just then, my brother appears from the kitchen. He's wiping his hands on a towel as his eyes find mine. We both smile before meeting each other halfway across the living room for a hug.

"How's the tour been?" he asks.

"Amazing. You'll come to the Austin show, right? It'll be the last one on the tour."

He rolls his eyes. "Of course we will."

For some reason, I almost tell Lucas right in this moment that I'm thinking about coming home to the whole family. I don't, of course, but it's right at the front of my mind. He'll be hesitant and protective about it, but he'll support me either way.

Remembering Jensen is behind me, I turn back to see him standing in my brother's living room with an expression of terror on his face.

Damn, he really is nervous, isn't he?

I return to his side. "Lucas, this is Jensen. Jensen, this is Lucas."

"You," my brother mutters, making my brow furrow.

"Lucas...Goode," Jensen mumbles.

"What's going on?" I stammer.

"You two know each other?" Sadie asks.

Then, Jensen turns toward me, scrutinizing my face as if it's the first time he's seen it. "Isaac...Goode."

Admittedly, I never mentioned my last name to Jensen for obvious reasons. I didn't need my father's transgressions to alter his opinion of me. Although, I never expected it would bother him this much.

"What's happening?" Lucas asks. "I'm so confused."

"I should go," Jensen snaps, turning away.

"What the fuck?" I grab his arm, but he only mumbles an apology as he tears it from my grip and heads to the door. "Jensen, wait. Tell me what's going on. How do you two know each other?"

"This is the guy you're dating?" Luke asks in astonishment.

I turn to him with aggression on my face. How dare he say that? How dare he...do whatever the hell he's doing right now?

"Someone please fucking explain to me what's going on," I bark loudly. Baby Henry's lip trembles as he stares up at me, and Sadie quickly scoops him up to comfort him. I hate this, and I don't even know what *this* is.

"He's Dad's replacement, Isaac," Luke shouts. Jensen is standing frozen near the door. "He's the new preacher at Redemption Point. He's been hounding me and Adam to come back to the church, but now, apparently, he's trying to recruit you too."

"That's not what this is," Jensen growls in anger.

"Lucas, stop," Sadie mutters.

"I didn't know. Obviously, I didn't know he was..." Jensen argues, meeting Luke's gaze. There is so much animosity between them I want to scream. My mind can't seem to comprehend what the hell is happening.

Jensen looks at me with an expression of sorrow and regret. "I knew this was a bad idea. I think I should just go." With that, he opens the front door and walks out toward his car.

My chest starts heaving. "No." In a panic, I rush after him and stop him. "Jensen, please."

With a wince, he puts a hand up. "Isaac, you should be mad. Dammit, be *mad*."

"Why? Because you..."

"Because I'm a liar and a fraud, and I can never be with you the way you deserve."

"I don't understand. You think I care that you preach at the same church my dad did? Why the fuck would I care?"

He throws his head back. "Because you should hate him! And I am just fucking like him, Isaac. Don't you see that? Every Sunday, I stand where that man stood, and I preach the same gospel he did. And do you know what's woven into that gospel, Isaac? Lies. Lies about people like us. The only difference is that I'm so fucked in the head, I believe them."

"Stop it," I say, my throat starting to ache with emotion.

"It's true, Isaac. Do you honestly think someday I'll be able to come out? Do you really think I can give you the life you deserve?"

"I can't come out either," I argue.

"Yes, Isaac. You can. People will love you regardless, but I've done bad things, Isaac. I am a preacher. I can't be gay."

"You're not making any sense," I whisper with tears in my eyes. "I don't understand."

He touches the handle of the car door with his head down. Then, he sadly mumbles, "I hope you never do. They ruined me, Isaac. I'm so sorry."

With that, he climbs in and doesn't look back at me even once. He just leaves me standing there alone. The comfort and safety I felt with Jensen are just gone. I don't know how long I stand there, watching the road after he's driven away.

Eventually, I hear a low voice behind me whisper, "I'm sorry, Isaac."

I don't respond. I just let everything build and build and build. Then, when I think I can't take it anymore, I shove it all deep, deep down.

Turning around to face my brother, I blink the tears from my eyes. I don't know how much of that he heard, but I just pretend he didn't hear any of it.

"I sure know how to pick 'em," I joke.

"Isaac," Luke says with a scolding tone.

"No, seriously." I laugh. "You could make a joke out of all the guys I've dated. A bartender, a dancer, and a preacher walk into a bar..."

"Isaac, stop."

"Then they all fuck me over and leave. That's the punch line."

No matter how much I try to laugh it off, Lucas doesn't even crack a smile. He closes the distance between us and wraps his arms around my neck, pulling me in for a tight hug.

"I'm sorry," he whispers.

"It's fine."

"No, it's not."

"It's..." My voice trails because if I speak another word, I'll crack and lose it. Instead, I let my big brother console me. It's nice, but he's not Jensen. Nothing compares to him.

TWENTY

JENSEN

The pins crash at the end of the lane, but I only stare numbly in the distance without truly seeing them. My mother cheers, and my dad gives her a high five, but I hardly move.

"You see that, Jens?" my dad asks, trying to cheer me up.

Shaking myself out of it, I force a smile. "Great job, Mom."

They both give me a pitying look. But they don't know what to say because they don't know what's wrong. I lied and told them I was just in a funk, and they accepted that.

I haven't spoken to Isaac since last night. He texted me later, asking me to call him, but I ignored it. Nothing has ever hurt so much.

I figured that hanging out with my parents would help tonight, but so far, I think it's making things worse. They want me to be happy. They've said that a thousand times throughout my life. My mother says it more than anyone.

And yet she was the first person to put the nail in the coffin. She was the one who signed me up for Eternal Harmony. The person who pushed me toward the ministry. The person who has set me up on the most dates.

She's the reason I can never be with Isaac. The reason I will never be truly happy.

Needing to get away, I stand from the chairs and walk over to the bar. My parents are distracted with their friends, so I grab a stool and order a tequila soda, imagining Isaac could be here to drink it with me.

After the first sip, a heavy hand lands on my shoulder. "Hey, son," my dad says as he takes the seat next to me.

"Hey, Dad," I mutter without emotion.

He holds up a hand for the bartender to bring him a beer. And for a few minutes, he doesn't speak. We just drink in silence.

Which is good. I don't have anything to say to him anyway.

My dad is a retired cop and about as tough and as masculine as it gets. He's tall like me but beefier and stronger. With age, his physique has changed, leaving him with a large beer belly and a balding head.

"So...things didn't work out with Gabby," he mumbles, with his pint glass to his lips.

I groan inwardly. "We're just friends."

"That's good. She seems like a good friend to have."

Nodding, I take another drink and think nothing of it. Then he continues.

"Friends are all good and fine, but at some point, I want you to find a partner."

I laugh at his use of the word *partner*. "Is this a cop metaphor?"

He doesn't even break a smile. "No, it's not."

I have to swallow, discomfort growing inside me. I stare straight ahead, not meeting his gaze as I casually reply, "I'm trying, Dad. I date but haven't found the right girl yet."

He clears his throat as if he's reacting to my statement. When I glance sideways at him, he's wearing a scowl and staring across the bar. What did I say?

We drink in silence for a few more minutes. Then, to my utter dismay, I hear a familiar song play on the radio. It's an old Theo

Virgil track, one of his breakout hits. The same one I had on my phone ringtone for a while. The one that made me obsessed with his music.

Tears prick my eyes, and I'm about two seconds from standing from the bar and hightailing it out of this bowling alley entirely.

"I like this song," my dad mumbles.

"Me too."

With that, it feels a bit more casual between us. My dad finishes his beer, throws down a twenty, and stands from his stool. I think it's done, and I've escaped any dangerous topics of conversation when he claps his hand on my shoulder again.

"I just want you to be happy, son. And I don't care what that looks like. I hope you know that. You only get one life. Don't waste it by trying to please everyone else."

With that, he walks away, and Isaac's song comes to an end. I sit at the barstools for a while, considering my next move, although I already know what I want to do.

But do I even deserve what I want?

Eventually, I stand from the bar and say goodbye to my parents.

"Oh, you're off already?" my mom whines.

"Yeah. I need to uh...do something."

My dad smiles as he picks up his bowling ball from the machine. Waving them goodbye, I leave the bowling alley in a rush. I'm in my car, driving without even really thinking about where I'm going. I have no destination in mind, just that familiar gravitational pull.

Before I know it, I'm texting him.

I don't deserve it but open the gate, please.

He reads the message, and a moment later, it starts to roll open slowly. I pull my car through and up to his house. Then, I'm out and practically running to the door.

He's standing in the doorway, a cold, emotionless expression on his face. He looks nothing like the star who takes the stage and commands a crowd. In a ripped muscle tee and a pair of tattered jeans, he looks like just a man. A brokenhearted man.

I stand two feet away, waiting to see if he wants to chew me out and curse my name. He doesn't say a word. He just stares at me.

Lifting my arms, I let them drop in surrender. What the fuck do I say?

I could tell Isaac that I'm sorry or that nothing has changed since last night. Everything still stands. Everything about our lives and futures.

But I don't want any of that darkness between us. So I close the distance between us without a word. Grabbing his face, I pull him in for a fierce kiss.

To my relief, he grabs me back, kissing me as passionately as I'm kissing him. His arms wind around my neck, and he lets my hands roam his body. I grip him by the ass and lift him a few inches off the ground. As I carry him inside, he clings to my neck like he needs me.

It should be a crime to be needed by Isaac Goode. He's been hurt by those who he needed before, and I am a monster for being the man he needs now. But I can't help it.

Because I need him too.

We stumble our way into the house. As we reach his living room, I'm tugging at his shirt desperately, and he's practically ripping the buttons off mine.

Our shirts come off in a rush, hitting the floor as we reach the thick plush rug in front of the dormant fireplace. I drop to my knees in front of Isaac and tear open the button of his jeans. His fingers wind through my hair, tugging so hard it makes my eyes water.

I like the pain he inflicts. I deserve it.

After jerking his pants down, I pull the elastic of his briefs with them. As his cock bounces free, pointing straight at me, I grab the length and pull it to my mouth. I am not gentle or teasing this time. I wrap my lips around him and suck him into the back of my throat like my life depends on it.

Instead of moaning with delight, he growls in frustration. His grip is still tight, and he's forcing himself deeper with each thrust. When I gag, spit flying from my mouth, he releases his grasp on my hair.

Grabbing him by the thighs, I wrestle him to the floor. He lets out a desperate sound, pulling my mouth down to his for a kiss. Then suddenly, he fights for control, rolling me to my back so he's straddling my chest.

Staring down at me with passion in his eyes, I can tell that he wants to scream at me. He's angry and I love it. I crave his fire. More than anything, I want Isaac to fight for himself, even if that means fighting me.

"You told me I could trust you," he says in a low, raspy tone as if he's speaking through gritted teeth. I've never seen him like this before.

"I know," I reply.

"Then you left. You fucking left." His palms are on my chest, his fingers pressing into me as if he wants to hurt me.

"You deserve better."

His anger only grows as he leans closer and practically shouts. "*I* will be the one to say what I deserve."

"Good," I reply flatly from the floor.

Suddenly, his anger starts to dissipate into sadness, and I find myself reaching for him. The moment I touch his face, the anger is back.

"I've been alone for a long time," he mutters. "I don't *need* you, not really. I just...want you. And I am so fucking tired of people telling me they love me and they care about me, and then they fucking leave. I'm so *tired* of being alone."

Tears well in his furious eyes.

"Take it out on me," I whisper. "I'm yours, Isaac."

"Don't make promises you can't keep," he snaps.

"No promises. I can't make a single promise to you."

He winces, throwing his head back as he fights the urge to scream or cry, but it's the best I can do. I hate it as much as he does.

"Is this what you want?" he asks in anger. "You want me to treat you like another hookup? A guy I fuck who means nothing to me?"

"No."

"Neither do I," he replies sadly.

To my surprise, he leans down and kisses me. I taste his rage and his hurt. And the harder he kisses me, biting and dominating my mouth, I realize he's doing what I told him to. He's taking it out on me.

His hands grip my hair again, pulling hard as he groans into my mouth. I savor every ounce of the pain. After breaking away from the kiss, Isaac stares down at me. His cock is still throbbing, resting on my chest. He glances down at it for a moment.

Then he starts to work his way up my body. Still holding my hair in his hands, he lifts my head and guides his cock to my mouth. I take every inch eagerly.

Isaac has come undone, and I adore him for it. He fucks my mouth, making me choke as he hits the back of my throat, and I know that if he didn't trust me, he would never let himself do this. He's comfortable with me, and it makes pride swell in my chest.

I want him to use me as much as he wants. I'm dying for him to make it hurt.

The harder he goes, the more it means to me.

Isaac's thrusts pick up speed, and my jaw and throat begin to ache. I'm ready for his release. I need it.

His breathing starts to get shallow and tight. His face is

contorted in pain, and I ready myself for everything he has to give me.

A moment later, he goes silent. Then warmth fills my mouth and I start to choke and spit while trying to swallow him down. He pulls out and strokes himself quickly through the rest of his climax. It's degrading as his cum lands in spurts on my tongue, but there's something intimate and sexy about that.

Isaac's spine curls around me as he continues to unload into my mouth. He's racked with pleasure and pain, shivering through his arousal.

My own cock is still stuck in my pants, throbbing with need, but I don't care. I won't touch it. This isn't about me getting off. It's about atoning for what I've done to him.

When he doesn't have another drop left, he rolls over and collapses onto the floor next to me. Out of the corner of my eye, I spot my shirt, so I grab it and wipe my mouth. Then I turn and stare at him. He's gazing, unfocused, at the ceiling as his chest heaves with the exertion he's just spent.

Finally, he turns to look at me. When our eyes meet, the moment feels far more tender than it did a moment ago. With a deep sigh, Isaac rolls toward me. He presses his face to my chest as I wrap my arms around him. My hand strokes up and down his bare back.

"I didn't mean to be so rough," he whispers.

"You weren't too rough. I wanted it that way."

Neither of us speaks. We're lying on a rug in his living room with nothing but the silence around us. He's completely naked, but there's a blanket on the couch nearby, so I just have to reach up to grab it.

Draping it over his body, I hold him close and kiss his head.

Then, with a shudder deep in my bones, I tell him everything.

Twenty-One

Isaac

Resting on Jensen's chest, I stare at his face as he takes a deep breath, clearly trying to garner the courage to do this. Whatever it is, I know my feelings for him won't change. They're too strong, ingrained in who I am, even after only a few weeks. He's become a part of me.

What I fear is learning something horrible about him and knowing what he's gone through. The idea of him hurting already sounds unbearable to me.

He stares up at the ceiling, an arm resting on the top of his forehead. "I've never come out to my parents or any of my friends. I'm forty years old, for fuck's sake."

"Why not?" I ask.

"Because I grew up thinking I could be changed, Isaac. I was taught that I was born with a defect. Brainwashed."

My brow furrows as I move to my elbow and stare at him. "Your parents taught you that?" And I thought Truett was bad. The worst he did was call me a sinner, which, okay, now that I think about it, is bad too. But a defect? What the fuck?

"No," he says, shaking his head. "My parents never spoke

about it. Deep down, they knew, but it wasn't them who told me that."

"Then who did?"

"It was a program called Eternal Harmony. They masked their practices by calling it a youth church group. My mother encouraged me to try it without telling me what it was. And at first, it was fine. They selected specific kids and made us feel special—like we were destined for greatness.

"First, they made us feel like we were a part of something virtuous. We were a community. I made my best friendships there. We met nearly every day after school and sometimes did trips out of town. They preached about family values and God's will."

He pauses, staring blankly in the distance as if he's lost in a memory. My heart aches, seeing the pain in his eyes. I already hate where this is going.

"As the years went by, I almost missed how subtle they were with their brainwashing. It took me nearly three years to realize they were targeting queer kids specifically. They built a hierarchy within the dynamics of the group, so before long, it was like they had tasked us with brainwashing each other."

Tears prick behind my eyes when I imagine the damage this place has done, not only to him but to so many others. It's not fucking fair. I want to beat the shit out of every single one of them.

"There was a specific pastor. His name was Derek, and he was young. He created these...mantras for us to use whenever something tempted us. Like little codes for our brains that never fucking go away. 'With God, change is possible. I don't have to be broken anymore. Together, we can be healed.'"

"Fuck," I mutter as my nostrils flare. I hate this. I hate it so fucking much.

"When I got older, Derek had these...tests."

I press my face into Jensen's chest. It's too much. I can't hear anymore.

"I failed them every time," he whispers with a quivering voice, and I don't have to look up to see that he's crying.

"He'd push me to drink with him. Ask me to kiss him. Ask me to touch him. So I did. Then, a day later…he'd punish me for it."

"Jesus, Jensen," I cry into his chest. The courage in his voice nearly kills me. My hands grip him so tightly, I'm sure it hurts, but he doesn't stop me.

Deep down, part of me knows…

If I hadn't run away, is this what my dad would have done to me? Would he have sent me away to a place like this? Hoping to "cure" me?

"Around the time I turned twenty-one, I had reached almost the highest rank within the program. I had so many kids under me. I even helped recruit them. I knew…" He takes a break to swallow and wipe his eyes. "I knew what we were doing."

His voice breaks as he sobs. Covering his face with his hands, he cries. There is anger in those tears and I feel it, too. How does he not just live his life with rage every day? How is he not fuming with hatred every moment of his life?

"It's not your fault," I whisper, pressing my lips to his cheek. "You were the victim, Jensen. You were just a kid."

He sobs a little longer, nodding along with my words but unable to show his face. When his tears subside, he wipes them away.

"I always knew it was bullshit," he says. "Deep down, I knew it was lies. But the longer I was there, the deeper I fell into their hole. I couldn't get out. They controlled everything in my life. My dating. My job. My family."

He lets out a fresh exhale.

"Then, one day, my dad made the local news. He was working a pride event that was attacked. He was a hero. But after Derek saw it, he tried to keep me from seeing him, my own dad. That was the final straw. I was twenty-five."

Holy shit.

"I was in a conversion program for nearly ten years, and everyone knew it. To this day, I hear their voices in my head. They still tell me that I'm a sinner. Not only that I *can* change, but that I *should*. That it's my fault. In a way, I never left."

Pressing my lips to his chest, I hold him as close as I can. "But you left, Jensen. You were smarter than them. They thought they had you, but they didn't. You made it out."

He doesn't look convinced, and it worries me. Did they really do so much mental damage to him he'll never truly recover? Will he ever be able to accept himself and truly *love* himself with the harm they've caused?

"You know the worst part?" he whispers, still not able to look at me. His face is wet and his eyes bloodshot.

"What?"

"They tried to ruin my relationship with God. They made me believe he would never love me. Don't we deserve God's love, too?"

I force his face toward me so he has to look me in the eye. "Yes, we do."

Suddenly, I see more vulnerability than I've seen before. It's like seeing the full-color picture of Jensen for the first time. He's taken down the walls between us. Bared his soul and cut himself open just for me.

Holding his face, I pull him close for a kiss. It's not passionate or heated. It's a kiss of love.

I rest my forehead against his as I murmur, "Thank you for sharing that with me. I'm so sorry that happened to you. It's not fair, but Jensen…" I say with emphasis. "They did not ruin you. Don't give them that much power. You can still heal and have a happy life, even with those memories."

He doesn't immediately argue, which is hopeful. Instead, he stares into my eyes just a few inches away. Sadly, he whispers, "I hope so."

✝

When I peel my eyes open the next morning, the space on the bed beside me is empty. Reaching over, I touch the pillow and find it still warm. Then I check my phone. It's nine thirty on a Sunday. He left for service.

The thought sours my stomach. I'm suddenly remembering what he told me last night. The shit he's been through. The brainwashing. The sexual assault. The shame they embedded into his sense of self. It's fucked.

How can he continue to work in a church after that? Maybe it's just me, but the shit my dad said when I came out tainted every bit of faith I had left in me. Why would I show up for God when it was clear He had no tolerance for me? If He can't love me the way I am, then fuck him.

But deep down, I do miss my faith. I miss the good parts, and there were good parts. I miss my relationship with God. I miss *believing* in him.

I only wish Jensen had stayed over longer today, but I understand. He has a job—

The coffee grinder whirs loudly downstairs. My eyes pop open and I climb from the bed. Padding quickly down the steps, I turn to find Jensen standing in my kitchen in nothing but a pair of *my* jeans.

"What are you doing here?" I ask.

He looks up in surprise. "Oh, I…called in."

"You called in?"

He smirks. "Yeah. There are other people at the church who can deliver a sermon, Isaac."

"Did you call in just to spend time with me?" I ask sheepishly as I walk into the kitchen.

"Of course I did," he replies, tipping his chin up.

I can't help but smile. Then, my gaze rakes over his body, and I shake my head, appreciating just how good he looks in my clothes.

"What did I tell you about this outfit?" I ask, gesturing to the jeans without socks or a shirt. It should be illegal.

"What, this?" He glances down and I notice that his jeans normally hang loosely from his hips, but mine fit him very snugly.

Stepping up to him, I press our bare chests together as I kiss the side of his neck. "Make your coffee, and then come back to bed," I mumble against his skin.

"Yes, sir," he replies with a sexy rasp to his voice.

Leaving him in my kitchen, I head upstairs and climb back into bed. I have to adjust the chubby state of my dick in my briefs as I grab my phone and open it to see if I have any notifications.

There's another text from Luke, checking on me. After dinner Friday night, which I stuck around for, I went home in a pretty foul mood. I then proceeded to spend the entire day yesterday moping around in a heartbroken state. Luke and Sadie took turns texting me throughout the day to check on me.

I quickly text my brother back now and let him know that Jensen and I have talked and I am feeling better. Then I leave it at that. Luke will be protective, no matter what. He's sort of a *one strike and you're out* kind of guy. Especially when it comes to me.

Then I notice another text. This one is from Caleb.

Since he and I saw each other almost two years ago, after one of my indie shows in Texas, he's only texted me sporadically and mostly just to share pics of his daughter, Abby. I can tell he doesn't want to overstep and pull me back into a relationship I'm not ready to be in.

This one is different.

I'm sorry to have to be the one to tell you this. I had no idea it was going to happen like this, but rich men have a lot of power in Texas and there was nothing anyone could do.

I won't get too legal on you, but the defense in Truett's case found a flaw with the prosecution, essentially voiding their entire case against him. He's been exonerated.

Adam doesn't want to put Sage through hell again, so they're not going to bother with any appeals.

Everyone is pretty upset.

We're all thinking about you. And we love you.

This was the news we were expecting, wasn't it? He's free. Truett Goode always comes out on top.

Lucas was always worried that Truett would find a way to ruin my career. That he would out me or sabotage me in some way, but right now, I'm not afraid for myself.

I'm afraid for my family.

Ever since I left, it seems they're falling apart. Caving in on themselves. Dad went off the rails. Then Adam followed suit, naturally. Caleb and Adam were fighting. Then Luke was just pissed at everyone.

I can't help but feel like all of this is my fault. My running away left my family in shambles.

Rereading Caleb's message over and over, I notice the last line and read it a little differently. I don't think Caleb is saying the family is thinking about me in a sympathetic way. I think he means they're all thinking about me...because they miss me.

Mom, Adam, Caleb, and Lucas are all struggling right now, and they're thinking about me because I'm missing. And while I know that I owe them nothing and being a part of a family doesn't really mean shit when it comes to responsibilities and ownership, I still feel a stronger pull than before.

They need me.

"Everything okay?" a voice asks from the doorway. Jensen is standing there with a cup of coffee in his hand, watching me with concern.

Suddenly, it's like I get instant amnesia and I can't remember a damn thing about my family. I toss my phone on the nightstand and recline on the pillow with my hands behind my head.

"Actually, everything is perfectly fine."

"Oh yeah?" he asks, stepping closer and taking a sip. "And why's that?"

"Because you..." I start, my voice trailing. Quickly, I pick up my phone and open the notepad. "Are perfectly mine."

Jensen hesitates a moment, waiting for my response. "What are you doing?" he asks.

"Sorry," I mumble, distracted. "Lyric idea."

With that, he chuckles. "You did call me your muse." He sits on the bed next to me with his coffee in hand. His feet cross at the ankles and he tries to sneak a peek at my phone.

I pull it away to hide it. "You can't see it yet. My manager said I could have some studio time next month while we're in New York. I want to have some material ready. Including your song."

"My song," he says wistfully. Then he presses his lips to my cheek. "I really like the sound of that."

Twenty-Two

I've never told anyone the story of what happened to me in Eternal Harmony. I think a part of me just didn't want to accept that it was real or that there was anything wrong with it. I just wanted to move on with my life.

I made it out alive. But in so many ways, I never made it to the *living* part.

After two amazing weeks, when Isaac and I were hardly separated, he had to leave again for his tour. His first stop is in Little Rock, but I have too many things at work I need to catch up on to go to that one.

The urge to climb onto that tour bus with him was so strong. But if we're trying to keep a low profile, that's probably not the way to do it.

So I'm meeting him in Nashville in six days. My bed is so lonely and cold compared to his when we can sleep together. Rolling over every night without having his body pressed up against mine is just downright depressing.

I haven't told him yet, but I'm fairly certain I love him. It was a hard emotion to grasp at first, mostly because a part of me has always loved Isaac. When he was just a celebrity to me, Theo Virgil, my favorite singer and songwriter, I loved him in a different way.

But now I know his heart, and I feel the way it beats with mine. He is the melody I've been waiting for my entire life. And for the first time, I believe that change really is possible. Isaac changes me. He changes the fear and shame into faith and pride. He's giving me back what was taken so long ago.

He's making me the man fifteen-year-old Jensen needed.

Sitting at my desk in the church, I stare down at my notes for Sunday's sermon. I've noticed the way my messages have changed over the last four weeks. I notice the subtle shift in myself, providing messages of hope, community and acceptance. I refuse to preach hate or judgment. I never did. But...could I do more?

Eternal Harmony still exists. They email me all the time, inviting me back.

The thought of them getting to my congregation makes me bristle with anger. I've let so many down before, but I won't let them down again.

With that, I erase the last line of what I have written. And I write a new one.

"God's love is unconditional. And if anyone tries to tell you differently, then they don't speak for him. They speak for themselves. And I know God's love is unconditional because I feel it. And I am a sinner, just like you."

It's a bit intense. And it might ruffle a few feathers, but I like it.

My phone starts ringing on the desk beside my paper. Isaac's name is displayed on the screen. With a smile, I pick it up.

"Hello," I say softly.

"Fuck, I miss you," he says with a groan.

"Then why aren't you video calling me naked?" I ask, keeping my voice down although my door is closed, and I know the place is mostly empty today.

"Because I'm at the venue. We had our dress rehearsal today."

"You sound tired," I reply.

"I'm exhausted. I could hardly sleep without you."

I chuckle in response. "Don't be dramatic."

"I have to be. I'm hoping if you hear how pathetic I sound without you, you'll fly out early to see me. I'm so pathetic, Jensen. Please. Save me."

Dammit, he's so cute.

"You do sound pathetic," I reply, leaning back in my office chair.

"I need my big, sexy daddy to come on tour with me."

My chair bolts upright as my eyes widen. Blood courses through my veins and straight to my cock at the sound of that word. I have never been called...*that* before because I never thought I'd like it, but holy shit...

I think I do.

"Too much?" he asks after a moment of silence. "It was a joke, Jens. I'm not going to actually call you that."

I clear my throat.

"I mean...unless you want me to," he adds.

"I hope you're alone," I say, my voice tight and deep.

"Well, Lola is with me, but she's used to it. She just made a vomit face, though, so I don't think she enjoyed that."

I can't help but laugh again. I still can't properly form words after he said *that*, though. It's only been two days since I last had him naked, but maybe it's the withdrawals that have me reacting this way.

"I miss you," I mumble. "Only six more days."

"Book a one-way instead of a round trip and just come with me for the rest of the tour. I'll keep you hidden. I promise."

"I wish I could," I reply sadly.

"I know you do."

There are sounds in the background and voices telling me he's no longer alone.

"I gotta go," he says despondently. "We have some press interview to do."

"Okay. Call me later then," I reply.

"I will."

The line hangs in silence as unspoken words linger between us. Words normally used at the end of a phone conversation between two people who care very much for each other.

But we haven't said it yet and I'm not about to say it first over a phone line.

"Bye, Jensen," he mumbles after a moment.

"Isaac, wait," I call. He pauses, so I quickly add, "I did like it."

With that, I hang up.

Smiling, I wait, staring down at my phone. Then, just as expected, a moment later, I get a text from him.

That was so hot.

It makes me laugh as I turn my attention back to the sermon I was writing.

✝

"Have a good night, guys," I say as I walk down the hallway from my office to the door. There are still people working, but I've finished my sermon, signed all the forms I have to sign, and replied to all the emails I need to.

But there's a lot that goes on behind the scenes that keeps others here far later than me. Community outreach, Bible studies, charity organizations, and so on, and so on. There's a sense of pride when I leave the office each night, knowing that we're a part of something *good*. That's what got me into this. Maybe it was an atonement for what I'd done with Eternal Harmony. Maybe it was trying to fix my own relationship with the church, but being here and making this place something amazing fills my soul with a richness I can't get anywhere else.

"Jensen, wait," a voice calls from behind me as I reach the door to the employee parking lot. I pause and turn to find Pete, one of the band members, jogging down the hall toward me.

"Everything okay?" I ask.

"Yeah," he mutters uncomfortably. "We were about to start rehearsal, but...there's a guy sitting in the pews that I think you should see."

My brow furrows, and I bristle internally as my mind runs through different scenarios and options.

"Is he showing signs of aggression?" I ask.

Pete shakes his head. "No, not at all. It's just... Come see."

Walking behind him, I clutch my bag tightly in my hand, squeezing the leather handle and reminding myself to breathe. Pete opens the door, and I stare down the aisle at the back of a gray-haired man's head. Hesitantly, I walk down toward him.

It's not often that people pose threats to churches, but it happens. We don't have security at the door, so it's not impossible that someone could waltz in here and do serious and tragic damage.

"I've got it, Pete. Thank you," I mumble to the man behind me, gesturing for him to stay back.

As I approach the old man in the seat, I think about Isaac. If I do get hurt, it would devastate him. I have to keep myself safe for *him*.

"Excuse me, sir. Our next service is Sunday at—"

"At nine. I know," he replies gruffly. I pause at the familiarity of his southern drawl. "And again at eleven."

I take the remaining steps until I'm standing close enough to take in the man's profile, and I nearly gasp in shock. He looks different than I remember. Gaunt, aged, tired. Nothing like the man who once stood at that pulpit.

He turns to me with a sad sort of smile on his face. "You must be my replacement," he drawls.

My heart picks up speed, and every breath becomes weighted as I draw air into my lungs. There's a sense of internal panic that somehow he *knows*.

But he can't know about me and Isaac. No one knows.

Regardless, I can't seem to wrap my mind around the fact that

Isaac's father is sitting in front of me. In a daze, I take the seat across the aisle from him and stare at him in shock.

"I'm Truett—"

"I know who you are," I stammer, cutting him off. "Truett Goode."

His mouth lifts in the corner in an expression of faded pride.

"What are you doing here?" I ask.

His smile fades. "I built this place. I stood up there for over twenty years."

If I close my eyes, I can see him standing there. Speaking words that brought goose bumps to my skin.

"I just wanted to see it again," he whispers sadly. I don't respond, still too struck that he's sitting here. So, he continues, "I loved being up there. People listened to me. They respected me. I meant something to this community."

Truett gazes longingly up at the pulpit like it's a long-lost lover, and I gape at him, trying to understand where it went wrong. How did a man fall so far? How do I avoid the same fate?

"You know..." he mumbles with a smirk on his mouth. "I didn't talk until I was six years old. And I don't know if it was because I couldn't...or because I was afraid to. People who speak up tend to be the first ones knocked down. Being quiet is safer. If nobody notices you, then nobody can hurt you."

My phone buzzes in my pocket, and I don't need to pull it out to know it's Isaac. I draw in a shaky breath as I stare at his father across the aisle.

"My daddy was a mean man, Mr. Miles," Truett says, and my brows pinch inward in confusion. Is this a moment of senility? What is he talking about?

"He brought us to church every Sunday and beat the tar out of us every Monday. But if I was quiet, he'd skip me. Beat my brother instead."

I swallow before glancing around to find that I'm alone with this man. He's talking like a man on the edge, a man about to lose control. But I stay steady, keeping him calm. I've heard what he did to Adam's wife. I know he's capable of violent rage. And if he knows about me and his son...

"I'm sorry to hear that," I murmur.

He chuckles to himself. Then he turns to me. "What do you think makes a good man, Mr. Miles?"

The fact that he knows my name without me having to tell him makes my blood run cold. I imagine him in some room somewhere, researching my name. Finding out about me and my family with some vendetta. Would he hurt me because I took the church he lost?

I swallow, and once again, I think of Isaac.

"I think being a good man has nothing to do with God or church. I think being a good man means that every night you can lay your head on that pillow and know that the world is a little better because you're in it."

He looks into my eyes, and I notice the hollowness in his. There's not much left in him.

Then his mouth breaks into a smile again. "I bet you make a good fucking preacher," he says with a laugh, and I wince before looking up at the cross hanging behind the pulpit. "But not a very good man."

My body turns frigid as I stare at him. "I think it's time for you to go, Mr. Goode."

"Yeah, I think so too," he mumbles sadly.

Before he stands, I put a hand out. "Can we pray?" I ask, hoping for some way to reconcile this.

He huffs with a shake of his head. "Don't bother."

With that, he stands and shuffles up the aisle toward the door. When I hear it close behind him, I take the first deep breath I've taken since I walked in here. Dropping my elbows on my knees, I stare straight at the pulpit at the front of the room as the weight of that conversation rolls over me.

Tears prick my eyes for no reason at all. There are so many thoughts and feelings in my mind at once that it's impossible to grasp just one. Fear, shame, relief, hopelessness, and regret all swirl together like some self-deprecating mental cocktail.

Will I become like Truett Goode?

Am I a fraud for standing where he stood?

Does my position hurt people like me? People like Isaac?

Am I a good man?

Isaac seems to think so, but I'm willing to bet there was a time in his life when he thought Truett Goode was, too.

TWENTY-THREE

ISAAC

I crash into the plush white bed of the hotel with a sigh. Today was never-ending. I nearly forgot how exhausting touring is. After a long night on the road, the bus ran into an electrical issue and had to go into emergency repair.

But on the bright side, they put us up in a four-star hotel with plush dream beds and showers with the best water pressure I've ever felt in my life.

In nothing but a white towel wrapped around my waist, I fall asleep for a few minutes. But then I'm awakened by the sound of my phone vibrating on the nightstand. Jensen didn't answer my last two calls, and I was starting to worry, so seeing his name on the screen fills me with relief.

"Hey," I say as I swipe the call.

"Hey," he replies. "Sorry I missed you earlier. I was...in a meeting." He sounds tense.

"Everything okay?"

"Yeah," he replies. "Where are you? Can I see you?"

"Fuck yeah, you can see me. In fact..." I hit the video call button. It takes a moment for Jensen's face to appear on the screen. He's at his house, the wall of his living room behind him.

"Whose bed is that?" he asks with a possessive quirk of his brow.

I spin the camera around the room. "This is the hotel treatment you get when your tour bus breaks down, apparently."

"Very nice," he replies. "But put the camera back on your face."

I spin it around and smile softly at my phone. "You sure everything is okay?"

He breathes out a sigh. "It is now."

My chest aches from missing him. I left four days ago, but I can't stand it already. I miss his touch, his kiss, his scent, everything.

"Work has just been...stressful," he says.

My features harden as I watch him through the line. When Jensen looks stressed or upset, he only lets me see a sliver of what he's really feeling. He hides himself too well, and it frightens me a little.

What he told me the last time we were together—about the conversion program he was in—has haunted me ever since. The more I think about it, the more appreciation I have for him. The more love I feel. He's endured something awful, probably more awful than even I know, but yet, he's so strong. He didn't let it darken his soul. He came out of all of that and still somehow managed to be the best person I've ever known.

"What can I do?" I ask, feeling helpless. I'm not very good at this boyfriend business.

Jensen reclines on his couch and props his phone up on the coffee table. I do the same, so we're looking at each other again as if we're in the same bed.

"This," he whispers.

"This I can do," I reply.

"Do you want to talk about it?" I ask, fully expecting him to stay quiet and keep his feelings hidden. To my surprise, he answers with vulnerability.

"Do you think I'm a fraud?"

My eyebrows pinch. "Are you serious? No, I don't think you're a fraud. Why would you ask that?"

"Because," he replies with a sigh, running a hand over his face. "I could explain away everything I've done up until this point. The hookups, the sex, the...urges. But I've never been in a relationship before—not like this."

"Let me ask you this," I reply, resting my head on my hand. "Do you think your congregation would lose respect for you if they knew the truth?"

"Some of them, yeah."

"Then that makes them frauds," I reply, thinking myself very clever. I smirk at him smugly as he smiles in return.

"Touché."

"Listen," I say with a bit more serious tone. "You're not doing anything wrong, Jensen. You deserve to stand up there as much as anyone else. And you deserve to have a hot boyfriend as much as anyone else."

He laughs, and the sight of it sends a shot of warmth to my chest. His smile creates creases in his cheeks that make me wish I could reach through this phone just to kiss him once.

"Thanks, Isaac," he says on a sigh. I'm filled with a sense of pride for doing even just a little to make him feel better.

"You're welcome, Daddy," I say, just to get a rise out of him.

He barks out another laugh as he shakes his head. "Isaac, stop it."

"Yes, Daddy."

"Isaac!"

We both laugh for a while, and my cheeks heat with a blush when I see him unable to stop grinning. Then that heat travels downward, causing my cock to twitch. When I wet my lips and roll the bottom one between my teeth, he stops smiling too.

"Isaac," he whispers.

"Yeah?"

"Are you naked?" he asks with that familiar look of arousal on his face.

I aim the camera downward to reveal the white towel wrapped around my waist. Jensen growls into the phone at the sight, and my body grows tight.

"Get rid of that," he says in a low, soft command.

Propping the phone on the nightstand so my entire body is within view, I tug the towel open to reveal my half-hard cock resting against my thigh.

Jensen moans again. I look up at the screen to see him biting his knuckle.

"Can I watch you? Will you stroke it for me?" he asks in a low, sultry tone.

"Haven't you figured it out by now?" I ask as I reach for my cock. Giving it a lazy stroke, I add, "I'll do anything you want."

He breathes loudly. "That's my good boy."

At the sound of his praise, my head falls back with a groan. The effect this man has on me is incredible. I've never wanted to please someone so much in my life. And it's more than just a want. I can't believe how much it turns me on to know I please him. I want more commands, more requests, more opportunities to hear him call me that.

"Lick your palm." His voice is even and focused. A deep, sexy order.

Bringing my hand up to my mouth, I lick my hand and coat it with saliva. Then I return my slick palm to my rigid length.

"How does that feel?" he asks. "Describe it for me."

Resting my head on the pillow with my eyes closed, I moan. "It feels so good," I reply breathily. "I'm picturing your hand instead of mine."

"It is my hand," he says, his voice tighter than before. "Now fondle your balls for me."

With the other hand, I reach down and cup my sack, gently massaging it in my grip. A guttural whimper escapes my lips.

"That's it," he urges me on. "Good boy. Keep going."

My stroking hand picks up speed. My heels dig into the mattress as I roll onto my back. With my eyes still clenched shut, I imagine it's Jensen's hand on my cock. Then, his mouth.

I groan out loud again.

"Look at me, Isaac," he commands, louder this time.

I turn my head and watch the screen on the nightstand to find that Jensen is stroking himself now too. His clothes are still on and the phone is farther back to capture his body on the screen.

We stare into each other's eyes as we fuck our palms together.

"God, I miss you," I cry out raspily.

"Miss me? I'm right here with you. That's my hand on your cock. Can you feel it?"

"Yes, I feel it," I reply, throwing my head back and stroking faster.

"Don't you dare come so fast," he says, noticing my reaction.

"I'm not," I reply, out of breath.

"Do you have lube?" he asks.

I glance around the room in a rush. There's lube in my tour bus, but I didn't exactly think to pack it in my overnight bag. I can't say I expected to need it.

My eyes catch a small complimentary bottle of lotion on the nightstand. If it's scented, it might burn like a bitch, but at this point, I don't care. Releasing my cock, I reach over and snatch it off the table.

"I want to see you finger fuck that pretty hole," he says, and heat shoots to my cock like an explosion. I swear to God, he never ceases to shock me with that mouth of his.

"Holy fuck, Jensen. You can't say shit like that if you don't want me to come."

"Just do it," he grunts.

Maneuvering myself to my knees, I squirt some lotion on my fingers. Then, with legs parted enough, I tease my ass. Just putting pressure on the rim makes my eyes roll.

"That's it. Lie down. I want to watch."

He's still stroking himself on the couch in his house as I move to my back, sideways on the bed, legs spread wide as I continue to tease myself. I put pillows under my head so I can continue to watch him while giving him a front-row view of my middle finger breaching my tight ring of muscle. He's removed his shirt, and his pants are splayed open.

My left hand continues pumping my cock as my finger slips in and out of my hole. Jensen groans salaciously, clearly enjoying the show.

"Fuck, you are so hot," he mutters. "And you're all fucking mine, aren't you? My good boy."

I'm breathing so hard I feel like I'm going to pass out. "Yes," I cry out. "Fuck yes."

"That's me in your ass, baby," he says between heavy breaths. "That's me, fucking your tight hole."

"Goddammit, Jensen. I'm gonna come."

My head is hung back, my neck extended as my cock starts to leak from the tip. I plunge my finger in my ass faster, imagining it is him. I can picture his face in my head, that look he gets right when he's about to come.

"Come for me, Isaac. Come for your daddy."

That's it. That does the trick. He just played the *daddy* card. The term I used earlier just to fuck with him and try to get a reaction has somehow turned into something so hot that I did not see coming.

"Fuck, fuck, fuck," I mumble incoherently as my cock unloads across my chest. My ears are ringing, but even through that, I can hear Jensen's familiar grunts and groans, meaning he's reached that point too.

Pleasure wraps around my body tightly, pulsing again and again and again, like it's carrying me down a stream I don't ever want to get out of.

Once it eventually subsides, I drop my arms at my sides, deadweight on the mattress as I try to catch my breath.

"You okay over there?" Jensen asks a moment later. He sits up on the couch and lets me feast on the sight of him, cum splattered all over his chest. It clings to his chest hair and makes me wish I were there to lick it up and then wash it off in the shower.

"I wish you were here," I mumble sadly.

"Me too," he replies. "But you have to admit...this was fun."

My head falls back as I laugh. "This was fun as fuck."

"I'll take you in the shower if you take me in the shower," he replies, picking up his phone and carrying it through his house.

"Deal." I sit up and do the same, smiling down at the camera as I take him with me into the shower.

Setting the phone on the ledge meant for soaps and shampoo, I turn the water on and watch him do the same. We don't talk as we wash ourselves in two different bathrooms in two different states. There's a sense of peace in knowing that Jensen will always be here for me, no matter how far apart we are. Other than my brother, I never had that sense of security before. Maybe I never really wanted it before.

But I want it with him.

Before turning the water off, after enjoying the comfortable silence together, I chuckle to myself.

"What?" he asks.

"I can't believe you played the daddy card."

He throws his head back and laughs, and so do I. I've never been in a relationship this comfortable, where vulnerability was so easy. I've never had anyone love me as Isaac Goode before, and that's exactly what Jensen has given me.

"You liked it," he replies with a shameless grin.

I turn off the water in the shower as I wink at the camera. "Damn right I did."

PART THREE

THE PRODIGAL SON

Twenty-Four

Jensen

The bell chimes over the door of the café while I watch in horror as the pink-haired woman sitting across from me douses her scrambled eggs in ketchup. The man at her side feeds a small bite of scrambled eggs to the adorable baby in the high chair at the end of the table. She claps her hands with a gummy smile as she chews.

As for me, I'm tensely holding my coffee cup, waiting for the eldest Goode brother to officially let me in on why I'm sitting here in the first place.

I know very little about the Goode family, but I do know a few things for certain after talking to Isaac.

For one, the only brother Isaac has had substantial contact with since he ran away is Lucas, the brother I met last week. That means, and I'm assuming here, that no one else in the family knows that he and I are dating.

And second, everyone in the Goode family has a personal vendetta against Truett Goode. All the more reason for this breakfast to be a little tense.

Finally, after Adam's breakfast is eaten, he sits back in his seat and stares at me with his arms crossed.

"I've given thought to your offer," he says with hesitation.

My offer feels like a conversation we had two years ago, not two months ago. Things have gotten a good deal more complicated since I last had breakfast with Adam. He just doesn't know it yet.

"Yeah?" I ask.

"I'm sure you've heard by now that my father was released early."

I nod, glancing back and forth between Adam and his wife, Sage. I haven't told Isaac yet about Truett's visit to my church because I don't want to stress him out, which means I'm certainly not going to tell his brother.

"I have," I reply.

"Mr. Miles, I just want to know that you're on our side. I know we haven't been exactly warm with each other, but I can't bear the thought of Truett ending up back at that pulpit."

Suddenly, I'm upright with my elbows on the table. "He is not coming for my job. That is *my* congregation."

Sage smirks at me. "I like you."

"Is that what you think? That we're going to let him back in just because he's out of prison?"

"I've seen worse," Adam replies with narrowed eyes.

"So have I," I reply. "But I can assure you, I have your side on this."

Forcing myself to calm down before I let anything slip, I lean back in the booth and let out a sigh. He has no idea just why I am so loyal to the Goode brothers instead of the patriarch. And it has nothing to do with him or the church and everything to do with the man I love.

"Adam, I know you think I'm cut from the same cloth as Truett, but I promise you, I'm not. I *care* about my congregation. I care about their faith and this community. I'm not here to pat another man's back in order to put me in a place of power. I am in that position at Redemption Point for a reason. Truett can try to take it from me, but I won't give it up without a fight."

Adam regards me from across the table. In the middle of our stare down, the baby in the high chair starts squealing impatiently, so he turns toward her with another bite of his breakfast on his fork. As he feeds it to her, there is a sudden softness apparent in him.

I see the dichotomy of fatherhood in one subtle flash of a moment. Softness and ferocity in the blink of an eye. The willingness to be present and vulnerable one moment while also protective and impenetrable the next.

"You've changed, Jensen," Adam says, looking up from his daughter. "Something happened to you since we met last."

You could say that.

"Maybe so," I reply. "But this will never change for me. I want to be good at my job. I don't need to be revered or remembered. I just want to make a difference. And I don't need Truett Goode to do it."

Sage is smiling brightly over her coffee cup now. "I like you a lot."

"Easy," Adam grumbles, making me snicker to myself.

"I'm relieved," Adam says as he hands the baby a small cup with handles that she clumsily drinks out of. "I hope you understand that I can't make an appearance at your church right now. It's just not the time. And without getting into our family drama too much, I just can't betray my brothers like that. Either we all come together, or we don't come at all."

Staring at Adam across the table, I think about Isaac. There's an opaque layer of sadness behind Adam's eyes when he says that, and I wonder how it must feel for him to miss out on so much of Isaac's life.

Isaac has mentioned how rough it's been for them to be without contact. I've supported his decision to stay without that contact, but now that I'm sitting across from Adam, I wonder if the pain for his brother is worse than Isaac realizes.

I see the resemblance between the two, more so than any of the other brothers. The same almond eyes. The same parentheses when they smile. Same sharp cheekbones and strong jawline.

It makes my heart ache with missing Isaac.

"I understand," I say softly.

Just then, the baby squeals again. She launches her cup at me, and I catch it before it topples to the floor.

"Shit, sorry." Sage laughs, but I just shake my head.

"Don't be sorry. She's adorable." Grinning, I hand the cup back to the baby. "What's her name?"

"Faith," Adam replies, looking like a proud dad.

Just then, Faith latches her tiny hand around my pinkie finger and brings it to her mouth. I laugh as she bites on it like some harmless little predator.

"She's teething," Sage says as she hands Faith a soft toy. "Careful, you could lose a finger." When she releases my hand, I wipe it on my napkin with a laugh.

Isaac is missing this. He should be here, sitting next to me. He'd adore every minute of this, playing with Faith, eating with his family. I told him once that I'd help him come home to his family and the one time we tried, I bailed on him. It wasn't fair, even if I was blindsided.

But I won't fail him again. If he's ready to come home, I will be here to help him.

"Do you want kids someday, Jensen?" Sage asks as she rests her chin on her open hand. She's a cute little thing. Pink hair, tattoos, and piercings. She looks nothing like the woman I normally see attached to men like Adam, and I like her even more for that.

"I...never thought about it," I mumble in response. It might sound odd, but it's the truth. I've spent the whole of my adulthood trying to live two different lives, avoiding relationships and running from my sexuality. I never once gave a second thought to starting a family. I was just trying to survive.

But now...I have someone I could imagine raising a child

with. I could see Isaac as a father. I could see us five or ten years down the road with a life like this, eating breakfast together, cleaning up after a messy and chaotic toddler, building something greater than ourselves.

But that nagging voice in my head shreds the vision to pieces before I have a moment to grasp it. Those hardwired mantras placed there over twenty years ago still have the ability to destroy any semblance of peace in my life.

Because I'm a sinner. I'm broken and unworthy. And wishing for anything more is futile.

Faith smiles up at me bashfully before banging her tiny cup against the table.

"Choosing not to have kids is totally valid," Sage says with a sympathetic expression. Then, she leans over and strokes the baby's soft black hair. "But as someone who honestly never saw it in the cards for myself, I have to say that it is kind of amazing. Having her sort of puts everything into perspective, you know? Like...all the things we used to worry about don't matter as much as we thought they did."

Adam kisses the side of Sage's head. He looks so content and at peace. I envy him for that. He and Sage might be opposites and look like an odd couple, but they'll never know the struggle that people like me and Isaac have.

Their daughter won't be subjected to cruel stares and harsh words. She won't see posters and signs from protesters and wonder if her parents are going to hell or are hated by God. They don't have to worry about the government stripping away their right to be a family.

Obviously, Sage and Adam have no clue about my sexuality or about me at all. But I'm willing to bet Sage doesn't realize that the things she has to worry about and the things I have to worry about are very different.

I don't respond as I sit back in my seat, lost in thought.

†

"I have to tell you something," I say in the car on my way home from breakfast with Adam.

"I'm listening," Isaac replies sleepily. His voice plays in the speaker of my car through the Bluetooth connection. I can't see him, but I imagine him lying in his plush hotel bed with his messy bedhead and those puffy circles he has under his eyes when he first wakes up.

"I had breakfast with your brother," I say bluntly. I don't want any more secrets between me and Isaac, and I'm aware that I'm not always the most forthcoming with information. I like to hold things close to my chest. Call it an old habit with a side of self-preservation.

"I have three. You'll have to be more specific," Isaac mumbles.

"Adam."

I hear the ruffling of the sheets, and I imagine Isaac has just bolted upright in response.

"Why? You didn't talk about me..."

"No, of course not. He has no idea about us," I reply.

"And Lucas isn't going to tell him," he says. "So, let me guess...this meeting was church-related, wasn't it?"

"Yeah, it was."

"Does he hate you?" he asks with humor in his voice.

"You mean he doesn't hate everyone?" I ask, matching his tone.

"Not that I remember," Isaac replies. "But I bet he's got a very bitter spot for anything related to that church after what our dad did."

"No, I don't think he hates me. In fact, today was the second time we met, and I think he's actually warming up to me," I say as I turn into my neighborhood.

"This must be really weird for you," Isaac replies with a loud breath. "The church connection and the secret boyfriend connection."

"It is, but it had me thinking," I say. Pensively, I chew on my lip before continuing. "I know the meeting with Luke was a disaster, but why don't we try again? Why don't we just...tell them?"

Isaac doesn't reply. He lets out a disgruntled sound. When I don't get my reply, I go on.

"With your father out of prison, I think solidarity right now is going to be the smart choice. Show him that you are all strong without him. He's not a threat to you anymore, Isaac. And it's time you took back your family. With me by your side, of course."

Still, silence.

"Isaac..."

"I'm thinking," he replies, sounding a little more awake now. "Aren't you worried about the public finding out?"

"I trust your family's discretion. They wouldn't do anything to hurt you."

"And if Truett finds out?"

"He won't," I reply astutely. I pull my car into my driveway and put it into park. Sitting in the front seat, I stare numbly ahead, waiting for Isaac's response.

"Listen," I say. "I'm not pressuring you into this, but I'm only trying to convince you because I know you're ready, and I know it's what you want. And I think that if we're going to do this, we tell them everything all at once. The truth about you and Lucas. The truth about you and me. The truth about me and the church. All of it."

"Jesus," he mumbles to himself. "I'll need alcohol for this."

With a wince, I let out a sigh. Isaac's natural reflex to reach for a drink hasn't gotten past me. It's not something we need to battle at the moment, though. We have enough hills to climb.

"Think about it," I say. "And I'm sorry if this is too much pressure, but...Adam brought his daughter to the meeting."

"Oh come on," Isaac replies with a groan. "Now I'm really jealous."

A smile stretches across my face. "She was pretty damn cute."

"You don't play fair."

"She threw a cup at me and tried to bite my finger off."

"She sounds feisty. I love her already," he says with a sigh.

"I just...don't want to see you miss out on time with your family when I could help you get that back."

"You're too good to me," he replies sweetly, and I lift my hand to my mouth so my neighbors don't come outside and find me grinning like a fool in my driveway.

"You'll see just how good in a couple more days."

"You tease," he replies with a groan.

This is that moment again when the call comes to an end and those three little words are on the tip of my tongue. I'm dying to say them. But I refuse to do it over the phone.

Three more days, and he's all mine.

TWENTY-FIVE

Eight days without Jensen was tough. Focusing on performing and songwriting when I know my family is in crisis is tough. Being on tour and in the public eye while all of this is going down is tough.

But none of those things are as tough as seeing my hot, older boyfriend at the end of the hall behind the stage at the arena and *not* being able to run into his arms and kiss him to death. That's just fucking torture.

Jensen looks so good as he stands with his hands in his pockets, watching me walk down the hall with the rest of my band behind me. Backstage is too fucking crowded. Why are there so many people around? They're all the crew and security and workers, none of whom need to see me kissing another man. Phones would come out so fast and ruin everything.

I lock eyes with Jensen as I approach him, and I know he's feeling the same pain. I put out a hand for a cordial handshake.

"Glad you could make it," I say with a beaming smile. He grips my hand so tight it hurts, and we give each other one of those awkward handshake hug things that guys do.

"Thanks for the invite," he replies, his eyes skating around the room as if to see everyone's reaction to our greeting.

Lola gives me a sad smile. "I'll let you have the shower in the bus first," she says with a hand on my arm. "Just don't take too long. We have to be back and ready for the show by five." Then she gives me a wink and walks off with the rest of the band.

Subtle. What a goddess.

"I love you," I mouth to her while no one is paying attention.

Then I turn to Jensen. "Care to have a beer with me while I get ready for the show?"

He shrugs. "Sure."

It feels like we're performing for an audience that isn't even paying attention. I walk first toward the back door, and Jensen follows. This early before the show, when the fans aren't even here yet, it's safe to come and go through the parking lot. Later tonight, it will be a madhouse out here.

Jensen and I don't speak on the trek to the bus. The anxious energy between us is palpable. Our feet move faster and faster with each step. When we reach the bus, the security guard outside opens the door for me and I thank him. His presence definitely means we need to keep it down inside.

"I've got beer. You like Shiner, right?" I ask Jensen as I climb the stairs.

"Sure," he replies.

Then, a moment later, the bus door is closed and we're alone. I spin on my heels and launch myself into his arms. His hands hold my face, knocking my cowboy hat to the floor as his mouth finds mine. Ravenously, he kisses me, licking his way into my mouth and nibbling on my lips.

My ass hits the counter as he backs me up. Then I push him toward the recliners and he falls into one. We barely break our kiss for a moment before I'm in his lap, kissing him hard again.

"Eight days has never felt so long in my life," he mumbles against my mouth.

His hands tug on my Wranglers, and I grind myself against

him as my cock swells behind the zipper. His mouth travels from my lips and down my jaw, biting me through the short hair. When he reaches my neck, he sucks hard on the tender, stubbly flesh and it takes everything in me to bite back my whimper.

"I've got time before the show," I whisper. "Take me to the bedroom."

He pauses, staring into my eyes with desire. "Not yet."

"What do you mean *not yet*?" I ask with surprise. "I've waited eight damn days."

He chuckles before giving me a peck on the lips. "I have something for you."

"Is it an orgasm? Because if it's not, I don't want it."

He smacks my ass playfully. "Get up. It's in my pocket."

With curiosity, I stand from his lap and lean against the counter and wait. He stands and I see not only the bulge in his jeans from his cock but also the bulge in his pocket. Consider my interest piqued.

I stare at him with furrowed brows as he pulls it out. "It's a good thing you gave me backstage access because I was afraid I wouldn't make it through security with this."

My brows pinch even more. It's a red velvet satchel. He loosens the top and pulls out a glass, mushroom-shaped plug.

"Oh, honey, the answer is yes," I say, holding back a laugh.

He steps up to me. "You already know what I'm going to say," he says with a sexy rasp in his voice.

"You want me to wear that while I'm onstage, don't you?" I ask, gazing into his eyes. My cock throbs in my pants at the idea.

He nods. "I want you dying for my cock by the end of the show, and I want to know your ass is ready for me."

"My ass is always ready for you," I reply with a smirk. Jensen laughs quietly with a shake of his head.

"You know what I mean, Isaac."

I can't help but kiss him. Wrapping my arms around his neck, I pull him close and let him kiss me so hard it becomes hard to breathe.

While our lips are still pressed together, he asks, "Did you do that other thing I asked you to do?"

"Oh, you mean this?" I ask as I pull away. Rushing to my room, I ruffle through the papers hidden in the drawer next to my bed. I pull out the one he wants to see. It's the one that says I am free of any transmittable diseases. He's already shown me his.

I hold it up for him to see as he approaches me with a soft expression of contentment. "Good boy," he whispers before planting a kiss on my mouth.

Letting the paper fall to the floor, I wrap my arms around Jensen and melt into his kiss. Later tonight, I'll have him to myself. All of him. Nothing between us.

It might seem like nothing, but I have never gotten to this point with a guy before. Even on the rare occasions that I was with someone for any length of time, we never took this step. This step is huge. It's the one that defines a level of intimacy I haven't seen before.

I'm certainly no hopeless romantic, but this stage of our relationship and the whole *I love you* thing feel very hand in hand.

God, what is happening to me?

Jensen smacks my ass again. "Get in the shower."

"I wish it were big enough for the both of us," I moan in complaint as I turn the water on.

"I'll be waiting for you to get out," he says, waving the glass plug in his hand. With his arms crossed, he watches me undress and climb into the small stall. Then he watches with interest as I soap up my body, taking time to stroke my still-hard cock.

"Enjoying the show?" I ask with a smirk.

"Yes, very much," he replies.

My shower is a bit more rushed than normal. Stepping out, I dry off but don't bother wrapping the towel around my waist. As I walk out of the bathroom, I turn to find Jensen sitting on the edge of my bed, fully clothed with lube in one hand and the butt plug in the other.

He pats his thigh. "Have a seat."

Nothing will ever compare as long as I live to how hot he looks in this moment. He looks like he owns me and he knows it. There's something about him. His willingness to always be what I need. To always be here for me, no matter what. It makes my heart swell in my chest every time I look at him.

I climb onto his lap, straddling his hips as I stare into his eyes. His stoic, hard expression melts into a smile that looks like love.

I want to say it. God, I want to say it.

But surely, this can't be the moment to whisper those three little words.

"You know," I say, wrapping my arms around his neck. "I have a little surprise for you, too."

"You do?"

"Yeah, but you have to wait for yours. At about...nine forty-five tonight."

He nods before pressing his lips to mine. As our mouths are entangled, his lubed fingers gently prod my ass, and I let out a moan of desire. As he starts to stretch me, I groan a little louder.

"Are you sure you don't want to just fuck me now?" I whisper against his lips.

He growls in response, which again seems to be my answer.

When the cool glass of the plug nudges my hole, I relax into his arms, allowing the toy to slowly penetrate. It's not my first rodeo, so I know this feeling.

I also know that tonight's show is going to be very...interesting. I guess I should just be grateful it isn't the remote-controlled vibrating type.

Once it's fully seated inside me, I shift my hips to feel it lightly grazing my prostate. I groan into Jensen's neck.

"I'm so fucked," I mumble, making him laugh. He strokes his hands up and down my back.

"You know you don't have to wear it for the show if you don't want to. You can always tell me no."

I pull back and look into his eyes. "You're sweet to say that, but trust me, I'd tell you no if I wanted to. You realize I'm a stubborn shithead, right?"

He gives me one of his signature crooked smiles. "Good. I want you to always tell me when you don't like something. And tell other people the same. Don't let anyone walk all over you."

My eyes narrow as I lean in. "Stop talking like you won't be around to protect me. I'm not worried about anything when I'm with you."

His arms wrap me tightly against his body, and he breathes into my neck. He doesn't respond, and it makes me a little unsettled. Jensen might be an enigma to me still, but it's the subtle darkness hidden deep inside that scares me most of all. But I'm convinced that if I hold him tight enough and love him hard enough, I can scare all that darkness away.

✝

It's at the end of a long instrumental bridge when I first curse Jensen in my mind. For a while, I almost forgot the plug was there, but once I started moving around onstage and playing harder, I was reminded.

Oh, there it is.

Now, I just have to pray that no one can see the hard evidence in front of my jeans. Fans might be thinking, "Wow, Theo Virgil *really* likes to play guitar."

And they'd be right. But it's mostly the prostate-teasing plug in my ass that has me smiling more than normal, hiding my erection behind the microphone stand, and running backstage at odd times in the show to adjust myself.

I made sure to find Jensen's seat before the show started this time so I could look out at the crowd and spot his smiling face—that smug bastard. I even grin down at him during his favorite song. On the next number, I do a little pelvic thrust move that drives the girls crazy. I hold hard eye contact with him for that part, and he narrows his eyes at me as I do.

But this instrumental bridge...this might be the death of me. It's the first time I've ever genuinely worried about coming in my pants onstage in front of a few thousand people. At least I manage to play the chords correctly. That's a new skill I didn't know I had —playing the guitar while on the brink of an orgasm.

The toy isn't the only reason tonight is different. I told Jensen I had a little something planned for him. And I'm slightly nervous about how it's going to go.

After the wild song and the instrumental bridge from hell, I decide to slow things down. My band all head backstage for a break, and one of the crew members brings me out a stool.

With my guitar on my lap, I sit on the stool and bring the microphone to my lips. Gazing out at the crowd, there is nothing quite like this feeling. Just me, alone, in front of twenty thousand people.

And yet, it's still somehow intimate.

I glance down at Jensen's section and notice him checking his watch. Nine forty-five on the dot. Then he looks up at me with a tilt of his head and a quizzical look on his face.

I strum a new melody softly on my guitar. "I'm doing something a little different tonight," I say into the microphone. I tug my earpiece from my ear, and it's so quiet in the arena that I can hear my guitar playing on my lap.

"I don't know if my record label is going to like this, but I'm going rogue," I say, and some of the crowd cheers.

"You see...I wrote this song just a couple weeks ago," I say, and they cheer again.

My hands are shaking, and for the first time, I'm nervous. It has nothing to do with the stage or the crowd, but rather, one person in it. And what I'm about to say.

Here goes nothing.

"Y'all know that stage of a relationship, when things are new, and you can't get enough of the other person, and they just make you so fucking happy?"

I brave a glance up and find Jensen in the crowd. He's watching me intently, the expression on his face serious.

"Y'all know that moment when you realize...that you're in love with the other person. And that moment just feels like... magic."

The crowd loses their minds, but my gaze doesn't waver from him. I can see the moisture in his eyes, even from here. Then he gives me a subtle head nod, and I know he feels the same.

"Well, this song...is about that. This is for you. You know who you are."

Twenty-Six

Jensen

Tears well in my eyes as I stand among a crowd of over twenty thousand people, watching the man I love stand alone on a stage and sing a song I listened to him write in the middle of the night just a couple weeks ago. *My song*.

Leave it to Theo Virgil to confess his love in the most dramatic and grand way possible. I wish I could do the same. I wish I could stand on a stage and tell the world that I love him.

I wish it didn't have to be a secret. I wish I could run up there right now, wrap my arms around him, and kiss him.

I wish our love wasn't such an offense to others.

This song is even more beautiful than I remember. Tender and slow. With lyrics that would pull on my heart even if it wasn't about me.

Isaac has a voice like a scorching campfire that crackles and burns with warmth and texture. As he sings, I close my eyes and I bathe in the sound.

This is when I feel closest to God. This keenness of music and togetherness and harmony. A powerful connection, so visceral it doesn't even feel like reality.

This was the sensation I chased every Sunday when I went to church growing up.

This song is my new hymn.

Isaac, my god.

When the song wraps up, I open my eyes and they immediately connect with Isaac's. For just a moment, it feels as if we're alone. His expression matches mine. I don't need to say the words that I'm thinking. He can feel them.

I love you. I love you. I love you.

As the crowd cheers, the band comes back out to the stage. They continue to play the rest of their set list. I don't hear the cruel voices that often pop up inside my head in moments like these. For a few blissful moments, it's quiet.

At this point, I have Theo Virgil's set list memorized. As he plays the last song before the encore, I shuffle out of the crowd toward the backstage. I hold up my badge to the bouncer near the exit, and he waves me through. This moment of anxious anticipation is the same after every show, although tonight is a bit different.

Not only did we essentially just say our first "I love yous," but I'm willing to bet Isaac is as hard as the Eiffel Tower in those jeans, and I can't wait to get my hands on him. Sometimes it takes over an hour between the end of the show and when we can finally be alone in his trailer, but I'll be damned if I'm gonna wait that long tonight.

After I make my way through the long hallways toward the backstage area, I lock eyes with Isaac. He and the band are about to run back out, the crowd screaming his name, waiting for their encore. It's dark, and the band runs out to the stage first, but before Isaac can disappear from my sight, I grab his hand and pull him toward me.

For a brief moment, we're alone. The crowd cheers louder, and I know I only have a few seconds left, so I press him up against the dark cinder block wall and I kiss his lips with ferocity. He growls against my mouth, tugging at my jeans desperately.

Reaching down, I grip his raging erection through his pants and he moans louder against me.

"Fuck!" he cries, seeking more desperately needed friction.

But we can't do this here. I have to tear my mouth away from his and my hand from his crotch.

Panting, I mutter, "Meet me in the greenroom after the show."

"Dammit. Okay," he replies, looking dazed. His pupils are blown wide with arousal. With that familiar sheen of sweat he gets when he performs, he looks so sexy it hurts.

I touch his face softly before he heads toward the curtain. The crowd is still screaming wildly, but before he steps out, I call for him.

"Isaac."

He stops and turns toward me in expectation.

"I love you, too," I say, and he smiles brightly before giving me that wink he always does and running out onto the stage.

I watch the last two songs from the wings with my arms crossed over my chest and a proud smile on my face. It's a different show every night, at least for me it is. The first time, I watched as a fan, then as a friend, and now through the lens of a lover.

He is mine, and as long as I am alive, I will keep him. Not Theo Virgil, but Isaac Goode, the young, carefree, and sometimes adorably obnoxious love of my life.

He plays the last song with more energy than ever, smiling brightly, strumming the guitar harder, jumping higher, and just before it ends, I leave the wings in search of the greenroom.

One of the staff points me in the right direction, and when she asks who I am, I simply explain that I'm Theo's pastor, of course, and after every show, he likes to say a private prayer. She doesn't ask any more questions, and it's not technically a lie.

The rooms they provide Isaac after all of his shows are always a little more drab and run-down than I expect them to be. And tonight is no different. The paint on the walls is chipped, the linoleum cracked. There's an old table with four chairs and a dusty old black leather couch. I pace the room with aroused anticipation. The bottle of lube that I took from Isaac's tour bus is in my pocket.

I feel like a deviant but in the best way. The last eight days without him have felt like so much longer. It's like I've forgotten the way his body feels. I crave it. I was *made* for it.

There's a rumbling of voices in the hallway, which I take to mean the show is over. I'm pacing with excitement when the door finally flies open and Isaac is standing there, chest heaving and eyes wild.

God, he looks so sexy like this. Sweat slicked and flushed from the exertion during the show. His usual dark cowboy hat sits on his head. His black T-shirt clings to his skin and the worn-out flannel hangs from his shoulders.

In a rush, he slams the door shut and locks it behind him with fumbling fingers. Then he's flying toward me. I gather him up in my arms, kissing him harshly and feeling him clutch tightly to my frame.

The fire that burns between us feels like it could stay ignited forever. I will never tire of his touch or the feel of his body in my hands.

"Fuck, that was the longest show of my life," he mumbles as he yanks my shirt up to slide his hands against the skin of my chest.

I tear off his flannel and yank up his shirt. He reaches behind his head and pulls his shirt off in one swipe. I do the same before we come back together, skin to skin.

"I was rock hard for that whole fucking show," he groans as he fumbles with the button on my pants. I jerk open his belt and slide it through the loops.

"So was I," I reply breathlessly as I cradle his head in my hands and kiss his neck. "But I'm always turned on while watching you."

Once I have his pants loosened, I slide my hand down the backside, over his ass, teasing down his crack until my fingers brush the flared base of the glass plug, making him shiver.

"Fuck me, I'm ready," he groans, clutching my arms like his legs have stopped working.

I chuckle with my face in his neck, breathing in the sweat-soaked, musky scent of him. "Not yet, cowboy."

Isaac is eagerly fighting with my zipper, and once he has it down, he dives his hand into my pants and wraps his fingers around my length. I have to bite my lip to keep from groaning too loud as I hold him in a harsh grip on the back of his neck.

He licks a line up the side of my neck. "What about now?" he mutters through clenched teeth.

"Fuck," I groan.

Roughly, I spin him around. He has to grab the counter of the vanity for support as I finish undoing my pants and shuffling them down far enough to grip my own throbbing cock.

After a few eager strokes, I tear down Isaac's jeans before letting out a gasp at the sight of him. He's bent over, his ass perched and ready with the glass plug wedged between his cheeks.

I press myself closer to him and we stare at each other in the mirror on the wall as I slowly ease the glass toy out of his hole. He nearly whimpers as it passes the ring of muscle.

"Please, Jensen," he cries. "I need your cock."

As I reach into my pocket for the lube, I kiss a line down Isaac's spine, starting between his shoulder blades. He arches for me, letting out needy cries as I uncap the bottle and coat my fingers.

When my fingers circle his sensitive hole, he pounds his fist quietly on the counter's surface.

"Jensen, come on," he growls, thrusting his hips back toward me.

"My boy is so impatient," I say, teasing him.

"Your boy is about to have a fucking fit," he replies. "I've been hard for hours, babe."

I chuckle again. I love seeing him so worked up.

"Give me hell, Isaac," I say as I uncap the lid of the bottle again, this time slathering up my cock. "It's going to be that much better when I shut you up."

Isaac reaches down and strokes his own dick, and I see in the reflection how red and throbbing it is. I'm willing to bet the inside of his boxers are coated with precum, and the thought is hot as hell.

He's groaning with impatience some more when I finally press my cock against his asshole. Instantly, he quiets.

Looking down, I savor the sight of his body taking mine, with nothing between us. As I watch my cock disappear inside him, my jaw hangs slack and my breathing seems to stop entirely.

"Mine," I mutter possessively as I slam the rest of the way in.

Isaac grips the counter tightly as his head hangs with a mumbling sound. "Fuck, yes."

I pull out to the tip and slam back in, and it feels incredible. The tight heat of his body swallows me up, sending warm electric shivers down my spine.

"You are all fucking mine, Isaac. Say it."

He looks up and meets my eyes in the mirror. "I'm all yours."

"Not the fans'. Not your family's. *Mine*. Understand?"

"God, yes, Jensen," he cries. "Don't stop."

"What did you call me?" I ask with strictness as I squeeze his hips tighter.

He meets my gaze in the mirror, looking surprised, maybe even hesitant.

"Try again," I mutter as I continue to fuck him.

"Yes...Daddy," he says before his eyes flutter closed. I've never been more turned on in my life. I am his daddy. I am his *everything*.

My hips are pistoning now. It's been too long to take my time with him. After everything, we both need this too much.

"Who takes care of you?" I ask, holding him tightly on the hips and pounding into him. With every thrust, his cock leaks from the tip. He's making a mess all over this greenroom, and it fills me with pride.

"You," he says on a gasp.

"Who makes you come?"

"You," he cries louder.

I no longer give a shit who is on the other side of that door. Let them hear Theo Virgil getting railed by the man who loves him. Let them hear how good I make this country star feel.

"Stroke yourself, baby," I mutter as the climax creeps down my spine.

He reaches down and grips his cock as I slam against his ass. The sound of our bodies coming together fills the room.

It's the instant reminder that when I do come, I'll be filling him up and marking him as mine, which eventually throws me into the storm of my own release. Pleasure courses through my body. My eyes close with my head thrown back as I slam home again and again before spilling into him.

When his body has taken every drop, I look down to see Isaac still stroking his cock. Grabbing him by the throat, I pull him upright and replace his hand with mine. I'm still buried deep inside him as I lick a line up the side of his neck and jack his shaft until he starts shuddering in my arms.

"That's it," I mutter as he comes. "Good boy."

The look of ecstasy on his face gives me goose bumps. He is so perfect and so mine. I don't deserve him—I never did. But I do love him, and I always will.

When his body starts to relax in my arms, he smiles like he's waking up from a dream.

"That was good," he says, leaning against me.

I kiss his cheek and then his neck. "Yes, it was."

Then he turns his head toward me and our eyes meet again. Reaching up, he strokes my hair as he softly mumbles, "I love you."

Smiling, I kiss his lips again. "I love you, too."

"This is crazy, right?" he asks. "We've only known each other a little over a month. Does it normally happen this fast?"

My arms squeeze around him affectionately. "Babe, you're a country music star and I'm a preacher. We are anything but normal."

He laughs. "Good point."

Twenty-Seven

Isaac

I'm onstage. *The lights just keep getting brighter and brighter the more I sing. It's hard to tell where the stage ends and I begin. The crowd and I are one. The mass of bodies is alive with energy, and I'm feeding off them, singing my heart out and dancing with the band.*

But then, the stage lights go out. I can't see the crowd, but I can feel them. They become a mob, and I'm holding the mic as they get closer, their low voices mumbling my name in a deep, terrifying cadence.

I cling to the mic and just keep singing. With my eyes tightly shut, I sing and sing and sing until I run out of song and I forget the lyrics.

The horde is smothering me, surrounding me until I can't breathe anymore.

"Jensen!" I shout into the mic, begging him to save me. But the moment his name comes out of my mouth, I realize I've said too much.

The crowd is angry now, clawing at me, punching me, trying to yank my guitar from my hands.

"Jensen," I cry, trying to get my instrument back, but they're too strong and the strings cut my hands as they steal it from me.

"I've got you," he whispers, but when I search for him in the crowd, he's not there. Just hazy visions of faces I recognize—Luke, my mother, Adam, Caleb. They're angry at me. For reasons I don't understand, they're shouting at me.

Someone shakes me, and I spin around to see my father. He slaps me across the face hard, and I start to cry like a child.

"Jens..." I sob.

"I'm here," the voice says again, sounding close but not close enough.

My father grabs my shoulders and shakes me again.

"Stop!" I shout.

The sound of my own voice jostles me awake. I stare into the darkness, someone else staring back. I panic, pushing him away until I can figure out who is hurting me.

"Baby, it's me," Jensen whispers.

I blink again, trying to make sense of his face in my bed. Then I glance around and see that it's not my bed.

It takes a moment before it all comes back, and I collapse onto the hotel bed.

"Fuck," I groan. "I'm sorry."

He comes closer carefully without touching me. "Don't be sorry. You had a bad dream. What can I do?"

Holding my hands over my face, I'm surprised to find moisture on my cheeks and temples. Shit, was I crying?

Taking deep breaths, I relive the whole thing in my mind. The terror feels fresh and real. The way the crowd turned on me. The way Jensen never showed, no matter how much I begged for him. The anger on my family's faces.

Where the hell did that come from?

"Isaac, you okay?" he presses.

"I'm fine," I mutter coldly as I roll out of bed and walk toward the bathroom. I can feel his concerned eyes on me as I leave him in the bed alone. It makes me feel like an asshole.

Once in the bathroom, I douse my face with frigid water. To my relief, Jensen doesn't follow me. He gives me the space I need because, well, he's fucking perfect like that.

I run a soft white towel over my face and stare at the man in the mirror. He has dark circles under his eyes. Is this exhaustion? Am I going too hard? But I can't stop. Not now. Not when everything is going perfectly.

Is it stupid to think of going home to my family at a time like this?

Is it stupid to think of coming out?

It's like everything in my life revolves around my career, and I want this fame so much I'm willing to sabotage everything good in my life to get it. Maybe that's why my family was yelling at me. Because I've put off going home to them for eleven fucking years while I've been out here building a fandom and giving my time to strangers instead of them.

Theo Virgil has it all at the expense of Isaac Goode.

When I eventually come out of the bathroom, Jensen is sitting on the edge of the bed with his head in his hands. He looks up at me with dread etched into his features.

"Wanna talk about it?" he asks.

I let out a sigh as I walk over to the bed, patting the pillow by my side. He lies down and I immediately crawl into his arms. The moment I show Jensen that I need him, he relaxes. His arms pull me closer and he kisses the top of my head.

"Sorry," I mumble. "I don't get nightmares very often. It just freaked me out."

"That's okay," he replies. "You don't need to apologize."

After a moment, he adds, "Isaac, I'm worried about you."

"I'm fine," I reply, and even I hear how unconvincing it sounds.

"You're under a lot of pressure and you're not giving yourself any time off."

"I know, but I promise, I'm okay. I can handle it."

"I regret bringing up your family the other day," he says,

running his hands down my arm. "You don't have to do anything you don't want to."

"That's the problem. I feel like I *can't* do anything I want to. I can't come out. I can't go home."

"Hey, hey, hey," he says, squeezing me tighter. "First of all, you are not under any deadline to do any of those things. And you know that you absolutely can come out if you want. If you lose fans, then they weren't your fans in the first place."

"What if it ruins my whole career?"

"What if it doesn't?"

I look up into his face. The confidence in his eyes calms me. He's fearless.

He presses his lips to my forehead and holds me tight against him. "You know that no matter what you choose, you don't have to do any of it alone. Not anymore."

Letting out a sigh, I hold him tighter and try to push that cruel dream out of my head. I don't know why my mind seemed to think Jensen wouldn't be there the minute I needed him. And I never want to feel that way again.

✝

I wake up the next morning to a pair of lips softly pressed against the back of my neck.

I hum with my arms wrapped around my pillow as Jensen leans into me, kissing his way down my spine.

"Is this heaven?" I murmur sleepily.

His deep chuckle buzzes against my back. "I was just thinking the same thing," he says as he reaches my boxer briefs, tugging on them with his teeth.

My phone lights up on the nightstand, and I peep my eyes open long enough to see it's an Instagram notification. Ignoring it, I wiggle my hips from side to side as Jensen continues to spoil me with kisses.

It lights up again.

Maybe my publicist posted some photos from the shoot or something.

Jensen straddles my hips with his stiff arousal against my ass. I groan into my pillow as I shift my weight backward like an invitation.

He lays his weight across my back. "I enjoy waking up with you."

"I enjoy waking up with you, too," I reply with a sleepy smile.

My phone is incessantly buzzing and lighting up like crazy on the nightstand.

"Fuck this thing," I growl as I reach for it with the intent to turn it off. But then I see the notifications. They're not just from Instagram. There are texts and calls and DMs.

"What the...fuck?"

"What is it?" Jensen asks.

I open my phone and start with the texts. There's one from my tour manager, telling me she's sending a car to the hotel to get me. Multiple from my publicist. Even a couple from Lola asking me to check in.

As I sit up, Jensen climbs off me and watches with concern. "Everything okay?"

"I have no clue," I reply.

I text Lola first because she's the easiest person to talk to.

> What's going on? I just woke up.

She replies immediately.

> Morning, sunshine. Your little performance last night caught some serious attention.

What performance?

Go look at your Instagram.

I quickly open up the app and immediately see myself on the stage. It's a video from last night of my song for Jensen. What's the big deal about that? It's not like I said who it was about.

Scrolling to the comments, I search for answers, but most of it is pretty expected.

Who is Theo dating?

Is it the actress from his music video?

Except for one...

Did you see pics of him with that guy?

Oh, God.

Immediately, I check my tags. And my heart drops. There are candid photos of me and Jensen. Photos of me and Lola. Of me and random guys at bars when I had no clue people even recognized me.

Sitting up, I dig my hand in my hair.

"Breathe, baby," Jensen says, rubbing a hand up and down my spine.

I'm trying to relax, but it feels like an invasion. It feels like they've just splayed open my life and slapped it on a platter for the whole world to see—my *personal fucking life.*

All this because I said I was in love? No one gave a shit before.

"They have pictures of you," I say, giving him a terrified look.

The calm in his expression glitches and I see the same look in his eyes I saw that night at Lucas's house. He's scared. He's just hiding it better now. Jensen has been shoving his feelings down for so long, but he's as frightened as I am. Maybe even more so.

"We'll deny it," he stammers as he stands from the bed, feigning confidence.

"Yeah," I reply, nodding my head.

"We're from the same town. We'll explain that I'm an old friend, a preacher, just like your father. No one will suspect anything..."

My breathing sounds heavy as I force air in and out of my lungs. As I meet his gaze, I give him a nod and an expression filled to the brim with forced conviction.

We said we would hide it, so that's what we'll do.

But things are different now, aren't they? Because we're not just hooking up anymore. We've established that this is the real thing. This could be...a forever thing. It feels wrong to hide it now. This relationship deserves better.

I watch as Jensen rushes to get dressed and I stare at him with doubts brewing in my mind. He said he loved me. He *meant* it. But was I filling in the blanks? Was I imagining that this could be a real relationship, even after he made it very clear that he could not, and would not, ever come out?

Does being in love make a difference?

What is wrong with me?

"What if we...don't?" I ask.

"What?" He stands up and stares at me with confusion.

"You said it yourself last night. You said what if this doesn't ruin my career? We have an opportunity to come out and just get it over with before someone else outs us first."

His shoulders slump and he wets his lips as he readies his reply, although I know what he's going to say already.

"I was talking about you, Isaac. Not me."

"What's the difference? Do it *with* me," I say, moving to my knees. "You said you would be here for everything, so be here, Jensen."

He wants to shoot me down. I can see it in his eyes, but he doesn't, not like that night at Luke's house. He won't run again. I know it.

"Let's talk about it later, okay? Don't make any rash decisions today. We'll...figure something out."

I swallow down the rising discomfort, and I remind myself that this is not his fault. It's not his fault that someone conditioned him for so long to be so afraid of coming out. I was too, but not like that.

"Okay," I reply.

We stare at each other for a moment before he quickly crosses the room toward me and pulls me into his arms. Holding me in a tight embrace, he whispers into my neck, "Everything is going to be okay."

I don't believe him, but I try.

TWENTY-EIGHT

Isaac and I leave the hotel room separately to avoid suspicion. I go first to check for fans or paparazzi in the lobby, but we're safe. It's mostly just the normal comings and goings of a downtown hotel.

Lingering outside, I wait for him. When he eventually emerges fifteen minutes later, he has on a ball cap and dark sunglasses, so he's almost unrecognizable. It throws me that this is his life. This is what he has to do to have a private life, and it's not fair.

The public's attention is fickle. They will obsess over him for the moment before they move on to the next hot topic of interest. I just hope he can get through this phase before anyone leaks anything damning against him.

I know he wants to come out, but at the same time, he's scared. I don't want some momentary nuclear situation to force him into something that should take time and thought.

As Isaac and I ride over to the local office where he's meeting with his tour manager, the voices in my head are louder than ever. Except it's not just voices. It's a familiar sentiment deep in my gut that's spreading like a parasite. It's a lot of things, but mostly shame.

I have to remind myself to keep breathing. He and I don't speak on the drive. He keeps his head down and stares at his phone. I don't have the guts to text anyone in the organization back home. I can't text the publicity manager and ask what to do if my name has been leaked as a lover of a famous country singer. I can't have this conversation with my colleagues. It's unfathomable.

So my leg bounces as I stare out the window on the drive.

The office is down an old street in an old part of the city that's been renovated. Various labels and companies have remodeled old brick houses into recording studios and galleries. Tall oak and magnolia trees line the street as our SUV pulls up to one of the brick buildings.

"Why don't I get a ride to the airport?" I say quietly, with regret.

Isaac looks up at me with surprise. "You're not supposed to go home until tomorrow."

"I know, but..."

The look in his eyes guts me. He's looking to me for support, and once I leave, he'll be alone, dealing with all of this.

Fuck it.

I reach across the back seat and grip his hand in mine. "Forget I said anything," I say. "I'll be here. Okay? I'll stay."

"Okay," he replies with relief. "Let me just go in and talk to them. I don't think it will take long. Then we can go find Lola and the others. We can still stay in a hotel tonight if you want."

I nod, although my stomach is turning with anxiety.

"Okay."

The driver opens Isaac's door and escorts him into the building while I wait alone in the car. My mind feels like it's falling into a familiar spiral. I close my eyes and breathe.

Then, it feels like retracing my steps. How did we get here? I went to a concert with a woman. I started a harmless conversation with a man. Then...

A montage of moments over the past month with Isaac cascades through my mind on a reel. It all seemed so natural. So... unavoidable. There was never a moment where I considered stopping. But so many opportunities.

How can one person have so many regrets and none at the same time? I don't regret a single moment with Isaac, and yet...

My actions are not the problem. I am.

Loving him is *not* evil. So why do I feel so sinful?

My head and my heart are at war.

The logic reminds me that it's what they did. The harm *they* caused. So why can't I just forget it? Why can't I function without it? Why can't I say to hell with everything and do what my heart so desperately wants? To tell the world that I love a man who loves me back and fuck anyone who has a problem with that.

My phone rings and I nearly jump. The driver is still standing outside, leaving me alone in the SUV. I pick up my phone to see my mom's picture on the screen.

My gut is telling me not to answer it. Deep down, I know she won't tell me what I need to hear right now. But that iota of hope that she will wins and I swipe the call.

"Hey, Mom," I say, forcing my voice to stay flat and calm.

"Hey, baby," she replies in her sweet voice. "I just got a call from Gabby's mom," she says, and I'm wincing before she even finishes that sentence.

"She said she saw you on Facebook with some big country singer. I told her you were going on a lot of trips out of town, but I had no idea you knew him personally."

She's doing a good job of masking her voice, but I know her too well. I can pick up on every single tell. She's not curious. She's worried.

I clear my throat. "Yeah, I do know him personally," I say.

"Really?" she says, and it's dripping with presumptuousness. "How do you know him?"

My eyes are stinging as I stare straight ahead, my gaze unfocused and my mind whirling. I'm tired of dancing around this unspoken thing. I'm tired of my mother and I pretending we can have a real relationship that is unharmed by the actions of the past.

"I think you know, Mom," I mutter lowly.

I can hear her breathing on the other line, but she doesn't respond. Not at first.

When the line grows too awkward, she rushes to fill it with something light.

"Oh, Jensen," she says, like I've just admitted that I failed to use a coupon at the grocery store. Not that I just admitted to a relationship she considers forbidden and sinful.

"Mom," I mutter.

"I don't know what you're telling me this for. That is *your* business."

"Mom, please."

"What, Jensen? You know that is a sin. You know it's wrong."

"It's not wrong. How could you say that to me?"

"Why are you mad at *me*?" she asks, sounding frantic. She's scrambling.

"I'm not...mad at you."

"Yes, you are." I can hear the quiver in her voice. I don't know if they are real tears or performative to make me feel bad, but I have an idea. "I'm not the one who will make your life hell when they find out, Jensen. I just worry about you and the way people will treat you."

I hang my head in defeat. A sardonic laugh escapes my lips.

"Is that why you sent me to that program? Because you didn't want the world to be mean to me?"

She's quiet again.

"What program?" she asks after a tense moment.

"You know what program, Mom. Eternal Harmony. Remember them?"

"Jensen, why are you bringing all this up now? What is going on over there? It feels like you're taking a lot out on me because of the way other people are reacting. I'm just trying to protect you."

When I blink, a tear falls onto my lap. I hear the sincerity in her voice. Maybe she's being honest, and this is all it was. A form of protection. Rather than embrace me and support me, she tried to change me for my own good. Maybe...she did have the best intentions.

And that's the most tragic thing of all. Because the thing she did to protect me is the same thing that's killing me.

In the corner of my eye, I see a door open, and Isaac emerges.

"Mom, I gotta go," I mutter with a sniffle.

I don't wait for her reply. Her upset voice echoes through the phone before I end the call. Quickly, I wipe my eyes and compose myself before the driver opens the door and Isaac climbs in.

"Everything okay?" I ask.

He shrugs and then looks into my eyes. He catches the emotion on my face, the side effects of my tears that I can't so easily hide.

"Everything okay with you?" he asks, frozen in fear.

Lying, I nod. "It's fine." Reaching across the seat, I hold his hand in mine.

The one thing I can count on with Isaac is that when it comes to heavy conversations, he'll avoid them. This means when I tell him everything is fine, he'll believe it—or at least pretend to believe it.

†

My knee bounces erratically on the drive from the label to wherever the tour bus is parked. Isaac wants to see the rest of his band because this involves them, but this entire thing has me feeling uncomfortable.

He wants to tell his band, and I'll support that, but it just feels like the more people that know, the more likely this won't stay under wraps for long.

His hand is the only thing I'm clinging to at the moment. I have to be here for him. He's going through this too, and while my job is at stake, his public image is much, much bigger than mine. He has far more to lose if this all goes south.

"Change of plans," the driver says, and I look at Isaac with concern. "The band is at the Hilton downtown."

"Where's the bus?" Isaac asks.

"The bus was public. Better security at the hotel."

"Better security?"

Just then, we turn down the street and my jaw drops. There is a horde of people outside the tall hotel building. They are holding cameras and microphones, and there is nothing to stop them from walking right up to our SUV when the driver pulls up to the curb.

A few big men in black shirts are stationed there to open the door for us, but it's immediately pandemonium.

"What the fuck?" Isaac mutters to himself. He releases my hand before the first bulb flashes.

Then, we're being escorted inside and it feels like there isn't a moment to breathe or think. I get out first, swept away by one of the guards.

There are cameras in my face and people yelling. Mostly asking Isaac invasive questions that I pray he's not answering. As I reach the door alone, I turn back to find him, but he's lost in the crowd.

Anger boils inside me when I spot him swallowed up by the paparazzi snapping photos. I barrel back into the mix, giving the security guard a rage-filled sneer as I shove camera-wielding men away from Isaac.

Wrapping an arm around Isaac's back, I shout, "Back up!" It does nothing. They ignore me and continue to block our path and get in our faces.

Isaac burrows himself against me as I plow through the mob.

"I've got you," I mumble to him just before we reach the

door. Finally, the security guards make themselves useful and stop the paparazzi from following us as we disappear inside.

Every ounce of cool I once had is gone.

The woman I recognize as Isaac's tour manager is there to greet us.

"Do those security guards work for the goddamn paparazzi?" I shout.

"Jensen," Isaac says with alarm as he stares at me. It takes me a moment to realize I'm still holding him close, so I let him go, and he steps away.

"You must be Mr. Miles," she says, putting out her hand.

I'm still fuming.

I don't shake her hand, but she picks up on that immediately. Putting her hands on her waist, she says, "Nobody panic. We have some damage control to do, and then we're leaving for the next stop on the tour."

Isaac and I follow her as she leads us to a room in the hotel to talk in private. As we walk, I just keep hearing *damage control* in my head. It feels like it's a little too late for that. Everything has gotten too out of hand, and the last thing I feel like we have at this moment is control.

Twenty-Nine

Lola sits across from me at a large conference table while my publicist and tour manager stand at the front of the room, discussing with each other how they can use this sudden onslaught of attention to their benefit.

I still can't understand what on earth we're even talking about.

"So I wrote a love song," I bark with my hands in my hair. "Who cares?"

"Theo, let us be very clear. We see no issue with the song or with any of the rumors," Martina, my publicist, says as her eyes dash back to Jensen, who is standing against the wall with his arms crossed.

"But with any good PR, it's always best to be three steps ahead and play the long game."

"What does that even mean?" I ask with a whine.

"It means...we have to have a plan."

"A plan for what?" I ask. I can hear how erratic and frustrated I sound. It's because I feel it. She's talking about getting ahead, but everything is flying at the speed of light. It hasn't even been twenty-four hours since I played that song, and already the public is speculating about my sexuality. What exactly am I supposed to get ahead of?

Martina sits down at the table and pulls up her phone. She slides it over to me face up. And right there on the screen is a video taken less than two hours ago, out front of the hotel.

Jensen is holding me to his chest—not like a friend, but like a lover.

I glance up at him and he rubs at his forehead. I can practically see the veins popping out of his neck from here.

"It'll blow over," I say with a shrug. "People will forget. We just have to say nothing and move on like it never happened."

Martina nods with a small smile. "Theo—"

"Isaac," Jensen barks. "His name is Isaac. If we're going to discuss his personal life, the least you can do is call him by his real name."

My heart bursts so large in my chest I can barely breathe as I glance up at him with adoration in my eyes.

Martina continues, "Isaac, we fully support your decision to either make a statement or stay silent in this scenario. However, we would be remiss not to warn you that making a statement of this caliber during your first major tour at the height of your success—and at the precipice of award season—could have a harrowing effect on the trajectory of your career."

It's like she's just placed hundred-pound weights on my shoulders.

"Jesus," Lola mutters with annoyance. I glance over at her and she gives a subtle shake of her head. I don't need her to say another word for me to understand that she's saying I don't need to listen to this corporate bullshit.

But Martina is right. And Lola is right. And Jensen is right.

And every voice in the world could be screaming at me at once and it wouldn't make any of this easier to decide. Or make any of these choices more right than the other. It has to be up to me and Jensen.

"I can't decide anything right now," I say with defeat.

"And you don't have to," Martina replies, touching my hand. "But if that's the case, we need to discuss behavior and boundaries."

"Like what?" I ask, narrowing my eyes at her.

"Staying out of the public eye for the next three or four days. After that, you should only be seen alone or with your band-mates. Don't give them any fuel for their fire. No more hotel stays. You have to go directly from your bus to the stage and back. And that's it."

The weight just feels heavier. I want to look at him so badly, but I'm afraid. What she's implying is that Jensen and I can't be together anymore, at least for a while. What if he agrees? What if he thinks this is more than he wants to deal with and I'm not worth it?

"Okay," I murmur sadly as I glance down at the video replaying over and over on her phone. He looks so protective in the clip. Because that's who he is—my protector. The only person in this room concerned with protecting Isaac over Theo. And I can't even see him anymore.

"You have a few days' break after your next show in Chicago and then some television appearances we have set up. It will be the perfect opportunity to redirect the conversation publicly. During your break, we can fly you back to Austin, and you can spend that time in your house, out of the public eye. Sound good?"

I swallow what feels like knives in my throat. "So I can't see him at all?"

The air in the room turns thick with that one question. In a tiny room full of my closest friends, and that one admission is stifling. I couldn't imagine it on a massive scale.

"Just for a little while," Martina says with a fake sweet smile. "You're right. It will blow over, mostly. But when the public sees there's something to grab onto, they will. Don't give them anything. At least not until you're ready. Then you just need to give us a heads-up first so we can devise a plan."

I nod. Everyone around me stands up, but I'm frozen in place. For the first time in a few minutes, I glance up at Jensen. There is so much stress on his face it breaks my heart.

"Can we just...have the room for a few minutes?" I ask.

Martina nods. "Of course. We'd be happy to escort Mr. Miles wherever he needs to go when you're done."

Her words land like cement in my stomach. I *hate* this.

"Thanks," he mutters angrily.

Rio shakes my shoulder in an act of support before he leaves the room. Lola gives me a tight smile. Waylon and Hugh both wave at me with sympathetic expressions.

As the door closes, I turn toward Jensen. There are no words left to say. Nothing we haven't discussed or faced. There is just the circumstance and its overbearing, suffocating weight.

And when there are no words left to say, there is only action. I stand from my chair and cross the room, hoping I make it into his arms before the tears come.

He closes the distance, pulling me tight to his chest. Burying my face in his neck, I squeeze out the tears in my eyes as I clench them shut tight.

"I'm so sorry," I sob.

"Don't be sorry," he replies. "It's going to be okay."

"You're just saying that," I argue. "But I'm scared."

"Scared of what?" he asks, forcing out a sad laugh.

"Scared you'll realize I'm not worth all of this."

"This?" he asks in astonishment. "You think this is bad?" His arms squeeze around me tighter. "Isaac," he mumbles, with his lips against my head. "I'd walk through hell for you."

I hold back a sob and squeeze my arms around him, gripping him so tight I wish I didn't have to walk away.

Kissing my head, he whispers, "You are worth everything to me."

When I pull my face from his neck, he holds my jaw gently

in his hand as he leans in and kisses me softly. I just hope he means the things he says. I feel it in his touch and the look in his eyes. But I wish I could look into the future and see that it's him and me at the end of it all. Only then could I properly relax.

†

To evade some of the drama in Nashville, we head out later that night to drive toward Chicago. We play in Chicago in two nights and then we have another week off because my publicist scheduled us for some TV spots.

Lying alone in my bed on the bus, nothing feels as exciting as it did yesterday. Suddenly, I don't care about performances on late shows or award show nominations. My life feels broken and in disarray.

Luke and Sadie call after they hear the news and I video chat with them for a while, doing my best to prove to them how *okay* I am. But I see the pity on their faces.

Talk about champagne problems. Please stop pitying the celebrity.

Jensen calls as soon as he lands in Austin, but our phone call feels empty and cold. I try not to look too much into it. This will pass. It has to.

I waste a couple hours on the drive watching mindless television and playing games on my phone. After falling asleep sometime between two and three in the morning, I wake up to the sound of my phone ringing around nine in the morning.

When I don't recognize the number, I hit ignore and go back to sleep. They call again. And again.

So when paranoia sets in, I open my eyes and answer it.

"Hello?" I ask with grit and anger in my voice.

I only hear breathing on the other end of the call.

"What the fuck," I mutter. "Who's there?"

Is this the kind of bullshit I have to deal with now? Random fans get a hold of my personal goddamn number and call just to hear me answer.

"Isaac?"

It's a deep, familiar voice that makes my heart seize up in my chest. My entire body is frozen as I wait for him to say something else.

"Is that you?" he asks, and my eyes widen, confirming my suspicion.

"What do you want?" I ask, trying to keep my voice steady. "How'd you get this number?"

"I saw your video on the internet. I had no idea... You're...a country star now."

My father's southern drawl sounds raspier than I remember, aged with time and poor life choices. It's like static that hurts my ears to hear.

"You can't...call me," I reply, trying to sound more confident than I feel. "You shouldn't even have my number."

"It wasn't easy," he replies. "I was up half the night, pullin' strings and makin' calls."

As soon as I signed with the record label, they offered to give me a new phone with a private number, but I didn't see the point. I had been Theo Virgil with this number for years. There was no reason to go and change it.

Now, I guess I understand the reason.

"What do you want?" I growl into the phone line. "You want to rub all this shit in my face now? You want to try and make my life even worse than it already is?"

"No," he replies, and I can't believe how different he sounds. Not at all the loud, boisterous father I once knew who used to yell at us boys as kids. He used his voice as his power at home and at church.

Now...it's meek and tired. He's been beaten down, and I guess he had it coming.

"I just wanted to say...I'm proud of you."

Sitting up in my bed, I drag my fingers through my hair as I let this moment set in. He's *proud* of me? The man who once waved a Bible in my face and told me I was going to hell. The man who used to smack us around when we didn't fall in line. The man who looked at me like I had killed his pride and joy the moment I told him I was gay.

I hate myself for the way it feels to hear him say that. To know I did what I had set out to do, to make him proud. From the first time I strummed a chord on my guitar, I have been doing nothing but trying to make him proud.

Even after everything.

I hate myself for how much I still want it.

"You're *proud* of me?" I ask with the threat of tears in my voice.

"I know I haven't been the best father, and I'll probably never get a chance to say it to your face, but I stayed up all night trying to get your number just to tell you that."

"Am I supposed to be grateful?"

He lets out a sigh, and he sounds so old as if he's withering away.

"Isaac, listen to me," he says, and it takes everything in me not to hang up right then. "Go home."

"What?"

"Go see your mother. She misses you more than you'll ever know."

"It's your fault I left," I bite back with tears in my eyes.

"I know, and I can't fix what I've done. But now that I'm gone, you should go home. Be with your family. And I won't bother you anymore."

I blink, and a tear slips over my cheek. Is he serious right now? Is this bullshit supposed to make me forgive him? He's trying to act like the hero—like he can make everything right?

I want to tell him to fuck off. I *should* tell him to fuck off.

But I don't. Maybe because it would feel like kicking an old man already on the ground. He's lost everything, so what would be the point? Even if he deserves to be told to fuck off.

When I say nothing for a while, he lets out another sigh, this one sounding more like relief.

"Well, that's all I wanted to say. That I'm so proud of you. And that I think it's time for you to go home. I love you, son."

In a panic, I hit the red end call button. Dropping my phone on the bed, I stare at it in shock. Tears stream down my face as I try to make sense of what the fuck just happened.

Eleven years ago

Isaac

My mother dishes me a piece of lasagna with a spatula and a smile. Dad is at the end of the table, droning on and on about some drama at the church, while Adam nods obediently at his side.

Caleb is sitting across from me. I make eye contact with him briefly, each of us doing a subtle eye roll in response to Dad's incessant complaining. Caleb got married last year and moved into his new place with his new wife, Briar. She's at Bible study with her mom and sister tonight, which means he could come home for family dinner like he never left.

I love nights like these. When two of my three brothers are back home. I hate being the only son left. It makes me the constant target. Mom smothers me with attention, which is nice sometimes. But for an almost eighteen-year-old, it would be nice to have someone around I could actually confide in.

And Dad just keeps pushing me to be more like Adam. Come to church. Go to college. Get a girlfriend.

I am like a bomb about to explode. The spark is nearing the end of the wick, and I'm not sure how much longer I have until I lose it.

"What the hell has this world come to?" my dad complains and I glance his way with a nudge of anxiety under my skin. "What happened to good old American family values?"

"I think we should give the Millers some grace," my mother says sweetly, looking at me with a wink. "Wouldn't we all want the same?"

"Grace?" my dad bellows. "They don't need grace, Melanie. What they need is a good study of the scripture. They want to have their queer son's wedding at our church and damn us all to hell."

"Truett," she says in a quiet, scolding tone.

I lift my head and stare at my father. "Wait, who wants to have their wedding at our church?"

"Just a new family in town," my mother answers for him. "They have a son about Adam's age, and they requested to have his wedding at our church."

My dad huffs in disgust. "Over my dead body."

"He's gay?" I ask quietly.

"I don't think this is an appropriate dinner table conversation," my mom says, trying to change the subject. "Caleb, tell us about your new car."

But no one takes the bait. Instead, Caleb and Adam are both watching me with caution. I can see by the look in their eyes that they're praying I won't cause a scene. Don't make a fuss. Don't explode. No matter how much you want to.

Dad glances up and stares into my eyes with a challenging expression. "Your mother's right," he says. "We don't need to talk about it anymore."

No one answers my question or approaches the subject again. Caleb eventually starts talking about the new car he just got, and Adam takes a call up in Dad's office. Dinner continues without incident, but I don't listen to a word. In my head, I'm just having a silent argument with my dad. How could this be what God intended? How could a man who preaches love and acceptance of their neighbors be filled with such hate and bigotry?

The longer I sit and stew on it, the more worked up I get.

By the time my mom serves the dessert, I look around the table and realize I'm sitting with the four people who are supposed to have my back. They're my family.

But they don't. They want me to be different. To be quiet. To be so small, I disappear.

There's a whole wide world of people out there who would love and accept me the way I am, but I'm forced to live between the same four walls as the people who would hurt me the most.

Maybe I should just disappear.

Maybe that way, they wouldn't have to worry about the son who's different. Or the gay wedding that would curse them all to hell. Or the mess I would make of their perfect little lives.

"You don't like your cherry pie?" my mom asks, touching my arm.

My expression remains flat as I push the plate away. "No, I don't."

As I stand up and walk out of the dining room, I hear my father bellow, "Isaac Goode, you get back here right this instant."

"Why should I?" I mutter under my breath.

"Because I told you to," he shouts, but I ignore him. And it only makes him more angry.

"Isaac, what has gotten into you?" Mom asks as she stands from the table, looking at me with a hint of anger in her eyes. My mother is never angry with me, but I can see now that she is. Why? Because I'm disturbing the peace, and she *hates* that.

Well, I hate a lot of shit I put up with around here, and I'm sick of it.

"What has gotten into *me*?" I argue. "You're all such hypocrites. You sit here and discuss another family and their gay son like it's such a fucking curse."

My dad stands up like a rocket. There is vitriol on his face, and I honestly have no idea how I'm related to him. How did I come from him? We are nothing alike.

"Go to your room," he barks, but I don't move.

"I'll go to my room," I reply in defeat. "Because you don't want to see me, right? You're disgusted by me, aren't you?"

"Stop it," he snaps.

"No, I'm done hiding and making myself smaller and quiet for you."

"Isaac," my mother pleads. "Stop it, baby."

"I don't want to stop it anymore," I reply, pulling at my hair in frustration. "None of you here really care about me. Not *really*."

"Don't say that," my mother argues with a gasp. "Of course we do."

I turn my enraged eyes on my dad. "Are you sure about that?"

"What in the hell are you going on about? What has gotten into you?" he asks with pained worry.

"I'm gay," I say flatly.

"No, you're not," he says, like this is something up for debate. Like I'm saying it just to anger him.

"Yes, I am. And I'm sorry if that makes me a disappointment to you."

"Go to your room," he bellows again, ignoring my argument.

"I'm just like the Millers' kid, which I guess means that my presence only curses you to hell. Isn't that right?"

"I said go to your room, boy. I swear…" He shakes his head in anger as if losing his temper would somehow be my fault. And tonight, I'm in the mood to push him. Maybe if I make him mad enough, he'll be the one to explode.

I've been tiptoeing around him for so long, I'm ready to push all of his buttons just to see how much damage I can do.

"Why should I? Because just the sight of me makes you sick? You think a good read of the scripture is going to *cure* me?" I hold up my hands to make air quotes.

Adam is watching us from the hall. "Isaac, stop it."

Caleb stands up, but he's looking at Adam. Neither of them knows which side to take or what to do. It's stupid of me to do this without Luke here, the one brother I always know will have my back.

"Why should I be the one to stop, Adam? Why can't I speak my truth?"

Dad takes a step toward me, and I watch him with worry. He hasn't laid a hand on me since I was a little kid and those were disguised as spankings.

My hands are shaking as I stare at my dad, trying to understand the look in his eyes. It's not just anger anymore. It's fear and sadness too. I'm not just making him mad. I'm breaking his heart.

"Go ahead, Dad. Say it. Tell me to get out. Tell me to leave forever because if you're going to be an ignorant bigot to the rest of the world, you have to be one to your own son—"

His hand slaps hard against my cheek, and I hear a collective gasp from everyone in the room. Facing the floor, I hold my cheek and feel the adrenaline course through my body.

"That's enough!" my mother screams as she rushes around the table and puts herself between us. She covers my hand with hers and strokes my back as a form of comfort. "You boys never know when to quit, do you? Always fighting. Always yelling at each other, and I can't take another minute!"

My eyes and throat sting as I fight off the tears. My father storms off to the living room as I force myself to feel the burn on my cheek from my father's hand. I want to remember this feeling. The pain, the anger, the torment. Because after tonight, when I'm gone, I'll need to remember why I left. I never want to forget this feeling because it will drive me for the rest of my life.

After tonight, I'll show him that I don't need him anymore. I'll show him just how good and amazing I can be *without* him, and it won't matter that I'm gay or that his God won't accept me this way. I will live a long, happy, successful life alone.

And I'll never have to see Truett Goode again.

THIRTY

"You just hung up?" I ask. My phone is resting on the pillow next to me, and Isaac's reclined on his bed on the tour bus.

"Yeah. I have nothing to say to him."

"Good," I reply with a nod. "I'm proud of you."

"I just...can't believe after all this time and everything he's done...he just called me."

I sit up and run a hand through my hair. Picking up my phone, I take Isaac with me as I amble into the bathroom to clean up.

"I can't even fathom trying to understand that man's decisions," I say before dousing cold water on my face.

"Neither can I," he replies.

"How are you feeling about it?" I ask.

Isaac shrugs. "He told me something that sort of...stuck with me."

"What?" I ask, hearing a car door slam in front of my house. I quickly grab a pair of sweats and a T-shirt draped over the chair in my room.

"He told me that I should go home."

My brow furrows as I pull the shirt on over my head. "Go home? What's that supposed to mean?"

"Like I think he was saying...now that he's gone, I should go home and be with the family."

I pause, tugging my shirt down. "Well, isn't that insightful?" I say with sarcasm.

"He's changed. A lot."

"Prison will do that to you."

"The old Truett was so self-righteous, he would have never budged on his convictions like that. But he...told me he was proud of me. Didn't say a word about you or the rumors. I mean...he told me he loved me."

"And that's a new thing?" I ask a moment before the front doorbell rings.

"Yeah. He never said stuff like that to us growing up."

"That's just sad," I reply as I make my way down the hall. My father was always affectionate with me. He tells me every day of my life that he loves me.

"Who's at your door?" he asks.

"I have no idea."

"Be careful," Isaac says. "Don't just answer it in case it's, like, paparazzi or something. I don't like you being there alone."

"I'll be fine, babe. But that's sweet of you to worry," I reply with a chuckle as I pull back the curtain in my living room and peek out to find a man standing on my front doormat.

Shit.

"It's your brother," I mutter without enthusiasm.

"Which one?"

"The one who hates me," I grumble.

"Luke hates everyone," he replies.

I pull open the front door with a flat expression. While staring at Lucas Goode standing in front of me, I hold my phone in my hand with Isaac on the other line.

"Isaac, I'll have to call you back."

"Be nice, Lucas," Isaac says loudly, but his brother doesn't react.

"Bye," I say before hanging up.

As I slide my phone into my back pocket, I step aside and let Luke enter my house.

"Want some coffee?" I ask as I shut my door and make my way into the kitchen. I wasn't exactly expecting company today, but it's not like I'm surprised he's standing here after the hailstorm of publicity his brother and I have received this week.

The only thing I don't know is if this is going to be a talking conversation or an arguing conversation. I'm ready for either.

"Yes, please," he mutters, sounding tired as he drops into a chair at my small kitchen dinette.

I get started making a pot of coffee and watch him out of the corner of my eye. I'll wait for him to start.

"I've given a lot of thought to you two," he says with an exasperated sigh.

"And?"

"He clearly cares about you a lot," he says.

I nod while scooping coffee grounds into the basket. "I care about him a lot. I love him."

"I could tell he loved you, even before the show that night. I know Isaac well, probably better than anyone. I know he puts up a front and pretends that everything is a joke or can be laughed off, but deep down, he's just scared and lonely like the rest of us. And just because your job doesn't bother him doesn't mean it's not a risk."

"I know that," I mutter as I turn toward him.

He relaxes in his chair and stares at me. "All that said...I think you could be really good for him, and I hope this works out."

My brows shoot upward. Then, a smile slowly creeps across my face. "That was unexpected."

He shrugs. "I'm an unpredictable guy."

For some reason, this makes me laugh, mostly because I know

he's full of shit, and he's probably the most predictable guy in their whole family.

"So, what changed your mind?" I ask, pulling down mugs from the cabinet.

"He did," Luke replies bluntly.

I pause and turn toward him with expectation.

"Eleven years ago, Isaac showed up on my doorstep with so much anger and resentment against not just our father but the world. Then, he turned that anger and resentment into fire. It has fueled him in every way since the day he left. He hides it well behind sarcasm and wit, but the truth is that even his career doesn't make him truly happy. Even his success is a by-product of what our father did to him.

"But since he met you...he's different. It's like...getting to see the real Isaac again. The one who isn't living in the shadow of that man anymore. His smiles aren't ironic anymore. He's just happy. And I think all along, what he really needed was someone who could prove to him that not all preachers are bad. Not all men of faith are cruel. Not everyone who comes into his life wants something from him or wants him to change."

Frozen in my kitchen, I stare at the man at the table who's talking about the person I love, and it suddenly hits me that it doesn't matter that this world is much bigger than me and Isaac. Because as long as I can be what he needs, and he can be what I need, then nothing else matters. Opinions and rumors don't fucking matter.

"I don't want Isaac to change at all," I say. "I love him very much."

Luke's chest expands with a long breath before he nods. "I know you do, so I will not bother asking you to take good care of him. Because I know you'll just tell me you plan to."

"I do plan to."

"That's the best any of us can do, right?"

"Right."

Turning around, I pour coffee into the mugs and bring them

over to the table before grabbing the creamer from the fridge. Then Luke and I have our coffee and make small talk, and for a moment, everything seems fine.

I don't tell him about Truett's call to Isaac because that's not my story to tell, but I am curious if Luke knows Isaac's plans to reunite with their family. But I let him bring it up.

"If he comes back home, you'll be with him, I hope," he says, taking a sip of his coffee.

"I wouldn't miss it," I reply.

"Good. You'll get a front-row view of my older brother murdering me on the dining room table. Right next to the mashed potatoes."

I can't help but chuckle. "You think he'll be that mad to learn that you've been taking care of Isaac all this time?"

"Livid."

"And what about your other brother? He won't be mad?" I ask, trying to keep them all straight even though I haven't met this other brother yet.

Luke makes an uncertain expression. "He'll be mad, but he's my twin. He won't let Adam kill me, but he might let him kick my ass."

I wish I knew what it's like having brothers. From the sound of it, they all give each other hell as much as they look out for each other.

"On the bright side," Luke says. "Isaac dating you might be distracting enough to keep me alive."

I laugh again as I finish the coffee in my mug. "I'm glad Isaac had you to run to. I'm glad he wasn't alone all this time."

"Me too," Luke replies with a nod.

"Sadly, sometimes the ones who stay suffer a worse fate."

Luke gives me a grim look. "True."

To my relief, he doesn't press the topic, and I don't expand on it. How I was one of those kids who stayed, and how I'm so grateful Isaac never had to go through what I did.

Just after Luke leaves, I get a text from Isaac.

I smile down at it before responding.

A moment later, his reply comes in.

†

The beauty of modern technology is that even when I'm home in Texas, I can log onto nearly any social media site and search up Theo Virgil, and at least one or two people have live stream footage or story clips of his concert.

Lying in bed, I watch him play on the stage, and it's moments like these I can't believe that he's mine. He's so talented I can hardly believe how easy he makes it all look. He memorizes the chords to every song, every lyric, every set change and every key of every song.

I've also noticed in the past few months, even before I met him in person, that Isaac, or should I say, Theo, has been throwing in more sex appeal into each of his performances. He clearly knows what the fans enjoy, so now he comes out with his shirt entirely unbuttoned, his sexy-as-hell washboard abs on display as he sings. Now I think he's doing it just to drive me crazy.

I can see how much he loves this. Music and performing are his passions. His real, true love. This is what has kept him going over the last eleven years and maybe even longer. Lucas mentioned how Isaac turned all of his anger into fire, and I can see that now.

He has taken every bad thing he's endured and turned it into something wonderful. Something that feeds the souls of others.

In the middle of the show, he takes a little break to address the audience. Girls scream his name and call out "I love yous" to him. He blushes onstage as he wipes the sweat from his brow before replacing his cowboy hat and grinning down at his adoring fans.

I know he was nervous about tonight. It's his first show since the whole fiasco and the first show since his secret song to me. The crowd still loves him, and I want to believe in my heart that they would continue to love him even if they found out the rumors were true.

"Play the new song!" someone screams, and he laughs behind the mic.

"You guys want to hear the new song again?" he asks.

They all cheer in response, mostly women shouting out, "Woo!" Then, every person in the stadium pulls out their phones to record.

"All right, all right," Isaac says with a chuckle. "I gotta change my guitar. Hang on."

They all laugh, like anything he says is hilarious. I see the slight difference between Isaac and Theo in moments like these. When he's performing, he's not a different person entirely, but there are just cute things he says and the way he talks that he does only for an audience.

The real Isaac, the man I know...I like to believe that's just for me.

He switches his guitar and the crowd quiets down. As he starts to strum, I watch the video with tears in my eyes, remembering the night he played it for me in his living room.

"This is for you," he mumbles into the mic. "You know who you are."

The crowd cheers as if he's dedicating it to them. I cover my mouth with my hand as I stare at him. He's thousands of miles away, still loving me.

The song is as beautiful as it was the first time I heard it. He's growing more comfortable with it, I can tell. Every time he plays it, he riffs on the bridge a bit more, and on that last chorus he adds some grit to his voice, practically growling out the last few lines. My heart nearly leaps out of my chest at the sound, and a warm arousal pools in my groin.

God, I miss him.

I wish I were backstage right now, waiting for him. I'd pull him into the closest bathroom, and I'd get on my knees for him in a heartbeat. I'd show him who his true biggest fan is.

When the song comes to an end, I lie down in my bed and prop up the phone to watch him as I fall asleep.

At some point in the middle of the night, my phone rings and wakes me. I pick it up and see his name on the screen. With a smile, I swipe the call.

"Hey," I rasp, still half-asleep.

"Shit, did I wake you?"

"It's okay," I mumble. "How was the show? I watched some of it on some grainy live stream."

"It was great. The crowd was crazy tonight."

"Good," I reply. "Where are you now?"

"On the bus in bed. I miss you." He sounds tired. His voice has a slightly gritty edge to it, like it often does after his shows.

"I miss you too," I reply sleepily. "I listened to the song."

"Did you like it?" he asks as if he needs my validation. As if *my* opinion matters. I chuckle lightly as I reply, "I fucking loved it."

"Good."

After a few moments of silence, I sleepily add, "Isaac..."

"Yeah?"

"I think I'm ready."

He pauses before replying. I know I don't need to clarify what I'm ready for. He already knows.

"I think I'm ready too," he says, and the sound of his familiar voice goes straight to my heart.

"You're coming to Austin tomorrow, right?" I ask.

"Yeah." There's a quiver in his voice, and it sounds like excitement.

"And you want to go to your mom's for dinner on Sunday night before you head out again for the TV appearances?"

He takes a deep breath, and I wish more than anything that I could hold his hand in this moment.

"Yeah, I do," he replies. "I'm ready."

"Then let's say fuck the rules. I'll be there with you."

"Once we tell them, Jensen, there's no going back," he says with a tone of caution.

"Good," I reply as I close my eyes again, my phone resting on my cheek. Already drifting back to sleep, I add, "I don't want to go back."

Thirty-One

Isaac

I'm sitting alone in my living room when the doorbell chimes, alerting me that someone is at the gate. I nearly leap out of my seat and run to the security panel.

Luke is in his car with the window rolled down, and I quickly buzz him through. He has dark tint on his windows, which is good because the last time I checked, there was a small crowd of paparazzi on the street, waiting to see me slip and, I don't know, accidentally make out with someone on the sidewalk or something.

If I want to come and go, I have to take a chauffeur, and I've been *advised* not to have any guests other than bandmates and family members. I'm only home for three days until I leave again. I'm supposed to be on some fucking late-night show next week, and I'm too busy stressing about public rumors to be excited about it.

It's not just a musical performance on the show. They want to talk to me. Apparently, fans eat up my interviews as much as my music, so I'm hoping I can shove all of this aside and pull out my winning personality for one night.

There's a lot riding on tonight first.

I got back to Austin the day before yesterday, and I've been completely alone since. Thankfully, most of the media attention has had a chance to simmer down a bit since that night in Nashville.

Luke pulls his car around and parks it in my garage for added privacy. I'm waiting by the door when I hear their car doors slam. Then, the door opens and Jensen walks through first.

A breath of relief pours out of me as I rush over to where he's standing and throw my arms around him. He holds me impossibly tight, breathing into my neck.

Pulling away, I hold his face as I bring his lips to mine. We don't bother saying *I miss you* anymore. It's redundant and unnecessary. I miss him even when he's standing right in front of me. So it's pointless to say it when he's states away.

Luke and Sadie walk in with Henry in a car seat carrier. Reluctantly, Jensen and I break up our kiss since it can't really get any hotter with my brother and his family around.

I hug Luke and Sadie next. "Thanks for bringing him. We couldn't risk him driving to my house."

"I understand," Luke replies. "And we're happy to help."

My brother checks on me with a hand on my shoulder. "You ready for this?"

"Are you?" I reply.

He tilts his head. "Stop deflecting and answer the question. Besides, I feed off people being angry at me. I'm not worried about our brothers."

"Yes, I'm ready," I snap with irritation. My hand is clutched in Jensen's as he squeezes it.

Sadie walks up and throws her arm over my shoulder. "If you want to bail at any second, just give me a wink and we are out of there, okay?"

I rest my head on her shoulder. "Okay."

Out of everyone here, it feels like Sadie gets it the most. We don't like heavy emotions, and more than likely, tonight, people will be crying, which means I am going to want to get as far away as I can.

But I need to do this like a Band-Aid. Just rip it off and be done with it.

"Okay, let's get this over with," I mutter, nodding toward the car.

After locking up the house, I climb into the back seat of Luke's car with Jensen. Baby Henry is in the rear-facing car seat, smiling up at the two of us on either side as we pull out onto the road.

Watching Henry smile up at Jensen calms my nerves. Jensen gently tickles under his chin and Henry giggles, drool hanging from his pudgy little baby lip.

I glance up at Jensen, noticing how enamored he seems with my nephew. He has a way with him that seems natural. Is this something he would want someday?

Hell, is this something *I* would want someday? To be honest, I haven't given much thought past my career. That was always the only goal. Relationships, family, future thoughts were never on my mind.

Just for fun, I try on the idea. Having a little kid in my life. A kid who would be mine. Who would call me Dad. A kid who would count on me.

Will Jensen still be in the picture? Is it too soon to think stuff like that? Probably, but I can't help it. I mean...look at him. He's a natural. Who wouldn't want to start a family with him?

Suddenly, all that *daddy* energy makes sense. He is legit *dad material*.

Then I think about the long term. A chance to do things right. To raise a kid in the right environment. To give our kids the chance we never had.

Those would be some lucky fucking kids.

Jensen glances up at me and our eyes lock as if we're thinking the same thing. It doesn't matter that it's way too early to be thinking stuff like this, because we're thinking it anyway. We're just two people who never thought we'd be in this situation or have this opportunity. I surely never saw myself settling down and Jensen obviously had no plans of ever attempting long term with anyone, let alone a man.

It feels incredibly freeing to finally imagine these things now.

"What's wrong?" Sadie asks Luke, and I glance up at them with concern. He looks in the rearview mirror.

"You see that car? It's been following us."

She turns around, as we all do. It's a black sedan I don't recognize, but there's nothing really out of the ordinary about it.

When Luke pulls off the highway at our exit, the black car does too. Then, to our relief, it turns in the opposite direction at the traffic light.

I glance up at my brother, who doesn't bother looking relaxed, and I'm assaulted by guilt. Is this how it's going to be now? Paranoia for the rest of my life. The sooner I come out, the sooner they can all get over it.

"See?" I say, turning forward. "Nothing to worry about."

A few moments later, Luke pulls up to my mother's house and all of the good feelings in my stomach turn to ice. Seeing this house again feels like being punched in the gut.

We discussed it earlier and decided to serve the family with the surprise of a lifetime, which means we haven't told any of them I'm coming. Why? Because I'm a dick sometimes, and while I know they probably could have used some time to mentally and emotionally prepare, I was slightly afraid that if I told them I was coming, I'd back out last minute and feel like shit for it.

So...*surprise*.

Luke pulls into the large circular driveway before anyone else has arrived. We planned to come early on purpose—for Mom. She deserves a few minutes alone with me before the chaos ensues.

Jensen and Luke both open their mouths to speak at the same time, but I quickly interject.

"If either of you asks if I'm ready again, I'm going to walk back home. Got it?"

They both close their mouths. "Got it," Jensen says.

Sadie winks at me from the front seat.

Henry starts to get fussy as soon as the car stops moving, so we all climb out of the car. It's like there's a weight on my chest as I stare up at the same house I walked out of eleven years ago.

This is the house seventeen-year-old me stood in while my father slapped me across the face for telling him I was gay—for calling him a bigot. This is where I stood that night when I promised myself I'd never return.

I freeze on the front porch steps. Jensen is by my side when he glances my way. Everyone stops and looks at me as if waiting for me to make the first move.

"If I walk in there...am I betraying the kid who ran away?"

Luke turns toward me with the baby on his hip. His eyes bore into me with severity as he says, "You're not betraying anyone. You got that kid out, Isaac. But you hold the power now, which means you can choose to leave. And having that choice is what really matters."

The tension melts away from my shoulders as I stare at my big brother.

Sadie reaches out and squeezes my arm. "You're not betraying anyone, Isaac."

I smile at her before nodding to Luke.

"Thanks. Okay...let's do this."

Luke reaches for the front door first. I stand behind him, sliding my hand into Jensen's. There are no cameras or paparazzi here. So he leans in and presses his lips to my temple.

Suddenly, I feel grounded and safe.

The first thing that hits me when I walk in the door is the scent. It's the smell of home, so deep within my psyche that I forgot it even existed. I couldn't put a name on it if I tried. It's my childhood and holidays and hugs from my mother all rolled into one.

"Hey, Mom," Lucas calls. "We're early."

The four of us step into the house with Henry in Luke's arms, and I'm hiding behind him like a scared child.

"Okay, darlin'," my mother calls from the kitchen. "I'm just putting the casserole in the oven." Goose bumps erupt over my skin.

I've spoken to my mother regularly since I left. She and Luke were the only two who had tabs on me the whole time.

But hearing her voice in person now, knowing she's in the next room, hits me with a tidal wave of emotion I wasn't expecting. Already, I want to turn and bolt out the door.

I force myself to swallow, although my throat feels like it's closing up on me at the moment. My molars clench so tight I can feel the muscles clicking in my jaw.

"Gimme that grandbaby," she says as she turns the corner into the foyer while wiping her hands on a kitchen towel and tossing it over her shoulder.

She falters when she notices two extra people in her entryway. She looks at Jensen first. Then, she looks at me.

My mother has aged so much in the past eleven years. Her light-blonde hair is mostly gray now and her skin seems so much softer. Otherwise, she is exactly how I remember.

Her eyes hold that motherly sense of intuition they always did. As if she knows everything, but will never let anyone see it.

Tears fill her eyes as she stares at me. I can't move. Maybe I should be the one to run to her, but I can't. It's hard enough to just pull air into my lungs at the moment.

Nobody moves for what feels like ages. Then my mom walks toward me. There's a shake in her hands as she wrings them in front of her. The others step aside, and when my mother reaches me, she places her hand on my cheek, smiling up at me with tears in her eyes.

"Welcome home, baby," she whispers.

"Thanks, Mama," I reply, feeling like a little kid all of a sudden. Her arms wrap around my neck and she pulls me roughly toward her for a hug. I have to practically fold myself in half to reach her, but I relax into her embrace.

I haven't had a mom hug in eleven years, and I hadn't thought much about how much I missed it, but now I'm remembering how good it feels. With the scent of an old perfume and fresh-baked cookies, she pats my back and squeezes me tight and makes everything feel just a little easier.

When she pulls away, her mascara is smudged under her eyes, and she makes a big fuss about fixing it. Then, she grabs my hand and looks at Jensen.

"And who is this?" she asks without hesitation.

My chest feels tight as I put my other hand out toward him. "Mom, this is Jensen Miles. He's my...boyfriend."

I see the moment in my mother's eyes when she puts it all together. I have no doubt that Melanie Goode has kept up with the gossip around Austin when it comes to the church and community she once helped build. I am quite sure she knows exactly who Jensen Miles is, if not by face, then by name.

"Oh," she says, looking at me and then him and back to me.

"Yeah..." I stammer with a nod.

It's going to be a long night.

"It's a pleasure to meet you, ma'am," Jensen says like the perfect fucking gentleman he is.

"You too, Jensen. Welcome to our home," she says.

Then, bless my mother's fucking heart, she turns to Luke and acts like absolutely nothing is out of the ordinary. She steals Henry and gives him big grandma kisses on the cheek like tonight is just any other night.

Luke and Sadie walk ahead of us, and I follow behind, with Jensen by my side.

"One down, two to go," I whisper.

"It's going to be okay," he replies.

As we step into the large dining room, I notice the table is much bigger than I remember. In fact, all the decorations in my mother's house are different. She's updated a lot. But the table is definitely the most jarring.

There are two high chairs pulled up to the table and what looks like six more chairs. It's now a table for twelve, and for some reason, seeing the visual representation of how much my family has changed since I left hits me like a truck.

Is this even still my family? Do I still have a seat at this table? They've moved on since I left. And I know they missed me, but it hurts a little to see that they moved on at the same time. But that's what life does, I guess. It moves on.

✝

No one sits. Maybe we're all a little too anxious.

So we stand around and wait for the others to arrive. Luke brings me a beer and I crack it open with relief. It goes down way too fast.

My mom asks me about the tour and how things have been this week, and I try to spare her from the gory details. I don't want her to worry. It's been intense, but I can handle it.

When we hear a car door close outside, we all tense. The foyer is out of view from here, so we just wait. I consider hiding, but that would be juvenile. It's not exactly the occasion to jump out from behind the couch and shout *surprise*. Although it sounds a lot easier and less tense.

I hear a female's voice outside and then a child's, so I know it must be Caleb and his family. Inching closer to Jensen, I watch the door with anxiety brewing inside me.

This shouldn't be too bad. I saw Caleb a couple years ago, and he got me up to speed on his family and the new addition—Dean —who just happens to be my *ex-boyfriend*.

So, yeah, I don't know why I'm worried. This shouldn't be awkward at all.

The door opens and I hear a little girl arguing with someone in the entryway.

"You cheated!" she shrieks.

"Don't be a sore loser just because I won." I recognize Dean's voice like a ghost from my past. I haven't seen him since I was fifteen years old. He was the first boy I kissed. The first dick I touched. The first person who let me say out loud that I was gay.

Then, one day, he just...disappeared. He stopped hanging out with me and stopped calling. Until poof—he showed up at my brother's house twelve years later and started fucking my brother and his wife.

I'm sure there was more to the story than that, but that's all I caught.

"Daddy, tell Dean he's cheating!"

"Please stop yelling, Peanut," my brother replies.

"You can't let her win *one* thumb wrestle?" Briar mumbles as the family walks into the house.

When they turn the corner and find us all awkwardly hovering around the dining room table, they freeze.

"What the hell—" Caleb mutters before his eyes collide with mine.

"Hey," I stammer as I wave at him.

"Who's that?" Abby says loudly, and I smile down at her. Immediately, I see my brother in her face. Brown hair, big eyes, freckles.

"That's your uncle Isaac," Caleb stutters before eating up the distance between us. "That's my brother."

He's smiling as he pulls me into a tight hug. Patting my back harshly, he lets out a laugh. "It's good to have you back."

To my relief, seeing Caleb again is far more chill than I'm sure seeing Adam will be. He pulls away from our hug and smiles brightly at me. "This is amazing. I can't believe you're really here."

"I'm here," I say, doing an awkward shoulder shrug. When I feel Jensen at my side, I turn toward him. "And this is my boyfriend, Jensen." *Damn, that feels nice to say.*

The two of them do their little handshake greeting. Then Caleb calls over his daughter, and I kneel to greet her as well. To my surprise, she throws her arms around my neck and squeezes me tightly, as if I'm not a complete stranger to her.

When I stand up with tears in my eyes, I make eye contact with Dean for the first time. We might as well be strangers at this point. I'm sure neither of us are the same people we were as teenagers.

"And you remember Dean..." Caleb says as he walks over and puts his arm around the man's back.

I thought I could prepare myself for what it would be like to actually see my brother with another man, but it still shocks me to my core. There's this unspoken conversation Caleb and I haven't had yet. The one where we face the harsh truth about him being queer this whole time and never telling me. Letting me take the brunt of our father's wrath when he could have spoken up, too.

And maybe he never knew. I guess that's a possibility—that until he met Dean and let himself finally admit those feelings, they were so repressed he was blind to his own sexuality.

That will be a fun conversation to have, but not tonight.

Dean has a stoic, cold expression on his face as he faces me. He always was such a serious guy that I know for sure we never would have worked out even if we had made it past fifteen together.

Instead of putting out my hand to shake his, I put my arms out for a hug. Although I'm the one coming home, I'm sure it's awkward for him, too. He's more a part of this family than I am at this point.

"I'm glad you're here," I mumble into our hug.

"I was just thinking the same," he replies as he pats my back.

As we pull apart, I hug Briar too, and introduce them all to Jensen. Then, it's just...normal. It feels like home.

It *is* home.

THIRTY-TWO

Isaac is fidgeting nervously on the sofa next to me. After we all greeted his brother, Caleb, Isaac's mother got a text message that Adam and Sage were running late. So we're in their living room, around the fireplace, catching up while we wait.

Caleb and Dean have gotten Isaac caught up on their lives. Then Isaac explained his rise to success, which everyone was already aware of, of course.

I'm impressed with the family's ability to focus on each other rather than dwell on all the negative things that have happened to them in the past couple of years, mainly involving the patriarch of the family.

But when Caleb turns to his twin and asks, "Were you shocked to see him?" everyone freezes with nervous tension. Isaac looks so uncomfortable that I want to whisk him away from this house to protect him.

No one says anything for a while as we all wait for Caleb to catch on. "What did I miss?" he asks, looking around.

"Isaac was staying with me, Caleb," Luke says bluntly. My

eyes widen at his boldness to just come out with it. Then I squeeze Isaac's hand in mine because I know he has to hate this.

"What?" Caleb asks. "What do you mean he was staying with you? Like this weekend?"

The air is so thick in the room, we could choke on it. I can see the regret in Luke's eyes as he shakes his head.

"No, Caleb. He's been with me since he left."

I slowly watch Caleb's anger build, and Isaac hangs his head as if to hide.

Caleb rises from the couch with hurt in his expression. "And you never told me?"

Suddenly, the two of them start bickering. Caleb harps on Luke for letting him worry over the last eleven years while Luke shouts back that his only priority was keeping their little brother safe.

Then, I look over and see Isaac's eyes clench shut before he pops up off the couch in distress. His brothers continue to fight as Isaac storms from the room, jogging up the stairs and away from the chaos in the living room.

His mother looks at me with concern on her face, but when she moves to follow him, I put a hand up. "I've got him."

Leaving the bickering behind me, I march up the large flight of stairs to the second story of the Goode house in search of Isaac. The house is massive. There's a wing to the right with closed doors, which I assume are bedrooms. To the left, I spot an open door and a shadow cast across the floor.

As I reach the room, I stand in the doorway and watch as Isaac pours whiskey into a short glass on an old bar cart in the corner of a massive office. There is a mahogany desk on the opposite side and an open Bible on the table next to a large leather chair.

Stepping into the room, I close the door behind me to block the sound of his brothers still arguing downstairs. Isaac quickly gulps down the whiskey with a wince before going to pour another.

"Hey, hey, hey," I say softly as I rest a hand on his to stop him. "That's not going to make you feel any better."

"I beg to differ," Isaac replies with a huff.

I peel his hand from the bottle and force him to face me. He seems so closed in on himself. He won't look at me or touch me and that's not like him. Which means I know he's in his head, probably blaming himself for all of this.

"Look at me," I whisper, and his eyes slowly drift up to mine. Then, he suddenly melts into my arms. With his face in my neck, he wraps his arms around my body and we just hold each other for a while.

"None of this is your fault. You know that, right?" I mumble against the side of his head.

"Does it even matter? My brothers are fighting because of me. Did you see how sad my mom looked? It's my fault I haven't seen her in eleven years."

Putting my hands on his face, I force him to look at me. "Isaac, stop. That was *his* fault. You did what you had to in order to survive, and that is never your fault. Your family knows that. They don't blame you for leaving."

Pain carves the features of his face as he closes his eyes and leans into my touch. "Just kiss me," he pleads. "Nothing hurts when you're kissing me."

The corner of my mouth lifts in a smirk as I bring his mouth to mine. Isaac's lips are like heaven, soft and sweet.

"Just say the word, baby. I never want you to hurt."

He smiles against my mouth as his arms hold me tighter, pulling me against him. We can't hear the argument downstairs anymore. It's like Isaac and I live alone in this bubble, safe from everything else in the world.

His tongue glides against mine, and a growling moan escapes my lips. What I meant as one soft kiss is quickly escalating into a heated make-out session.

It takes everything in me to pull away. "We can't be doing this here."

"Why not?" he asks, pulling me in for another scorching kiss. He's clinging to me desperately, forcing a whimper out of me when he squeezes the back of my neck and bites hard on my lower lip.

I'm growing hard behind my zipper as my hands rest on his hips, no matter how much I want to grip him tightly. It feels wrong to be getting so aroused in his mother's home with his family so close by.

"Isaac," I whisper between kisses, but it's no use. He's forcibly trying to seduce me in what I assume is his father's old office while his family is downstairs, and honestly, it's working. I don't know if it's because we haven't seen each other in days or because he just always has this effect on me, but it doesn't matter because when it comes to Isaac Goode, I'm a weak, weak man.

Then he slides a hand down over my pants, squeezing the bulge as he whispers, "Please, Daddy."

"Oh fucking hell," I growl as I clutch his hips in my hands and turn his body, slamming it against a bookcase. When he calls me that, I am powerless. I want to give him everything he wants. I want to *be* everything he wants.

Isaac smiles triumphantly as I kiss him hard, grinding into him until he is moaning against my lips.

"If we get caught, it's your fault," I mutter as my hand slides up, encircling his throat in a gentle grip. "When you say things like that, I lose control."

"I want you to lose control," he replies wickedly.

Reaching down, I hook a hand under his thigh and lift it so I can grind myself even closer. Our cocks align through the thick fabric of our pants, and something about the pressure and the friction is divine.

He throws his head back as I drive my hips against his. Seeing his neck extended before me, I lean in and suck hard on the sensitive flesh.

"Fuck," he cries breathlessly.

I can feel the pulse in his neck as I reach down and quickly undo his pants. I can't believe I'm wrapping my hand around his cock while his family is still right downstairs. We were supposed to be here for his mother's casserole and suddenly, I'm stroking his dick upstairs in his dad's office.

Deviant. Sinner. Wrong, wrong, wrong.

I shove the thought away as I drop to my knees and quickly take Isaac's cock down my throat.

"Oh fuck," he whispers as he grips hard on the bookshelf behind him.

My mouth was made for this cock. I wish I could spend every day of my life worshipping it. Making Isaac feel good is what makes me feel good, and there's nothing sinful or wrong about that. It all feels so right.

He slides his cock along my tongue and I suck gently on the head with every stroke, feeling it grow more and more engorged with each pass of my lips.

If I keep working him like this, I'll have him coming in seconds. Which I should probably do. It's not like we have all the time in the world up here.

But I don't stop. I need his cum too much. I want his pleasure on my face and in my mouth. And I certainly don't give a shit anymore who is waiting on us. Everything in this room is all that matters.

He pulls at my hair as I suck him hard, my eyes cast upward to catch the euphoria on his face. When I feel his cock harden and swell, I hold my tongue and stroke him to his release.

"Fuck, fuck, fuck," he whispers before the orgasm takes him. His boots scrape against the hardwood floor as he comes on my tongue. A few drops of the warmth land on my cheek and I revel in it.

My cock is throbbing in my pants, and I fully intend to let it go, but Isaac takes one look at me with his cum on my face and lets out a growling sound.

"Come here."

With one hand on my throat, he pulls me to my feet. Then,

with a ravenous look on his face that is burned in my memory, he sticks out his tongue and licks a long line across my cheek, cleaning up his own release from my face.

"Holy shit, that was hot," I whisper before kissing him hard. Our tongues tangle salaciously, the saltiness of his release bursting with flavor in our fused mouths.

He's still eager for more as he fumbles with the zipper on my pants. I really should stop him, but I can't help it. It's been days since I felt his touch and I miss it. When he slides his hand in to grab my cock, I stifle a groan.

"Get on your knees, and let me feed you my cock," I whisper into his ear with a hand on his shoulder. He moves to the floor without hesitation. I have to bite my bottom lip with how sexy he looks as he kneels in front of me. He's staring at me as if he's starving for my cock.

Holding my length at the base, I place the other hand on the back of Isaac's neck and slowly slide my shaft between his lips. He sucks on it noisily.

"Better keep it down," I whisper to him. "We wouldn't want anyone to walk in and find you on your knees for me."

He moans quietly around my cock as his head bobs up and down. Getting the base nice and wet, he grips it firmly and strokes it in time with his mouth. I let myself fall into the ecstasy of it. Staring across the room, I take in the large desk where his father once sat.

In some filthy fantasy, I imagine that I'm proving to that man who Isaac belongs to now. He's *mine*. He will always be mine.

Isaac picks up his pace, tightening his lips around the tip of my cock, and it's so intense I can't last another minute. "Shit, Isaac, I'm coming."

Shivers roll up my spine as my body seizes around him. I hold tight to Isaac's head as my cock reaches the back of his throat. He spits and sputters, trying to take every drop of my cum. I'm so strung out on the pleasure of the climax that I almost miss the heavenly sight of Isaac swallowing down every bit. Not a single drop lands anywhere else.

"That's my good boy," I whisper as I stroke his head lovingly.

We're both locked in some post-orgasm haze, and I'm not sure how long we stay like this. Eventually, I pull him to his feet and gather him into my warm embrace.

"We should...get cleaned up for dinner," he says with his face in my neck, and I can't help but laugh. Soon, we're both lost in a fit of quiet laughter. My arms wind around him, holding him close and soaking in this moment.

"Let's get down there."

†

When Isaac and I come out of the office, the fighting downstairs seems to be over, which is a relief. I'm sure that casserole is ice cold by now, but after the appetite Isaac and I just worked up in that office, I'll eat it, anyway.

After a quick stop in the bathroom, we descend the stairs and find that the family is no longer in the living room. Instead, they are gathered around the table. It would appear Adam never showed up after all.

Everyone is staring at us as we enter the room, and a blush rises to my cheeks. Caleb is laughing under his breath as Isaac and I walk down to the empty seats at the table.

"Sorry," Isaac says, clearing his throat. "I didn't know you guys were eating. I just needed to get away for a second."

"It's okay, darling," his mother says. "We just sat down. Haven't even said grace yet."

"Where's Adam?" Isaac asks as he takes a seat at the table.

"Something came up at work," his mother says with a grimace. "We didn't tell him."

Sadly, Isaac nods. "That's okay."

The tension between Caleb and Luke has seemed to die down enough to make things bearable. The man with the buzz cut at

Caleb's side has his hand on his leg in comfort, and I think it's doing a lot to settle his nerves.

"Jensen," Isaac's mother says sweetly. "Would you like to do the honors and say grace tonight?"

I pull in a deep breath before turning toward Isaac to gauge his reaction. I've never even prayed with Isaac before. It feels like my work as a preacher and my life with Isaac are two very different lives.

He gives a subtle nod as his lips press together.

"I'd love to," I reply before turning my gaze downward.

For the briefest moment, a flush of shame courses through me. I'm a fraud. A liar.

You're a failure. You don't deserve to speak to God.

Closing my eyes, I push those thoughts away.

"Heavenly Father, we thank you for the blessing of this meal and for bringing this family together. Tonight is especially meaningful as they gather for the first time in so long, with hearts full of joy for the safe return of Isaac. Bless this food that was so beautifully prepared by Melanie. May we always cherish these times and remember those who are not with us tonight. Amen."

"Amen," Isaac mumbles at my side before the rest of the family joins in. He's staring at me as if he's noticing something for the first time. He doesn't seem put off or uncomfortable, which is a relief. I know it can be jarring to see someone in their element for the first time.

"That was beautiful," Melanie says from the head of the table.

"Thank you," I reply softly.

As we eat, I glance around the table at Isaac's family. I see so much love at this table, but I see pain, too. I can only imagine what they've endured these past few years. Now, Isaac is here, and they are one step closer to being whole again.

Everyone makes casual conversation, and it feels so normal. This is exactly what Isaac needs. The family he deserves.

THIRTY-THREE

ISAAC

Sitting in the back seat, Jensen's hand is in mine, and I feel on top of the world. Even without seeing Adam, which I'll admit was the one I was most anticipating, I'm at peace. It's like there's an entire part of me that can relax for the first time in over a decade.

Leaning my head against the seat, I stare at Jensen beside me. Even though I can see the tension he's trying to hide, I'm grateful he was with me. I would have hated walking in that door alone.

I just hope I wasn't asking too much of him, calling him my boyfriend. To be *out*, even if not publicly. It's still a scary thing for people to know something you've held locked in for your entire life. I should know.

But my situation is a little different than his. His scars run deeper than mine. Sometimes, I worry that his being *out* won't be as liberating as it should be. I'm afraid that the conditioning his mother subjected him to will ruin that monumental occasion for him.

He should only feel love and acceptance, but I'm worried he

won't. I'm worried they've rewired his brain to only feel shame and guilt instead.

I squeeze his hand tighter in mine as if I can hold him here with me—like he might float away on a breeze if I don't.

When we reach my house, I look at him with nervous anticipation. I want him to come in. *Obviously*, I want him to come in. But if he doesn't want to risk it, I understand. But that nervous kid inside me doesn't want to appear too vulnerable or eager.

Luke pulls up the long driveway in front of my house. "Will you stay?" I whisper with Henry sleeping in his car seat between us.

Jensen's dark eyes shimmer in the moonlight as a gentle smile causes them to narrow. "Of course."

My heart leaps with gratitude as he and I climb out together. We take turns hugging Sadie and Luke good night.

Then Jensen and I walk into my house and straight up to my room. I think he knows I don't really want to talk much about how tonight went. It's something I can revisit later, but it was all so heavy that I don't want to hash it out or refeel it all. I just want to bask in this newfound peace.

Everything feels right.

We take turns showering, and when I come out, I find him lying on my bed in nothing but a pair of *my* boxer briefs. Stopping in the doorway, I dry my hair with a towel as I gawk at him like a drooling teenager.

He sets his phone down. "I stole a pair of your underwear."

"Please explain to me why that's so hot," I say, tossing my towel in the hamper.

"I think," he says with a sexy smirk as he puts his hands behind his head and leans against the pillow. "Because it means I'm yours."

I don't bother putting on any underwear as I climb onto the bed, straddling his thick thighs. "That must be it."

When we're alone like this and Jensen can just be himself, it's like I get a better version of him. Like he's all mine. And I wish I could keep him here forever.

But our time is limited. It's *always* limited.

That nagging worry deep in my gut threatens to ruin our evening, so I ignore it.

"Speaking of sexy..." I say, leaning down to kiss his stomach. "Listening to you say grace at dinner was criminally hot."

"Isaac," he says with a laugh as I work my lips up to his pecs. "There is nothing hot about that."

With a raspy chuckle, I bite gently on his left nipple. "When you do it, there is."

"No, there is not." His voice is breathy and tight as I switch sides and play with his other nipple. I can feel his cock hardening beneath me. And I refuse to believe it's just the nipple play causing it.

"Come on," I moan before biting it again.

He yelps and his back arches off the bed.

"Let me hear a little prayer," I beg.

He grabs my hair and wrestles me to my back. With his body draped over mine, he boxes me in with his arms on the bed by my ears.

"I am not saying a prayer in bed," he growls.

"Please, Daddy," I whine, but he only shakes his head.

"That won't work on me again." Leaning down, he kisses my neck, and it lights a fire inside me. I'm smiling from ear to ear with my legs wrapped around his waist.

Jensen finds my hands and interlaces our fingers, pinning them to the bed above me. As he kisses his way down my neck and over my collarbone, I lose my jokes and witty comebacks. He certainly has his ways of shutting me up.

"Besides," he mumbles before licking his way up my neck and putting his mouth next to my ear. "You'll be the one talking to God when I'm done with you."

I practically melt right into the mattress. "Fuck me," I say on a gasp as goose bumps cover my body.

"I plan to," he replies with a wicked grin.

His lips find mine, and he kisses me hard, grinding himself against me. When he has me nearly breathless, like a worthless aroused puddle beneath him, he reaches into my nightstand and retrieves the lube.

I love that we don't need condoms anymore. I love that we've reached this point together, that we trust each other this much. I've never imagined a long-term relationship in my future, but I want that more than anything with Jensen. I want him in my life forever. And it might seem crazy to claim that after only a couple of months, but when I'm with him, it's like all the broken parts of me are whole again. He is the glue.

He takes his time working me open. Kissing my neck and teasing my nipples, he presses my thighs up higher as he slides three fingers inside me. Honestly, he takes more time than he needs to. As if he's so concerned about hurting me, and I love him for that. Not that I mind a little pain, but I have never felt more taken care of and protected in my life.

Jensen never takes, only gives. He never hurts, only heals. He is the redeemer. My salvation. My love.

I watch with adoration and arousal as he slides his boxer briefs off and settles between my legs. Lining up our cocks, he rocks against me as he looks into my eyes.

"I love you," I whisper, staring up at him. With anyone else, I might be embarrassed to be so emotional or that they'll notice the moisture in my eyes, but with him, I'm safe.

He touches his forehead to mine. "I will love you until the day I die."

My eyes close and I have to swallow the lump building in my throat. Then, as we breathe the same air, he presses my legs up and eases his cock inside of me.

He slips past the ring of muscle, and I let out a groan. He quickly kisses it from my mouth while his hips thrust deep and slow.

"I was made for this," he whispers as he presses my legs higher and pushes in deeper.

"We were made for this," I reply breathlessly.

I am so incredibly full, and it's a sensation I savor. Normally, with sex, I wanted it to be fast and hard because there was never a connection like this before. Never another person I wanted to be closer to. It was just about me and this aching *need* to be desired, fucked, made for pleasure for others to derive. I used to have sex just to feel something.

Now, with him, it's something else entirely. Sex isn't dirty or filthy. It's cosmic and beautiful. We are more than just two bodies —we're two souls. We give without taking, a mutual pleasure that's far more rewarding than anything I've ever felt before.

Jensen reaches between our bodies and wraps his hand around my cock. The motion of his thrusts drives his hand and when he pegs my prostate, a bit of cum leaks from the tip.

"God, yes," I groan, clutching tighter to him.

Jensen chuckles as he grinds his hips upward at the angle that makes my body tense and my eyes roll.

"What is so funny?" I ask tightly while trying not to come too soon.

"I told you."

"Told me what?"

"That you'd be talking to God."

A smile tugs at my lips, but only until he slams into me again. Then my smile is wiped away and I'm on the brink of an orgasm.

"Shut up and fuck me harder," I cry out. He quickly takes my mouth in a kiss, and I hear him groaning deep in his chest. He's trying hard to hold on too.

We're no longer sweetly making love. He has me practically folded in half as he pounds hard into me, and I have a pleasure-laced scream at the tip of my tongue.

"God, don't stop. Fuck, I'm right...there," I mumble incoherently.

"I'm right there too," he mutters. "Tell me to come inside you."

"Yes, please, Daddy. Fill me up," I shout.

"You come first, baby." He sounds like he's on the razor-thin edge of control.

His hand around my cock squeezes the head on the upstroke as he nails that spot inside me again, and I'm a goner. The climax digs its claws in and I'm powerless against it. Warm cum lands against my chest and neck while I'm riding out the waves of ecstasy.

"I'm coming," he groans as he slams in a couple more times before stilling. His cock pulses as he comes, and I love the idea of being filled and claimed by him.

We both collapse at the same time, and I instantly feel his heart hammering in his chest as he lies on top of me. It's like heaven, catching our breaths together. Our hearts pounding together. Cum-covered and satisfied.

Eventually and begrudgingly, we both get up. He goes into the bathroom first and comes back with a warm, wet washcloth. I lie in bed, feeling like his filthy little sex toy as he gently cleans my chest and between my legs.

"What are you grinning at?" he asks when he sees my face.

"Nothing," I reply with a big stretch. "I just love this."

He pauses, gazing down at me. "Me taking care of you or the post-orgasm haze altogether?"

"All of it. But mostly just having you here."

He goes into the bathroom and tosses the washcloth in the hamper before washing his hands. I get to stare at his sexy ass the entire time.

"You know," I say, rolling to my side. "You could just leave some underwear here."

"I thought you liked me wearing your underwear?" he asks as he picks up the ones he discarded on the floor before sex and pulls them back on.

"I do, but I sort of love the idea of you keeping your things at my place more."

He stares at me with his thumbs in the waistband of his briefs. "I could do that," he says with hesitation.

"You could stay here too, you know. When I'm not here. Sleep in my bed. Swim in my pool. Jack off in my shower."

He smirks as he climbs into the bed and lies next to me. "Isaac, are you asking me to move in with you?"

"Am I moving too fast?" I ask, hearing how ridiculous this probably sounds. I've never even been to his place, and yet, I'm asking him to live in my house. This is probably too much, but I don't care. I just love him so much and I want moments like this all the time. I want all the stupid domestic boyfriend shit every day.

He licks his bottom lip as he thinks it over. "I love that idea, too," he mumbles, and I grin wildly at him.

"Really?"

"Really." He nods.

Then we're both grinning like idiots. He hooks an arm around my waist and tugs me toward him until I'm hugging him tight.

As I rest my head on his chest, I realize that everything is working out. Nothing that threatened to tear us apart has, and we might have been worried about everything for nothing. Truett can't hurt us. Jensen's past can't hurt us.

With time, we'll come out and either they'll accept us or they won't, but either way, we'll be okay. We're together, we're in love, and everything is going to be just fine.

Better than fine. Everything will be perfect.

Thirty-Four

JENSEN

Isaac smiles on the screen, large dimples indented on his cheeks while the audience laughs at whatever adorable thing he just said.

The camera loves him. In a tight flannel shirt around a snug white T-shirt, he looks like such an all-American country boy. With the worn-out cowboy hat and boots too, of course.

The audience adores him too. They laugh at everything that comes out of his mouth, and I swear he's leaning on the chair like that on purpose because he knows just how hot it makes him look.

The host pulls out a picture from Isaac's last show, and the audience screeches like a pack of horny hyenas. It's a photo of him onstage in nothing but a pair of holey jeans. Suddenly, Isaac is blushing and hiding his smile like a fool.

I laugh out loud from my couch as I watch him. My phone is in my hand and I can't wait to text him when this interview is over. He's a natural, but there's a subtle possessive part of me that gets a little turned on by how much everyone swoons over him.

You can lust after him all you want, but he's mine.

"So, did you forget your shirt?" the host asks, making the audience laugh.

Isaac grins harder. "Yeah, I did. I couldn't seem to find it backstage, and you know what they say…the show must go on."

They laugh again.

The host avoids any questions about Isaac's personal dating life, as they agreed to before the show. His publicist has a very thorough plan that involves using this interview to guide the conversation toward Isaac's overall swoon factor rather than focus on his sexuality.

Isaac clearly hasn't told her it's only a matter of time before he'll come out on his own, anyway.

The host asks Isaac something about his songs, and the conversation settles down for a moment. Not so much blushing and grinning. But when Isaac gets to truly talk about songwriting and music, he turns into a different person. He's passionate and brilliant, and I swear I fall more and more in love with him the longer he speaks.

Unexpectedly, my doorbell rings. I glance down at my watch to see it's past nine. I'm not expecting any visitors, so I consider ignoring it. I don't want to miss Isaac's interview, but I guess that's the beauty of modern technology. I can rewatch it online as much as I want.

With a groan, I get up from the couch and walk to the front door. It must be my mom or dad. Or maybe one of Isaac's brothers to talk about dinner the other night.

I pull open the door, and the blood immediately drains from my face.

"Hi, Jensen. Sorry to just show up unannounced, but you don't answer my calls or emails."

"Derek," I mutter. My stomach coils immediately with a sick, cramping sensation.

Pastor Derek has changed a lot over the years. Back when I was still a teenager, he was younger than I am now. After twenty-plus years, he's aged with salt-and-pepper hair, a few extra pounds on his slender frame, and heavy bags under his eyes.

"What are you doing here?" I ask, trying to remain casual.

"Just checking up on you, of course. We haven't spoken in...it seems like forever. What's it been...four years?"

My stomach cramps turn to nausea. Four years. That's how long ago I attended an Eternal Harmony conference. Call it a relapse, but I was in my mid-thirties, going through either a mid-life crisis or, I don't know...an identity crisis. My sexual escapades had turned promiscuous, and I felt like I was going down a lonely, dark path.

They reached out, and for the first time in nearly ten years, I answered.

I've regretted it ever since. And I haven't told a soul.

If Isaac found out...

"Well, aren't you going to let me in?" he asks with that charismatic smile.

The voices in my head drown out my own thoughts. Somewhere in there is a voice telling me to shut the door in his face and tell him to never call again. But old habits die hard and I was never the kind of man who would do that to a pastor, a *friend*.

Not a friend, Jensen. Not a friend.

"Of course," I mutter under my breath as I step aside. Derek enters my home, and my skin buzzes with anxiety. He's just here for a little chat. We'll catch up and then he'll leave, and everything will go back to normal.

When Derek enters my living room, Isaac is still on the TV, talking about his music before smiling at the audience. It makes my heart lurch in my chest.

I wish he were here so I could hold him.

I wish I were a different man for him.

Derek smiles at the TV before giving me a knowing glance. "I'm a big fan of this guy. According to the media lately, so are you." He takes a seat on my couch, in the exact spot I just sat, so I hover nearby and force myself to act normal.

"Can I get you something to drink?" I ask, without looking him in the eye.

"That depends," he asks. "Are we behaving ourselves tonight?"

Bile rises in my throat. "Derek, I—"

He laughs. "That was a joke, Jensen. Relax. Water is fine."

With a shaky breath, I go to my kitchen and pour two glasses of water. Taking them back out, I notice the show has gone to a commercial break, so I hand a glass to Derek and take a seat on the opposite sofa, as far from him as I can get.

"So, how've you been?" he asks, staring at me with intensity.

"Fine," I say, looking at the opposite wall instead of at him. "I'm preaching at Redemption Point now."

"Yeah, I've heard. That's incredible. Congratulations."

"Thanks."

We make small talk for a bit. He mostly talks about his work with the program and how much they've *accomplished*. I feel sick.

"And what about your initiative?" he asks, leaning forward with his elbows on his knees. My *initiative* is the plan Eternal Harmony assigned each of us. Our job was to identify our triggers, the temptations in our lives that caused us to stray from the path. Then we had a prescribed course of actions to take to help deny and resist those temptations.

I am a forty-year-old man. I haven't had an initiative since I was twenty-five, so why can't I just say that to him now? Why do I suddenly feel like an unruly teenager who's been caught with his hand in the cookie jar?

"I said I'm fine," I mutter without looking at him.

"Good," he replies with a head nod. Then he shifts seats, bringing him closer to me, and I stiffen. "Jensen, I'm only here out of concern. When I saw the photos online, I reached out to your mother and she told me where I'd find you. I've heard the rumors like everyone else. It breaks my heart to see someone fall from their path of righteousness. I know temptations can be mighty and hard to resist, but it's your soul I worry about. Your eternal peace."

He lays a hand on my leg, and I freeze.

He's so full of shit. His words never match his actions, but his ability to manipulate my mind is some sort of sick talent.

"I'm here because I care. You know that, right?"

Lifting my gaze, I meet his eyes for the first time tonight. Instantly, I'm shrunk down to nothing but an inferior being. I'm a child. A fiend. A sinner.

Because I know he wants me to be compliant, I nod.

"Your actions have great significance, not only on you but on him, too." He nods toward the TV, where Isaac is now performing with the band. He's so far away from me, not just in distance but in thought too.

In just a few intense moments, Derek has made Isaac feel like a distant memory to me. Someone from another life.

"We're friends," I stammer unconvincingly.

Derek just ignores me. "You have an opportunity here, Jensen. Let me help you."

His hand squeezes my knee, and I tremble deep in my bones. I pray he can't feel it. "I'm fine."

"You're a public figure now, Jensen. People know your affiliation with Eternal Harmony. If we just...make a statement. Show your support. Don't let down these kids."

My stomach turns, and I nearly vomit. Before the sickness catches up with me, I stand from the couch and pace away from him.

"No. I have no...affiliation," I stammer.

"Your church has donated to our cause, Jensen. *You* did that."

"No."

"Does *he* know that?"

"You should leave. I can't...I can't do this," I argue, but my mind is a mess. Thoughts swirl and nothing catches. I can't seem to find the things I need to say. The things I want to say to him. It's all lost in noise and voices.

"If people find out about him with *you*, of all people, Jensen, it will ruin his career. You think the scandal is bad now? Imagine how much worse it could be. A heartthrob country musician and a conversion therapy counselor?"

"I was just a kid!" I shout, fire brewing in my bloodstream. "You...you made me..."

"A kid? Were you a kid four years ago? Were you a kid in your twenties? Don't blame me for the choices you made."

"Fuck you, Derek," I grit out with my fists clenched tight at my sides. "You fucked my head up, and I won't support you fucking up more kids like me."

I expect him to back down, but he doesn't. Instead, he barrels toward me and shoves me hard against the wall. "If the media catches wind of your past, it will be at the expense of everything I've built. They won't just tear you apart, I have a reputation to uphold, you motherfucker."

I shove him away from me. "You think I give a shit about your reputation? You can't hurt me anymore."

"Think so, Jensen? You don't think I can go to the media. Tell them what you did to all those kids in the program?"

My brow furrows as I glare at him with rage. "What the fuck are you talking about? I didn't hurt anyone, you sick fuck."

"Didn't you?" he says, his voice like poison. "Didn't you touch them? You tempted them. Made those boys do all kinds of perverted things."

My blood runs cold. "That was *you*," I whisper in disbelief. Even saying such disgusting things out loud to him makes me sick. "That was *you*! You did all that shit to *me*!"

He closes in, and I feel like a kid again. He's just an old man in his fifties now, but it takes one look, one repulsive memory to turn me into a shaking, scared teenager again.

"What good times we had, Jensen. From what I remember, you were the easiest one, too. What a desperate little slut you were."

Rage bubbles up in me like boiling water. My fist flies,

connecting hard with his face, and he stumbles across my living room, hitting the TV where Isaac once played. The television goes black, and I have to talk myself down from hitting him again. I'm afraid if I start, I won't stop.

"Get out of my house," I growl angrily.

He takes his time standing up, holding his nose as it gushes blood down his shirt and onto my floor.

"You think I can't hurt you, Jensen?" he asks with blood all over his hands. "I don't need to. You're ruining your own life. And his. I'm just here to make sure you don't take us down with you. Because it's clear you only care about yourself. You always did."

"I said get out." My nostrils are flaring, and I can only stare at him and force myself to breathe.

Then he looks up at me, and I am pierced with the intensity of his condemnation. "God doesn't love men like you, Jensen. You don't deserve that congregation. You had a chance to live a good life, but you were too weak. Always were too fucking weak. Now, you'll drag that boy down with you."

He turns his back and walks to the front door of my house. I'm shaking so hard, one gust of wind could blow me over.

"Go to hell, Derek," I mutter.

"Only one of us is destined for hell, Jensen. Just be sure you don't take anyone else with you."

When he disappears through the front door, I reach for the nearest thing, which is the glass of water I had given him only fifteen minutes ago. It flies with force from my hand to the front door, crashing and sending glass and water everywhere.

My heart is pounding so fast I have to pull air into my lungs, one large breath at a time. There's a tremble in my hands that is so violent they tingle and feel numb.

Deep breath. Deep breath. Deep breath.

I struggle in vain, trying to calm my body and my mind, but it's futile. The voices are back and louder than ever. Suddenly, I'm a teenager again, scared and alone and *stupid*.

"God doesn't love men like you, Jensen."

I'm no man. I'm a fraud. A liar. I've tricked everyone into believing in me, including Isaac. I've manipulated him into trusting that I could be different. That I could be with him. That I could be righteous. That I could be anything at all.

I've conned him into loving me.

I'm as bad as Derek.

It's like I'm standing between two land masses being ripped apart, and when I can't seem to grasp onto either side, my nails digging desperately into the surface, trying to keep my feet on the ground, I fail and plummet into the depths.

Where I belong.

All I can do is let out a deafening, roaring cry of anger.

Everything hurts. And I'm not sure I'm ever going to crawl back out of the darkness again.

THIRTY-FIVE

"**H**ey, babe. You must have fallen asleep early last night. And...you're sleeping in late today. I hope everything's okay. If I don't hear from you before the show tonight, I'm going to have to send Lucas over there, and you know how much fun he is."

I force a laugh when I can't feel an ounce of humor in me.

"I love you. Maybe your phone broke or something. Or you just need a break from me. I don't know. My mind is coming up with crazy scenarios, so please stop freaking me out. I love you. Did I mention that? I'll say it again. I love you, Jensen. Please call me back."

I feel sick. Like physically sick. I called Jensen after my TV interview last night, but he didn't answer. I expected to wake up to a text this morning, but still nothing.

I don't know if he's mad at me or ghosting me or lying dead in a ditch somewhere, but the constant worry is making me physically ill. My body aches and I have no appetite.

It's past noon back in Austin, and we're supposed to do a promo video tonight for some brand sponsorship, but I can't even get myself in the shower, let alone dressed for photos.

Everything was great when I left town a few days ago. Did I push him too hard with the family stuff? And then the moving in.

I let out a groan as I bury my hands in my hair. Because I have nothing else to do, I pick up my phone and ring him again. According to my call log, I've called him twelve times today.

Needy much, Isaac?

It rings and rings just like it has all day. Then, to my relief, it stops ringing like he's picked up.

"Jensen?" I ask, my voice buzzing with anticipation.

"Hey," he mumbles.

"Are you okay? Jesus, you scared the shit out of me."

My pulse is pumping in my ears as I let the relief flow through me. He's okay. We're okay.

"I'm fine." His voice is low and raspy. It's him, but not him at the same time.

I clear my throat, not sure what to say. "Did you see the show last night?"

The line is silent for a few minutes. My knee bounces, waiting for him to just speak to me like the real Jensen that I know and love. Inside, I'm panicking that somehow everything I thought I had is slipping through my fingers.

"Isaac, listen..."

I freeze.

"I can't do this anymore."

No.

"It's not your fault." His voice cracks.

Stop.

"I just...don't think I can be the man you need."

"What happened?" I ask while staring at the blank wall of my room on the bus.

"Nothing happened," he lies. I can hear it in his voice.

"Don't lie to me, Jensen. What...happened?"

"Isaac, please listen to me."

"No!" I shout. "You're not going to fucking break up with me over the phone!" I stand up in a rage, my heart pounding in a panic. "We love each other, Jensen. You can't do this."

"Isaac, stop!" he shouts through the phone.

"No, you stop! Did those motherfuckers get in your head? What happened? Did you talk to one of them? Or was it my dad? Did he find you? Don't listen to their bullshit!"

"It's not bullshit, Isaac. It's real life, and we can't just pretend we live in a bubble all the time because no matter what we do, we have to answer to God."

It feels like he's just punched me in the stomach. "You think God would judge us for the way we love each other? Is that what you honestly think, Jensen?"

He's quiet. All I can hear is his breathing, and it sounds like my soul shattering.

"I have to believe that, Isaac."

He's crying. I can hear the pain in his voice, the tears on the line. And I'm filled with so much anger and sadness I don't know how to react. I can't handle the agony.

"You were never going to be there, were you?" I ask, and it feels like my heart is splitting in half. "I was never going to be anything more than your dirty secret."

He makes a hiccuping sound and I fight the urge to scream.

"Answer me, Jensen. You're breaking my heart, so you can at least give me this much. Tell me the truth." My voice reeks of vitriol as I spit my words at him through the phone.

"No," he whispers sadly. "We never had a future."

I squeeze my phone so hard it feels like it could crack. The pain morphs into rage. My face feels bright red as I clench my teeth and shut my eyes tight.

"I'm so fucking stupid," I whisper.

"Isaac—"

Before he can say another word, I punch the end call button. My legs are bouncing erratically, like I might detonate at any moment. I'm so mad at him. So mad at myself. So mad at my stupid fucking heart for thinking he could change for me. He tried to tell me. He tried to warn me that he had been through too much. That he could never give me himself, but I didn't ask for much. I just wanted to love him.

I still want to just love him.

Why can't we just do that? Even in the privacy of our own homes. We could just be happy together. Why, why, why.

The worst part is that he actually thinks the lies they've put in his head. He tried to make me believe it too. He thinks we're a sin. I'll never be able to change his mind. Never.

There's a knock on the door to my room. "You okay in there?"

"No," I murmur with my face in my hands.

The door opens and Lola walks in. She takes one look at me and her expression morphs into pity. Then she crosses the space, crawls onto the bed next to me, and pulls me into her arms.

I can't cry. I'm too angry.

Why would he do this? Over the fucking phone.

None of this is adding up.

"Want me to call Martina and reschedule the shoot?" Lola asks.

"No," I mumble. "I need the distraction."

"Are you sure?" she asks, patting my back. I can't stand the idea of being coddled, so I remove myself from her hold and stand from the bed.

"Yes, let's just get the fuck out of here."

With a look of remorse, she nods and follows me as I march angrily off the bus.

✝

"This attitude is working," the photographer says as he clicks the camera again. "Now, let's give the girls a smile, can we?"

I try to smile. I really do. But it's only the bottom half of my face contorting, and I don't feel an ounce of joy behind the expression. I can tell the photographer is disappointed.

"Broody and sexy it is," he mutters as he snaps a few more from different angles.

All day, I've been thinking about Jensen. I check my phone every five seconds. I've written and rewritten about a hundred texts to him, but none of them feel right. It's like I'm talking to a version of him I don't even know.

I just want to scream at him, "It's me. Stop acting like this."

Not once in our relationship has he ever spoken about God, other than the times when he was baring his soul about what he went through. He has never used God against me the way he did today.

That's not him. That's what those monsters at Eternal-whatever taught him to think. They fucked him up. They have to be in his head. That's all this is.

But if that's all this is, then maybe he needs me. Is it wrong of me to let him push me away when he so clearly needs me to remind him what's real and what's not?

We're traveling to our next tour stop tomorrow.

"Do you need a break?" the assistant says as she sprays water on my chest.

"What? No," I reply, shaking my head out of the stupor. "Let's get this over with."

"Then you have to give me some emotion," the photographer snaps with irritation.

I manage to make it through the rest of the shoot somehow. The entire time, I just have to do my best not to think about Jensen, but it's impossible. Anxiety replaces the anger I felt earlier. I can't sit around and do nothing. I have no intention of just getting over this. I'm not going to let him go that easily.

After the shoot, I get in the car with Lola. The minute the door closes, I blurt out, "I have to go home."

"What?"

"The rest of you can go to Charleston, but I need to go see him in person."

"Tonight?" she asks with shock.

"Yes. I'm looking up flights now."

When I find one that takes off late tonight, I quickly book it without another thought. I have to get home to him immediately. I'll explain to my tour manager, and I'll be back in time for dress rehearsal the day after tomorrow.

I've been crawling out of my skin ever since I got off the phone with my tour manager. She sounded frustrated with my decision. But I don't care. If Jensen thinks I'm just going to let all of this go over one bad day, he's wrong.

I've walked away from love before. I walked away from my own family. That was for my own good because that love didn't serve me anymore, but I won't walk away from Jensen. I will never walk away from him.

Thirty-Six

*Y*ou're weak.
You always were.
God doesn't love men like you.
You are a sinner.
You only care about yourself.
You'll only bring him down with you.

Over and over and over. These are the words that greet me the moment I open my eyes. There is no way out. No beacon of light anymore. Just every hard truth I've been hiding from for years.

Because that's what they are. The mantras and the voices were never lies. They were enlightenment.

That's why they are so loud. They ring with truth.

The room is dark. It must be night again. Isaac's voice echoes through the phone line even though he's long since hung up.

I just wish I could stay asleep longer. Because every time I open my eyes and the memories and voices come back, they hurt. Everything hurts.

I am such a fool for trying to live a normal life. I feel so stupid for thinking I could change.

What is wrong with you?

You have done terrible things. He would never love you if he knew.

No one would. Not even God.

I pull the covers back over my head and try to quiet the thoughts in my head, but they just won't stop. I try pinching my skin, hoping the physical pain will distract me from the emotional pain.

I don't feel like myself anymore. I'm made of shame now. Regret, pain, anger.

The night is long and agonizing. When I climb out of bed, hoping for a distraction, I see the broken glass and water still covering my floor. The broken TV. And it brings back everything. The things Derek said. The memories it brought back. It was a kill switch. He knew exactly what to say to make it all hurt again.

Because it's all true.

Letting go of Isaac was the right thing to do. Dragging him into a relationship for this long was wrong of me. So it's just better if he goes and is free of me. The public will eventually forget I was ever in the picture. He'll have a long, happy career. He'll meet someone who will give him what he needs. Someone to be there for him. To hold his hand when he comes out. Who loves him proudly.

I won't be here to see it. I can't.

The weight of this hurt is more than I can carry. It's enough to drag me down and make the entire world feel against me. I can't take another second of it. This anguish. It's like being stabbed by a thousand blades at once. I can't numb it. Can't drown it out. There's only one way to escape it.

Standing in the bathroom, I stare at the shell of a man staring back. It's too late for me. Too late to fix what I've done. Too late to make myself a man worthy of God's love. Isaac's love. Too late.

In moments of darkness, some people speak about hearing the voice of God or searching for His strength, but I am not reaching for God. I am hiding from him.

Reaching into the medicine cabinet, I know this has always been the road I was on. The end I so desperately needed. The sweet relief.

This is not a tragedy. It's not even the easy way out.

This is mercy.

THIRTY-SEVEN

ISAAC

The plane lands early, and I briefly consider going to a hotel to sleep off the jet lag, but I decide to just go straight to his house. I couldn't rest if I wanted to. Not being this close to him and having so much to work out together.

When I land, I switch my phone off Airplane Mode, and there's one text from Jensen that chills me to the bone.

I'm sorry.

But when I call, it goes to voicemail. He must be sleeping.

I practically run to the taxi stand. It's six o'clock in the morning, but it doesn't matter. I'll wake him up if I have to. We just have to talk this out and everything will be fine. I'll probably be on a plane back to South Carolina by tomorrow morning.

I've never actually been to Jensen's house, but I have the address, so I give it to the driver and wait anxiously in the back seat as he drives us there.

Jensen still doesn't pick up.

The drive is agony. It's only twenty minutes, but it feels like hours. I distantly recognize my song playing on the radio and how incredibly trivial it feels. It's just a song. And I'm just a singer. Like either of those really fucking matters compared to love and the people in my life who make it worth living.

Would I really put my love for Jensen aside because of this one stupid fucking job?

When the cab driver pulls into a nice suburban neighborhood, I feel closer to Jensen. I sit upright in my seat and eagerly wait for him to stop in front of one of the houses. It's a white brick two-story house where we stop, and I pay him so quickly, I'm tempted to just toss him my credit card and run.

When the transaction is done, I leap out of the car and dash up to the front door. I bang on it loudly and pull out my phone to call him again.

No answer on either.

"Jensen!" I shout, although drawing attention from neighbors probably isn't a good idea either.

When a few moments pass without a response, I decide to try the knob. To my surprise, the handle turns and it opens. He leaves his door unlocked at night?

Pushing it open slowly, I call his name once more. But again, no answer.

When I step inside, I hear the crunch of something under my boot. My eyes cast downward in confusion. There's water and glass on the floor.

Something isn't right here.

My skin buzzes with panic as I scream his name. "Jensen!"

Barreling into his house, I notice the broken TV in the living room, and I worry for a moment that he was attacked or someone broke in. He's nowhere to be seen downstairs, so I head for the stairs, calling his name with worry the entire time.

He has to be okay.

He's just sleeping.

I run first for the door on the right, which appears to be a primary bedroom. The curtains are pulled closed, and the bed is unmade.

Then I run into the connected bathroom and stop in my tracks. He's sitting on the floor, his back against the tub with his knees bent and his head hung between them. It reeks of vomit.

"Oh my god," I shout as I launch myself toward him, putting myself between his legs and forcing his head up to look at me. He's pale, like *really* pale. His face is sweat-soaked and his eyes dazed. It's a sight I'll carry with me for the rest of my life, burned into my memory like a scar.

"Jensen, what did you do? What's wrong?" I cry in a panic.

His face contorts in anguish as he starts sobbing. "I... fucked up."

"Baby, what are you talking about?" I ask as I look around him on the floor. My eyes stop on the orange pill bottle on the white tile floor. I breathe fast, the panic setting in.

"Did you take something? Did you..." My voice trails as I shuffle in my pockets for my phone.

Jensen continues to cry, his head hanging limply from his body. The next few minutes pass in a blur. With trembling fingers, I dial 911.

Jensen mumbles incoherently, and I can't take my eyes off him as the lady on the line asks me so many questions I can't answer. My entire body trembles and when he starts to daze out, I grab his shoulder and shake him violently.

I barely hear the woman on the phone, but when she says the ambulance is on the way, I drop my phone on the tile and hold his face. Tears are running down my face as I hold him close to me.

"I'm sorry," he sobs against my shoulder. "I tried to... stop it..."

"It's okay," I cry. "Just stay with me. Please stay with me."

"I can't do this anymore," he sobs. "It hurts too much, Isaac. It hurts. You have to let me go."

"I'll never let you go," I say through quivering lips, stroking his face and looking into his lifeless eyes. "What did they do to you?"

He floats harrowingly in and out of lucidity as he stares forward without truly seeing me. It's like his mind is already gone, and I shake with fear.

"I love you," I whisper, trying to hold him to this moment.

Delicately, he repeats after me. "I love you." There is no feeling in his voice. No heart. No Jensen.

Then he starts to cry again and my heart shatters. It breaks into a million shards of glass and leaves me as nothing but a hollow shell. He looks like he's in agony, so much pain. I wish I could take it from him.

"Do you think God is mad at me?" he cries and if I had anything left in my chest, it would kill me to hear him say that, but I've shut off all of my feelings. It's like my mind is protecting me from feeling the gravity of this moment. Letting the fear in would mean accepting what Jensen has done. It means grasping the severity of the damage they've caused. It would mean knowing just how bad he's been hurting and never seeing the signs. Instead, I just hold him and whisper how much I love him.

I hold him until the ambulance comes. I keep him awake until the paramedics drag me away and tend to him.

I feel nothing. My face is tear-soaked and my heart is numb.

They usher me out of his room entirely. And everything happens in slow motion. I hear him retching and crying. I sob alone downstairs on his couch because none of this is fair. Nothing.

I'm alone, and I'm so fucking tired of being alone. So I pull out my phone and I call my brother.

Luke picks up on the first ring, probably alarmed by my calling so early in the morning. And in an emotional rush, I tell him everything. I manage to hold it all together until they bring Jensen downstairs on a stretcher. His eyes are closed and he has an oxygen mask on his face.

I just want to hold him. I want to tell him how much I love

him and for no one to give us a hard time about that. Aren't we allowed that much? In this day and age, I thought we were finally free, but we're still not. It's all an illusion.

"Where are you taking him?" I cry, and the paramedic gives me the directions.

Then they're gone and I'm sitting alone in Jensen's house, waiting for my brother.

"I'm coming, Isaac. Don't move. I'm coming!" Luke shouts into the phone. I hear his car door slam in the background.

When he pulls up a few moments later, every ounce of composure I once had is gone. I break down as soon as his arms go around me. I don't just cry; I wail. My voice is cracked and deafening as I scream into my brother's shoulder. I cry for Jensen and for me. I cry in pain and anger. I let everything I've stowed away in the past eleven years come flooding out.

I don't feel any better when it's over because I won't feel an ounce of relief until I know he's okay. So, after shutting the door to his house, I rush out to the car with my brother. He drives me to the hospital in silence.

There's not a single thought in my head. Not a song lyric. Not a memory.

When it feels truly quiet in my mind, I close my eyes. And I pray.

✝

They won't let me back to see him because, of course, I'm not his husband or his brother. They act like being his boyfriend means nothing. So Luke and I are stuck in the waiting room. I've had about two hours of sleep all night and I am wired and restless.

The hours tick by. I keep asking for an update, but they can't provide one. If they could at least just tell me he's going to be okay, then I could at least go home and try to relax.

No, I couldn't. Who am I kidding?

Since the moment I met Jensen, there has been an invisible

string between us, and the distance always felt like torture. Now, it's unbearable.

Luke gets us coffee as he sits down next to me and whispers, "Don't be mad at me."

I turn my head in confusion. "What?"

"I made some calls."

"To who? Local news stations. You told them where to find me, didn't you?"

He rolls his eyes. "No. You'll see."

Five minutes later, Caleb strolls through the door. He looks panicked until his eyes meet mine. Then he's running toward me, pulling me into a tight bear hug.

"Holy shit, Isaac. I'm so sorry."

"I'm fine," I say, but it's a lie. Probably the most popular lie out of all of them.

"What can I get you? Are you hungry? Need some sleep?"

"What, are you gonna sleep for me? I wish you could."

He doesn't laugh at my joke. "I'm here for whatever you need." He takes the seat opposite Luke, and we continue to wait together. No one says anything, and I realize how much I missed this.

Having brothers. Knowing they'll be there for me whenever I need it. No matter how mad we get or how hard times are. When I call, they come.

It feels instantly more comfortable with them on either side of me. It certainly doesn't solve any of my problems when it comes to Jensen, but it reminds me that no matter what happens, I won't be alone.

Part of me wonders if I should feel bad for running away from this all those years ago, but if I've learned anything this year, it's that I won't regret a single decision I've made. It brought me success in my career. It brought me a person I love more than anyone.

I just need him to come out of this alive. The rest we can deal with. He needs time. He needs counseling or treatment. We'll get it all. We can handle anything that life throws at us together.

I rest my head on Luke's shoulder and drift off when the automatic doors open again. The bright light from outside shines through, so I almost don't recognize the tall figure who rushes in.

But as he comes closer to me, my eyes focus until I'm staring at Adam. I freeze in place, as does he. He looks so much older than I remember. He has a dark beard. Longer hair. Weathered features.

Before I can even register what I'm doing, I launch out of my chair and cover the last few steps between us. Neither of us says a word as we collide. My arms wrap around him as he holds me, and the damn breaks again.

I cry silently into his shoulder, shuddering without a sound.

"I'm so sorry this is happening to you," he mumbles next to my head.

"I'm sorry I left," I cry. Because I am. Right now, realizing how much I missed my older brother, how much I needed him, I am sorry. I wish it hadn't happened this way.

"Don't be sorry. You did what you had to. I'm not mad at you."

"Thank you for being here," I reply with a hiccuping sob.

"I'll always be there. No matter what. You just have to call."

There's nothing left to say, so we just hold each other for a little longer. Maybe it's my exhaustion or what I've been through today, but my emotions feel wrung out and beat up.

When I pull away from the embrace and finally look at my brother, it feels like I've never left. He's the same guy he always was, just a little older.

He ruffles my hair with a sad smile, and I try to paste a smirk on my face, but I don't have one.

What I do have are my three brothers here on the worst day of my life.

✝

I fall asleep on Luke's shoulder for a while, but then I wake up after about an hour to the sound of Jensen's name being spoken somewhere in the lobby. I peel my eyes open and watch as an older couple rush into the hospital with terror on their faces.

I lift my head and watch them as they wait for the nurse behind the counter to give them an update on their son. I can tell by the height of the man and the woman's eyes that those are Jensen's parents.

I rise from the chair and slowly approach them. There are a lot of things I'd like to say to these people. How could you put your kid in conversion *trauma* for ten years? How could you do that to your own child? That is why he is here. That is why he is in so much pain. What monsters would do that to their own flesh and blood?

But I see the fear on their faces. So, I don't attack them—yet.

"Hi," I say from behind them. The mother turns with a yelp. I can tell by the red lines around her eyes that she's been crying. Then I watch as her gaze focuses on my face and she recognizes me.

"I'm...Isaac. I'm..."

"I know who you are," the mother snaps while staring at me. She looks like she wants to say more, but her lip quivers and she turns away instead.

I look up at the man, but he doesn't turn away from me. Instead, he gives me an expression of remorse.

"They won't give me an update or let me back there with him."

The man nods his head before resting a comforting hand on my shoulder. "We'll get some answers."

Jensen's mother won't turn back toward me. When the nurse comes out, we all look at her with eager hope.

"He's stable, but he's not in a room yet. You two can come back to see him briefly."

My mouth opens to ask, but his dad beats me to it. "What about him?" he asks, pointing at me.

"Who are you?" she asks like I haven't been sitting here in this waiting room for hours. If I wasn't so exhausted and desperate, I'd be furious.

"I'm his boyfriend," I say with my shoulders back.

She gives me an expression of pity. "I'm sorry. Family only."

Every bone in my body freezes. Jensen's mother scurries off with the nurse while his dad hangs back with me.

Suddenly, I feel my brother at my side. "This is bullshit," Adam argues. "He was the one who found him. He's the reason he's still alive and you won't let him back there because he's not family?"

"Richard, come on," the woman says to her husband, who is still looking at me with pity in his eyes.

"I'm sorry," he says. "I'll see if I can pull some strings. You deserve to come back there, too."

"Thank you," I whisper, appreciating the compassion. "Just tell him...I'm here."

"I will."

Meanwhile, Adam slams a fist on the counter in outrage to get someone's attention.

"This isn't right. Family, my ass. That's just a cover for their small-minded bigotry. I'll have that nurse reported."

I glance sideways at him and feel a smirk growing on my face. "Sit down, Karen. We can wait. They have to let us back there, eventually."

"How can you just sit there while they discriminate against you?" he argues.

"Because getting kicked out of here isn't going to get me back to see Jensen any sooner."

He looks unsatisfied as he drops into a chair across from me. As the four of us carry on a casual conversation, I can't get the look on Jensen's mother's face out of my head. I know that look very well. And I know the damage it can do.

Part Four

The Redeemer

Thirty-Eight

I've never felt so tired in my life. My limbs feel like lead and I have to fight to keep my eyes open. There's a doctor shining a light in my eyes, and my throat burns like I've recently swallowed fire. A machine beeps somewhere in the room, and I glance around to see my mother hovering nearby. Her eyes are rimmed with red and she's holding a tissue under her nose. My dad is behind her, looking concerned and slightly angry.

I just want to go back to sleep.

"He'll be transferred to the psych unit for monitoring," the doctor says to someone else. Like I'm not lying right here—like I'm a child. "But vitals are strong, and I don't see any signs of liver or kidney failure."

"Thank God," my mother mumbles as she starts to cry again.

"Mr. Miles, can you hear me?" he asks.

I grumble, fighting the urge to close my eyes again. As he talks, telling me what I've done as if I don't fucking remember, I try to replay everything in my mind.

"You've ingested a near-lethal dose of diazepam, causing respiratory depression. We've administered an antidote, but we have to keep you here for your safety. Once you're cleared, the psych unit can speak to you about discharge options."

I nod, feeling shame creep up my spine.

It was still dark out when I made the decision. I remember thinking that it would just be better if I could just go back to bed and never wake up. It would be that easy. No more pain. No more memories. Just quiet.

Then I went to bed. As I lay there, feeling the effects slowly take over, I thought about Isaac. I wanted him to be my last thought. Our good times. Then, I distinctly remember the moment I changed my mind. I recalled all the promises I made him. Promises to never leave. To always be there for him, no matter what. How could I break those promises? How could I do this to him? I scrambled from my bed to the bathroom in a panic. I sobbed on the bathroom floor as I tried to expel every one of those pills from my body. By that point, I was too far gone to call 911. That's when everything got blurry.

"Isaac," I say with my voice like gravel.

"What's that?" the doctor asks.

I don't respond as I piece together moments from this morning. He was there. He was in my house. He held me and cried in terror. He called the ambulance.

He saved my life.

"Where's Isaac?"

"They only let family back, dear," my mother says as she pats my hand. The sleepiness wears off, and I'm fueled only by adrenaline as I try to sit up. My brow furrows and my nostrils flare.

"What?"

"Relax, Jensen. You can call him when the doctor releases you and we can take you home."

"Where is he?" I reply with a growl. "He saved my life. Has anyone given him an update?"

The heaviness of the drugs weighs on me and my limbs collapse down onto the bed like lead.

"He should...be here," I slur breathlessly.

"Sweetheart, you need your rest." My mom pats my hand and I stare behind her at my dad standing alone. His brows are curved upward, and I give him a pleading expression.

"Please," I murmur.

When he offers me a subtle nod, I melt into the bed. I'm just so tired. On an exhale, I close my eyes and drift off to sleep.

†

I wake up to the sensation of being punched in the stomach, or at least that's what it feels like. With the soreness in my muscles, every inhale aches like I've never felt before.

Earlier, I had the remnants of a drug-induced high to cover the pain. Now, I'm forced to feel it all. My body revolts, angry at me for what I've done. My throat, my head, my lungs, my stomach. All of them are screaming in pain, and I'm forced to endure it all.

I should be grateful for this. Even in agony, at least I'm alive.

Lying in the dim room of the hospital, I feel every ounce of the pain like a sacrament.

With a groan, I lift my head and glance around in search of my mother. But she's not here. There is, however, a man sleeping on the tiny blue couch next to the window. He's about twice the size of that sofa, with his blue jeans and boots hanging over the arm. There's a weathered old cowboy hat covering his face while he sleeps.

I smile to myself at the sight of him. He's here.

Immediately, I'm assaulted by guilt for what I put him through today—or yesterday, or whenever it was. I hate that he had to endure that, not only finding me in that state but for almost losing me. I can't explain or even fathom why I did what I did right now, but I know the reasons are buried deep within me. Seeing Derek triggered me in a way I can't explain away.

I won't put Isaac through this again. Which means I have a long road ahead of me.

I clear my throat, and he immediately stirs. Pulling his legs down from the couch, he lifts his cowboy hat and stares at me across the room. His eyes grow misty at once.

Then he's rushing toward me to stand by my side.

"You're awake," he cries quietly as he holds my hand.

My mouth opens to utter something trivial, but I can't find the ability to speak. There is too much to say. Instead, my eyes sting and moisten. Just staring at him, I try to convey every unspeakable thing I'm feeling.

He nods as if he can read my mind. As if he knows every little thing I want to say without me having to actually say it.

Then he launches himself at me until his face is in my neck and I can lift my heavy arms to hold him.

"I'm sorry," I mumble as tears leak from my eyes. "I'm so sorry, Isaac."

"That was the scariest moment of my life," he whispers. "I'm just glad you're okay."

Words evade me. They're just not enough.

I'm sorry is just two words. Three syllables. Seven letters. It will never be enough to convey this feeling in my chest. It couldn't possibly express the different shades of remorse I need it to.

After a moment, Isaac pulls away and stares down at me. He has dark circles under his swollen eyes. He looks like he hasn't slept in days and has been to hell and back.

"Isaac, listen to me," I say, gripping his hand tight in mine.

"Please don't," he says, stopping me. Then, to my surprise, he climbs onto the hospital bed so he's seated next to me. "Whatever you're going through, I understand it's a lot, but please, please, please don't push me away again. Let me be here for you."

Suddenly, I wish the physical pain were worse to distract me from how much it hurts to see that look on his face.

I try to sit upright and pull him closer. Touching his face, I swallow down the emotion building in my throat.

"I'm not pushing you away," I whisper. "I'm sorry for doing that to you."

"Then help me understand," he begs. "Open up, Jensen. Tell me what happened."

Opening up isn't something I do easily. There is too much darkness hidden behind the fake smiles and confident facade, but I know Isaac is right. If I want to keep him, then I have to let him see everything that I am.

So I tell him everything. From the visit with Derek to the terrible things he said to me. The accusations. The blackmail. The slimy way he weaseled into my subconscious and knew all the right buttons to push.

I even confessed to going to Eternal Harmony four years ago. Donating church funds. Speaking at their conference.

I'm not proud and I expect him to walk out the door, but he doesn't. He touches my face and sees the good in my soul, latching on to it like a raft out in a dark, endless sea.

"I'm so sorry he did that too, but he was wrong, Jensen. He can't hurt you. Not really."

"Yes, he can," I argue. "He can hurt *you*. And nothing would devastate me more."

"Can he tear us apart? Can he take away the one person in my life who understands me? Can you honestly say that *one fucking guy* can break us up?"

My brow furrows as I stare up at him. "No, of course not."

Isaac leans forward and presses his forehead to mine. "Then he can't hurt me. Not really. My job is just a job. Your job is just a job. But this..." He looks down at our clasped hands. And I see what he sees. Love. Family. Forever. "This is all that matters to me."

My throat stings worse now, but for different reasons. Latching a hand around his neck, I pull him against me, wrapping him up as tightly as I can.

"I love you," I whisper.

He repeats the sentiment, clutching tightly to my body. Then, I scoot myself over in the bed and he lies down next to me, his head on my shoulder. If I close my eyes, I can pretend we're not in a hospital and there's not an IV sticking out of my hand. We're just in his bed or in a hotel or on his tour bus. Everything is fine.

But everything is not fine, and we both know it.

When a few minutes pass, and I feel ready to speak again, I stroke his head and squeeze him tighter.

"You know I can't just go back to the way things were, right?"

He winces before he nods. "I know."

"The damage they did runs deep, and I can't risk this happening again. I'll never, ever do this to you again," I say as my voice grows raspy with pain.

He squeezes me tighter. "I know."

"I'll need to go away for a while. I want to be able to fully commit to you. I want to be able to come out without the fear of another spiral. This isn't something I can just brush off anymore." When I blink, a tear falls over my cheek, and it feels like a weight is pressing down on my chest.

I hate having to do this to him. I hate asking more of him. It's not fair. But I know he'll wait for me. I know he'll support me every step of the way, but I also need him to understand the most important part.

"While I'm gone, I need you to do something for me."

He sniffles and warm tears seep through my hospital gown and onto my chest. When he doesn't respond, I continue.

"I need you to go back on your tour and do what you do best. I need you to focus on you, Isaac. I couldn't live with myself if I got in the way of your success."

"Don't I have a choice in this? It's my life."

"You do. Of course you do. But I'm asking you, Isaac. Please. Let me get the help I need so that when I can be with you for good, I'm giving you the man you deserve."

Turning my head, I gaze down at him with tears in my eyes. He looks up at me as he cries and I press a soft kiss to his lips.

"Will you do that for me?" I whisper.

"Of course I will," he replies. "I'll do anything for you."

Isaac rests his head on my shoulder, and I close my eyes for a few minutes. I'm not as fatigued as I was earlier, but I can still feel the effects of the drugs in my system. It's a terrifying feeling to know how close I was.

When the door opens and a nurse walks in, she stops in her tracks when she finds a six-foot cowboy in my bed. But with a shrug, she just continues to go about her business, checking my vitals.

"Sorry, ma'am," Isaac mumbles as he rolls out of my bed.

"That's okay, sugar," she says with her sweet Texas drawl. "When I'm done, you give him all the love and cuddles you want. He needs it." She runs her soft hand over my forehead and it pulls on my heart.

"I plan to," he replies with a smirk.

"And his daddy didn't cause that big ol' fuss for nothing," she adds as she takes my temperature.

"What are you talking about?" I ask.

Isaac is smirking like a fool next to my bed. "Your dad sort of caused a scene. It was pretty fucking cool."

"He did?"

"He sure did," the redheaded nurse replies before walking over to the window to throw open the curtains, revealing the morning sun. "I'll let you tell him." She winks at Isaac and I stare at him in amazement. My dad? Cause a scene?

"The psych doc will be back again in just a few to talk to you," she adds before walking out, leaving us alone. I turn toward Isaac in anticipation of this story.

"One of the ladies up front wouldn't let me come back to see you before they put you in the room. He came out threatening to file a discrimination lawsuit. She was shaking in her boots. It was incredible."

He blushes a little as he sits back down at my side. But I can tell there's some hesitation there too.

"I don't think your mom is too happy with me, though," he stammers uncomfortably.

"I don't care," I say with conviction.

"It's your mom, Jensen."

"I know, but…she and I have some things we need to work out on our own. I'm starting to realize that maybe she never wanted what was best for me. I just keep making excuses for her."

He nods in contemplation. "Well, I wish I had a dad like that growing up."

"I wish you did too," I say, taking his hand in mine.

After a few minutes, he kicks off his boots and crawls back into bed with me.

"When do you have to go back?" I ask as I stroke his hair.

"I have a show in Charleston in two days," he replies. "I'm supposed to be at dress rehearsal tomorrow."

"I want you to go," I say as I press my lips to his forehead.

"I don't know if I can." His voice is quiet, and he sounds so young. Sometimes I forget that he's only twenty-eight. He's been through so much in his short years. When he was forced to run away and be on his own at only seventeen, he was forced to grow up, but in a way, he preserved his youth at the same time. He will forever have that scared teenage boy inside him to protect.

"Of course you can," I reply. "You got this far on your own, Isaac. This is your moment. Don't let me or anyone else ruin that for you."

"Will I be able to talk to you while I'm gone?"

"I don't think so."

"But if you need me, you'll find a way to tell me, right?" he asks with a quiver in his voice.

"I promise."

"I have two more months of this tour," he says. "Our last stop is back here. Then I'll be here, waiting for you, for as long as you need."

I wince. I'm not sure how long I'll be gone or even where I'll go at this point. It's not something I can rush. Eight weeks feels so long, but if I'm going to do this, I'm going to do it right. Eight weeks for the rest of my life.

More if I need it.

"Play my song, baby," I reply, kissing his forehead.

"I will," he whispers. "I'll play it every night."

I don't know how much longer it is until I drift off to sleep, but when I wake again, he's gone. My dad is back, alone. They keep me in the psych unit for another two days for evaluation. The psychiatrist works with my dad to get me signed up for a treatment center called Pathways.

On my last day in the hospital, my dad brings me clothes, and I sit across from him at a small table in the cafeteria. He looks terrified, and honestly, I feel terrified. Whatever these next two months bring, I know they won't be easy. I know it's going to hurt, but I need to do it.

"Your mother is staying with her sister for a while," he says after clearing his throat. And that's all he says. I nod my head in understanding. I don't ask any more questions because I don't know if I can.

Moments later, the nurse comes to tell me that the car is here to take me. My father looks across the table at me with desperation in his eyes. Desperation to make things right. Desperation to save his son's life.

With shaking hands, I wrap my arms around him for a tight hug. Then, I follow the nurse as she leads me out the door and into the car. No matter what the next phase of my life brings, I'm ready for it. For *him*. For *us*. For *me*.

THIRTY-NINE

ISAAC

"I'll be on a plane first thing tomorrow morning," I mumble groggily into the phone.

"Are you sure?" Lola asks with concern. "You've been through a lot, Isaac."

I let out a sigh as I stare out the window. Adam is in the driver's seat next to me, and I can't help but agree with Lola here. I have been through a lot. This month has been pure insanity, but I made a promise to Jensen. I told him I'd keep going.

Not to mention, I need to be on the stage again. What others don't understand is that performing isn't work to me. It's cathartic. It's when my mind gets a break from all the noise, chaos and pain. It doesn't hurt onstage.

"Well, maybe you should consider getting some support of your own," she says, and I love her for saying that. The motherly concern coming from such a badass is the most wholesome thing I've ever heard.

Choosing not to mock her for it, I simply nod. "I will. You're absolutely right."

She gives a haughty chuckle. "I know I am."

"See you tomorrow, Lo."

"See you tomorrow, Isaac."

After hanging up the phone, I'm suddenly alone with my brother, Adam. The brother I haven't seen for eleven years, other than the dramatic moment yesterday morning in the waiting room nearly twenty-four hours ago.

"Everything okay?" he asks.

I shrug. "Yeah. Everything is fine. I'll get there in time to run through the set list before the show. I missed some local news spot and the official dress rehearsal, but that's the least of my worries."

He nods as he drives. I can see the tension in his posture and expression. I'm sure there's a lot he wants to say to me, and honestly, there's a lot I want to say to him too, but I'm just so fucking tired.

I hardly slept all night. I was lucky the nurses let me stay the night with Jensen in his room. Most of the time, they kick you out after visiting hours, but after the show Mr. Miles put on, waving around his badge and threatening a discrimination lawsuit, they didn't say a word to me.

It's morning now, and I am in desperate need of a shower and some real food, not the vending machine bullshit I survived on yesterday.

When Adam pulls up to my mother's house, I notice the other cars in the drive. He puts the car into park but doesn't move to get out. Instead, he turns to face me.

"You've been through a lot, so I won't burden you with anything now, but I just want to take a moment to say…"

He pauses and I watch as his eyes fill with tears. "I'm so fucking proud of you."

My mouth lifts with a crooked smirk. "Thanks, Adam, but—"

"You know I'm not talking about your career, right?"

I freeze, staring at him across the center console of the car. I'm cried out and talked out and just so sick of all the goddamn feelings, but hearing my older brother, the one I looked up to my whole life, tell me he's proud of me...

It cuts deep. It's been a long road for both of us to get here, one I'm sure we'll discuss more in time—now that we have time.

Without a word, I lean over and pull him into a tight hug. "Thank you, Adam."

"It doesn't matter how much anyone missed you. It doesn't matter who it hurt when you left. You understand that, right? You did the right thing, Isaac."

Tearfully, I nod against his shoulder.

"You're the best. The rest of us are a fucking mess, but you... you're the good one."

I didn't know I had any tears left. But I cry them into Adam's embrace, anyway. Adam was the hardest person to walk away from, not because I missed him but because I saw the path he was headed down, and it felt like I was losing him. In a way, I think I left so I didn't have to watch my closest brother turn into our father.

Instead of me losing him, he lost me.

Then, to see him fight for me yesterday was the second biggest relief of the day. Adam grew into the man I knew he could be instead of the man I was afraid he'd become. He grew into the father I always needed.

"We should get inside," he says, eventually pulling away. "Mom made breakfast, and I'm sure you're starved."

The word breakfast has my stomach growling audibly.

"Shower first. Then breakfast," I reply with a smile.

He nods before we both climb out of the car.

✝

I stand under the hot water for what feels like hours. I needed this. If I could wash away the last forty-eight hours, I would.

When I come downstairs after my shower, wearing the clean clothes Adam brought over for me, I'm greeted by all of my brothers in one room. They're sitting around the table, chatting like it's just a regular Tuesday morning. It feels like sliding the last puzzle piece into the puzzle.

"Hey, baby," my mother says as she stands from the table with her coffee cup in hand. "You hungry?"

"Starving," I reply.

Adam grabs me a plate and my brothers rush to fill it with eggs and bacon and biscuits and pancakes. I grin softly at them as I take the plate. "Thanks, guys."

"Here," Adam says, pulling out the chair next to him. "I saved you a seat."

We stare at each other before I sit down next to him. Luke is across from me, watching me like the protector he is. Caleb tries to act natural, picking food off his plate. And my mother is at the head of the table to my left. She looks content and I don't take that for granted for a moment.

Then we fall into easy conversation. No one brings up Jensen or church or Dad or anything. We mostly joke and catch up and poke fun at each other. It's nice. *So nice.*

I needed this. We've never had the opportunity to be together like this without our father around. Just brothers.

Adam tells us that Sage wants to start trying for another baby already. Caleb makes a sex joke, and Luke immediately replies with some jab about him having the most sex since he has *two* spouses, and my mom winces next to me.

"You boys behave!" she says, covering her ears. "Mothers are not supposed to hear this stuff."

We all laugh so hard my cheeks hurt. It seems wrong after what the last two days have entailed, but it feels good to smile now.

My first thought is that I want to tell Jensen about this. Eventually, I will.

Getting an idea, I pull out my phone and open the Notes app. It's filled with lyrics and ideas, and I open a new one.

Breakfast at my mom's, my brother bringing up threesomes.

I'll keep a running note of everything I want to tell Jensen until I see him again. It'll keep me occupied over the next two months. And it will always remind me of how lucky I am that I will have the opportunity to tell him.

Even after breakfast is done and we clean up the table, we still sit down together and talk. No one is in any hurry to leave this.

That is until there's a knock at the door.

"Expecting company?" Adam asks my mom. She shakes her head.

"Not that I know of," she replies as she stands from the table. "It's probably one of the neighbors. I'll get it."

My brothers and I watch as she walks to the front door. We all glance at each other with confusion, expecting her to greet one of her church friends.

But then I hear a voice that sends chills down my spine.

"I don't think you should be here," my mother says gently.

"He's my son too, Melanie. I just want to see him."

Chairs fly from the table as my brothers bolt up in unison. I'm too frozen to move, but I hear footsteps as someone enters the house.

Then I see my father pausing at the entrance of the dining room, his eyes immediately landing on me.

All three of my brothers move to stand like guards between him and me.

"Get the fuck out," Adam barks first.

I rise from the dining room chair, feeling helpless as I watch my brothers fume with rage at our father.

"Now," Caleb adds.

Truett puts his hands up in surrender.

"Boys, please," Mom pleads. "I don't want anyone fighting today. Hasn't your brother been through enough?"

"Then tell *him* to leave," Luke says with spite.

"I'm not here to hurt anybody," my father cries, his voice shaking as he tries to get a look at me. Caleb and Luke keep blocking his path. "I heard what happened. I just want to make sure he's okay."

"He's fine," Adam bites back. "We're taking care of him. Now leave."

My dad tilts his head to get a glimpse of me. There is a heaviness in my chest at seeing him again.

Caleb steps toward our dad with a look of hatred on his face. "Mom, call the police."

Before I know it, I'm stepping forward with my hand out. "Stop."

Everyone looks at me. And I meet their gazes with empathy. "Please. No cops or fighting. Just...let me talk to him for a minute."

Caleb's nostrils flare with anger and Luke's jaw clenches, but I see Adam give me a gentle nod. My brothers would fight my wars for me if they could, probably to make up for all the times they never did, but I'm not a kid anymore. I'm a man now, and I refuse to solve every problem with fighting.

If Truett wants to talk, I'll listen.

But I have some things to say too.

"We'll be right outside," Adam says with a hand on my shoulder as I nod toward him.

"If you need us, just holler," Caleb says before placing a hand on my shoulder.

"Thanks. I'll be fine."

Luke gives me a silent nod before he leaves. I hear the back door close as the four of them escape to the patio, leaving my dad and me alone in the dining room.

As he stands before me, I take in his appearance. He looks nothing like I remember. Thinner. Older. Broken. Honestly, with that shaky breathing and gaunt appearance, he looks like he's standing at death's door. I honestly wonder how much time he has left in this condition. The past few years have been hard on him.

"Let's go into the living room," I say. As he walks to the other side of the house, I notice the shakiness in his steps. I had myself mentally prepared to take the brunt of his judgment and wrath, but now I see this old man can hardly stand on his own.

He has no power over me.

With a shudder in his limbs, he sits down in the old leather armchair by the fireplace and I settle onto the right side of the couch. I have no idea if I'm supposed to talk first or he is, so I sit in silence and wait.

When he looks at me, I try to define the expression on his face. It's not anger like I expected. Then I remember that phone call he made to me a couple weeks ago. He told me he was proud of me. Nothing that I expected with him is happening and it has me feeling guarded.

"Are you okay?" he asks, his voice laced with concern.

"I'm fine." There're those two words again. The biggest lie of them all.

But it's not like I'm about to open up to this guy.

"Is he..."

"He's fine," I reply. "How did you hear about it?"

My dad scrubs a hand over his face. "I got a call. They told me who it was. I've met him before, you know? He's a good man."

Hearing my dad talk about Jensen sends chills down my spine. "And you know about us?"

He looks up. "I heard."

Anger brews inside me. This little dance he's doing, traipsing around the topic he doesn't want to face, is pissing me off.

Leaning forward, I put my elbows on my knees and glare at him. "You know why this happened, don't you? You know what his mother did to him? She put him in fucking conversion therapy when he was just a kid. They taught him to hate himself. A local program called *Eternal Harmony*. You've heard of it, I'm sure."

Truett fidgets in his seat, avoiding my scrutiny.

"Don't sit there and pretend I wouldn't have ended up in the same place," I mutter indignantly.

His head snaps in my direction. "You seriously think I would have done that to you?"

My jaw drops. "Yes, I do. When I came out, you slapped me across the face. Remember that?"

There's a tic in his jaw as he looks away.

"I told you I was gay, and you tried to tell me I wasn't. You waved a Bible in my face and told me I'd go to hell. Don't act like you are better than them."

There's a wild fury in his eyes as he stares back at me. "I was terrified, Isaac."

I let out a huffing sound of shock. "*You* were terrified? You've got to be fucking kidding me."

"Yes, I was terrified," he argues. "I knew what you would face. I knew what the world would do to you, but I never once thought of sending you away. All this time, you've been mad at me for something I didn't even do."

I open my mouth to argue, but the words die on my lips. What's the point? What is the point anymore of telling men like him or people like Jensen's mom that children shouldn't need protection from their own parents? They are the ones who are supposed to protect us, not change us.

He clears his throat as he looks away. "I had a stroke in prison," he mumbles. My eyes widen, but I try not to show it. "I'm not telling you that for your condolences..."

"Okay..." I mutter.

"I don't know how much longer I've got left, and it's made me realize just how bad I was. How much I hurt you kids."

"You're realizing this *now*?"

"I'd like to do something better with the time I have left," he replies before he starts coughing. I hear the rattle in his chest. "Especially for you. I want to make it right."

Truett's eyes grow moist, and suddenly, I'm hit by a revelation like lightning. I see him in a totally new light. I see a man in desperation, and it makes everything make sense all at once.

"Oh my god," I whisper. My entire childhood replays in front of me like a slow-motion reel, and it all makes perfect sense. The sound of pride in his voice when he spoke to me. The smiles he saved just for me. The way he'd bounce me on his knee while the music played. Being the baby of the family, I always sensed a hint of favoritism from everyone. But now...I realize it was mostly from him.

He quickly blinks his tears away as he stares at me. "What?"

"I think I just figured it all out."

"Figured what out?"

"That you really loved me. Didn't you? Maybe the most."

He shifts in his seat, his eyes growing wet again. This time, he doesn't bother to blink or wipe them away. I've never seen him cry once in my entire life.

"And if that's true," I continue, putting the pieces together in my mind. "Then that means...it tore you up when I left. Maybe even broke your heart. That's when you went off the rails, wasn't it? That's when you started sabotaging your own life. You lost your little boy."

He flicks a tear off his cheek as he stares at the cold and empty fireplace. Sitting in this room, I remember the night my mom set up a makeshift stage right over there. I remember standing behind the curtain, feeling like the most special kid in the entire world because my dad was cheering for me. That pride I felt when he smiled at me, shouted my name, called me his boy...that feeling never left. That feeling...created me.

"I did all of it for you, you know? My music, my career, the fame."

He glances up, looking a little shocked.

"I just wanted to make you proud," I say. "That was all I ever wanted. If you had just supported me. Protected me. Maybe I never would have left. And honestly, Dad, I'm not mad at you. Unlike my brothers, I don't hate you. In fact..."

I raise my head and level my gaze in his direction. "I pity you."

His nostrils flare as another tear slips over his cheek.

"But I can't let you dictate my life anymore. You've made your bed, and now it's time to lie in it. If this truly is the end for you, then I hope you go knowing that I don't hate you. I'm not even mad at you."

Choosing not to sit around and let his sadness affect me anymore, I stand from the couch and walk toward the back patio where the rest of my family is.

Before leaving, I turn back to face him.

"I know you prayed to God for me to be different. But you know, Dad, I wish you were different."

He turns toward me, his eyes red and bloodshot, as he softly whispers, "I am proud of you, Isaac. I'm so proud of you. You were right. I always loved my boys, and when you left, it nearly killed me."

The words wash over me like oil on water. I give him a lazy shrug as I reply, "It doesn't matter anymore. Bye, Dad."

With that, I leave him sitting alone and join the rest of my family, where I belong.

FORTY

JENSEN

Four weeks later

"What are you afraid of, Jensen?"

I wind my arms around my waist as I close my eyes and find the same old fears and voices waiting for me. Each of my hands taps in time—left, right, left, right—something he has me do whenever I have to answer this question.

"That God will hate me," I reply. "That I'm letting people down. My congregation. My family. Myself."

"And is that true?"

I take a deep breath. Left, right, left, right.

"No."

"What is true?" he asks from across the room.

Digging deeper, I pull out the first thing that comes to mind. They're buried beneath the lies and I imagine pulling them from some deeply locked case within my head.

"I'm not letting anyone down. There's nothing wrong with me."

"What about God?"

Tears sting behind my eyes, but I'm not afraid to let that happen anymore. The fear that one tear will lead to a tidal wave is no longer there.

"The God I worship loves me the way I am."

"Good," he mumbles. "Open your eyes."

I let my hands relax at my sides. Kyle is smiling softly at me from his seat across the room. "Deep breath," he says.

I do, and it feels just as good as it does every day, like breathing out something heavy and toxic.

"How do you feel?" he asks.

I nod. "Better."

"Tell me more," he says, and I do.

I've learned to regard my emotions differently since I came here. They don't terrify me the way they once did. It's like a sieve has been opened inside me and I can let out every dark thought, every vulnerability, every fear and confession. There is no judgment, least of all from myself.

Of course, not every day is effortless. In the beginning, it felt as if I was just getting worse. Feeling and talking about the hardest, darkest parts of myself felt like falling down a dark hole I'd never climb out of again. But with time and treatment, I started to feel better—better than ever. And it's going to be work for a long time. I don't think I'll ever be truly healed. Those ideations might always be there. But I can still live a full, happy life with the right care.

And that's the thought that keeps me going every day. Through all the one-on-one therapy, the group therapy, the EMDR, the meditation, the tears, the rage, the pain, the loneliness, the regret...all of it. I just keep thinking of him.

Every night when I put my head on the pillow, I imagine the life Isaac and I could have. I picture our future. In my fantasy, we move into a new house. Somewhere he can enjoy some privacy on his time off. He's wearing my ring on his finger and I'm wearing his on mine. I see us with a family of our own. Children we can pour all of our love into. A real legacy to leave behind.

I imagine him lying in the bed next to me. When I close my eyes before I sleep, I remember the feel of his skin against my lips. The taste of his kiss. The warmth of his body.

For the chance to live that life, I keep going every single day. Because I deserve that happiness. I deserve *him*.

At the halfway point of our treatment plan, the counselors suggest we have a family member visit. I couldn't be less enthused about this part of the program. Just when I am starting to feel good and relaxed, I have to face the one person who threatens to tear it all down again. But as Kyle has reminded me a hundred times already, feelings need to be felt. Which is just a cruel and rude thing to say, honestly.

My mother is sitting at the small table alone in the middle of the garden when I emerge from my room to see her. She looks nervous, wringing the handle of her purse and bouncing her knee as she waits for me.

I feel like a jerk for making her be here and listen to things I have to say, but it's not up to me to make her life painless. It's only up to me to heal and part of that means making my mother aware of the pain she's inadvertently caused.

"Oh, Jens," she whispers when she sees me. "You look so good, honey."

She stands from the table and pulls me in for a hug. I embrace her back with hesitation. I know that I look good on the outside to her. I've been running and working out every day. The treatment center has a pool that I do laps in every morning. I've shaved off my beard and I actually get sleep every night now, so yeah, I'm sure to her, I do look better.

It's not a reflection of what I feel like on the inside.

"Thanks, Mom."

I take a seat across from her and watch her fidget nervously. Avoiding awkward silence, she launches into small talk.

"I've been at your aunt Maureen's since you came here. You should see her new house up in the hills. Vineyards for miles. It's gorgeous. And your cousin just got married there."

I give her a moment of rambling before I cut her off. "Mom."

"I'm sure your father has already told you, but Gabby is dating someone new. I guess she brought him to bowling night, but I missed it."

"Mom, please stop."

I reach across the table and take her hands in mine. They're shaking and she tries to pull them away, but I hold her in place.

"I don't know if I can do this, Jensen," she cries.

"You're free to leave at any time," I reply.

Her lips are pressed together, and I swallow my guilt for making her sad. But I need to say this—for as long as she'll listen.

"I'm just afraid you're going to tell me it was my fault." Her voice quivers with emotion. "Your father seems to think it is."

I shake my head. "I'm not going to tell you that."

"You're not?" Her brows rise with hope.

"No. That's for you to work out on your own," I reply, and her brows instantly drop back down.

"Then...what do you want to say?" There is so much fear in her eyes, and it breaks my heart.

"I want to tell you..." I drag in a long, slow breath, and after letting it out, I look at her steadily. "I'm gay."

Her brows pinch inward. "I know that, Jensen."

"I know you know that, but I could never tell you. And I needed to say it."

"I don't care that you're—"

I hold a hand up. "Mom, please just listen. Don't talk for a moment. I just want you to hear me."

She swallows and presses her lips together with indignation.

"When I was fifteen, I was signed up for a conversion program without anyone fully explaining to me what I was attending and with no consent from me, and I have spent my entire adult life feeling very resentful of that."

"I—"

I hold up my hand to stop her again.

"I felt betrayed, Mom."

She starts to cry, letting out a whimpering sob as she covers her eyes with her clenched hands. She can choose not to hear what I have to say, but I'm going to say it anyway. I *need* to say it.

"That program was *wrong*. Evil, even. It caused serious damage to my self-worth, my mental health, my faith, my confidence. My future. I was sexually and mentally *abused* there. I need you to hear that part. But I am working through all of that now. I'm healing from the harm they caused, and I am going to be okay."

She sobs again.

"I knew it. I knew you were going to tell me this was my fault."

My eyes sting. "I didn't say that, Mom."

"Yes, you did. You don't understand, Jensen. I was just trying to protect you."

I swallow and look down at my hands on the table. Kyle warned me it could be like this, that she would think only of herself, although I never once directed it at her. That's her guilt talking. Not mine.

"I want you in my life, Mom," I mumble without looking up.

She gives a little gasp. "Of course, I'll be in your life, Jensen. I'm your *mother*."

This is the hard part. The part that feels like a dull knife jabbed in my chest.

"I can't have you in my life unless I know I have your support."

She tsks, straightening her spine. "I'm doing my best."

I look up at her as I continue. "I'm in love with Isaac. Eventually, I want to marry him. I would like your support."

"What about your job?" she asks, and my shoulders fall in defeat. Hanging my head, I dig my fingers in my hair.

"I don't care about my job, Mom. You're not listening to me."

"I am listening to you, Jensen. I'm listening to you tell me you are struggling. That your whole life has been a struggle and you want to just make it worse and worse. I'll support you. Of course I'll support you, but I can't change who I am, either. You and your father seem to think this should be so easy for me, but neither of you understands how hard this is for me."

The dull knife digs deeper and deeper as she continues.

"I can't just change my beliefs overnight, Jensen. I was raised to believe that it's a sin and excuse me for not wanting my son to go to hell. So, yes, I did try to help you. I didn't want to change you, Jensen. I wanted to *cure* you. There is a difference."

"I don't need a cure, Mom. There's nothing wrong with me."

She huffs. "I can't change my beliefs, Jensen. I won't."

I open my mouth to argue, but there's no use. This conversation is going in circles, and I assume it always will unless I remove myself. There's nothing in my power to change her response or beliefs. All I can do is walk away. And it hurts, probably more than anything has ever hurt before, but I have to do this.

"Okay, Mom," I stammer quietly as I move to stand.

"Where are you going?" she cries.

"I'm saying goodbye," I reply.

"Why? Because I'm upset? Because I want to defend myself? Am I not allowed to be sad?"

"Of course you are." I open my arms for a hug from her. She's reluctant, probably because she knows I'm offering her my last hug. After today, I will have no choice but to cut her out of my life—for my own good.

It's not her fault she doesn't get it, and I'm not even angry at her. I'm not mad that my mom can't be the mom I need her to be. Just like me, she was brainwashed, too. She grew up in a world that fed her lies, but it's not up to me to fix her.

It's up to me to protect myself and the future I have planned.

"Goodbye, Mom," I say, my voice shaking with emotion.

She whimpers with a cry as she stands up. "I only wanted you to be happy."

I pull her into my arms, hugging her tight. "I will be happy. Don't worry."

As she cries against my chest, it's like a weight has been lifted. This was probably the hardest conversation I've ever had to have, but I had it. It's over. It's not the outcome I wanted, but it's the one that will give me the most peace.

I hope it's not forever. I hope my mother learns to grow and change and is someday ready to accept me the way I am. I want that vision of Isaac and me in our home with our children to involve my mother, being the grandmother I know she wants to be. I hate that she's depriving herself of a relationship with me.

But with every hard decision I make, I'm one step closer to him.

One step closer to us.

Forty-One

Isaac

I'm pacing the greenroom of the stadium in Atlanta. I keep stopping to check my appearance, but it's not like there's much to check.

Black cowboy hat, check.

Tight jeans, check.

Unbuttoned flannel, check.

Tight white T-shirt that will end up on the floor by the second half of the show, check.

"I know I've said this a thousand times already, but if you're not ready, you don't need to do this."

I pause to glance at Lola on the couch, chewing on her lip and toying with the new piercing in the center. Grinning at her softly, I nod. "I know. I'm just nervous. I can be nervous and ready at the same time, right?"

She shrugs. "How should I know?"

We both let out a nervous laugh and I start bouncing on my feet. I'm ready. I know I'm ready. I've been thinking about this and planning it for weeks now. The rumors have started to die down and the ball feels back in my court.

I've discussed my plan with my publicist, and they've made it very clear that they are behind me one hundred percent. There's no pressure in either direction, which makes it feel like the right time.

I pull out my phone as we wait and open the mile-long note I've been writing to Jensen since he left. It's a mess at this point and I'm not sure I'll ever be able to properly translate it all into English, but it helps so much I can't stop.

I'm so fucking nervous, but I'm also so fucking ready. I'm ready for all of my closeted days to be behind me. Whatever the world throws at me, it couldn't be worse than what I've already been through. So give me your worst.

Then I finish the note like I finish all of them.

I miss you.

It's been six weeks and three days since he checked himself into the facility. I haven't spoken to him at all, but I do keep in touch with his dad. He has assured me that Jensen is doing great and will hopefully be out next month.

I would never rush him. I want him to have all the time in the world, but at the same time, I miss him so much it hurts.

The only contact we've had is a handwritten letter that his dad sent to me while I've been on the road. I've read it no less than fifty times.

Jensen asked me to give him time, so I am. He asked me to live my life, and I am. He asked me to trust that his love would never die, and I have never trusted anything more in my life. My eyes won't stray an inch.

There is only Jensen for me. Forever. I believe the universe has a way of bringing people together who truly need each other, and I know that's what happened with us. He would call that divine intervention, but I don't think it matters who gets the credit. It doesn't make it any less true.

Jensen is my soul mate. And I'll wait forever if he needs me to.

There's a knock at the door and I jump, looking up at it as if there's something evil lurking behind it. "Fifteen minutes," someone calls.

Lola looks at me with wide eyes. "Deep breath."

"Got it."

As we come out of the room and meet the rest of our band and crew backstage, they're all looking at me. Everyone knows what's happening tonight. I would never spring this on anyone, but I can see the tension on their faces. Maybe they think I'm not ready, or they're worried about how tonight will go.

For all I know, everyone in that stadium could boo me and leave. That would really fucking suck, but I'm prepared for that. I'll be fine if that happens. Might cry a little...rightfully so, but I also know the chances of that happening are pretty slim.

As everyone stares at me expectantly, I place my hand in the middle. Taking a deep breath, I realize what a big moment this is, not just for me but for all of us. We're nearing the end of our tour. For some of them, this was their first—like me. Some of us have been together since the beginning.

Either way, it reminds me that every moment is so fleeting but still just as significant.

"I want you all to know that I appreciate every single one of you for being on this journey with me. Having you behind me, both literally and figuratively, has given me the strength to stand here and do this today. You're the best fucking band and crew in the world. From the bottom of my heart, thank you."

"We love you, Theo," someone says, making me tear up.

"Yeah, we love you," Lola adds, nudging my shoulder.

They start hooting and cheering and soon, we're all jumping and shouting and getting pumped for the show. I feel like crying already, but I manage to hold it together before we run to our places.

The lights in the stadium go down and the crowd goes wild. Lola starts on the guitar and I wait for my cue.

No matter what happens tonight, I'll be fine. I've done far worse things than this. And I've already built this fan base from nothing. If I have to, I'll do it again. I'm Theo motherfucking Virgil. I can do anything.

With that, I run out onstage and stare out into the bright lights at the sound of my adoring fans.

†

We play the first half of the set to an energetic crowd. They sing along louder than ever, and it gives me hope that this won't be a complete disaster.

Toward the middle of the show, the audience is pumped and I do the same thing I do every night. The band goes out for their break. Someone on the crew brings me out a stool and I take a seat in front of the mic to sing Jensen's song.

Tonight is just going to be a little different. Normally, I talk about writing this song and being in love and I keep things vague for a reason.

But as I sit down on the stool and stare out at the crowd through the bright lights, I sense Lola and the others watching me from the wings.

"I'm doing things a little differently tonight," I say, holding my guitar on my lap. It's like my security blanket. I strum it quietly between words.

I can only really see the people closest to me, and it's mostly women huddled together in the GA pit, holding phones and staring up at me with adoring smiles. I grin down at them and take a deep breath.

"I wrote this song when I fell in love with someone. Most of my other songs are about me growing up in a religious household, breaking away to find peace in my life, making friends and finding myself along the way."

When I take a moment to gather my courage, the crowd starts to cheer, growing louder and louder, and it honestly takes my breath away. I glance up through the bright lights and I see my own face on the large screens on either side of the stadium. The cameras are homed in on my face and the tears brimming in my eyes.

When I bring my mouth back to the mic, the crowd quiets again. I close my eyes, and I speak my truth. Not just for myself and not just for Jensen. But for every single person out there who has been afraid to be themselves. For everyone who felt they had to hide. For everyone who has thought the best thing to do is to run away—either like I did or like Jensen tried to.

I want them to know they're not alone.

"It occurred to me recently that I sing this song to you every night, but I've never told you about the person I wrote it for. There's been a lot of speculation about who I've been dating. I know everyone is curious, and I've kept the truth from you for so long because…it's so vulnerable and a little scary. I don't know how people will react, and I only want love and acceptance like everyone else. Like everyone deserves. The truth is…"

Deep breath, Isaac.

You're not alone.

"We love you, Theo!" a female voice screams from the pit nearby. I smile into the mic as she's joined by a cacophony of voices shouting variations of the same thing.

When they quiet again, I lean forward and let it all out.

"The truth is…that I'm gay."

It's like walking off a cliff. One step and I'm off the edge. There is no going back. No unspeaking the words that just came out. There is just the fall.

The fall feels like a beat of silence.

And then…thunderous sound.

I open my eyes, chills breaking out over my skin as the twenty thousand people around me cheer and scream and clap. I squint against the bright lights, trying to see them, but I can't.

I can just feel them. Men, women, everyone.

In my periphery, Lola and the band are jumping up and down in celebration.

My hands stop playing, and I just sit with the sound. My eyes are red and moist as I let it all sink in. Clinging to the mic stand, I smile out at the crowd.

I've never felt more vulnerable in my life. But I've also never felt more brave.

For a moment, I can't believe I did this.

Tearfully, I mumble, "Thank you," and they cheer more.

I turn and stare at Lola, who is still bouncing with excitement in the wings. If people are angry or disappointed or are marching out of the stadium right now, I can't see them. They can feel whatever they want to feel, but they can't hurt me. Because right now, I'm on top of the world.

I realize at some point that I have to quiet them down, or we could go far too late like this. Leaning into the mic with a bashful grin, I mumble, "Wow. That was...incredible. Y'all are incredible."

"We love you!" they scream, and I wink at one of the fans down in the pit. "I love you, too."

I chuckle into the mic and they cheer some more. "So...now that we've gotten that out of the way..."

They laugh and I eat it up. "Y'all ready to hear this song?"

More applause.

Then I do what I do every night. As I start to strum the guitar to the familiar tune of his song, I whisper into the mic, "This is for you. You know who you are."

The crowd gets a little extra kick out of that. As I start to sing, I realize that with all of these cameras pointed at me he could be somewhere watching. I hope he is.

And I hope he's proud of me.

FORTY-TWO

I replay the video of Isaac on the stage over and over in my mind. I don't have access to my phone while I'm here, so my dad showed it to me on one of his visits two weeks ago. I've asked to watch it again and again on each visit since.

I've never seen anything so brave in my life. He must have been terrified, but if I know Isaac, then I know he put a lot of thought into that. And it was the most perfect thing I've ever seen.

Sitting on the grass, I stare out at the setting sun over the hills in the distance. Tomorrow is my last day at Pathways. Eight and a half weeks have felt like a lifetime. But at the same time, I worry that it isn't enough.

I had the option to extend. I could have stayed longer, and I've been mulling it over a lot. Will I ever feel ready? There are moments where I don't feel healed at all, and then there are moments where I feel like a different man than the one who came in here. I've cried, sobbed, really. I've confessed and mended and cut people out. I've written letters and even burned a few.

At this moment, in my heart, I feel confident that I will never do what I did again.

But what happens when things go wrong, or I'm triggered by the past? What if I'm not as healed as I thought? Are my convictions enough to get me through?

Are they ever enough to get anyone through?

Wrapping my arms around my bent knees, I close my eyes and pray.

"Dear God, give me strength. Please. I need you. I'm afraid," I whisper.

Tears moisten my eyes as the sun sinks below the horizon. A gentle sigh escapes my lips as I bury my face in my folded arms.

"Please, don't leave me. Not when I need you the most."

Call me crazy, but I swear God hears me better now. I feel his acceptance in a way I've never felt it before. His gentle touch on my shoulder. His guiding voice in my ear.

I talk to him every night, but tonight feels the most terrifying because my future is so unclear. Will Isaac still want me after all this time? Do I have a following left at our church? Is there a home for me in the ministry? Even after everything, I still miss it. The congregation. The community. Will they still want me? If not, what will become of me or of my church? I don't know who I am without this job.

It's dark when I finally feel ready to stand and head inside. It's my last group session tonight, and I wouldn't miss it for the world.

✝

"Have you talked to him?" my dad asks from the driver's seat.

"No," I reply. "I don't want to bother him while he's finishing up his tour. He still has a week left, and I just want him to focus on that."

"His last show is here, isn't it?"

I turn to face my dad with surprise. "Yeah. How did you know?"

He shrugs. "I have a life, Jensen. And I know how to use a computer."

"You didn't buy tickets, did you?"

"What? I can't go to concerts now?"

My head tilts as I glare at him. "Dad."

"What, son? You realize you're not a burden on him, right? You're his boyfriend, and you deserve to be there. Don't you think he'd want you there?"

My jaw clenches as I turn forward. "I don't know…"

He picks up my phone from the center console and tosses it in my lap. "Then call him."

"I will," I argue. "I just got out. Can you give me some time, dammit?"

He chuckles, his large stomach shaking as he drives. His smile is infectious and I have to admit that it's nice to be back to this new vision of normal. The last two months have been heavy, and they will continue to be heavy for a while.

My mom hasn't come home from her sister's. My dad told her not to, and while that's not something I can really carry right now, I still feel the guilt of it. He asked me to live with him for a while, but I told him I really needed to do this on my own. I didn't go through those eight weeks for nothing. I'm ready to live my life now.

"What about work?" he asks.

"I meet with the board tomorrow."

"So you're going back?" He glances my way with uncertainty, but I give a solemn nod.

"I want to. There is still a lot of good I can do."

Technically, the board decides, but I built a following. I brought it back to life. I worked hard to save it from ruin and scandal, so I have every right to keep my position. But if I lose my attendees, I lose the church. And if that happens, then I'll find another. There are always options. Nothing is hopeless.

Reaching across the seat, he places a large hand on my shoulder. "I'm proud of you."

With a subtle smirk, I nod. "Thanks, Dad."

✝

"Home sweet home," my dad says as he opens the door to my house. I have my duffel slung over my shoulder as I step inside. He rushes into the kitchen while I stand on the mat.

The broken glass is gone. The TV replaced.

"I stocked the fridge for you. Plenty of water and soda and stuff to make dinner if you feel like cooking. Or...I can cook you something if you want. I bought a couple T-bones. I can fire up the grill."

I smirk at him. "Thanks, Dad. I got it. I promise."

He lets out a sigh, and I can see his discomfort. Leaving me here must be harrowing for him.

"I promise I'm going to be okay."

"I know you are," he stammers while rubbing the back of his neck. "But I'm your dad. It's my job to worry."

Walking in, I drop my bag on the floor. "I'm just going to do some laundry and throw a frozen pizza in for dinner. Call it an early night."

He nods while looking at me with mischief on his face. "And maybe make a phone call."

I shake my head with a laugh. "Yeah. Maybe make a phone call."

My dad walks up to me before pulling me in for a bear hug. He pounds a hand on my back affectionately. As he pulls away, he holds my arms as he says, "Don't forget to check in."

"I won't."

"And let me know how the meeting goes tomorrow."

"I will," I reply with a nod.

Before letting go, he gazes into my eyes like he wants to say more. "They're lucky to have you," he adds. "Just the way you are."

I give him a tight smile, and as much as I hate to admit it, I've needed that. Just a boost of confidence that I can do this.

"Thanks, Dad."

With a fatherly nod and a pat on my arm, he walks toward the front door. Just after opening it, he turns back toward me. "Oh, I went ahead and wrote the night of that concert on your calendar in the kitchen. So you don't forget."

With a laugh, I shake my head. Then he's gone.

And for the first time in eight weeks, I'm truly alone.

Immediately, I busy myself. I empty my bag in the laundry room, throwing all of my clothes in the wash. Then I preheat the oven for the frozen supreme pizza. Stopping by the fridge, I pull out a bottle of water and notice the date on the calendar that my dad circled with purpose.

It's next week. Isaac's tour ends in a week, and he'll be home in Austin. While the oven heats, I pull out my phone and check his schedule on his website. He's not playing a show tonight. He'll be in New Orleans tomorrow. Houston, a few days later. Then Austin.

My stomach clenches with anxiety. Every time I start to spiral with thoughts of Isaac moving on without me or me ruining a good thing with what I did, I stop and ask myself... What do I know to be true?

I know I love him more than anything.

I know he loves me.

I know he promised to wait.

I know I told him I'd call him as soon as I could.

And now...I can. My phone is sitting in my hand, waiting for me to make the move. So what's holding me back? It's just one small step in the direction I want to go in, so what is my problem?

Pulling open his contact, my finger hovers over the call button. But at the last minute, I click on the text icon instead. It feels like the cowardly thing to do, but at least it's something.

Hey. I hope you're doing well. I just wanted to let you know that I'm home. But please don't feel obligated to...

"Ugh, I suck at this," I mumble to myself as I delete the whole thing.

Hey. I'm home.

"No, no, no. I wasn't out for milk," I mutter to myself. *Delete.*

The oven beeps when it's heated and I set down my phone to put the pizza in. After setting the timer, I pick up my phone again and close my eyes, imagining Isaac in my hospital bed that day and everything I did to him. The stupid phone call I made to him. The way he found me. I told him he needed to finish his tour without me dragging him back down into all of my shit.

But he deserves to at least know I'm home.

> Hey. I just got home from the recovery center. I still need some time, but I just wanted you to know. I've been watching you on your tour. You're doing amazing. Keep going. When it's over, I want to see you again. I hope you still want to see me.

I'm chewing on my lip as I hit send. Was that too impersonal? Too cold?

I pace some more while I wait. What if he doesn't respond at all? What will I do? I'd have to move on, I know that, but it would be miserable.

Then my phone pings with a message and I nearly drop it as I scramble to see it. And when I open the text message thread, I let out a soft whimpering sound.

It's a selfie of him lying down in his bed with a soft smile on his face. Below the picture, it says...

> Best news I've heard all year. When you're ready, I'll be there.

And just like that, all of my anxiety dissipates. Just his face and those comforting words. He knew exactly what I needed.

Composing myself, I hold up my phone with the selfie camera on. I snap a picture with the softest smile.

After I send it, I write:

> I can't wait.

†

"You're the pastor, Jensen. They hired you for a reason."

"I know that," I reply with my hand around my coffee mug. Adam is sitting across from me at the diner, and I'm replaying the entire meeting today with the board at the church. Redemption Point has a large team, including the two other preachers who stepped in while I was gone, but Adam is right. At the end of the day, I am the one they want.

"Are you thinking about stepping away?" he asks, and that is the question that's been hounding me.

"No," I say without hesitation. "I love my job."

"Okay, start over. Tell me exactly how the meeting went," he says as he leans his elbows on the table.

Setting my cup down, I cross my arms over my chest. "I sat in front of the entire board, and I told them everything. I told them that I'm gay. That I have a public boyfriend. That I won't be stepping down. I worked for that spot and that church. If they want to fire me, they can face a discrimination lawsuit."

"What did they say?"

It's my turn to tilt my head toward him. "A couple of them threw a fit. Tried to bully me out of the job. But some...were supportive."

Adam is wearing a smug smirk as he tosses a piece of bacon in his mouth.

"What is that look for?" I ask.

He chuckles. "I wanted that job more than anything. I thought I was going to be the man standing at that pulpit, but my father made sure that never happened. And now...the church belongs to *you*. His son's boyfriend."

"I call that irony," I say with a smile.

"I call it providence."

With a tight-lipped smile, I nod.

"So tomorrow is your first sermon back," he says as he continues to pick at his breakfast.

"Yeah."

"You ready?" he asks.

I shake my head. "I don't know if I'll ever be ready. I wrote this sermon the entire time I was gone. But no matter what I try, I can't seem to find the right words."

"Speak from the heart," he says. "They'll listen."

We sit in silence, my back straight against the diner booth. For the first time in a long time, I'm starting to feel like myself again.

"You'll be there, won't you?" I ask.

Adam looks up at me with a subtle nod. "Yeah, of course I will."

I smile softly at him, lifting my coffee to my lips when he adds, "We'll consider a trade."

Pausing, I ask, "A trade for what?"

"I'll come to your service if you...come to his show."

The corner of my mouth tics with a hint of a smile. "His show?"

"The whole family is going on Friday night. We have room in our VIP section, and you belong there. You know it."

Hearing his brother say that feels amazing. To be truly accepted by his family is more than I ever expected. And to be honest, I was planning on going to that concert, regardless. After my dad brought it up, I knew I wouldn't miss it for the world. But now, to be invited by his family is the icing on the cake. Truly, nothing could stop us now.

Lifting my coffee cup to my lips with a smirk, I reply, "I wouldn't miss it for the world."

FORTY-THREE

Isaac

If I thought my life was chaotic before, I had no idea. My little coming out onstage went viral, *really* viral. Since then, I've been swamped with podcasts, interviews, photo shoots. Lola keeps showing me these fan edits of me that make me blush. She says my courage and vulnerability made me sexier to the general public, which I did not expect.

But I like it.

There was some backlash—because of course there was—but I found it pretty easy to drown it all out. Everyone who had something negative to say about me and my sexuality just yelled at each other in their own void.

The next day, the phone calls came in. Country star legends reached out to offer their support. Politicians, movie stars, other musicians. It was the wildest two weeks of my life. For a whole seven days, *my name* was trending on social media.

Since then, things have started to die down a bit, which is a blessing. Song lyrics are coming back to me again. Even with Jensen gone, I hear the music because I know he's alive. He's getting better. He's coming back to me. Admittedly, the songs I'm writing these days are heavier than normal, but if I've learned anything in my career, it's that the fans love to hear what's real. Everyone is just craving connection, and that's the beauty of art. Even country singers have the words to explain things so profound and personal.

Ever since Jensen texted, I haven't been able to relax. I know he said he still needs time, but I have a feeling that's just him giving *me* time. He thinks I need to focus on my tour and all the media attention, but what I really need is to remember that I'm a real person with a real life.

I'm not *really* Theo Virgil.

Amazingly, things with my family have been great as well. My new lock screen is a photo of me and Abigail, and her drawings now cover the small fridge on the tour bus. I talk to my brothers nearly every day.

Dean and I play *Grand Theft Auto* together while I'm on the road, which is a great way to reconnect with him without having to address the fact that he's now banging my brother and sister-in-law.

They're all coming to my last show in Austin tonight, and I can't wait to see them. Afterward, we're hosting a huge party at my house with the band and crew and our families and people from the label.

While I'm walking back from the stadium after a dress rehearsal, I get a text from my mother. It's a link to a video, which takes me by surprise. Especially when I see Jensen's face on the screen. My heart hammers in my chest as I click the link.

It takes me to a clip of him in his church, and I assume for a moment that it's an old clip of him preaching from before...which would be strange for my mother to send it. But then I watch for a few moments...and realize this was from today.

He paces confidently across the stage, looking handsome in a pair of black slacks and a tight blue button-down shirt. His hair is longer than I remember, and the muscles through his shirt seem more defined.

"In Leviticus, it tells us that man shall not lie with another man, for that is an abomination."

My skin grows hot and my eyes widen. Glued to my phone, I watch him as he stops pacing and faces his congregation with the Bible in his hand.

"But, my friends, as we have seen through history, so much of the Bible has been twisted and misconstrued over time through translations and misunderstanding of the world then versus now. But I have spoken to God, and like you have, I feel his love. For me. For who I am."

"Holy shit," I mutter. Pausing between the building and my tour bus, I watch the video and my pulse quickens. He speaks with such conviction. Such passion and confidence. It makes my heart swell in my chest to hear him.

"Tell me, if we know that God created all creatures in his image..." He pauses, looking down with contemplation. As he gazes up, I see the emotion in his eyes. *"Am I any less in his image than any other man or woman?"*

It's happening, I think as Lola steps up behind me. "Everything okay?"

I turn my phone toward her, and she stares at it in confusion.

"Listen to this," I say with a quiver in my voice.

"My friends, I have struggled with my sexuality, and I am here to tell you I struggle no more. Yes, I am a gay man. Yes, I am a preacher. I have faced moral infractions the same as every person in this room, and yet... When I speak to God, he listens. When I reach for his love, I feel it."

"Did he just...?" she mumbles, and I nod with tears in my eyes.

"He's really doing it."

She wraps a hand around my shoulders and squeezes me tight as we watch the rest of Jensen's sermon. It's beautiful. Probably the most beautiful thing I've ever listened to. Lola and I make our way onto the tour bus and prop the phone up on the table as we listen to the rest of it.

We can see a few people getting up and leaving his sermon, but what's more important are the people who stay. The warm bodies filling those pews who nod along with Jensen, who offer him their support, and, at the very end, pray with him.

I can see in the video that Adam, Caleb, Luke, and my mother are among them, and it chokes me up to see them. My family and his family are together in that church.

The video cuts off at the end, and it makes me miss him so much it hurts. I wish I were there for him so I could hold him after that and tell him how stunning it was.

The fact that Jensen plans to continue preaching makes me love him so much more. He's not willing to sacrifice his faith for his sexuality or the other way around, even when others try to convince him he has to. He sees the good in spirituality, even when I couldn't. Because there is so much. I walked away from my faith years ago because I was convinced it was the only way to stay true to myself. But Jensen represents everything I *wanted* when I was in the church. He doesn't just see the good—he *is* the good.

After watching his video, I text my mom back and thank her for sending it and for going to support him. She immediately replies.

You've got yourself a good one.

With a smile, I reply.

I know.

After that, I open a text thread to him. Biting my bottom lip, I type something from the heart. I don't want to push him—I just want him to know that I'm here and that I support him.

> I just watched your sermon. That was so
> incredible, Jensen, and I'm so proud of you.
> You make that church a better place. In fact,
> you make the world a better place. I love you.

Nervously, I hit send.

✝

"Fifteen minutes," someone calls after a quick knock on the greenroom door.

I look over at Lola and our expressions both carry the heavy weight of nostalgia and sadness. This is our last show. Appropriately, it's in Austin. My entire family is out in the stands, and while I'm sad about the tour ending and this phase of my career coming to a close, I'm anxious about what comes after this too.

I'm eager to see Jensen again. We haven't spoken since that one day last week when we sent each other selfies on the day he came home and the small message of support I sent him after seeing his sermon online. I've given him space while he's dealing with his own coming out. I'm hoping that means he'll let me focus on our relationship after this.

Lola moves toward the door, but I grab her arm and pull her in for a hug. She stumbles into my arms and lets me squeeze her in a tight embrace.

"What's this for?" she mumbles against my shirt.

"I just want to say thank you for always being there for me."

She squeezes me back. "Of course, cowboy."

After our hug, we head out of the greenroom to meet the rest of the band. As I put my hand in the middle, I glance around at all of their faces. I'm filled with so much gratitude that they've stuck with me through so much.

I try to keep our last pep speech light and not too cheesy. We've already been through so much together.

"Thanks for being the greatest band on the planet," I say with tears in my eyes.

After one final celebration, we take the stage with more energy and enthusiasm than we ever have before.

The crowd is wild. Even through my monitor, I can hear them singing along. With my limited view through the lights, I can see them all dancing and celebrating with us. It's incredible.

During the first half of the set, I peer out into the crowd whenever I can to see if I can spot my family. They're in the VIP section and each time I barely make out someone new. Sadie is the easiest to spot with her vibrant red hair and the fact that she is dancing and jumping the most.

I pick out Sage too. She's tiny and blends in with Adam's tall frame, but I can see her tattooed arm held up as she sings along to the songs.

During each of the songs, I feel a sting of pain. For one, this is the last time we'll be performing them in this show. I want to believe I'll have another tour in the future, but sometimes these things aren't guaranteed.

The other reason, of course, is because I miss him. I miss the beginning of the tour when I could feel him watching with pride, knowing that he would be waiting for me after every show. I try to imagine he's out there. I swear I can feel his eyes in the crowd.

Regardless, I play for him.

As we reach the middle of the set, where the band takes a break and I pull out my stool, I sit on it and smile at the adoring fans who cheer for me.

"I just want to take a moment," I mumble into the mic. "And savor this feeling on our last night."

The din of cheers and applause reverberates through the stadium, so I pull out my earpiece and just take it in. My face is on the jumbo screen, so I can see and feel the tears in my eyes as I soak in this moment with my fans.

"This tour has been so incredible," I say, hearing my voice

echo back to me. "It's been such a ride, and I have every single one of you to thank for supporting me and loving me along the way."

As usual, a few of them shout their adoration for me and it hits home that I might not hear this for a while.

"You know what?" I say, holding my hand over my eyes to block the lights. "Can we shine the lights out there so I can see the crowd? Just this once? I want to see your beautiful faces."

I squint up at where the tech crew is stationed. They take a moment, but eventually, they flip the lights so they're shining on the crowd. The view of my fans jumping and cheering for me takes my breath away.

While I sit on the stage and stare at them, I think about how far I've come. I think about the day I left my home and ran away in search of a dream like this. I wanted to *be* more. I wanted to prove to a bitter old man that I could still accomplish so much, even if I was a sinner. Even if I wasn't the son he wanted.

I found adoring fans who love me.

I found a good man who loves me.

But maybe more important than all of that is that I've reached a point in my life where *I* love me.

I didn't reach this milestone out of spite. I reached it because I wanted it. Because I deserve it. Because I love myself enough to work for it. To fall and stumble and mess up along the way but to keep going no matter what.

Squinting out at the VIP area, I wave at my family and they scream so loud I can hear them above the others. My mom, Adam, Caleb, Luke, Dean, Sadie, and Sage. They're all here—for me.

There's a familiar, robust man with a mustache near my mom, and my gaze catches on him before traveling to the tall man beside him.

All at once, the blood drains from my face as our eyes meet.

The crowd melts away. I don't hear a single clap or cheer. I see no one else. It all turns to a far-off echo as my eyes soak in the sight of him.

Jensen is smiling proudly, clapping those large hands for me. He's in the VIP area with my family, who are all now looking back at him. My face is still displayed on the enormous screen, but I'm no longer smiling.

There's not a single thought in my mind except for him. No stage. No fans. No show.

Scrambling, I drop my guitar on the floor and take off in a sprint toward stage left, where a security guard is staring at me in shock and confusion. I practically leap off the four-foot platform and onto the floor, security swarming me in alarm.

The cameras are following me as I run up the aisle between fans who are screaming and jumping for me, but I only have one goal in mind.

He's here.

When I turn the corner between sections and see him standing in the aisle with wide eyes laser-focused on me, my legs take me even faster. I sprint up the aisle toward him, and there is no hesitation. There are no questions in my mind of decorum or discretion. None of that matters.

As I launch myself into his arms, my hat flies off my head and his arms wind tightly around me. The sound of the people in the stadium is deafening. Pure pandemonium.

But here, in his arms, it's quiet. Every sensation is a revelation. The strong crush of his arms. The familiar scent of his skin. The cadence of his heart pounding against mine.

I don't know exactly how long we hold each other, but it occurs to me in our embrace that Jensen might not be ready for public affection. A hug might be all right, but anything more could be triggering, so I don't move for a kiss.

But he does.

Taking my face in his strong hands, he pulls my mouth to his and crushes our lips together. Distantly, I hear the crowd screaming again. Home run, touchdown, big game win type of cheering.

It's not a hot kiss, at least not as hot as I plan to make it later, but it's the best kiss of my life. As good as the first one. That night in a hotel, when everything felt so new. When he cornered me in an elevator for *just one more*. This one beats every single kiss we've shared combined.

As we pull apart, I smile at him, and he tearfully grins back. Even if he did say something, I'm not sure I'd be able to hear it. So we don't talk with our voices; we talk with our eyes instead.

And they say, *I love you.*

It occurs to me at this point that I'm in the middle of a concert and tens of thousands of people are staring at us. I'll probably have a whole fucking meeting tomorrow with my publicist about this, but I don't care. Nothing could get me down now.

After squeezing his hand, Jensen mouths, "Go," as he nods toward the stage.

Reluctantly, I pull myself away, but even as I'm running back to the mic, I'm grinning like a fool. I climb back up to where I belong and jog over to the stool and the guitar discarded on the floor.

With shaking hands, I put everything back in place, including my earpiece. Then, I sit back down on the stool and grin sheepishly at the crowd.

"Sorry about that," I mumble into the mic. "My boyfriend is here."

The crowd cheers again, and I honestly wonder how they have any voice left at all.

Strumming quietly on the guitar, I start his song, and I set out to make it the best version I have ever sung. The last time on this tour.

And just before I start singing, I find his eyes through the bright light. With my lips near the mic, I smile. "This is for you. You know who you are."

FORTY-FOUR

JENSEN

My hands are shaking as I watch him sing my song. I've heard it hundreds of times at this point, and it never fails to knock me off my feet.

A hand claps on my shoulder and I look over to find my dad smiling at me. When the song ends, Sadie is wrapping her arms around me lovingly. His entire family pulls me in, smothering me with love and acceptance.

He does the rest of his set with renewed energy. This is the part of the show where he loses the undershirt and dances around with those tight abs and that flirty smile. The fans eat it up.

His family and I dance and sing along, celebrating all of Isaac's accomplishments together as we should. I couldn't be prouder of him.

And I couldn't be more eager to get my hands on him later.

When the concert comes to an end, the cheers for the encore are the loudest I've ever heard. My own voice will be hoarse after this. I glance over to see his brothers all cheering and whistling for him. Sadie is practically screaming his name. Even my dad is piercing ears with that whistle of his.

For the last two songs, Isaac comes out and puts his all into them. They are the crowd's favorites. The ones everyone fell in love with years ago when he was just an indie performer, hustling on social media and in small bars and venues. These are the songs that captured hearts. They certainly captured mine.

I can almost remember where I was the first time I heard them. I knew there was something special about him even then. The lyrics captivated my soul and spoke to me in a way no other songs ever had. He speaks about the struggles of living in a way that makes them both relatable and beautiful at the same time. Who knew songs about loneliness and depression could also have a good beat you could dance to.

Isaac is a prodigy. He's a miracle. Quite simply, he's the greatest person I've ever had the privilege of knowing, and I'm the lucky bastard who somehow gets to call him mine.

✝

After the show, his entire family and I head toward the backstage area. The security guards wave us all through and we wait in a group for Isaac to run out after his final bow.

His mother is crying as she watches him from the wings. And when he finally runs off after his final bow, I stand back and watch everyone swarm him with love. My heart swells at the sight. He deserves this.

He almost missed this. Who would be standing here for him if he hadn't gone back home? Who would be here if I hadn't gone to that show where we met? I've never been more grateful for the opportunities I've been given than I am right now as I bask in the happiness on his face.

After hugging his entire family, he spots me. I'm itching to hold him again, so I don't hesitate. I pull him into a tight embrace. I kiss the side of his face and breathe in the musk of his sweat-soaked body. I want him exactly like this.

I don't care that there are people around. I pull Isaac's face to mine again and kiss him because I can. Out here in the open. Only slightly less public than the one during the concert. This time, I lick the seam of his mouth and he parts his lips for me. When our tongues collide, I feel whole again for the first time in months.

His hands grip my sides as he pulls me toward him. When he moans into my mouth, I know that if we don't stop now, we're going to cause a real scene. And neither of us wants to go to jail tonight.

"Get a room," Sadie calls after us, and we peel our mouths apart.

"Where are you staying tonight?" he whispers, gazing into my eyes.

I chuckle because it reminds me of our days on the road, but we're not on the road tonight. We live here.

"Where are *you* staying tonight?" I reply. Winding my hand around his waist, I slide my finger into one of his belt loops and jerk him toward me.

As he runs his fingers through the overgrown hair at the back of my neck, he winks with a seductive smile. "Between your body and my bed. All night."

"I was hoping you'd say that," I mutter before leaning in and kissing him again.

"There's an after-party at my place," he says as he gazes into my eyes.

"Good." I smirk before running the back of my hand along the stubble of his jaw. He leans into my touch and it sends heat down my spine.

"All right, seriously, you two," Luke mutters as he leans close to us. "Mom is here, and she wants a picture of all of us together."

"Shit, yeah. Good idea, Mom," Isaac says as he links his hand with mine. His entire family huddles together while the bassist takes someone's phone. Isaac wouldn't let me out of his grasp if I tried. So I stand slightly behind him. He slings his other arm around Luke and we all squeeze in close.

Smiling brightly with Isaac in my arms, I can't remember the last time life felt this good.

†

The crowd out back waiting for Isaac is like nothing I've ever seen. His entire family is escorted to their cars while Isaac and I are ushered together toward a black SUV. The security team clearly doesn't want him stopping to talk to the massive crowd, but Isaac digs his feet into the ground when the big guys in black shirts try to push him forward.

I adore his boldness as he beelines straight for the crowd behind the rope. They scream his name as he comes toward them. One girl starts crying immediately as he signs her album. Another one reaches out, just wanting to touch him. He takes a few selfies with them as I stand at a distance and watch.

"Can he get in it too?" one couple asks. My eyes widen as Isaac waves me over.

"You want to?" he asks.

"Me?"

"You did kiss me in front of the entire world." He laughs as he grabs my hand and tugs me into the horde. We pose for a few selfies and fans are clearly excited for just a fraction of his time. They snap pictures of me, even when I'm not expecting it. And when I lean in close to Isaac, they nearly lose their minds.

Fame is weird. It's like some small part of him belongs to his fans. They crave his attention or an iota of his life, but as someone who started out as his fan, I get it. I wanted to be in Theo Virgil's realm too. Although, now I have to say I prefer Isaac Goode even more.

"All right, I gotta go," he says, waving to everyone he didn't get to speak to. They call out his name, telling him how much they love him as he intertwines his fingers with mine and walks with me toward the SUV.

Security opens the door for us and we quickly shuffle inside.

The moment it closes and we're nearly alone—except for the driver—Isaac buries his face in my neck. I hold him against me in the back seat, squeezing him so tight it's as if I can squeeze out all the time we've been apart. If I hold him tight enough, it'll be like those weeks away never happened.

"I'm so glad you're here," he whispers.

"I didn't want to overshadow your big day," I reply, stroking the side of his face.

"You don't overshadow anything, Jensen. You make everything better."

With that, I tip his face up toward me and I kiss him softly and quietly.

"I missed you so much," I mumble against his mouth when our kiss comes to an end.

"I missed you more," he replies with a smirk. "I kept a notepad on my phone; it's full of all the things I wanted to tell you. It's very, very long."

I chuckle before leaning in for another kiss. "I can't wait to hear it all."

After a moment of heavy silence, Isaac looks into my eyes. "Did you get all the time you need? How are you feeling?"

It makes me smile to see how empathetic he is. "I am much better. I wouldn't have come back to you if I wasn't ready, I promise."

"I'll do whatever you need," he replies. "Anything."

I settle him on my chest and rest my chin on his head. "Right now, this is all I need."

FORTY-FIVE

Isaac

My house is packed to the brim. It feels like I move from one conversation to another all night. If I turn away from one of my brothers, I walk right into a bandmate. And it's like that for hours.

Jensen stays close all night. I don't know why, but I'm afraid if I let him out of my sight for a minute, he's going to slip back out of my life, which is ridiculous. He's here to stay. I know it.

"Do you want something to drink?" he asks over the sound of music and people talking.

"Just a Dr Pepper," I reply, making his brow furrow. As he stares at me, I shrug. "I sort of...cut back."

Which is true. I could feel myself slipping over the last year, indulging in alcohol to escape. Using it to numb the pain. Turning into my father. Quitting has given me some of that power back, and I don't know if it's forever or not. I just know...I don't need alcohol to feel good, especially not in this moment. I'm ecstatic without it.

He kisses my forehead before escaping to the kitchen and coming back a moment later with two sodas in his hands. As I sip my drink, I mentally jot down some lyrics I could use for an upbeat song I've been working on.

You take the edge off when you take your clothes off

Chuckling to myself, I laugh at the cheesiness of it. I could still make it work.

During a brief break in conversation, I ease out of my living room and into the bathroom downstairs off the main living room. On my way out, Jensen snatches my wrist in the hallway and presses me against the wall.

He kisses me so hard my knees get weak. God, I've missed this.

"What do I have to do to get you to ditch this party and come upstairs with me?" I ask as I pull his weight against me.

"Just ask," he replies while kissing his way down my jaw.

"Let's go," I say without hesitation. He laughs against me before brushing a curl off my forehead. "You earned this party. Stay here and celebrate. I'm not going anywhere."

Moaning, I pull him closer and kiss the soft skin on the side of his neck.

"Fine."

He takes my hand and pulls me back into the party. It goes on for at least two more hours. Sadie gets so tipsy she starts a Theo Virgil karaoke contest that is both humiliating and hilarious. I have video blackmail of Adam singing that I will hold on to until I die. Sitting next to Jensen on the couch, we watch everything cuddled close.

It's past two when the last of the guests finally file out of my house. When I lock the front door, I turn to find Jensen is nowhere to be seen. Heading up to the second floor where my bedroom is, I turn the corner and hear the shower running in the en suite.

As I enter, I smile at him as he prepares the shower for both of us. Well, I assume both of us. I hope he knows I'm not getting in there alone.

It's so surreal to have him back in my home. There's a sense of gratitude in my mind alongside the fear. We were so close to losing this. While I'm so grateful beyond words, I acknowledge that there's a version of us in an alternate reality where I'm mourning him instead of holding him. And my heart breaks for that version of us.

When he sees my gaze turn soft and contemplative, he pulls me into his arms and kisses my cheek. It's like he can read my mind.

"I'm here," he murmurs in my ear. "I'll never be able to undo what I did to you, and I'll regret it for the rest of my life, but I'm here now. And I'm not going anywhere."

The corner of my mouth lifts as I squeeze him tighter. "Good," I whisper. "My life is infinitely better with you in it."

He kisses the side of my head. "Likewise."

I tug my T-shirt over my head as he pulls off his button-down. We each shed our pants and boxers until we're both naked. He holds my hand as he pulls me into the shower.

Once we're under the spray, he kisses me hungrily. His hard body against mine is all I need. He must have had time to work out in the recovery center because his abs are tighter and the soft ring of flesh around his midsection is gone.

The hard length of his cock is pressed against my hip, and a spike of arousal hits me at the sensation. I want him more than I've ever wanted anyone.

"I need you," I whimper against his mouth.

"Patience, baby."

He reaches for the soap and starts up a lather in his hands. Then, he proceeds to torture me by working the warm bubbles all over my body. He tenderly massages my shoulders, pecs, and traps, working his fingers into my sore muscles until it feels like I'm melted wax in his hands.

Then he lowers to his knees in front of me. When I look down and see Jensen kneeling with my hard cock jutting out toward his mouth, my lips part and my eyes dilate with arousal.

He soaps up my cock slowly, and it leaks from the tip while I try my hardest not to come. The water sluices down my body, rinsing the soap from my chest and cock. It all feels so good I might lose my mind. Then he massages my balls and I have to press a hand to the shower wall to keep from crumbling to the floor.

"Fuck," I grit out.

With his soapy hand, he slides his fingers between the crack of my ass to gently massage my rim. I spread my legs a little farther for him and look down to see his tongue out to welcome my cock between his lips.

"Oh, God."

He takes my length all the way into his mouth as his soapy finger continues to press against the ring of muscle. I try to relax for him and allow him in. As he slips inside, my eyes roll and I let out a guttural moan.

I rest my foot on the shower wall to give him more room as he sucks down my cock and works me open at the same time. His finger thrusts deeper and deeper inside me, adding a second as he goes. I won't last long. That's for sure.

His mouth bobs eagerly up and down, taking me deep as he swallows around my cock. Then his fingers hook, hitting my prostate, and I'm a goner.

"Jesus fucking Christ, Jensen," I call out with one hand on the wall and the other gripping his wet hair. I can't keep my hips from thrusting toward him as my orgasm pummels me hard. I'm drowned in pleasure as I come and come and come.

He doesn't stop sucking, swallowing down my release while I'm seeing stars and trying not to fall over from the intensity of it.

A bone-deep shiver rolls through me, and he finally pulls his lips from my cock. When he finally stands, I collapse into his arms. He holds me against him as he mumbles in my ear, "Who takes care of you?"

With a wicked grin, I reply, "You, Daddy."

Laughing, he holds me tighter. "That's fuckin' right."

+

After our shower, we wrap the towels around our waists, but we don't bother getting dressed because this night is far from over. I don't plan on sleeping anytime soon. I have the rest of my life to catch up on sleep. Tonight, I need to reacquaint my body with his. It's been too long to prioritize sleep over sex.

He's sitting at the head of my bed, watching the door when I emerge from the bathroom. The only thing he's wearing is a satisfied grin and a look of pure heat in his eyes. Tearing off my towel, I walk over to him and climb onto his lap, holding his face in my hands.

"What are you going to do now that your tour is over?" he asks.

"I guess work on my next album," I reply. "And have lots and lots of sex with my hot boyfriend."

He chuckles, capturing my lips with his.

"You know…" I say as I pull back. My hands are linked around his neck, playing with the hair at the nape. "My offer still stands. For you to…you know…move in. But I mean, if you just want to start with a drawer, that's fine too. I don't want to pressure you before you're ready—"

Thankfully, he kisses me at that moment to shut me up.

"I do still want to," he replies. "I thought about it a lot while I was gone."

"You did?" Excitement courses down my spine. I love the idea that he thought about me at all while he was gone, which is a little ridiculous. Of course he thought about me. "What else did you think about?"

His fingers grip my ass, pulling me closer as he reclines against the pillows. He watches me like I'm his favorite thing to look at, and it makes me hotter than I already am.

Lazily drawing his hands up my thighs and waist, he stares into my eyes. "I thought about you—a lot. I thought about us and the future we could have together."

My mouth tugs in a crooked smirk. "What do you see?"

Shooting me a look of disbelief, he asks, "This doesn't freak you out? Talking about us long term."

"Fuck no," I snap. "I see you in every vision of my life. That doesn't scare me. Does it scare you?"

He shakes his head. "It comforts me."

"Good. Then tell me what you see," I reply as I lean over him. With our cocks pressed against each other's between our bodies, mine is already getting hard again.

He takes my hand and kisses my knuckle tenderly. "I see my ring on your finger. I see us in a big house, all our own. I see... kids."

My brows shoot upward, my heart hammering wildly in my chest. Just imagining the future we could have has me excited to start living it.

"Oh yeah? How many kids do you see?"

He shrugs. "Doesn't matter. As long as they're ours. We could give them the life they deserve. The parents we always wanted."

With my forehead pressed against his, I close my eyes. "I like that future a lot."

"You do?" he asks in a sultry, sexy tone.

He pulls me down for a deeper kiss, licking into my mouth and caressing my tongue with his. Heat gathers at the base of my spine, and I start grinding myself against him.

We're breathless and ravenous for each other when I pull my mouth away and whisper, "I like any future with you in it. Especially the immediate future where you're fucking me, please."

He chuckles against my lips. "I like that one too."

FORTY-SIX

JENSEN

The feel of Isaac's naked body in my hands is heaven. His kiss, his skin, his mouth, all heaven. Almost as good as the prospect of getting to spend the rest of my life with him.

He grinds against me eagerly as my mouth traces its way down to his neck, sucking and nibbling on his skin just to hear him whimper and feel him tremble.

"Get the lube," I mumble against his throat.

Without leaving my lap, he reaches into his nightstand drawer and pulls out the bottle. Passing it back to me, he collapses back into my arms, letting his lips travel down my throat and across my collarbone.

The angle is awkward, but I manage to coat my fingers and reach behind him to prep him for my cock.

"I'm ready," he mutters eagerly against my lips.

"No, you're not. I will not hurt you."

He lets out a petulant sigh, and I smile at the idea of Isaac being a little brat. It makes the moments when he obeys and submits that much more rewarding. He doesn't fuss anymore as I work him open. He melts into my arms, moaning against my chest as my fingers thrust inside him.

My own cock is lying neglected on my belly, but I know the moment I'm inside him, it will be a struggle to keep from coming too soon. I've waited so long for this. I didn't touch myself while I was in the center. I wanted to have this moment to look forward to. I wanted Isaac to be the reward in more ways than one.

"Please, Daddy," he rasps playfully against my earlobe. He likes to use that pet name as a joke, but I also see how much he genuinely likes it. Isaac wants me to be the man who takes care of him, and I am more than happy to oblige. This is what I was born for. To please and love him more than anyone.

"Lift up," I say as I reach for the lube and apply a generous amount to my cock. The moment I start slathering it up, my muscles tense and my climax creeps closer. "I'm not going to last long, baby. So I hope you're up for another round when I'm done."

"I don't want to sleep a wink all night," he replies.

Isaac eagerly takes my cock in his hand and guides it toward his ass while he slowly sits back.

"Easy, baby," I say, trying to slow him down, but it's no use. He's too impatient for it. My cock breaches the ring of muscle as he slides down as far as he can go. The moment his ass swallows my cock, my back arches and I struggle to maintain my composure.

But Isaac isn't interested in taking anything slow tonight. He starts moving without hesitation, bouncing and grinding his hips on top of me to chase his own pleasure.

"Fuck, fuck, fuck," I mutter with my head hanging back. He feels so good, all tight and warm and perfect. I manage to hold out longer than I expect to.

Isaac's eyes find mine as he moves on top of me. My fingers dig into his hips while his claw at my chest. I can't breathe or move or speak. I'm being swept up in a landslide of pleasure.

"You feel so good," he cries out as he moves. His cock bounces with his body, so I reach up and squeeze it in my fist. He lets out a whimpering sound, and it sends me over the edge.

"I'm coming," I say before the wind is knocked out of me by a torrential wave of euphoria.

"Fill me up," he says with a raspy growl as he continues to bounce on my cock. The sensation steals my breath as I drive my hips upward into Isaac. My cock pulses as my balls empty inside him. Judging by the length and intensity of the orgasm, I know it's a lot. The idea of my cum leaking out of him only adds to the pleasure of my climax.

My body collapses against the bed. I'm still buried deep inside him as he replaces my hand with his and strokes his cock with vigor while staring into my eyes.

It only takes him a moment before his own climax hits him for the second time tonight. He groans loudly with what's left of his voice after a long night of performing. Warm, wet jets of his release land on my chest. I wear them like a badge of honor.

When he eventually lifts up, I make him do it slowly so I can watch it drip down his leg.

"I know we should clean up, but I don't want to," I say as I grin lazily up at him.

"You want to just lie in bed and cover each other with cum?"

I pretend to contemplate this. "Yeah, I think I do."

He falls onto his back beside me and stares up at the ceiling. "Fine. Give me fifteen minutes."

✝

The sun blazes through the crevice between the curtains in Isaac's room. I know it's long been up because it was rising by the time Isaac and I fell asleep.

I've never fucked so much in my life. Before last night, I didn't even know I was capable of three orgasms in one session, but he proved it to me. My muscles feel like gelatin when I roll over in the bed and spoon my body around his.

He gently stirs as I kiss the back of his neck.

"What time is it?" he murmurs sleepily.

"Doesn't matter."

Isaac lets out a humming sound as he falls back to sleep. Seeing him so content and comfortable is all I need. I plant a kiss on his cheek before getting out of bed. I slip on a pair of his boxer briefs because he loves it so much, and because I don't have any here, *yet*.

I take my phone and head downstairs. I brew a pot of coffee while watching the footage of our kiss last night from nearly every angle in the stadium. I don't even see the trolls in the comments, although they're there. I'm too focused on all of the kind comments. People were ready to see love displayed like this. They needed it.

Fearless, shameless, proud, uninhibited love. Regardless of gender, age or background. Just love.

It dawns on me that somewhere, Derek is seeing this, and his reaction to it doesn't affect me at all. He could try and retaliate, but there's nothing he could do that could hurt me now. Tarnish my name. Take my job. Spread lies and rumors. I don't care.

I was afraid for so long of letting this happen that I never bothered to look on the other side and see how free I could feel. I would have lived in that closet forever because I was terrified of what the church would say or how my life would change. I had no idea it could be this good.

I finally asked God for strength I should have begged for ages ago. If I had listened to him, rather than all of them, I would have known in my youth that God's love is unconditional. That is what we preach because that is what we feel. That is what we know.

Everything else is just noise.

I pour myself a cup of coffee and I take it to the back patio. Sitting outside, I close my eyes and I say a silent prayer in my mind. It's nothing eloquent. Just a moment of gratitude. For this life. For this love. For this mercy.

"Oh, Abigail can FaceTime me now, and she likes to FaceTime when she's supposed to be asleep in bed, so that's been fun. I won't tell on her, of course."

I chuckle as I lean back on the couch with my feet in Isaac's lap. He's reading me updates from the note app on his phone.

"What do you guys talk about?"

He shrugs. "She mostly tells me about the drama in her class, but it's third-grade drama, which is cute."

"That is cute."

"And Lola started dating a new guy. He's Italian and very handsome, but he lives in New York, so she has to do the long-distance thing for a while."

"Well, now that the tour is over, she can go there."

"Psh. She won't travel anywhere alone. She's going to make that man come to her."

"Good for her," I reply.

He scrolls his app, but instead of telling me another thing from the list, he sets it down and looks at me. I can feel the intensity of his gaze on my face, and I know by that look that he wants to talk about something serious.

I pull my feet from his lap and turn to face him. It's not like Isaac to want to talk about anything heavy.

"That was the worst day of my life, Jensen."

My heart splinters down the middle, and the pain of it is sharp and intense.

"I'm so sorry, Isaac." I reach for his hand and press my lips to the back.

"I don't want you to feel bad," he whispers in response. "I just...want to make sure I'm there for you the next time..."

Lifting my head, I stare into his eyes to make sure he grasps the weight of my words. "It's not up to you, babe. It's up to me. And I hope you trust that I'm going to take care of myself now. I'm going to see a therapist. I never want to feel that way again."

"It's not fucking fair," he says with disdain on his face. "You never should have…"

"It doesn't matter now," I say, wanting to ease his worries.

"Yes, it does."

Pulling his face toward me, I look into his eyes as I stroke his cheek. "All that matters right now is everything in this room. I'm alive. You're alive. No one can hurt us. Not your dad. Not that pastor."

He nods before resting his forehead on my shoulder. "I love you."

I gather him closer, feeling his breath on the pulse in my neck. The cadence echoes, *I'm alive, I'm alive, I'm alive.* And while Isaac is right, it's not fair. None of this is, but where they attack us with hate, we will fight back with love. Because we are stronger and more resilient, and even against the strongest storms of injustice, we will prevail.

Love always does.

FORTY-SEVEN

Isaac

Six months later

"Let's run that last verse again. I want to try something," I say into the mic. The producer in the booth gives me a thumbs-up and signals for me to run the chorus again.

On the second round, I give the lines a bit more grit and texture in my voice. I want to really charge the words with more power.

This new album needs to be strong, *really* strong. On the one hand, I believe my name will sell records as it is, but this is my sophomore album, which means the pressure can either be crippling or motivating. So far, I'm somewhere in between.

"That sounded great," the producer says through the speaker. "We can add a bass track to that to really make it hit harder."

"Cool," I reply distractedly as I pull my phone from my back pocket. It's ringing with a call from Jensen, who never calls. Worry fills my veins like a rising tide.

"I gotta take this," I say as I stand from the stool and swipe the call. "Hey, you okay?"

"Hey," he replies. Immediately, I hear the tension in his voice. "I'm sorry to bug you while you're in the studio, but your mom just called."

"Is she okay?"

"Yeah...it's your dad. He had a heart attack."

The blood drains from my face. "Is he..."

"He's in critical condition in the hospital. She wanted to know...if you wanted to see him."

"Seriously?" Why the hell would I want to see him?

"I didn't answer for you, but I figured that if you wanted to say anything to him...maybe this was the time. There's no wrong answer here, babe. Whatever you want, I'll support you."

I chew on my bottom lip as the question weighs on my chest. It's not a choice I want to make.

"Your mom said your brothers are coming to her house. They'll make a plan from there."

I let out a deep sigh. "Okay. I'll head that way."

"Want me to meet you there?" he asks with loving concern.

"No, that's okay. I need to do this on my own."

"I understand," he replies. Then, after a beat, he adds, "I love you."

"I love you too," I mumble before hanging up. It's at this moment that I realize my hands are shaking.

Without thinking too much about it, I let my producer know the situation. We were about to wrap it up anyway, so it's not a total loss. Then, I drive directly over to my mother's house. My brothers' cars are all parked outside, and I have to take a deep breath when I get out of my car and walk through the front door.

Everyone is sitting around the table when I walk in. It's just the four of us and Mom. No spouses or kids or boyfriends. I take a seat across from Adam and wait to see what they have to say before I speak up.

It's Caleb who breaks the tension first.

"Good job, Isaac. Your little publicity stunt killed him."

"Caleb!" my mother shrieks.

Luke snorts and I break out in a full-belly laugh. I look up to find Adam shaking his head at us while trying to hold back a smile. It feels good to let go of this stress I've been holding.

"Me? You threw your boyfriend's underwear at him."

"Boys, stop it!"

"To be fair," Adam adds. "I did release a sex tape we filmed in his office."

Luke chuckles. "I mean, who here hasn't desecrated his office?"

"I have," I reply, holding up my hand.

"We know," the twins answer in unison.

My poor mother is at the head of the table with her face in her hands.

"Sorry, Mom," I stutter uncomfortably.

"Yeah, sorry, Mom," the others reply.

She eventually pulls her hand away and takes a deep breath. On the exhale, she glances around at all of us, and we wait for her to speak next.

Finally, she shrugs. "I may have sent him a little revenge video of my own."

Our jaws drop collectively. "Holy shit, Mom!" Luke says in an outburst with a shocked smile on his face.

"Excuse me?" Adam asks. "With who?"

"Don't answer that," Caleb answers with a look of discomfort.

Meanwhile, I can't keep my laughter in.

"What?" she asks with a shrug. "I was just as mad as you boys were. But that is not the point." Waving her hand, she tries to maneuver the conversation back to the topic at hand. "I wanted you all here to tell you I will be going up to the hospital. I'd like to make peace before he goes. Your decision is up to you, and I won't be mad at you either way."

"Okay, Mom," Adam says, placing a hand on her shoulder. "I'll go with you, so you're not alone."

"I'd like to go too," Luke says next. "I think saying goodbye will give me some closure."

Caleb nods. "As much as I'd like to knock his lights out, I think I'll regret it if I don't at least say goodbye."

Everyone looks at me, and a tightness builds in my throat. I have nothing left to say to my father after what I told him at the house when he came here. I said my goodbye. But what if I don't go, and I regret it? I don't care about Truett Goode anymore, but he is still my dad. If I go to say one last goodbye, it would be more for me than for him.

"I'll go," I mumble. "To say goodbye."

My mother gives me a tight smile while my brothers nod in unison. The air in the room is thick with tension, and I almost wish someone would crack a joke again to lighten it, but they don't. Because sometimes, even the tough stuff needs to be felt.

†

My family and I all arrive at the hospital about an hour later. My mom leads the pack, walking with us behind her down the hall toward the room where the nurse told us to go.

The hospital brings back tough memories of when I visited Jensen here, and it makes me miss him. As soon as this is over, I'm going to rush home to him and let him wash away all the stress of this day with his mouth and his hands.

My mom presses the door to our father's room open slowly, and we all file in together. The first thing I register is the sound of a machine beeping with the cadence of a heartbeat. Then we shuffle around his bed and I see my father lying unconscious with tubes and wires coming from his body.

From the moment I see him, I know it's over. He won't wake up from this. He's never walking out of this hospital. He has the look of a man on the cusp of death.

It really shouldn't hit me with a wave of emotion, but it does. Maybe deep down, I assumed my dad might change. I figured somewhere far down the road when Jensen and I are married and have children, my dad would come around. He'd apologize and become a changed man, and then we might have some semblance of a second chance.

It was a pipe dream all along, but I still hoped for it.

I look over at my mother to find her crying quietly as she stares at the man in the bed, even after everything he's done to her. I have to remind myself that he was her husband. Her partner. The person she was meant to go through life with. And even if that didn't work out the way she wanted, it probably still hurts to see him dying.

Even Adam has tears in his eyes, and I realize that all of this is heavier and more complicated than we expected. Most of the people in this room have at least once in their lives promised this man they would dance on his grave. But now...seeing him actually dying...is harder than we anticipated.

"He doesn't deserve any of our forgiveness," my mother says quietly with a sniffle. "But maybe...if we gave it to him anyway, we'd find some peace."

Adam puts an arm around her. "Yeah, Mom. You're right."

"We deserve peace," Caleb adds.

The five of us settle into the hospital room. We reminisce together on memories from our childhood—the good ones only. Our dad doesn't wake up, but it's like he's still in the room with us. The kinder version of him. I like to imagine that somewhere along the way, we broke the cruel, hatred-filled man who was raised on spoonfuls of spite and bigotry. Somewhere in there was a man who loved his family and his community. I'll mourn him, but I won't mourn the version that used to treat us like he hated us and refused to accept us the way we were.

I don't think even Truett wanted to be that version of himself. Not really. The power ruined him.

The long day stretches into night, and the entire time, we stay together as a family.

And sometime around three, the beeping stops.

We huddle around our mother as she weeps. A nurse comes in to call his time of death. And that's it.

Just like that, it's over. Three decades of fighting and animosity. Three decades of trying to make that man proud. Three decades of proving to him what a man I could be.

Losing a parent is strange. It feels like flying from the nest without wanting to. Like having a pair of wings slapped on my back and being shoved into adulthood. Which is strange for someone like me who has lived without his parents for over a decade.

But now that Truett is gone, I feel a different type of freedom. And I'm not sure I want it. Because now I have to actually prove what I can do. Now, I'm a man without a father, and the gauntlet has been passed.

Adam, Caleb, Luke, and I hug each other tightly in a huddle and I know they feel it too. We no longer exist in his shadow. Our existence is no longer defined by trying to prove him wrong. We are finally at liberty to be the men we want to be.

After taking my mother home and making sure she's settled, I head home to Jensen. He's asleep on the couch when I arrive as if he couldn't even go to bed without me. I crawl into his arms sometime around daybreak.

"Welcome home, baby," he whispers.

He just holds me. His hand runs up and down my back in a comforting motion until I fall asleep.

✝

About a month after my dad's death, Jensen and I are hanging out on the couch when he gets a text from his dad to turn on the local news. I have my guitar resting on my lap, strumming the chords of a new song, when he changes the channel and I see the headline on the screen.

Local Pastor Arrested for Tax Fraud and Misconduct

"What the…"

I don't recognize the mugshot on the screen or the man being hauled off in cuffs, but Jensen looks like he's seen a ghost.

"Who is that?" I ask, although I have a suspicion.

"That's Derek," he says softly as he grabs the remote and turns up the volume to hear the report.

"A local pastor was recently arrested on charges of tax fraud and misconduct after incriminating files and emails were sent to authorities from the late Reverend Truett Goode, who passed just last month. It is believed that Pastor Derek Reedus, chief administrator of the Eternal Harmony program, was not only laundering funds costing his organization their tax-exempt status but the email also detailed allegations of sexual abuse of minors in the Eternal Harmony program. Reedus is due to face trial without bond."

"Holy shit," I mutter quietly as I stare at the screen. The news anchor changes gears to another story, but Jensen and I are still mutely gazing in disbelief.

"Did that just say…" he starts.

"My *dad* sent emails to the police?"

Jensen turns to stare at me. "Why would he do that?"

"I have no clue," I reply numbly.

When the news gets around, I get calls from my brothers, who are also trying to figure it out, but it's too late to get answers, and until this asshole goes to trial, I guess we won't know. None of us plan to actually go to that trial, anyway.

But it's not until I crawl into bed that night and cuddle up to Jensen's side that I figure it out. And the realization is heart-shattering.

Maybe I'm wrong. Or maybe this is just wishful thinking, but as I cozy up to the man I love, I realize that maybe my father changed. Maybe he did that for me after all.

He took a look in the mirror and recognized the monster

looking back. And given the opportunity to make it right, he took it. I don't know if those emails were falsified or if somehow he was able to frame the man who hurt my boyfriend, but I'm not sure it matters at this point.

A bad man does bad things for himself, but a good man does bad things for others. And I think my father just used his power for good. It only took a few emails, but he helped bring down the monster that hurt someone in his family. With his dying breath, he did something truly benevolent.

It was the only thing he could do for me at that point. Our relationship was tarnished, as were all of his family relationships. He broke them all.

I choose to believe that after everything, we might have changed him a little. I choose to believe that love has the ability to warm a cold soul, open a closed mind, and heal a broken heart.

But in the end, it was never about him. It was about us—his sons. My brothers. About the men we became, about how after all the mistakes and all the heartbreaks and all the rebellions, what truly remains are good men.

Jensen's Epilogue

Two years later

Henry waddles down the aisle with the tiny white pillow in his hands. His red hair is combed to the side, and he's wearing a cheesy grin as the photographer snaps photos of him.

Behind him, Faith bashfully rushes down the aisle toward her mom, who's squatting in the front row with her arms outstretched. Rather than dropping a few petals as she goes, she dumps the whole basket before jumping into Sage's arms.

It's about as traditional as weddings get, honestly, but that's what I wanted. And it really didn't matter to Isaac either way. He said that as long as we leave here married, he doesn't care how modern or traditional it is, and I agree.

I walk down the aisle first with my dad by my side, and Adam is at the altar, ready to officiate with a teary-eyed smile. When I reach him, I turn and hug my dad. He slaps me hard on the back as he chokes back his tears. "I'm so proud of you."

I can't respond, or I'll start crying, so I just nod.

My mom chose not to be here today. I invited her although

we hardly speak anymore. She just said that no one would want her there anyway, and my therapist didn't even have to remind me that it was just her way of playing the victim in a situation she created.

After all this time, I'm not mad at her. I have no resentment toward my mother. In the end, I pity her. I wish things were different, but I won't let it dictate my happiness anymore. At the very least, she can rest knowing her son is happy. That has to be enough.

After a deep breath, I turn and watch as Isaac starts his walk down the aisle with his mom at his side. He takes my breath away. In a black suit with a blue vest that brings out his eyes, he smiles at me as he meets me at the altar.

After hugging his mom, he takes my hands. We stare at each other while Adam starts the ceremony. Then, right there in the church his father built, that I now lead, in front of our friends and family, we vow our lives to each other. It's the easiest promise I've ever made.

I promise to love and care for him. To be faithful and true. I promise to always put him first and commit to this union. I promise to be at his side, no matter what, until the day I die.

He slips a gold band on my ring finger as he looks up into my eyes and winks. The inscription around the band reads: *This is for you. You know who you are.*

I fight the urge to cry as I slip a braided silver-and-gold band on his finger. On the inside of his ring, it says, *Eternally yours.* Because he is the only eternal I need. He is the harmony. Forever.

After we say our vows, Adam's voice cracks on the last part. With tears in his eyes, he says, "I now pronounce you married. You may kiss your groom."

Isaac practically leaps into my arms. I hold him tighter than I've ever held him as I kiss his mouth with passion. We're both grinning wildly as we come apart, and the people in the pews cheer on their feet.

It's the happiest day of my life.

Hand in hand, Isaac and I walk back down the aisle toward the door of the church. Everyone meets us out on the lawn for pictures and to throw confetti on us while we kiss.

Our photographer will release the photos to the media because Isaac wants them to. Ever since the *very* viral moment of our reunion at his concert, Isaac's fame skyrocketed. We became icons overnight, and while some of that has faded over the last couple of years, people are still ravenous for a glimpse of our life—our story.

And we're proud to share it. This is love. And now, this is marriage.

Isaac's second album went platinum within a week. He is truly a force, and I admire him every single day of my life. I'm still amazed that he and I found our way to each other. Against all odds. In a world that tried to keep us apart.

I often think about what might have become of us if I hadn't heard his song on the radio one day. Or I hadn't taken that extra concert ticket. The scariest outcome is that we would have continued on the path we were on when we met. Alone. Afraid. Ashamed.

Together, we are none of those things.

My ministry has found new life in the last two years. I did lose a large chunk of my congregation when I came out, but like a beacon, I found so many more who needed a home like Redemption Point—which is honestly such an appropriate name. Now, the pews are filled with people who refused to sacrifice God's love when the community tried to force them out. Faith like I've never felt before fills these walls every Sunday.

With the tithings and money we've raised, our church has been able to provide mental health care to conversion therapy survivors like me. And with a lot of work in the coming months, we hope to bring pivotal legislation to the state courts to have programs like Derek's banned for good. I wish I could abolish it overnight, but hate always seems to persevere in some form. Until then, I'm going to do everything I can to right their wrongs.

After our photos are all taken, the wedding party takes off for the reception venue. We will meet them over there, but first, I want to close up the church and have a moment alone with my new husband.

Isaac side-eyes me with mischief as we disappear into the building and make our way down the long hallway toward my office. We're practically running, and if there wasn't still staff on site, I'd be grinding him against a wall out here.

The moment he steps into my office, I slam the door shut and throw Isaac against the surface. My mouth is on his in a heartbeat, kissing him vigorously after that chaste one we shared in front of our friends and family.

Our bodies are pressed together as I kiss him. Between breaths, he mumbles, "Holy shit, we're married."

"We're fucking married, baby," I reply, kissing my way down his throat.

He groans loudly as I grind him against the door, and right now, I don't care who's on the other side. They should probably get out of the hallway if they don't want to hear two newlyweds going at it.

My hand winds around the front of Isaac's throat as I mutter with my lips against his, "Now, be a good boy and get your daddy's cock out."

He grins wickedly as his fingers fumble for my belt. I lick my way into his mouth as he works my pants open. And the moment his hand wraps around my cock, I let out a loud moan.

Looking down, I stare at the ring on his finger as he grips my rigid length. He slides his fingers delicately along my shaft, teasing me, and it feels so fucking good.

We've been talking about this moment for months. The first time we could be together as a married couple, and it's honestly even better than I imagined. For us, it honestly never felt like we'd get here. We were both in a place where it felt like marriage was never in the cards for us, and now that I'm here, there's no one else I'd rather experience this with. How do people wait until their honeymoon?

Dropping my hand from his throat, I move to strip my husband of his clothes. I fumble with his jacket, vest, and button-down shirt. We're both working to undress each other as I back him up into my office more.

When his bare ass hits the edge of my desk, he smiles up at me. "How do you want me, Daddy?"

I let out a growling sound as my cock twitches in my hand.

"God, I love you," I mumble before taking his mouth again.

I should probably care that we're in a church and there's a large photo of Jesus on the wall behind my desk, but honestly, I don't. This is what we were made for. This is the purest form of love and devotion. There is nothing truly wicked in our hearts when I'm with Isaac. It's only good and pure.

Although, when he looks at me like that and I think about all the filthy things I want to do to him, I do feel a *little* wicked.

Hooking my hands under his thighs, I lift him onto the desk and position myself between his knees. He leans back and stares up at me with his bottom lip pinched between his teeth, and I have to admire just how stunning this man is. And he's all *mine*.

I stroke my cock lazily as I take my fill. Isaac reaches behind him into the top drawer of my desk to find the lube I keep stashed there for...*emergencies*. He shoves it at me, but I press it back toward him.

"Let me watch you prep yourself," I mutter huskily.

"Yes, Daddy," he replies with a wink. Taking a step back, I watch as my hot-as-hell husband sprawls across my desk, one foot up on the surface, as he preps his tight hole for me. It takes everything in me not to come just from watching.

My eyes catch on the new tattoo adorning his right forearm. It's a line of sheet music with the notes of our song, the one he wrote for me early in our relationship.

His jaw hangs slack and his eyes are hooded as he works in a second finger. My cock leaks from the tip and I almost lose it.

Grabbing the lube from the desk, I flip open the top and squirt a generous amount on my cock.

"Come here," I bark as I slap away his hand and drag his ass to the edge of the desk. Holding his balls in my palm, I sink my wet cock into him. He throws his head back with a groan.

"Your ass is heaven," I say, my voice tight and breathless.

"You feel so fucking good," he cries out. His head is hanging off the opposite side of the desk as I fuck him. Pulling out to the tip, I drive my cock back in forcefully.

Isaac is stroking his cock slowly and I watch as cum leaks from the tip with every one of my thrusts. I swipe a bead of it with my finger and lift it to my lips. The flavor explodes on my tongue.

I want to be consumed by him. Taste, touch, smell—I want it all.

"Harder, Jensen. Fuck me harder." He's stroking himself faster now, the other hand buried in his hair.

"What my husband wants, my husband gets," I reply with a smile. He opens his eyes and grins at me. This connection between us is more than I ever imagined love could be. He is everything to me. My own soul. My own beating heart.

Tugging him even farther toward me, I hook both my hands under his thighs and pound into him unrelentingly. He cries out louder. At this point, I'm no longer fighting my climax but rushing toward it. I can't take my eyes off his pleasure-laced expression and the vigorous movement of his fist as he fucks it.

I want him to come first, but I'm so close I don't know if he'll get there in time.

"Come for your daddy, Isaac," I growl, tilting my hips up to find that spot inside him that shoves him over the edge. His cock unloads immediately, spraying his fist and chest with his cum.

My legs shudder as my orgasm barrels into me. I can't breathe as I come hard, filling Isaac with my release. He's still in the throes of his own orgasm, back arched and stroking the life out of his cock.

Moments later, we're both wrung dry and exhausted, panting

and waiting for our hearts to slow. With a sex-dazed smile, he stares up at me before taking my left hand and running his fingers over the gold band there.

After slowly pulling out of him, I grab some tissues and quickly clean him up. Gripping his hand in mine, I help him up and wrap my arms around him so our naked bodies are pressed together.

His breath tickles my neck as he whispers, "Thank you for loving me."

With my lips against the side of his head, I whisper, "You don't have to thank me. I'll love you until the day I die, Isaac Goode."

He smiles against my neck. "Right back at you, Jensen Goode."

Pulling away, I tip up his chin as I smile. "Oh, I love the sound of that."

"Me too," he says before planting his lips on mine again.

The decision for me to take his name was easy. Isaac had just returned to his family—I didn't want to immediately take him away. And sure, a name is just a name and changing it doesn't actually signify leaving one's family at all, but in all honesty, I just wanted to be a Goode too.

Isaac and I put our suits back on and clean up the mess on my desk. My office smells of sex, and I shamelessly love it.

We walk out together, hand in hand, to head for the off-site wedding reception, where our families are waiting. I open his door for him, and he climbs in with a sated smile. As I walk around to my side, I look back at the building behind me, and gratitude swells in my chest.

I made it. By some miracle, I was one of the lucky ones, and there's not a day that goes by when I won't be eternally grateful and try to pay this mercy back in any way I can.

Letting out a sigh of contentment, I open my side of the car and climb in. My husband waits for me with a soft smirk, and I take his hand in mine, kissing his ring finger.

With that, we drive away from the church that started it all, the rainbow flag flying proudly over the door.

Isaac's Epilogue

Ten years later

"Sorry I'm late," I call as I run into the living room. "Got caught up in the studio."

"Shhh..." Jensen replies as he points to the sleeping toddler currently taking up residence on his chest. Maya doesn't sleep well at night, and never has since she was placed with us over a year ago, so we take these naps when we can get them.

Tiptoeing closer, I brush her tight black curls from her forehead and kiss her softly. "Damn, she sure is cute," I whisper.

Jensen pulls back to stare at her pouty lips on his chest. Stroking her back, he smiles with love in his eyes. "She really is."

The foster system placed Maya with us, along with her brother Milo, fifteen months ago. We're already in the process of adopting them, but from experience, we know we have a long road ahead.

I made Jensen promise me that after this adoption is finalized, this is it. Four is enough. We have to be done.

He *promised*, but I'm not sure I buy it. We joke about wanting more, but honestly, seeing him as a father is compelling enough. I'd give him a hundred kids if he wanted them. When I see him with ours, I know he was made for this. I regret that he didn't get a sooner start, and I often think about how close we came to never having this.

But I won't look back in fear. I only look forward in gratitude.

"Da-da, sit down!" Milo calls. "We're almost ready!"

"Okay, okay, I'm sorry," I say as I toss a stuffed animal off the couch and plop down across from Jensen.

An old floral sheet hangs from a rope strung across the living room. Behind the sheet, ten-year-old Sami and five-year-old Milo are whispering frantically to each other.

Milo sticks his head out with a bright smile. "We're almost ready."

Jensen and I laugh before I glance around the living room and notice someone is missing. "Where's Maddox?"

"Where do you think?" Jensen replies, turning his eyes up to the second floor of the house.

I rise from the couch and start toward the stairs. "I'll be right back."

"Good luck," Jensen replies with a smirk.

When I reach the second level, I turn down toward Mad's room at the end of the hall. We had this rustic farmhouse built eight years ago. It was far too big for the two of us, so we made quick work of trying to fill it.

Over the years, we've housed and cared for dozens of kids who've come and gone. Even for a short time, I wanted to give them a happy home full of laughter, music, family, and love.

Shortly after we started fostering, they placed Sami with us. She was a bubbly little girl that my mother says is just like me when I was little. When she became eligible for adoption, we couldn't file the paperwork fast enough. She belongs with us.

It was a while later before we fostered again. The two years when it was just the three of us were so special. Our family was new and being fathers was the greatest feeling on this planet.

We opened our family again when Sami turned five, and that's when we got Maddox.

"Incoming," I say after knocking on his door. I press it open to find an empty bedroom with the latest emo band blaring on the speakers. "It smells like body spray and Doritos in here," I call, but there's no reply. That's when I notice the open window and the cool breeze blowing into the room.

Peering my head out, I find fifteen-year-old Maddox sitting alone on the slanted roof with a look of determined bitterness on his face.

"Hey, kid," I say softly.

"Don't tell Dad I'm out here," he mutters indignantly.

"You realize I am one of your dads, right?" I ask as I climb out the window and take a seat on the roof next to him.

"Yeah, but you're the cool one."

"Thanks," I say, nudging him with my shoulder. "I will gloat about that for years to come."

He chuckles. Then it's quiet.

"Anything you want to talk about?" I ask.

He shrugs. "No. I'm just in a bad mood."

I nod in understanding. "That's fair."

Maddox has a lot of bad moods. Understandably, he's had a rough start in life, and even when they dropped him off, I could see the resentment in his eyes. Resentment toward a world that handed him an unfair deal.

I know that look all too well. But the moment I realized the life I was given was unjust, I ran from it, which is my biggest fear with Maddox. I worry he'll think he could do it on his own or that we could never understand the things he's going through. I know how that feels because I was once in those shoes. Maddox reminds me so much of a young Isaac, so full of spite and loneliness.

How do I hold him close while giving him room to grow at the same time? I want to smother him with love, but I know if I do, it'll make him fight even more to leave. All Jens and I can really do is love him and give him a family that supports him no matter what. But the fear never really goes away.

"I get it," I reply nonchalantly. "I get in bad moods, too. When I was your age, I hated my home so much I ran away and never looked back. And you know what I found?"

"Let me guess," he huffs with annoyance. "You're gonna tell me how terrible it was to try and scare me from doing it."

Laughing, I shake my head. "No, actually, it was awesome. It made me stronger and more independent and taught me how to work hard for what I want."

Maddox glares at me with his brows pinched together. "What is wrong with you? Why are you telling me this?"

"Because you have something I never did," I reply.

"Two annoying dads?"

"Very funny." I shove him playfully on the shoulder. "No, two parents who accept you exactly the way you are, moods and all."

He rolls his eyes. "Whatever."

"Also, a dad with lots of money and good connections who could find you before you cross county lines."

"I'm not gonna run away, okay?" His tone is argumentative and hostile, but that's just what I've come to expect from Maddox. He's at that age, and I assume he'll grow out of it someday. Or maybe he won't, and I can send him to my brother Luke's house so they can be grumps together.

"Good. Because my point is...you don't have to. You can have as many bad moods as you want, but you do have to stop climbing onto the roof alone. If you fall off, your dad will lose his mind."

I sling an arm over his shoulders and pull him toward me for a hug.

"We love you, Mads."

He rests his head on my shoulder for a brief second. "I love you, too."

The moment is wonderful but ends too quickly.

Trying to remain aloof and cool, I climb back into his bedroom. I give him a stern glare, and he finally rolls his eyes and climbs back in behind me.

"Thank you," I say before heading to the door.

He drops down onto his unmade bed and picks up a video game controller.

Before leaving, I lean in and add, "If you're interested, we're going to watch Milo and Sami put on their show in the living room. You probably don't want to, though. That's fine."

I smile to myself all the way back down to the couch where Jensen is sitting without a toddler on his chest. He must have successfully put Maya down in her crib, which is a miracle worth celebrating.

He's helping Milo tuck in his shirt as he looks over at me. "Is he coming?"

"I give it two minutes," I reply.

Jensen smiles at me. Once Milo's shirt is tucked, he disappears back behind the curtain. I scoot closer to my husband, cuddling my head into the crook of his arm.

"How's the album coming?" he mumbles.

"Good, so far," I reply as I kick my feet up on the ottoman. "We're on track to finish by the end of the year."

"That's great, babe," he replies, kissing me softly on the side of the head.

The last couple of years have been busy with so many new projects and developments. I've taken up a new role as producer, helping to bring new artists to the country music scene. More artists like me, of course. Now, I'm recording my fifth album, and it feels like a dream come true.

Jensen is still at Redemption Point, but he doesn't go in as often as he used to. He's still the senior preacher on staff, but there are enough people under him to keep it going. He's taken up more of a role with the kids, although we're privileged enough to have a lot of help between nannies and my mom, who loves to watch them when she can.

Jensen's fingers link with mine, the two wedding bands next to each other as I turn to smile up at him, love exploding in my chest. With a gentle smirk, he kisses my forehead.

It's almost criminal how much hotter Jensen has gotten since turning fifty. He's grown more gray around the ears in the past few years, and I love it.

And I thought he had the sexy daddy vibes before...

"Okay, kids, we're ready! Your audience is waiting," I call.

Milo and Sami whisper to each other before one of them pushes the curtain open and they both step out. Sami has a guitar strung over her shoulder, and Milo is holding the microphone.

Sami plays a couple of chords, but when I notice her finger placement, I whisper a couple of cues to help her fix it. With her side-parted blonde hair draped over one eye—*because she likes it that way*—she beams up at me and continues to play.

Milo sings while Jensen records it on his phone.

A moment later, I see a figure descending the stairs. Maddox tries not to look too enthusiastic as he sits down on the opposite sofa, watching his siblings with a flat expression on his face.

More than once, I catch his mouth twitching with a smile, but he successfully hides it.

When Milo and Sami's song ends, we clap and cheer for them, even Maddox. Sami is beaming with pride. I see so much of myself in her, and I know that if she sticks with it, she will do amazing things one day.

As we all cheer for the kids, Maya cries from the next room. When I move to get her, Maddox puts a hand up. "I'll get her."

Jensen and I look at each other with surprise.

Maddox comes back a moment later with the two-year-old in his arms. But instead of sitting on the opposite couch, he plops down right next to us. His icy cold demeanor thaws as he kisses Maya's cheek and places her on his lap. He holds her while the other two play another song, this one much messier than the first, but we clap and cheer just the same.

It's one of those brief moments that I know we'll always remember. One of those instances where life is truly perfect. I share a home with my soul mate and best friend. I have four perfect kids. Our home is filled with love.

The lyrics and songs pour from me now. I am surrounded by my passions: music and family.

These are the things people write songs about, and I have. These are the moments where I thank God for the mistakes I've made and the choices that led me here.

These are the moments when I realize that I wouldn't have it any other way.

Resources & Ways to Help

Youth exposed to gender and sexuality conversion efforts are **twice as likely to attempt suicide** compared to their peers who do not undergo such harmful practices (The Trevor Project, 2019). Despite growing awareness and opposition, **over 1,300 active conversion therapy programs** continue to operate in the United States as of 2022 (Williams Institute, UCLA School of Law).

What You Can Do to Help:

1. Donate to Organizations Fighting Conversion Therapy:
   ◦ **The Trevor Project:** The leading national organization providing crisis intervention and suicide prevention services to LGBTQ+ youth.
   ◦ **Born Perfect:** A campaign dedicated to ending conversion therapy through litigation, legislation, and public education.
   ◦ **GLAAD:** Works to accelerate LGBTQ+ acceptance and advocate against harmful practices like conversion therapy.

2. Support Legislative Efforts:
   ◦ Contact your local representatives to advocate for **bans on**

conversion therapy in your state. There are still 18 states without any laws or policies banning conversion therapy. To see the full list: click here.

3. Educate & Raise Awareness:

° Be vocal. Be an ally. Elevate voices of those affected to highlight the harm caused by conversion therapy.

° Support LGBTQ+ youth in your community. Be someone's safe space.

4 Volunteer:

° Get involved with local LGBTQ+ centers or national hotlines like The Trevor Project to support youth in crisis.

A Personal Note:

Stories have the power to heal, connect, and shine light into dark places. If you're reading this and have ever felt like you had to change who you are to be loved or accepted, I want you to know—you are perfect exactly as you are. No one should ever feel pressured to hide their truth.

This story was written with love, but more importantly, it's a reminder that you are *not* alone. Whether you're seeking support or looking to help others, I hope these resources guide you toward hope and healing. Together, we can create a world where everyone is free to love—and live—authentically.

If you or someone you know is struggling:
- **The Trevor Lifeline:** 1-866-488-7386
- **Trans Lifeline:** 1-877-565-8860
- **National Suicide Prevention Lifeline:** 988

ACKNOWLEDGMENTS

Well, friends, we've come to the end. This series started out as something I felt I needed to write. I spent a long time worried you wouldn't like it. It was far darker and heavier than my previous series, but you, my readers, blew me away with your response.

So, thank you. Thanks for showing up, for having faith in me, and for sharing your stories with me. I've had a blast overcoming religious trauma with you.

As for my team, I can't possibly finish up this series without saying some very heartfelt thank you's.

I didn't write this series alone. Jill, you've been by my side through it all, listening to my wild ideas, bouncing ideas around with me, and being my shoulder to cry on when things got tough. Thank you for putting your heart into this series. It's better for it.

If someone had told me five years ago that I'd be writing sermons (or pieces of them) in my books, I would have called them a liar. Thankfully, I had Becca in my corner. Thank you for helping me keep my portrayal of the church accurate, critical, and respectful. It certainly wasn't easy at times, but we did it.

Phil, the bond we've shared through this series is one of my most treasured experiences. Thank you for your valued input and enthusiasm. I can't wait to write more books with you.

There's no way I could have made the time to plot, write, and edit if it wasn't for my team behind the scenes. Misty and Lori, thank you for being my biggest supporters, my fiercest friends, and the world's best assistants. I love you immensely, and I couldn't do this without you.

Working with Erin Spencer with One Night Stands studios

on the audio of this series has been such a seemless and enjoyable experience. You guys don't get enough thanks, but I hope you and every single one of my narrators knows just how much I adore and appreciate you all. Thank you!

My agent, Savannah Greenwell, deserves acknowledgement for the way she treats my career with so much care and encouragement. So thank you so much for always fighting for me.

Adrian, thank you for always reading my work and giving your honest and generous feedback.

My editors and proofreaders who take my mess and make it tidy and wonderful—Becky, Rumi, and Rose. You three are invaluable.

The amazing and talented designers who create these incredible covers—Emily Wittig and Lori Jackson.

My PR teams at Hambright and The Author Agency. You are both so dedicated to getting my books to the world and I couldn't thank you more.

And last, to anyone who has ever shared their experiences or trauma with me while reading this series. If these stories helped you in any way, please know that you were the ones that helped me write them.

Thank you.

Handsome Devil

Bully romance

Burn for Me

Wicked Hearts Series

Delicate

Dangerous

Defiant

About Sara Cate

Sara Cate is a USA Today bestselling romance author who weaves complex characters, heart-wrenching stories, and forbidden romance into every page of her spicy novels. Sara's writing is as hot as a desert summer, with twists and turns that will leave you breathless. Best known for the Salacious Players' Club series, Sara strives to take risks and provide her readers with an experience that is as arousing as it is empowering. When she's not penning steamy tales, she can be found soaking up the Arizona sun, jamming to Taylor Swift, and watching Marvel movies with her family.

You can find more information about her at
www.saracatebooks.com